Fourth Debt
INDEBTED #5

PEPPER WINTERS

Fourth Debt (Indebted #5)
Copyright © 2015 Pepper Winters
Published by Pepper Winters

All rights reserved. No part of this book may be reproduced or transmitted in any form, including electronic or mechanical, without written permission from the publisher, except in the case of brief quotations embodied in critical articles or reviews.

This is a work of fiction. Names, characters, businesses, places, events, and incidents are either the products of the author's imagination or used in a fictitious manner. Any resemblance to actual persons, living or dead, or actual events is purely coincidental.

This book is licensed for your personal enjoyment only. This book may not be re-sold or given away to other people. If you would like to share this book with another person, please purchase an additional copy for each person you share it with. If you are reading this book and did not purchase it, or it was not purchased for your use only, then you should return it to the seller and purchase your own copy. Thank you for respecting the author's work.

Published: Pepper Winters 2015: **pepperwinters@gmail.com**
Cover Design: by Ari at Cover it! Designs:
http://salon.io/#coveritdesigns
Proofreading by: Jenny Sims: http://www.editing4indies.com
Proofreading by: Erica Russikoff: http://www.ericaedits.com
Final Proofreading by: Ellen Blackwell & Ellen Windom
Images in Manuscript from Canstock Photos:
http://www.canstockphoto.com

This story isn't suitable for those who don't enjoy dark romance, uncomfortable situations, and dubious consent. It's sexy, it's twisty, there's colour as well as darkness, but it's a rollercoaster not a carrousel.

(As an additional warning please note, this is a cliffhanger. Answers will continue to be delivered as the storyline resolves. There are six in total.)

Warning heeded…enter the world of debts and payments.

If you would like to read this book with like-minded readers, and be in to win advance copies of other books in the series, along with Q&A sessions with Pepper Winters, please join the Facebook group below:

Indebted Series Group Read

OTHER WORK BY PEPPER WINTERS

Pepper Winters is a New York Times, Wall Street Journal, and USA Today International Bestseller.

Her Dark Romance books include:

Monsters in the Dark Trilogy
Tears of Tess (Monsters in the Dark #1)
Quintessentially Q (Monsters in the Dark #2)
Twisted Together (Monsters in the Dark #3)

Indebted Series
Debt Inheritance (Indebted #1)
First Debt (Indebted Series #2)
Second Debt (Indebted Series #3)
Third Debt (Indebted Series #4)
Fourth Debt (Indebted Series #5)

Her Grey Romance books include:
Destroyed

Upcoming releases are:
7th July 2015: **Ruin & Rule (Pure Corruption MC #1)**
Late 2015: **Forbidden Flaws (Contemporary Romance Standalone)**
Late 2015: **Final Debt (Indebted #6)**
Late 2015-Early 2016: **Je Suis a Toi (Monsters in the Dark Novella)**
January 2016: **Sin & Suffer (Pure Corruption MC #2)**

To be the first to know of upcoming releases, please join Pepper's Newsletter (she promises never to spam or annoy you.)

Pepper's Newsletter

Or follow her on her website
Pepper Winters

VAUGHN

FUNNY HOW LIFE plays practical jokes.

The past few days—that had to be a fucking joke, right?

No logical answer would make sense of what I'd seen, heard, and lived the past seventy-two hours.

My sister.

My best friend and twin.

This was what she'd been living with? This was how she'd been treated?

This was what she wanted to *return* to?

Motherfucking *why*? Why would she ever want to return to this insanity?

We'd been raised in a broken home, chained to an empire that absorbed us right from birth. But we were kept safe, warm, and loved. We grew up together. We shared everything.

But now...I had no fucking clue who my sister was.

But then *she* came to me.

A woman I never knew existed.

The most stunning creature I'd ever seen.

Only she didn't come to me on feet or wings of an angel. She rolled into my life and demanded my help.

And for better or for worse...

I helped her.

Nila

"LET ME GO!"

Daniel cackled like a mad hyena, his fingers stabbing into my bicep. Without breaking his stride, he stole me further away from the parlour and into the bowels of the house.

I didn't want to go. I didn't want to go *anywhere* with him.

"Take me back!"

He can't be dead!

Just because he lay unmoving and bloody didn't mean he was gone.

That's exactly what it means.

I shook my head, dislodging those awful thoughts. *He's alive.* He had to be.

I couldn't tolerate any other answer. I refused to live in a world where evil triumphed over good. That wasn't right—life couldn't be that cruel.

It's always been that way.

My mind filled with images of my mother. My father's desolation. My broken childhood. Evil had puppeteered us from day one. Why should now be any different?

He's not dead!

I swallowed a sob.

Please don't be dead...

I fought harder. "Let me see him. You can't do this!"

Daniel cackled louder. "Keep begging, Weaver. Won't do you any good."

He's not dead!

I locked my knees, fighting him every step. "Stop!" Looking back the way we'd come, the door to the parlour seemed so far away—a bright beacon at the end of a festering corridor. "They were your brothers, you insane psychopath. Don't you feel anything?!"

Please let me go to him. He has to be alive...
Please let my twin stay alive...
Let all of this be a nightmare!

I couldn't cope with Jethro murdered; I'd go clinically insane if they killed V, too.

"I feel relief. I no longer have to put up with their simpering bullshit." He flashed his teeth. "Cut did us all a favour."

Cut will die.

He was evil incarnate. He deserved to die in excruciatingly painful ways.

I refuse to believe they're dead.

"I said *stop*!" I wriggled harder, only succeeding in Daniel's fingers tearing into my flesh. Goosebumps covered my skin while ice steadily froze my veins. Every second was endless torture. I couldn't live without Jethro.

It can't end like this!

"You won't win, Weaver." Daniel tugged harder. "Accept what's fucking happened and *obey* me."

The vacantness I'd endured when Jethro and Kes collapsed hadn't lasted long. The moment Cut had given me over to Daniel—the exact *second* he'd delivered my life into his sick son's control—I'd lost that blanket of numbness.

Agony I'd never experienced cracked my heart into tiny irreplaceable pieces. My every thought bled with murder and death. My wails had mixed with Jasmine's. Vaughn's curses and shouts drowned out by grief.

It was a never-ending loop.

He's dead.
He's dead.
He's left me.
He's dead.
He's dead.
He's gone.

God, I wanted it to stop. I wanted this to end—for the curtain on this madhouse production to fall and for the director to shout 'cut.' For it all to be make-believe.

But what if it's true?
He's dead.
He's dead.
He's abandoned me.

I sagged in Daniel's hold, bombarded with incapacitating sadness. If it was the truth, what else mattered? Why did I care what my future entailed when I no longer had anyone to fight for?

Vaughn...fight for him.
Tex...fight for him.

My lungs crushed. I could fight for them—but ultimately, they didn't need me. Not like Jethro had needed me. He'd finally opened up to me—finally let me in and given me a new home in his love. But now I'd been cast out all over again; I couldn't stomach the empty wasteland without him.

He's dead.
He's dead.
He's lost...

I tripped, succumbing to the weight of the boulder on my back, the rock of eternal grief. I didn't bother trying to stabilise. I wanted to curl up into a ball and never move again.

He's...dead...

"For fuck's sake." Daniel hoisted me on to my feet. "Get a grip! Walk. Do what I say or—"

"No!" My voice ripped down the corridor, frigid with fear. Somehow, my mourning lashed into a violent whip, lacerating my insides with fury. "I'll *never* do what you say. You might as

well end it now because I *refuse* to listen to scum like you!" I scratched his hand holding my arm, but just like Cut when he'd dragged me from Jethro's bedroom, he didn't twitch or respond. "Never! Do you hear me? I'm *done*."

Desperation tore raging holes inside my mind. I wanted to collapse by Jethro's side and scoop up his blood and feed it back to him—to force him to come back to life. I wanted to hold my twin and tell him it would be all right—to wash away his panic. And I wanted to say goodbye to Kestrel—to send him to the ether knowing how grateful I was for what he'd done.

But I couldn't do any of those things.

Daniel's pincer grip caged me, leaving me to rot in his deluded embrace.

Bastard.

Sick and twisted *bastard.*

My temper screeched out of control, and for the first time in my life, I gave in to it. I opened my arms to the tornado of loathing and screamed at the top of my lungs. "Fuck you, Daniel. Fuck you! Fuck you and fuck Cut and fuck *all* of you!"

The world stopped.

Daniel froze.

I trembled.

Then, he slapped me.

My head snapped sideways. His handprint decorated my cheek with blazing fire, and everything spun out of control.

"You little cunt." He yanked me forward. His inertia gave me no choice but to stumble into him. "Have your little tantrum. Go on, scream and make a spectacle of yourself. But it won't change facts." Trailing his fingertips over my flaming cheek, he murmured, "You just contradicted yourself. First you said you wouldn't obey me, but then you said you'd fuck me…" He chuckled. "I'm taking the 'fuck you' part literally." Digging his fingers into the sides of my cheeks, he kissed me. "You don't have to listen for me to fuck you. You don't even have to obey me. Whatever power you had over my brothers is over, Weaver. You'll see."

Jethro...

Letting my face go, he grabbed my arm and tugged me down the corridor.

Further and further from Jethro, Kestrel, and Vaughn.
Further and further into hell.

He's dead.
He's dead.
He's nothing...

Everything inside shrieked with disbelief. He couldn't be dead. He just *couldn't*. I needed to see him again. How could I go on when I didn't believe what had happened? How could I hope to breathe and exist when all I wanted was to give up like he had?

I swallowed another tsunami of tears. My soul didn't believe. But my circumstances said otherwise. This was my life now—this endless misery.

"You won't get away with this."

Daniel snickered, looking over his shoulder. "Get away with what?"

Murdering my future.
Murdering any chance of happiness I ever had.

"Everything."

Only thing is...they've gotten away with it for centuries.

Every step I died a little more, leaving my beating heart beside Jethro as his body grew cold. The further apart we became, the less human I felt. It was as if the tether binding us would snap at any moment, leaving me smarting, empty, and alone.

He's dead.
He's...dead...
It's...truly...over...

Cold tears stained my cheeks, putting out the fire from Daniel's slap.

Thick lethargy hijacked my limbs. Sleep...it beckoned me.

All I wanted was to fall into its fluffy cradle and disappear.

Daniel dragged me deeper into the house, past foyers and alcoves, and into a wing I'd never entered.

Every step pained me; every breath a blade. My eyes never rose from the monogrammed carpet. I wanted to give up, but an incessant need to fight never left. I forced myself to stand up to him, no matter that it was pointless. "Your father just killed two of your family members. Aren't you afraid he'll do it to you? Too many people know, Daniel. The media, online—"

"You think a few fucking tweeters and social media posts can stop us?" He propelled me into his arms with a vicious yank. "I thought you'd stopped being delusional." His lips turned into a sneer. "Then again, you willingly came back. That makes you a dumb bitch who deserves what's coming to her."

I came for him.

But now he's gone.

I recoiled in his arms. The last liveliness in my heart vanished. I'd witnessed the love of my life die in front of my eyes. I'd been audience to two murders and too many ruined lives. I couldn't...I couldn't cope any more.

I sank...

I gave in.

I evaporated inside.

I'm in shock.

Daniel chuckled, continuing to tug me down corridors I didn't recognise. I stopped paying attention, following like a good sheep, stumbling over a threshold I'd never crossed before.

He shoved me forward. "Welcome to your new home, bitch."

I tripped forward, arms whirling, mind fighting against vertigo.

A loud slam ricocheted from behind me. A door. A prison gate.

I spun around, breathing hard. I didn't have any words or energy left. I was sick, terrified, heartbroken. But through it all,

I was numb.

I'd accepted my fate, acknowledged the truth, and finally seen what it all meant.

He's truly, truly dead.

Daniel stalked toward me.

Automatically, my feet shuffled back—not from conscious instruction but some primal need for self-preservation. In reality, I no longer cared what happened. It was as if I watched myself from the safety of the ceiling, peering down at the poor unfortunate Weaver, no longer caring what happened to blood and bone when I no longer inhabited it.

He's dead.

He's dead.

I want to die, too.

Daniel never stopped corralling me around the space. Through blurry eyes, I took in the rich emerald brocade on his four-poster bed, the priceless antiques, and moss-coloured walls. The shades of green looked like we'd traded indoors for some woodland glen.

He was the hunter, raising his shotgun to shoot the dismal deer.

I'm that deer.

His hands outstretched; face alight with manic lust. "You're all mine now, Weaver. Locked in my room, bound to my rules, at my mercy. Fuck, this is gonna be good."

My ears rang with his voice. My eyes smarted with his appearance. I wanted to leave—to chase Jethro into the stars. Suicide didn't compute. Taking my own life didn't register. It wasn't a matter of life and death, killing or surviving, but about transcending from one world to another.

He's not dead.

He's just…evolved.

And I didn't want him to leave without me.

We were a pair. A duo.

I'm done with this existence.

My mind was gone—unfocused and slow. But my body

still wanted to survive. My feet tripped backward for every one of Daniel's, but there was no finesse. I moved like a robot with no one at the controls.

From my sanctuary in the ceiling, I pitied the delusional girl below. Why was I backpedalling? Why prolong the inevitable? The sooner Daniel caught me, the sooner he would hurt me and ultimately send me to Jethro.

Let go.

Let it happen.

The numbness inside would block external pain, surely.

It was best to stop everything. To stop thinking, stop breathing, stop surviving.

My knees locked. I stood steadfast.

Daniel quirked an eyebrow. He stalled when I didn't continue our morbid dance. Cocking his head, he searched for a trap. "Giving up so easily, whore?"

I didn't respond. Not a whisper of a shrug or a flicker of an eye. I stared right through him—at a new dimension that promised a fresh beginning with Jethro and an end to hardship.

Daniel growled under his breath. "You're seriously just giving up?" Stomping forward, he grabbed my hair, fisting it in his sweaty hands. "You're not going to fight me like you did my brother?"

I was right.

No pain registered. No agony or discomfort.

My senses were meaningless decoration.

"Fight back! Where's the fucking sport if you just give in?"

He tugged my hair, raising my eyes to his. If I focused, I would've brought his putrid face into vision. I would've cringed at the sharp bone structure, small black goatee, and swept back dark hair. If I still had my sense of smell, I would've inhaled his musky excitement, unable to be hidden beneath thick notes of aftershave. And if I had sense of touch, I would've felt his body heat infecting mine, seeping into me like a disease.

But I had none of that, so I noticed none.

All I saw, heard, felt was a void: nothing but silent wind

across my face and emptiness before me.

His mouth twisted with rage. "Fuck you, Weaver. You're mine now. What do you have to say for yourself?"

The burn in my scalp chased away the icy tears on my cheeks. My heart had given up the moment a bullet slammed into the love of my life. If he wanted a reaction, he wouldn't get it.

Not this time, you bastard.
Nothing.
I have nothing.
"My brothers are dead. How does that make you feel?"
Nothing.
I feel nothing.
"Answer me, cunt! Tell me how much you don't want me to touch you. How much you're afraid of me!"
Nothing.
I care about nothing.

Jethro was gone. I'd never seen anyone die before. Never been to a funeral or witnessed a pet succumb—even my own mother just vanished rather than died. My first participation in death and it'd been two men who'd captured my affection, turning me into a completely different person.

The old Nila died the day she entered Hawksridge. But this new Nila was a fading photograph, vanishing piece by piece while her lover bled out on priceless carpet.

Daniel threw me away from him. "Snap out of it!"

Vertigo caught me in its sickening embrace. For once, I didn't fight it. I tumbled to the carpet, letting a whirligig of rollercoasters and nausea take me, thanks to my broken brain. Normally, it was the worst kind of punishment, but now it was better than facing reality.

Vibrations in the carpet alerted me to Daniel's closeness. He towered over me, rage painting his face. "Pay attention to me, Weaver!" His boot shot like a black meteor, connecting with my belly.

Air exploded from my lungs.

Pain crept over my senses—pain I didn't want to feel because it reminded me I wasn't dead...wasn't free. I was still here—in this pointless game of madness and deception.

He's dead.

He's dead.

I'm all alone.

Daniel kicked me again.

His boot crunched against my belly, sending white-hot agony up my chest.

Agony.

And with agony came life.

You're not alone.

Vaughn. My father. I still had family who mattered. People I couldn't abandon.

I'm not dead.

I don't have the luxury of giving up.

Jethro and Kes had been murdered by men who'd polluted the world for long enough. I'd made a promise to my ancestors to end this. I now made a promise to them.

I will kill your family.

I will end this once and for all.

My eyes shot wide. Energy zapped into my limbs. Agony made me reckless, granting false courage. I was stronger than this. Hadn't I proven as much with what I'd lived through? Each debt I'd endured, I'd evolved from naïve little girl into a woman.

I'm braver than this.

Scrambling backward, I put as much distance between Daniel's next kick and myself as I could.

He placed his hands on his hips, laughing coldly. "Finally decided to play, huh? Took you long enough."

Coughing, I held my bruised belly and forced myself to stand.

He didn't approach me, giving me time to regroup. He enjoyed me fighting—he wanted me alive and screaming.

Bastard.

"I'll kill you," I whispered, wincing with every breath.

He chuckled, moving toward me. "What did you say?"

Standing taller, I locked eyes with him. My ribs bellowed from his kick, but steel entered my tone. "I said *I'll kill you.*"

He ran a hand through his dark hair, smiling. The evil tainting his soul suffocated him—he wasn't attractive even though outwardly he had good bones and sex appeal. To me, he was a troll, a stinking pile of excrement.

"I'd like to see you try." He closed the distance between us one boot at a time.

I parried backward. "You won't see it coming."

"You won't be able to get close enough to do it." He winked smugly. "You're nothing compared to me."

I bared my teeth. "It'll happen when you least expect it."

"It will never happen." He flexed his muscles. "I'm invincible."

"You're human."

And that makes you killable.

Every word filled me with power. Conviction and confidence shoved aside my numbness and grief.

Jethro and Kes were dead. But it wasn't the end for me. I had a purpose. I would *complete* that purpose.

"Want to know why I came back? Why I didn't run or hide?" The snow in my veins made its way into my heart. "I came back to ruin you." Spit pooled in my mouth. If I'd been braver, I would've spat it all over his face. "I came back for *him*, but that's over now."

I'll avenge him, so help me, God. Kestrel, too. And myself. And my brother. And my mother and grandmother and generations of Weaver women.

This was the beginning of the end.

The Debt Inheritance was null and void—Cut had seen to that. It was time to slaughter the Hawks and extinguish a dynasty of torture. Every second made me stronger, filling me with a strange acceptance. Happiness wasn't my life path—but destruction was. I would be that instrument of destruction.

Daniel shook his head, positively glowing with insanity. "You came back to watch him die? How thoughtful."

"Wrong. I came back to end this." Darkness settled around my soul, blotting out any remaining light.

He's dead.
He's dead.
But I'll keep my promise.

I hadn't been able to save Jethro, but I wouldn't abandon him. "I made an oath to myself." I narrowed my eyes, glad that they'd stopped watering—that I could look at him with strength rather than terror. "Want to know what that oath was?"

He stiffened. "Don't want to know anything about you, Weaver." He licked his lips. "Scratch that. I want to know three things and three things only."

I shivered in disgust. "My oath was to destroy you. To end your father. To end you. No matter what you do—"

He shot forward and slapped a hand over my mouth. His palm silenced me, sending my heart chugging with hatred. "Ah, that's fucking rude. You were meant to ask what three things *I* want to know, not spout ridiculous bullshit." His golden eyes—so similar to Jethro's and Kestrel's—glittered. "Go on…ask me."

His fingers pulsed on my cheeks as I shook my head. I couldn't speak, but it didn't stop me from screaming with every molecule.

Never!

His temper eddied around us. "Fine. Don't need you to ask, 'cause I'll tell you anyway." He crowded me, pressing his body against mine. "Three things, bitch. I want to know how your screams will sound in my ears." His fingers dropped from my mouth, tracing my lips with his salty touch.

"I want to know how your tiny hands will feel fighting me off." His palm drifted down my throat, over my diamond collar, to my breasts.

I closed my eyes as he kept going, lower and lower and

lower.

My teeth clamped on my bottom lip as he cupped my core with rancid fingers. The thin knickers and t-shirt I wore from sharing Jethro's bed left me vulnerable. "And I want to know how your pussy will taste on my tongue." Without any warning, he plucked me from the carpet and threw me against a wall.

My shoulder slammed against a portrait of waxy fruit. I slithered to my knees. Pain flared, fear swelled, and vertigo did its best to steal me away.

He's dead.
He's dead.
Don't you dare give in.

"I'll show you that I get what I want. I'll teach you to fucking respect me." He towered over me, fists clenched. "Isn't that what you think of me? That I'm some spoiled brat who was the *'mistake'*? That I was never good enough for this family or to have my own Weaver to torment?" His voice deepened with rage. "Saw the tampered video, Nila."

I struggled to stand, never taking my eyes off his boots.

He stood poised, ready to kick. "Always knew Kes was a pillock, but I never took him for a fucking dreamer. Anyone could tell that wasn't you with Cut. And it was a fucking mockery to believe I'd buy the badly spliced images of me with some whore. He couldn't even overlay your face onto her body right. Not to mention the fact I remember the night I disfigured that bitch and Jethro tried to save her."

His hand lashed out, grabbing my hair. "She could've survived if he'd tried. He killed her—said it was what she wanted. That it was the only way she could live with what I'd done. I call fucking bullshit."

He shook his head, eyes wild. "He's always been a pussy, and Kes was always a fucking sap. Jet drugged and lied to us—but fool on him. Cut will make you repay the Third Debt. Kes screwed up with that shoddy film—it could've been the best-edited video in all of bloody Hollywood, and I wouldn't have bought it." Slowly pulling me to my feet, he hissed, "Know why?"

Kes had been a true friend. Jethro had been a true lover.
They're dead.
They're dead.
Two friends gone.

My heart cracked all over again, but instead of sinking into depths of despair, something happened. My temper warmed, growing brighter and stronger, nudging aside grief.

Something was changing...building, *evolving*.

"Answer me!" Daniel shook me. "Tell me why I would never have bought that fucked-up video."

Temper turned to rage, which turned to fury, creating a bubbling concoction of revenge.

I stood before him proud and undefeated. "I know why. Because you're a sick, deranged pervert who remembers things like rape and torture."

He barked with laughter. "Well, fuck me, you do understand."

Breath by breath, I sold my soul to the churning anger inside. I gave up my innocence. I traded all resemblance of peace and purity, letting the blackness consume me.

Jethro had confused me—making me believe the debts were liveable. That, in the end, we'd win because we deserved to. His kindness outshone his cruelty, mixing the messages he sent.

But Daniel.

There was no more confusion.

I knew as surely as the sun would rise, Daniel would rape, maim, and kill me. There was no compassion or affection inside him.

That fantasy was done.

But with that knowledge came clear-headedness. I no longer wanted to fight hate with love or pain with tenderness.

I meant to meet Daniel in the abyss and kill him before he killed me.

"I know enough to destroy you, Daniel Hawk."

My heart beat for the last time, frosting over—protecting itself for what I would do. I'd never planned on becoming a villain. But I'd never planned on losing my soul-mate, either.

Daniel snarled, "You're a dead woman." He squeezed my throat below my diamond collar, wedging me against the wall. "I mean to fill your final days on Earth with suffering. You'll see. You'll *beg* me to kill you before I'm finished."

I gasped. Every instinct urged to scramble at his tight fingers. But I didn't beg or plead. The numbness turned to coldness, and I understood my predicament better than ever before.

I'm a killer.

I just needed a weapon to fulfil it.

"Buzzard!"

Daniel froze, turning to face the door. His hand never let go of my throat, anger filtering through his grip.

I couldn't turn my head, but in my periphery stood my second target. The man I would kill after dispatching his youngest son.

Bryan Hawk.

"Let her go for a moment. There's a good boy." Cut tapped a key against his chin—the key which no doubt unlocked the entrance to Daniel's bedroom. Inching over the threshold, he came further into sight.

Daniel gathered me close, spinning me around so I squashed against his front. His breath wafted in my ear as his hand fisted my breast like I was a trophy to be touted.

I didn't care. My body was as numb as my soul.

My eyes widened as a red-faced, tear-stained Jasmine rolled in behind her father. If I hadn't locked away my pain, I would've burst into tears and shared her grief.

Why was she here? How could she stand to be around her father after what he'd done?

Two of her brothers, gone.

Half of her family obliterated by the man who should've protected them from everything.

He'd tried to kill her, yet she willingly breathed the same air as him.

Why?

"What are you doing?" Daniel grunted, kneading my breast. "You said—"

"I know what I said." Cut prowled closer, his gaze taking in my dry eyes and balled hands. His jaw ticked, but that was the only sign of emotion. "Something has come to light."

Jasmine looked at me. Something didn't seem right. Her cheekbones sliced through pale skin, her normally sleek bob messy and tangled. But she had an edge about her speaking of unpredictability and almost...deranged mania.

He's dead.

He's dead.

Of course, she wouldn't cope.

"Get out!" Daniel took a step back, hauling me with him. Our legs entwined, but I didn't fight. I had the power to kill him, but we had to be alone. That was the only way.

Cut tucked the key into his pocket. "Buzzard, listen—"

"No, listen to *me*." Jasmine shoved the rims of her wheelchair, barging past Cut and coasting at supersonic speed toward us. "Let her fucking go, Dan!"

Daniel flinched.

Jasmine cursing was wrong—as if she'd never sworn in her life. She looked too perfect to stoop so low. However, the unhinged glint in her bronze eyes and whitewashed face held no hint of weakness from watching two brothers die.

She looked livid rather than heartbroken.

What is going on?

Daniel's gaze swooped to Cut. "What the fu—"

"Do as she says," Cut ordered.

I swallowed as Daniel tweaked my nipple. "Like shit I will. She's mine. We've all decided."

"Listen to your father, child." Bonnie appeared, entering the room and resting two hands on her walking stick.

Shit, they're all here.

My hackles rose.

In my melancholy and newly budding fury, I'd forgotten about Bonnie. I'd counted only two victims. Two men who would suffocate in dirty graves, eaten by worms.

I have three targets.

Three lives to steal to avenge so many others.

Daniel stepped back, dragging me with him. "No chance. Get out. The lot of you. The door was locked for a motherfucking reason."

Bonnie growled, sounding like a grizzly bear about to teach her cubs a lesson. "Drop her. Don't make me say it again."

Drop her? Like I'm some dog's chew toy.

The bubbling darkness inside wanted to strike and rip out her voice box. I wanted her bleeding at my feet.

Just like him.

Jethro's blood stained this house.

Hers will, too.

"This is bullshit," Daniel spat, shoving me away from him. The moment I was free, Jasmine rolled toward me and captured my wrist with cold fingers.

My stomach churned.

I didn't like this turn of events. I didn't want any more confusion. Daniel was black and white. *I* was black and white. Death or life—those were my two choices. This scuffle was a grey area and if I let myself lose my cut-throat mentality, I wouldn't be able to continue.

He's dead.

He's dead.

He's not coming back.

The grief threatened to wash me away again.

"She's mine. I'm the oldest." Jasmine spun her chair, dragging me to face Bonnie and Cut. "You agreed. Tell him."

I looked over my shoulder at Daniel, hating the fact he was behind me. I didn't want to take my eyes off the little creep.

You're a dead man walking, Buzzard.

My mind raced with images of my pilfered dirk sliding between his ribs. Of slashing his throat. Of cutting off his balls.

"You have a valid argument, Jasmine." Bonnie nodded. "And we'll discuss it further when the mess of today is over with."

I swallowed a gasp. The *mess* of today? She talked about the murder of her two grandsons as if it was an inconvenient *mishap*.

Who are *these people?*

"No, I want to hear that she's mine. Right now." Her fingernails dug into my flesh, breaking my skin, imprinting crescent moon cuts.

I didn't flinch.

Jaz's eyes met mine. They were just as lifeless and cold as me. A switch had triggered in both of us, leaving us lost in this new world.

"You belong to me, Nila Weaver. You're the reason my two brothers are dead." Yanking me down to her height, she hissed, "You'll pay. I'll make you pay so damn much for what you've done."

What?

A cloud worse than numbness consumed me.

She'd lost everything back in the parlour. She'd even lost herself.

Who *was* this woman? Sure, Jasmine had never been ultra-friendly with me. In fact, she'd asked me to die the last time I'd visited her to save her brother. But I'd never seen someone so remote and vastly changed.

Then again, what did I expect? Why would she soften toward me now that the worst had happened?

Cut jumped in. "We'll discuss it at greater length. But I do agree; Daniel doesn't get full rights to her. You are my daughter and the successor matriarch. You know our empire inside out, whereas Daniel is yet to be trained. It's only fair that you have joint ownership of the final debts, and the pain she is required to pay."

I bit my lip, unable to tear my eyes away from Jasmine. What did this mean? Would I have to dig four graves instead of three? I never wanted to kill Jasmine. But I would if she gave me a reason.

It was me versus them now. I wouldn't back down again.

I'm done being tortured.

It was their turn.

Daniel stomped forward, throwing his hands up in a bad boy tantrum. "But, you fucking promised."

Cut sniffed. "I promised nothing. You will still inherit, but as I'm tearing up all the rules lately, there might be a dual inheritance. Primogeniture is over. I'm looking at all bases now."

"But that's not fair! There are rules, contracts!"

"Yes, and if I'd followed those rules, you wouldn't have her either, you fucking ingrate," Cut snapped. "I need a few days to unscramble this shit-storm. Then we can proceed correctly once the documents have been amended."

Wait. Documents? What amendments?

Daniel laughed, slipping beside me and wrapping his hand in my hair. The long strands tangled around his wrist, providing a perfect rope to jerk me away from Jasmine.

Only, she didn't let go. Her nails dug deeper into my wrist, keeping me pinned between the two fighting siblings.

"Let her go. She's mine!" Jaz slammed on her brakes.

"You can have her when I've taken what I want." Daniel yanked me toward him.

I cried out, tripping and swaying, two parts of me caught by two Hawks.

Oh, my God.

I was a piñata in the middle of a feuding family—tugged and devoured and ultimately beaten until I'd split open and die.

I laughed out loud at the insanity stinking up the room.

Jasmine was as bonkers as the rest of her bloodline. She would have to go, too.

He's dead.
He's dead.
He was good where they're all bad.

"Quit it!" Cut roared at the same time as Bonnie screeched, "Behave yourselves!"

The Hawk siblings quit squabbling like brats. We looked at Cut and Bonnie, panting hard, trapped in a cycle of idiocy.

"For fuck's sake." Cut dragged a hand over his face. "You're acting like two-year olds. I have a good mind to take the strap to both of you." His gaze fell on his children, searing and intense. "She'll be locked up until we have a family meeting. Then we can decide who has her first and what punishments shall be divided."

Jasmine sneered, "See, Dan. Let her go."

"You let go first."

"God, you're such a moron." Jasmine relinquished her hold. Instantly, blood seeped from the slices she'd given, trickling down my wrist.

"You're just an invalid who's never been laid." Daniel threw me away. "You always had it so easy, sister. Ever since your 'accident.'"

My ears pricked. The aura of mystery surrounding Jasmine only grew thicker. I wanted to know everything about her before I ended her. Just like I wanted to know everything about Bonnie, Cut, and Daniel. I would wear their history like a talisman. I would be the last person to know their tales before they faded into obscurity.

Jasmine sniffed. "You're pissed that your worthless *invalid* sister has won. I'm the eldest now; therefore, my word is law."

"Don't get ahead of yourself, Jaz," Cut said.

Daniel ignored him. "That's not it at all." Slamming his hands on the handrails of Jasmine's chair, he hemmed her in. "Now I have two women on my shit list instead of one." He dragged a finger across his throat. "I'd watch out if I were you."

Pushing off, he deliberately shouldered Cut out of the way, scowled at Bonnie, and stalked from the room.

The moment he disappeared, my muscles quivered. Somehow, I'd avoided whatever would've happened. I'd slipped into shock and come out ready to murder. And I'd been given to yet another Hawk who hated me.

Cut shook his head, looking at his mother. "They never fucking learn."

Bonnie laughed. "Neither did you, dear. Not for a long time."

He wrapped an arm around her brittle shoulders. "I can't imagine ever being so terrible."

My fingernails dug into my palm as I witnessed a seemingly normal bond. How could evil have so many layers? How could it be so obvious one moment, then hidden by family ties and hierarchy the next?

Bonnie tapped her cane against Cut's foot. "You're not forgetting what you did, are you? Because I have news for you—you were worse. A lot worse." Moving forward, she dislodged his hold. "But I straightened out the mess you made. I put things right. I have every faith you will, too."

Cut nodded. "Damn right, I will." His eyes strained but apart from a few cracks in his smooth veneer, I would never have guessed he'd pulled the trigger on two of his children.

He's dead.

He's dead.

All because of me.

Inching closer to Jasmine, I whispered so only she would hear. "He tried to shoot you, but Jethro saved you. Do you have no shame?"

Her eyes zeroed in on mine. Thoughts and emotions flickered over her face but she didn't reply.

Her betrayal hurt. Jethro and Kes had loved her. They'd *died* for her. Who could claim to love them in return yet continue to be in the same house as the man who'd shot them?

My stomach twisted. "You make me sick."

Her hands tightened around the rims of her wheels. Shutters slammed over her eyes, but still no response.

Tears stung but I had nothing else to say. Only one promise that she might as well hear, so she'd know who truly loved her brother. "I'll kill you for this. Just like I'll kill them."

She sat taller. Locking eyes with me, she said icily, "I guess we'll see, won't we?" Raising her voice, she pointed at the door. "Your fate will be discussed and decreed. Go to your room. Leave us."

I rubbed my wrist, smearing the blood she'd conjured. When I didn't move, she herded me with silver wheels toward the exit.

"I said leave." She didn't stop, pushing me between Cut and Bonnie.

My skin crawled as Cut reached out, gathering me to him. He brushed aside black hair that'd stuck to my clammy cheeks. His golden eyes shone with power. "I'm afraid our timeframe has accelerated since you've arrived. Emma was in my control for a delightful length of time. I'd hoped Jethro could manage the same. But…I raised lacklustre sons and have to hope my daughter can do better."

Jasmine nudged against the back of my thighs. "Let her go, father. She has to be trained in obedience." Her legs remained covered with a rose-coloured blanket, but temper flared her cheeks. "That was her issue with Jet. She never listened. I'll teach her otherwise."

How did I judge someone so wrong? All this time, I thought Jasmine was half-way sane—a crutch for her brother and stronger than all of them combined. But she was just as diabolical.

"If anyone can do it, it's you, Jasmine." Cut released me. "I have no doubt."

Bonnie smiled, leaning on her stick. "Jasmine is an exemplary student. She'll rise to the challenge."

"You never have to doubt, father." Jasmine's frosty voice sent goosebumps over my skin. "I'm ten times the man my brothers were."

Who *was* this person? This cold-hearted harpy who didn't

care. How could she sit there and speak to the man who'd killed her brothers, let alone agree to torture me.

He's dead.

He's dead.

He's free from this insanity.

I couldn't control the frothing animosity any longer. My lips pulled back. "You're all monsters. Every single one of you. You'll all pay."

Cut sighed, "You were told to leave, Ms. Weaver. I suggest you listen."

Bonnie swatted the back of my calves with her stick. "Move, you little guttersnipe."

"Wait, grandmamma." Jasmine wheeled herself in front of me with a few expert manoeuvres. "I have something else I want to say."

The room sucked in a breath, all of us waiting.

Her gaze fell on mine, dead and empty. "You, Nila Weaver, are the reason my best friend is dead. You are the reason I am now sister to only one brother. And you are the reason my family is falling apart." Her face darkened, manicured eyebrows shadowing angry eyes. "I asked you once to let the debts take place. I asked you to give your life for him—like it has always been. But you didn't listen."

Rolling away, she waved at the door. "Go to your room and think about that. Because this time, I'm not giving you a choice.

"This time, I'll make you pay."

Nila

I WOULD NEVER sleep again.

Not while Daniel roamed the corridors and Cut held my life in his hands. I would never relax while they breathed. I would never drop my guard while they plotted my demise.

But while they plotted, *I* plotted.

Together, we would meet in hell, and I was past caring who would win. As long as I exterminated them, I would happily trade my life for justice.

Twelve hours passed.

Twelve hours where my heart bled for Jethro and every minute erased his imprint on this world.

Twelve hours where I'd been alone.

I hadn't seen anyone but Flaw. He'd knocked on my door around 9:00 p.m., bringing venison stew and crusty baguettes. He'd looked as bad as I did—his piercing eyes fogged with stress, his dark hair a turbulent mess. He was a direct mirror of grey disbelief and desolation. I'd wanted him to stay—to protect me if Daniel decided to pay a nocturnal visit, but the moment he'd delivered my dinner, he left.

Food was ash inside my mouth, but I forced small bites, painstakingly swallowing and providing energy to the only weapon I could rely on. Once I'd eaten every morsel, I'd sat cross-legged in the centre of my bed and tightened my grip around the ruby-encrusted dirk.

I couldn't lie down because Jethro's smell laced my sheets.

I couldn't close my eyes because his handsome face and blazing love haunted me.

And I couldn't relax because I needed to be ready to attack if any Hawk came for me.

Only, they never came.

Daybreak brought a smidgen of peace, illuminating Hawksridge—yet again, hiding the filthy evil that seemed so obvious at night.

My cheeks itched from the salt of my sadness, and my head ached from dehydration.

For one heart-ripping moment, I permitted myself to fall face first on the bedding where Jethro had told me everything. I allowed grief to grab me with thick arms and smother me in terrible tears.

I relived his touch and kisses. I punished myself with memories of him slipping inside me, of him saying he loved me for the first time. I came completely undone as I hugged my knife and inhaled the last reminders I would ever have of him.

I had no photographs, no love letters.

Only a few texts and recollections.

They weren't worth any monetary value, but in a blink, they became my most prized possessions.

Once I'd shed a final tear and drugged myself on his subtle flavour of woods and leather, I hauled myself out of bed and into the shower. Stepping into the hot spray felt like a betrayal to Jethro—as if I washed away the past, moving into a future without him.

I thought I'd cried my final tear, but beneath the waterfall, I purged again, letting my tears swirl down the drain.

I will kill them.

And I will dance on their graves when I do.

Dawn morphed to morning, one hour blending into

another, drifting me further from Jethro's memory.

I tried to leave. My body was weak, needing fuel, mimicking my aching heart with emptiness. But the doorknob refused to spin.

They'd locked me inside.

Could I break it down? Destroy it? But why should I waste my fury on an innocent door when Cut and Daniel deserved to be torn into smithereens?

So, I did the only thing I could. I sat on my chaise and gripped my cell-phone with chilly fingers, begging for a miracle to happen.

Text me, Jethro.
Prove it's all a big mistake.

Over and over, I repeated my prayer, only for the stubborn phone never to answer. It remained blank and unfeeling, the battery slowly dwindling. The battle to keep going drained me to the point of exhaustion.

I could call for help. I could ring the police chief who'd taken me back after the Second Debt. But they'd wiped my file when I did the *Vanity Fair* interview. I'd cried wolf and they wouldn't believe me—especially as most of them were bought by Cut.

Plus, I can't leave Vaughn. I couldn't risk giving them ammunition to hurt him.

Indulging in the past, rather than dwelling on a desolate future, I opened every text he'd sent, reliving the rush and sexual frustration of forbidden whispers.

Kite007: *Me and my wandering hand missed you.*

The intoxicating innocence when I didn't know it was him.

Kite007: *If I said I wanted one night of blatant honesty, no douchebaggery, no bullshit of any kind, what would you say?*

The first crack in his cool exterior, revealing just how deep he ran.

Kite007: *I feel what you feel. Whether it be a kiss or a kick or a killing blow. I wished I didn't, but you're mine. Therefore, you are my affliction.*

The first taste of truth when he told me his condition in riddles.

Kite007: *Don't go into the dark alone, little Weaver. Monsters roam the shadows, and your time is officially up.*

The last darkness inside him that'd vanished entirely the night we revealed everything.

All of it.

Every letter and comma were still tangible, while the author had now vanished. I would've given anything for him to reappear—to magically reverse tragedy and come back to me.

Jethro…

Hunching over my phone, I let go again.

Wracking sobs, heaving ribs, and a dying soul screaming that nothing would ever be the same.

He's dead.

He's…

dead.

At lunchtime, Flaw appeared.

My only visitor and I didn't know if he was friend or foe.

For the past while, I'd stared into space, picturing gruesome ways to end it.

I couldn't cry anymore.

I couldn't read Kite's texts anymore.

All I could do was exist in a room where scents of love mixed with smells of war, settling deeper into hate.

Flaw didn't speak, only delivered a meal of salad and cured ham. With sad eyes, he retreated from my room and locked the door.

It'd taken over an hour before I had the energy to move from my crumpled, soggy ball. Along with the agony of grief, I'd surpassed the craving of hunger, leaving me blissfully blank of basic necessities.

I shivered, but I wasn't cold.

My stomach growled, but I wasn't hungry.

My heart kept beating, but I was no longer alive.

I wasn't human. I was a killer waiting for first blood.

Blood.

The thought of extracting hot, sticky red from Cut and Daniel kick-started my energy. My hand curled around my blade as I crawled across the carpet and poked the food.

Eat.

Stay strong.

Kill.

The ham settled like salty concrete on my tongue. Every mouthful wasn't about nutrition or satisfaction—it was about building power so I was ready for war.

Minute by minute, my anger solidified. The Hawks had been untouchable for long enough. They believed no amount of treason or rebellion could dethrone them.

They were wrong.

Their reign was over. It was time for a new ruler. One who stood for justice rather than debts. One who would avenge those she'd lost.

They've underestimated me.

And they would die because of it.

Dusk crept silently across my carpet.

The tentative darkness sucked the light from glittering sequins, sinking into rich velvet from the fabric bolts on the walls. Every minute its gloomy fingers made their way stealthily from window to bed, reminding me that my world might've ended yesterday, but the rest of the globe didn't care.

The sun still rose.

The moon still set.

And my heart still beat regardless.

My ears pricked as the harsh scrape of a key echoed from the opposite side of the room. I sat up in bed, rubbing my eyes, grabbing my dirk from the covers.

The door swung open.

I shifted to my knees, wielding the knife. After my shower last night, I'd dressed in black leggings and an oversized cream cardigan. But no matter how many layers or quilts I snuggled beneath, I couldn't eradicate the chill of loneliness.

My ears still echoed with gunshots.

My mind replayed the moment when Kes collapsed with blood blooming on his shirt, and Jethro dove to protect his sister.

The sister who didn't deserve to be saved.

My jaw clenched.

Jasmine.

She was in equal running for my dislike with Daniel. In fact, she was worse. Always coming across as gentle and removed from her mad family—when, in actual fact, she'd been the instigator and in cahoots with Bonnie.

Flaw appeared.

Peering around the door, he wore his typical outfit of jeans, black t-shirt, and Black Diamonds jacket. His gaze drifted to the knife in my hands, raising an eyebrow. "If you don't want that confiscated, I'd hide it if I were you."

My hands shook. "Why are you here?" I didn't see any trays of food. A social call was out of the question. Shuffling higher, I narrowed my eyes. "Why do you care if they take my knife or not?"

He ran a hand through his hair, opening the door wider. "Don't like this situation any more than you do."

His voice sounded loud and obtrusive, spilling secrets. It was the first time I'd spoken to someone since I'd been locked up; I'd forgotten how to do it.

My heart ached. "You miss them, too?"

Jethro…

Kes…

The only ones not tainted by Hawk insanity.

He nodded. "Kes has been a close friend for years. Didn't have much to do with Jethro until recently, but he proved he was a good bloke. Almost as good as his brother."

His comment hurt irrationally. To me, Jethro was better than anyone. Then again, my heart was biased. Kestrel was a genuine, caring friend who'd sacrificed far too much for people who didn't deserve him.

Myself included.

I hugged my knife, stroking it with the thought of spilling Cut's blood. "He was the best. His death won't go unpunished."

Flaw came closer, his boots silent on the emerald W carpet. "Words like that can get you into trouble."

I ran my thumb along the sharp blade. "I don't care. All I want is for them to die."

He cleared his throat. "Can't say I don't understand or feel your pain, but it's best to stop saying such things." Inching closer to the bed, he held out his hand. "I was told to bring you."

My head snapped up. "What?"

The last time someone had come to take me somewhere, the maid made me dress in breaches and cheesecloth, then delivered me to the worst poker night in history.

I tightened my grip on the dirk. "I'm not going anywhere with you."

He scowled. "Don't make this harder than it already is."

I moved away from him, inching to the other side of the bed. "Tell me why."

"Why?"

My heart cantered faster—almost as fast as Moth, the day Kes took me for a ride. I should've been nice to him. Kinder. Less suspicious.

I bared my teeth. "If this is to re-do the Third Debt, I'm not going. I'll kill you first." My threat wasn't empty. I boiled with the urge to do it—to prove I was done being weak.

Flaw jammed his hands in his back pockets. The action made him appear personable and less threatening.

I didn't buy it.

He'd been there that first night when Jethro stole me from

Milan. He'd witnessed what they'd done to me in the months I'd been there.

"I haven't been told anything. I guess you'll just have to come and find out for yourself."

"Tell Cut he can come for me himself."

My eyes darted around the room. I had weapons here: needles, scissors, scalpels for sculpturing lace. If I could entice Cut into my nest, I could ambush him with tools I knew how to wield.

He wouldn't stand a chance.

"Look—" He shrugged. "I was told not to tell you, but fuck it. They're in the library. And they have guests. I doubt they'll do anything of a…family matter…in front of an audience."

No, but they keep such blatant evidence.

Their audacity at keeping mementos of my ancestors' pain infuriated me. Once I'd killed them, I'd gather up every video and document and burn them. I'd demolish every evidence and set my ancestors' souls free.

Why not turn it into the police?

I shuddered. The thought of men in suits—men who the Hawks might've paid to turn a blind eye for so long—watching video-tapes of my mother's agony almost made me black out with a vicious vertigo wave.

Gripping the sheets, I let the dizziness subside before blinking my vision clear.

Flaw hadn't moved; a relaxed employee who knew I'd have to obey eventually.

"Why should I trust you? What's to stop you from lying?" He might've been Kes's friend, but he was still a Black Diamond. And they weren't to be trusted.

"Because I might be the last remaining friend you have in this godforsaken place." His face tightened for a moment, filling with thoughts he refused to share. "You need more? Fine. I happen to know the guests are lawyers." Holding out his hand, he said, "Happy? Now, let's go."

"Lawyers?" I shook my head. "Why?"

What on earth are lawyers doing here?

Flaw gave half a smile. "Instead of all the questions, how about you just get it over with?"

I didn't want to move but I couldn't deny he had logic on his side.

With one last glower, I swung my legs off the bed and padded toward him. The room wobbled from getting up so fast, but other than that, my bloodlust for Cut's life kept me focused on an anchor.

Jethro is no longer my anchor.

I was once again a shipwrecked boat, drifting on an ocean of misfortune.

Flaw's gaze fell to my knife. "You planning on taking that?"

"Do you have a problem with that?"

I waited for him to snatch it from me. To confiscate it. Instead, he pursed his lips. "I'm not the one on your shit list."

"Not at the moment, you aren't."

He sucked in a breath.

Rebellion and power siphoned through my blood. I didn't trust Flaw, but he wasn't my enemy. Holding eye contact, I hitched up the hem of my slouchy cardigan, tucked the dirk in my waistband, and concealed it.

He didn't say a word.

I was playing with fire. He was on their side. He could tell them I had it and leave me defenceless, but at the same time, I had to push and search for allies. Flaw had been kind to me whenever we'd crossed paths. He'd escorted me to my room late at night if Daniel caught me sneaking to the kitchens. He'd been there whenever I'd popped in to see Kestrel, laughing and seeming normal and carefree.

Anyone who was friends with Kes couldn't be too bad—Kes wouldn't tolerate it.

And I learned that the hard way.

He's dead.

Just like his brother.

My heart panged. No matter how strong I forced myself to be, I couldn't stop the lacerations of grief. It was like a rogue wave, lapping at my soul, tugging me under with its rip.

Flaw crossed his arms, challenge sparking in his eyes. "You know the knife won't be enough."

"I know."

He cocked his head. "Then why bother?"

Running my hands through my hair, I twisted the black length to drape over my shoulder. "Because they won't expect it. And the element of surprise can make a tiny knife become a sword."

He chuckled. "Deep. Sounds like Confucius or some other metaphorical bullshit."

I shrugged. "Doesn't matter. I know what I mean. I know what I'll do." My tone slid to ice. "And I suggest you stay out of my way and keep your mouth shut."

He laughed quietly. "Hey. As long as you stay away from me, I don't have a problem. Always knew things would change. Ever since Kes told me what Jethro planned to do on his thirtieth, I knew my lifestyle was up."

I froze.

He'll never age another day.

Jethro's corpse would forever remain twenty-nine—immortal and unchanging.

"What? What was he planning?"

"He didn't tell you?" He crossed his arms. "I thought you were deep as fucking thieves. That was the reason all of this grew out of control."

Breathing hard, I swallowed sadness. "No, he didn't tell me."

Flaw softened. "Sorry."

I swiped at my face, dispelling any sign of tears. "So, what was he planning?"

He's dead. But he's still here...holding me...guiding me.

Learning more about Jethro, even though he was gone,

was awfully bittersweet.

Flaw looked behind him at the open door. His face shadowed, and for a moment, I thought he'd refuse to say, but then he lowered his voice. "Once everything was his, he planned on ripping up the contracts. Ending it."

My eyes grew wide. "Forever?"

"Yup."

"He would have that power?"

Flaw turned rigid, his thoughts obviously on topics he didn't enjoy. "Of course. He was a Hawk. They made the contract. They had the power to absolve it. Jethro planned to split up the estate equally between his brothers and sister and ban Cut and Bonnie from the grounds." He rubbed his chin. "I only know that because Kes told me in a couple of years they might not require the Club to transport shipments because the shipments would stop altogether."

"He didn't want to smuggle anymore, either?" *Wow*. All this time I'd grown close to Jethro, yet we'd never shared our future together. Never lain in bed and murmured about what we wanted or dreamed.

Because our future was bleak.

Death for me. Heartache for him. Why focus on a fantasy when the reality threatened to destroy us?

Flaw moved toward the door. "Would you continue doing something illegal when you had more money than you could ever spend in hundreds of lifetimes?" His eyes darkened with nostalgia for his friends. "With the estate broken up, everyone could've gone their separate ways. Kes planned to take a few years off and spend it in Africa injecting some of the money taken from its soil back to its people." He sighed. "Like I said, a good man."

Placing his hand on the doorknob, he tilted his head. "Enough talking. They'll be waiting. Better get you there before they suspect something."

The cold steel of the blade wedged against my back. It gave me courage but couldn't stop my sudden tremble. "Will you give me your word you're not taking me somewhere for those psychopaths to hurt me?"

His jaw clenched. "I just told you insider information that could get me killed if you said anything. Doesn't that deserve a little trust?"

"It does if it was said out of understanding rather than manipulation. I've fallen for the kind act far more times than I'm comfortable with."

Flaw frowned. "Would it help to know I give you full permission to gut the next bastard who tries to hurt you?"

My heart stuttered. "Permission? You think I need your *permission*?" Moving toward him, I stood close enough to smell his spicy aftershave and leather from his jacket. "Give me something better than your permission, Flaw."

He straightened. "Like what?"

"Like freedom." I waved at the window. "I could've run. I could've somehow found my way to the boundary and vanished, but they have my brother. Bring V to me and we'll go. I'll take my family and disappear."

And then I'll come back and murder them in their sleep.

His eyes burned into mine. "You know I can't do that."

"So, all your talk of a better future and good men...that was what? Empty words?"

He scowled. "There are things going on that you don't know about."

I threw my hands up. "Oh, really? Funny, I've never heard that before."

Once again, thoughts flickered over his face, secrets shadowing his eyes.

"If that's true, tell me. What's going on?"

He looked away. "I can't answer that."

I laughed morbidly. "No, of course, you can't."

"That's not fair."

My temper frayed, entirely unleashed. "That's not *fair*?" I poked him in the chest. "What's *fair* about me being subjected to more Hawk insanity? What's fair about having the love of my life shot in front of me? What's fair about waiting to die?!"

His hands fisted.

"You know what; I'm done." Shaking my head, I brushed past him into the corridor. "Just take me to them like a good minion and get out of my sight."

He growled under his breath. "Don't judge me. Don't judge my actions based on what you can't see." Stomping in front of me, he said over his shoulder, "I know who I am, and I know what I do is right."

Animosity flared between us.

I stayed silent, following him down the corridor toward the wing where I'd spent most time with Kestrel. We passed the room where he'd given me the Weaver Journal and headed into the hall where the library was located. My mind flickered back to the afternoon he'd found me, asking if Jethro had been to see me since completing the First Debt.

At the time, his question wasn't too unusual. But now it took on a whole new meaning. He wasn't asking about me. He'd been asking about his brother—keen to know how absorbing my pain had affected his empathetic sibling.

God, how bad had Jethro felt? How much did my thoughts destroy him?

"In there." Flaw stopped outside the library.

So many memories were already stored in this place. So many breakthroughs and breakdowns as I grew from girl to woman.

Not making eye contact, he muttered, "They're waiting for you. Better get inside." Without a goodbye, he turned on his heel and left.

His retreating back upset me all over again. He was the last connection I had to Kestrel's kindness and to Jethro's ultimate plans.

Come back.

My soul scrunched tight as the ghosts of Jethro and Kes haunted the walls of their home. In twenty-four hours, I'd gone through the cycles of bereavement: disbelief, shock, despair, rage…I doubted I'd ever get through acceptance, but I embraced my anger, building a barrier that only clearheaded, cold-hearted fury could enter.

I didn't want any other emotion when facing Cut and Daniel.

Touching the dagger hilt, I straightened my shoulders and pushed open the library doors.

My eyes widened as I stepped into the old world charm of book-bindings and scripted letters. The large beanbags where Kes had found me dozing still scattered. The window seats waited for morning sunshine and a bookworm to absorb themselves in fairy-tale pages.

This place was a church of stories and imagination. But then my gaze fell on the antichrist, polluting the sanctity of peace.

"Nice of you to join us, Nila." Cut waved at the one and only empty chair at the large oak table.

My teeth clamped together. I didn't reply.

"Come." He snapped his fingers. "Sit. We've waited long enough."

You can do this.
Obey until an opportunity presents itself.
Then…
kill
him.

I drifted forward, drawn by the multiple pairs of eyes watching me.

Bonnie, Daniel, Jasmine, Cut, and four men I didn't recognise waited for me to join them. The four men wore sombre black suits and aubergine ties—a uniform painting them with the same brush.

I drew closer to the table.

Daniel stood up, wrapping a vile arm around my waist. "Missed you, Weaver." Planting a kiss on my cheek, he whispered, "Whatever happens here tonight doesn't mean shit, you hear me? I'm coming for you, and I don't fucking care what they say."

I shuddered with disgust.

Withdrawing the hate from his voice, Daniel transformed into a cordial smile. "Sit." With a gallant act, he pulled out the empty seat. "Take a load off. This is going to be a long meeting."

I wanted to touch his pulse, count his heartbeat, relish in knowing they were numbered.

Soon, Daniel...soon...

Locking my jaw, so I didn't say anything I might regret, I sat down.

The men in matching suits never looked away. They ranged in age from sixties with greying hair to mid-thirties with blond buzz cut.

Daniel kicked my chair forward so my stomach kissed the lip of the table. I sucked in a breath, straightening my spine uncomfortably in order to tolerate the tight arrangement.

His golden eyes met mine, smug and vainglorious.

I'll cut that look right off your face.

My fingers twitched for my knife.

Daniel sat beside me, while the person on my other side hissed, "No speaking unless spoken to. Got it?"

My eyes shot to Jasmine. Her hands rested on the table, a cute gold ring circling her middle finger, while her seat perched on a small ramp, bringing the wheels in line with the chairs of the other guests. She looked like a capable heiress, dressed in a black smock with a black ribbon around her throat. She was the epitome of a mourning sister.

I don't buy it.

I'd misjudged her—thought she was decent and caring. She'd fooled me the most.

Tearing my gaze from her, I glanced at the remaining Hawks. Just like Jasmine, they all wore black. Bonnie looked as if she'd jumped into a jungle of black lace and fastened it with glittering diamond broaches. Cut wore an immaculate suit with black shirt and tie. Even Daniel looked fit for the opera in a glossy onyx ensemble and satin waistcoat.

I'd never seen so much darkness—both on the outside and inside. They'd discarded their leather jackets in favour of mourning attire.

All for what?

To garner sympathy from outsiders? To play the part of grieving family, even though they were the cause of murder?

I hate you.

I hate all of you.

My hands balled on the table. I wanted to say so many things. I wanted to launch onto the table and stab them with my knife. But I heeded Jasmine's warning and stayed put. There was no other way.

Cut cleared his throat. "Now that we're all here, you may begin, Marshall." His gaze pinned the oldest stranger. "I appreciate you coming after work hours, but this matter has to be dealt with quickly."

Bonnie reclined in her chair, a faint smile on her lips.

Every time I looked at the old bat, I got the feeling she was the meddler in all of this. She was the reason Cut was the way he was. She was the reason why Jasmine was disabled and Jethro and Kes were dead. I guessed she was also the reason why Jethro never mentioned his mother.

I'd been in their lives for months, yet no one had uttered a thing about Mrs. Cut Hawk.

Unless it was a miracle conception and Cut carved his children from his bones like some evil sorcerer, she had to have existed and stuck around long enough to give Cut four babies.

Where is she now?

Images of Jethro and Kes reuniting with their mother in heaven gave me equal measure of despair and comfort.

If she's even dead.

She could be trapped in the house, on a floor I didn't know, in a room hidden from view. She might be alive and not know that her husband killed two of her sons.

God, what a tragic—

The stranger coughed, stealing my attention. "Thank you, Bryan." Meticulously, he aligned a wayward fountain pen beside his tan ledger before looking at his colleagues. "I'll start, gentlemen."

His grey eyes locked on me, gluing me into my chair. "You must be Ms. Weaver. We haven't had the pleasure of meeting up till now."

My back bristled.

Any man who'd studied the law and permitted the Hawks to continue to get away with what they did wasn't someone I wanted to speak with.

Daniel nudged me. "Say hello, Nila."

I clamped my lips together.

"You don't want to be rude." He snickered. "These guys have met all the Weavers. Isn't that right, Marshall?"

My heart stopped.

What does that mean?

Marshall nodded. "That is correct, Mr. Daniel. I, personally, am lucky enough to have met your mother, Ms. Weaver. She was a fine young woman who loved you very much."

I thought the pain of Jethro's death had broken me past any other emotional agony.

I was wrong.

The mention of my mother *crippled* me. A sob wrapped wet tentacles around my lungs.

Don't cry. Do not cry.

I would never cry again. Not as long as these people lived.

I'll slaughter you all!

Jasmine arched her neck condescendingly. "Instead of torturing an already tortured girl, let's get on with it, shall we?" Her eyes gleamed. "Leave the emotional battery to me once the legalities are straightened out."

Cut chuckled, eyeing his daughter with newfound awe. "Jasmine, I must say, I never knew you were so capable."

Bonnie preened like some proud mother hen. "That's

because I told you to leave her to me." White tendrils of hair escaped her chignon, wisping in the low-lit room. "She's stronger than Jet, Kes, and Dan combined. And it's all thanks to me."

I wanted to vomit. Or slash her to pieces. Either would work.

How could someone of that age, who should be tender and kind, be so heartlessly cruel?

Jasmine merely nodded like a princess accepting a compliment and turned her attention back to the life-stealing, blood-sucking, soul-leaching lawyer. "You may continue, Mr. Marshall."

Marshall stretched his wrinkly face into a smile. "As you wish, Ms. Jasmine." Waving at his partners, he said, "Ms. Weaver, before we begin, we must honour the common niceties. I am principal director of the firm Marshall, Backham, and Cole. We have provided legal counsel and been sole conservator of the Hawk family for generations. My father was proud to be of service and his father and his father before him. There is nothing about the Hawk legacy that we are not a part of." His eyes narrowed. "Do you know what I'm saying?"

I stopped breathing.

A part of everything?

So outsiders were aware of what went on inside these walls? Lawyers knew what the Debt Inheritance entailed and yet they were *okay* with it?

My body throbbed with another flush of fury.

I didn't just want to steal three lives but theirs, too. The corridors of Hawksridge Hall would flow with blood by the time I eradicated the amount of people in on this ancient serial killing spree. Their innards would drape the walls, and their bones would rot the foundations with their malicious ideals.

That's all they are.

Rich, eloquent, intelligent murderers hiding behind false pretences of contracts and signatures.

Would they sign a new contract giving me the right to

slash their throats and tear out their hearts in payment for atrocities committed?

It doesn't matter.

I didn't need their permission.

I focused on the table, on the swirls of wood grain, rather than his face. If I looked up, I wouldn't have the strength to stay in my chair. "You're saying you presided over my ancestors' executions? That you helped bribe away the truth and protect these sick bastards?"

Cut shot to his feet. "Nila!"

I ignored him, my fingernails digging into my palms. "You're saying you helped change the law and enabled one family to destroy another? You're saying you had my ancestors *killed*?"

I slammed my chair back, my voice reaching a glass-shattering octave. "You're saying that you can sit there, talk to me, tell me whatever bullshit you're about to do, all the while *knowing* they mean to chop off my head, and you don't have a *problem* with that?"

Jasmine snatched my wrist. "God's sake, sit your arse down."

"Let go of—" I cried out as Daniel grabbed my hair and shoved me forward. I lost my footing; my face smashed against the table. Instantly, blood spurted from my nose, pain resonating in my skull.

Sickness drenched my senses with agony.

"Drop her, Daniel!" Cut yelled.

Daniel's fingers were suddenly torn from my hair, letting me slouch backward, landing in my chair. Jasmine fought off her brother, slapping him away. "Don't fucking touch her. What did I say? *I'm* in charge. *I'm* the oldest."

My eyes watered as more blood gushed from my nose. I didn't think it was broken, but the room spun with an induced vertigo wave.

God, what was I thinking?

The plan was to remain cool and invisible, looking for the

perfect chance.

Now I couldn't think straight with pain.

"You're not in fucking charge, Jaz. She's mine." Daniel pointed at Marshall. "Tell her. Amend it, so my sister can shut the fuck up about the rules."

Marshall looked awkwardly at Cut. "Sir?"

Cut ran a hand over his face, slowly sitting back down. "No, the conversation we had yesterday still stands." His lips turned up at the rapidly building stain from my nosebleed. Every red drip redecorated the table and the front of my cardigan. "Someone get her a damn napkin."

Jasmine shuffled in her wheelchair, pulling out a white handkerchief. "Here." Shoving it into my hand, her eyes flickered with compassion.

It only made me hate her more.

Scrunching up the material, I held it to my nose, getting sick joy from destroying the white perfection. The stuffiness made me breathless, and my eyes drifted to the corner where initials had been embroidered.

JKH

I dropped it.

Oh, my God.

My hand splayed open, tinged with crimson and sticky but unable to hide the two tattoos on my fingertips. JKH.

Jasmine kept her brother's handkerchief.

Why? To rub salt in already hollowed wounds or to laugh over fooling him just like she'd fooled me.

I locked eyes with her, pouring all my rage into my stare. "You'll pay for what you've done." Glancing at Bonnie and Cut, I added, "You'll *all* pay."

Marshall cleared his throat loudly. "I think the little interlude has come to an end. Shall we continue?"

"Yes, let's," Bonnie sniffed. "Never seen something so unruly in all my life." Sniffing in my direction, she tilted her chin. "Another word out of you, Weaver, and you won't like the consequences."

Daniel moaned, "But Grandmamma—"

"Buzzard, zip it," Cut growled. "Sit down or leave. But don't fucking talk again."

Daniel muttered under his breath but plonked back into his chair.

Jasmine grabbed the red-sodden material and shoved it under my nose. "Hold this, shut up, and don't get into any more trouble."

The skirmish ended; no one moved.

Silence hovered thick over the table.

The only sound was the heavy ticking of a grandfather clock by the gold ladder leading to the limited editions above. Side lamps had been switched on, filling the large space with warm illumination, while curtains blocked any remaining light that dared trespass on priceless books or fade cherished words.

Finally, Marshall sucked in a breath. He rearranged his fountain pen again. "Now that we're all on the same page, I'll carry on." Looking at me, he said, "For the rest of this meeting, you may address me as Marshall, or by my first name, which is Colin. These are my colleagues."

Pointing to the man closest to him: a potbellied, watery-eyed bald guy, he continued, "This is Hartwell Backham, followed by Samuel Cole, and my son Matthew Marshall."

My nose ached but the bleeding had stopped, leaving me stuffed up. I glowered at the men. There wasn't an ounce of mercy in their gazes.

They were here to do the job they'd been entrusted. Their loyalties were steadfast. Their intentions unchangeable.

I doubted they saw me as human—just a clause in a contract and nothing more.

Daniel poked me under the table. "After your little stunt, the least you can do is be nice." His voice deepened. "Say hello."

Yet another way to make me obey. He didn't care about pleasantries—only about making me submit to his every childish whim.

I sat straighter.

I'll do nothing of the sort.

Jasmine nudged me. "If you won't listen to him, listen to me. Do it."

I glared at her. "Why should I?"

"Because you belong to her, you little cow." Grabbing her cane, Bonnie struck her chair leg as if the furniture would turn into a horse and gallop her away from there. "Start. Now."

Marshall launched into action. "Of course, Madame Hawk. My apologies." Slapping open the file in front of him, his partners copied. Ledgers flung open and pens uncapped.

"Let me assure you that we're honoured to once again provide service to your impeccable family," Marshall twittered like a buffoon.

Cut groaned, steepling his fingers. "Lose the arse kissing. Did you bring the file or not?"

Paper scattered the wooden tabletop like fallen snowflakes, reminding me all over again of the icy way Jethro protected himself—the arctic coolness and thawing as I slowly made him want me.

The pain in my nose shot to my heart.

He's dead.

He's dead.

Don't think about him.

Marshall selected a certain page. "I did." Looking at his son—the blond buzz cut douchebag—he pointed at a box by the exit. "Grab that will you, Matthew?"

Matthew shot to his feet. "Sure." In a whisper of cashmere suit, he went to retrieve the large white box.

Curiosity rose to know what was in it. But at the same time, I was past caring.

More bullshit. More games.

None of it mattered because I was playing a different game. One they wouldn't understand until it was too late.

Jasmine scooted her wheelchair back a little, giving Matthew access to the table.

He smiled in thanks, placing the heavy box before his father. Marshall stood up and opened the lid while his son sat back down.

I sniffed, trying hard to clear my nostrils of blood. The pounding headache made everything fuzzy—a struggle to completely follow. I wanted to be coherent for whatever was about to happen.

No one spoke as Marshall removed reams and reams of paper and stacked them in neat piles on the table. The more he withdrew, the more aged the paper became. The first pile was pristinely white, neat edges, and uniformed lettering from a computer and printer.

The next stack was thin and cream-coloured, smudged edges, and the fuzzy blocks of a typewriter ribbon.

What is going on?

The third was yellowed and crinkled, shabby with torn edges, and the spidery scrawl of human penmanship.

And the final stack was moth-eaten, the colour of coffee, and swirling calligraphy of an art lost long ago.

That colour...

Its coffee bean shade was similar to the Debt Inheritance scraps Cut had given me at my welcome luncheon.

Could it be...

My attention zeroed in on Cut.

"Do you hazard a guess as to what that is, Nila?"

I shivered at the fatherly way he said my name, as if this was a family lesson. Something to be proud of and honoured to be an exclusive member.

I don't need to guess.

I cocked my chin. "No, I don't."

He chuckled. "Come now. You already know. I can see it in your eyes."

"I don't know what you're talking about."

Jasmine huffed. "Just be honest. For once in your life." Her voice dropped to a harsh curse. "Don't make this any worse, for God's sake."

Whoa...

After everything she'd done. After cuddling up to her father after he shot Jethro and Kes and promising me a world of hurt for being responsible for such a tragedy, she had the *audacity* to make it seem as if I were unappreciative and uncooperative.

Not going to fly anymore.

Screw being meek and quiet.

I'd tried that.

Now, I snapped.

Turning to face her, my hackles rose. The claws I'd grown when I'd first arrived unsheathed, and I wanted nothing more than to drag them across her face. "I'd watch what you say to me...*bitch*."

The room sucked into a dark hole, hovering in space, glacial and deadly.

The curse hovered between us, not fading—if possible, only growing louder the more the silence deafened.

I never swore. Ever. I never called people names or stooped to such a crass level. But since Jethro had died, I'd sunk steadily into profanity, and the power of that simple word bolstered my courage a thousand times.

I *loved* the righteous power it gave me.

I loved the shock factor it delivered.

Jaz gaped. "What did you just call me?"

I smiled as if I had a mouthful of sugar. "Bitch. I called you a bitch. A motherfucking bitch, and I think you'll find the name suits you."

Bonnie slapped her cane onto the table, cracking the palpable tension. "Watch your tongue, hussy. I'll have it ripped out before you can—"

Jaz held up her hand. "Grandmamma, let me handle this." Her eyes narrowed to bronze blades. "Let me get this straight. *I'm* the bitch? I'm the bitch for loving my brothers so much that I now want to avenge their deaths by killing the person who took theirs? I'm the bitch because I gave everything to

Jethro, including the use of my legs, and don't deserve to honour his memory by making you suffer?"

Her face turned red. "Excuse me if you don't think I'm worth that, Ms. High and Fucking Mighty. Perhaps, we should kill your brother and see what sort of person *you'd* turn into."

My heart exploded at the mention of harming Vaughn. "Don't you *dare* touch him."

"Address me properly and we'll see." Jasmine shoved her face close to mine. "Behave yourself and your twin will walk away when you die. Don't, and his head will be in the basket beside yours."

Oh, my God.

I couldn't breathe.

I couldn't even speak through the horrors of what she'd said.

"If you so much as touch him—"

"You'll what? Kill me? Yeah, right." Jaz rolled her eyes. "Like anyone believes you're capable of that, little Weaver. Even Jethro knew you could never hurt him and that's why he—"

I slapped my hands over my ears. "Stop it!"

Daniel broke out into loud guffaws. "Well, fuck me, sis. You're kinda badass."

Jaz looked at her younger brother. The harsh glint in her eyes increased with maliciousness. "You have no idea, baby brother."

Cut clapped his hands. "Marshall continue. My mother must rest, and we have a lot to cover. Ignore any further outbursts and get on with it."

Marshall nodded. "Yes, sir. Of course."

Jasmine twisted away from me, facing the lawyers. She breathed steadily with no adverse reactions to our verbal war.

The lawyers shuffled and stacked their files. No one was fussed that Jaz had just announced every sordid detail. That she'd admitted to holding me and my twin hostage or that they callously planned a double homicide.

And why would they?

They belonged body, heart, and soul to the devil born Hawks.

Marshall pointed at the piles of paperwork. "Mr. Hawk has advised me that you were shown the original document labelled the Debt Inheritance. Is that correct, Ms. Weaver?"

My muscles quaked with the need to bolt or fight. Both would be preferable. Sitting sandwiched between Jaz and Daniel only wound me tighter.

My mind ran with profanity.

Fuck you.

"Answer him, Nila," Cut said.

"You already know that that's correct."

Marshall warmed to his task, finally having one of his questions answered without Armageddon breaking out.

God, I wish you were here, Jethro. Sitting beside me, granting me strength.

I was all alone.

"Fantastic. Well, that document is just the first of many that you're about to become acquainted with." Laying his hand on the oldest looking stack, he lowered his voice. "These documents are the originals, passed down through our firm and our connection with the Hawks to keep safe and protected. In here exists every note, amendment, and requested clause update. It has been lodged in accordance with the times and royals in power, drifting through kings, queens, and ultimately, prime ministers and diplomats."

My headache came back at the nonsense he spouted. "You're telling me people in power kept signing these...when they knew all along what it was?"

Hartwell Backham answered, his voice rich as burnished copper. "Don't underestimate the power of a family crest or the name of the oldest law firm in England. We have garnered centuries of goodwill, and our clients sign what we suggest. They trust our judgement and don't have time for consuming activities such as reading every document that crosses their tables."

There was so much wrong with that sentence, it astounded me.

"You're saying that—"

Marshall interrupted me, doing what Cut had told him and powering through my retaliation. "Over the years, the Debt Inheritance has had to...how shall I say? Adapt."

I couldn't argue. I couldn't win.

All I could do was sit and silently seethe.

"All contracts are amended at some point or another, and this is no different." Marshall uncapped his fountain pen. "I hope that's self-explanatory, so I can skip to the next topic."

"No, it isn't self-explanatory." I snarled, "What you're saying is all this talk of being set in stone and law-abiding is actually not—it's revised to suit your benefits with no input from my family?"

My stomach roiled at the unfairness. How could they change the rules and tote it over our heads like gospel? How could they notarise something without both parties agreeing?

Who were these corrupt, money-grubbing lawyers?

Cut tutted under his breath. "Don't force me to gag you, Ms. Weaver." His eyes blackened as if I'd offended his moral code.

What moral code?

He was scum.

"Everything we do is within the parameters set by our current law. We've made sure nothing is carried out until it's first written, signed, and witnessed."

"Even rape and murder?"

Bonnie leaned forward. "Watch your tongue."

Cut clasped his fingers. "I'll allow that one last question. Perhaps, if you finally understand that all of this is meticulously recorded, then you might stop thinking you've been indisposed and suffering an injustice."

Sitting taller in his chair, he buffed his fingernails on his cuff. "Things outside the realm of understanding can become approved if it's drafted and agreed to. What do you think war is, Nila? It's a contract between two countries that men in their comfy offices sign. With one signature, they deliver countless resources and sign the death warrant of so many lives. That's murder. And it's all done with no comeuppance because they had a *contract* stating they had the full use of enlisted men's lives all for greed, money, and power."

I hated that he made sense; hated that I agreed with my archenemy. The world had always been twisted in that respect. Sending men off to war, only to die the moment they landed on enemy soil...then to send yet more men to the exact same battlefield, knowing the outcome would be death.

That was homicide on a negligent global scale, and those in power never paid for their crimes.

I sat silent.

Cut smiled, knowing he'd gotten through to me in some way. "When I say everything was done by the law, I do mean *everything*." He nodded at the stacks of paper. "In there, you'll find every deviation from the Debt Inheritance along with a Hawk signature and a Weaver's."

My heart skipped painfully. "You're saying my family *signed* this?" I snorted. "I don't believe that. Did you force them under duress?"

Marshall huffed. "At no point would my firm accept such a thing. We have iron-clad records that protect our client's reputation. We have proof to show there was no hardship signing the amendments."

Like I believed him. He let murderers get away with it for six hundred years.

Plucking a piece of paper from the fourth pile, he handed it to me. "See for yourself."

Part of me wanted to crumple it up and throw it in his face, but I restrained.

Calmly, I accepted the page and scanned it.

The scraps Cut had given me in return for serving them lunch had been taken from this document. The Debt

Inheritance was there in its entirety.

My eyes highlighted certain lines, remembering the ridiculous contract.

For actions committed by Percy Weaver, he stands judged and wanting.

Even I agreed with that after he'd sent an innocent girl to her death by ducking stool and a boy to be raped for twelve hours.

Bennett Hawk requires a public apology, monetary gain, and most of all, bodily retribution.

How much money did Weaver pay? Was it enough for the Hawks to somehow leave England, find their diamonds, and became untouchable through wealth?

In accordance with the law, both parties have agreed that the paperwork is binding, unbreakable, and incontestable from now and forever.

That part I didn't believe, but it wasn't arguable. In the minds and pockets of the Hawks, Weavers had to pay continuously toward the bottomless debt.

But Jethro would've ended it.

We could've been the last generation to ever have to deal with this brutal nonsense.

Percy Weaver hereby solemnly swears to present his firstborn girl-child, Sonya Weaver, to the son of Bennett Hawk, known as William Hawk. This will nullify all unrest and unpleasantries until such a time as a new generation comes to pass.

So the boy who'd been raped for Weaver's gambling debts was the one who'd carried out the first Debt Inheritance? Had he taken great joy in hurting the daughter of his enemy, or had he hated it as much as Jethro?

This debt will not only bind the current occupancies of the year of our Lord 1472 but every year thereafter.

How something had lasted for so long was a testament to feuds and grudges of wealthy madmen.

Once I'd reached the bottom, Marshall handed me another page. "This was the last amendment to the contract before today's meeting."

Doing a switch, I scanned the new document. The page was white and modern—only a few years old rather than decades.

In the case of the last surviving line of Alfred 'Eagle' Hawk and Melanie Warren, the succession of the Debt Inheritance will go to Bryan 'Vulture' Hawk over his recently deceased brother, Peter 'Osprey' Hawk.

I frowned, absorbing the legal jargon.

What did it mean?

I looked at the very bottom, sucking in a breath as I double-checked the feminine sweep.

No.

My mother's signature.

"What—"

I read it again. No matter how much I wished it wasn't true, it was. My mother's signature inked the paper, prim and proper, just as I remembered her writing style to be.

Right beside hers was Cut's masculine scrawl.

My brain scrambled; I glared at Cut. "You weren't firstborn."

Cut smiled slyly. "Never said I was."

Bonnie's red lips spread into a sneer. "Sad day for all involved." She tapped her fingers on the table. "I'd groomed my firstborn to be a worthy heir. Peter would've been a good leader but circumstances I didn't foresee came to light." Her gaze narrowed at Cut, full of reproof and history.

Cut shrugged. "A little mishap. That's all."

Bonnie coughed. "Call it what you want. I still haven't forgiven you."

Cut only laughed.

What on earth happened in that generation? What about the ages of the men? How was Cut allowed to claim my mother? Was that why she'd had children? Hearing that the firstborn Hawk had died, had she believed she was unbound to the debts?

If that was the case, how did she know what the future

entailed when I hadn't been told until Jethro appeared in Milan? *Tex kept it from me. Emma might've been forewarned.*

So many questions. So many scenarios.

When did Peter Hawk die?

If he died when my mother was young, maybe that was why she fell so hard for my father. Drunk on the thought of freedom, she'd started a family far younger than she might've done thinking we were all...safe.

What a horrible, terrible joke.

Questions danced on my tongue. I chose the most random but most poignant. "What happens when you run out of Weavers to torture? I won't have children. Vaughn won't. What then?"

Daniel laughed. "Remember that sister I joked about?"

Oh, my God. It's true?

Cut interrupted. "You have no other siblings, Nila. I would've told you if you did. Merely a farce."

Daniel scowled. "Thanks for fucking ruining my fun. Had her believing that for months."

I hadn't believed it...but I'd wondered.

"So, it was all nonsense?"

Cut shook his head. "Not quite. You have a cousin. A few times removed but still bearing the Weaver name. We would look at all avenues if the future required it."

Poor cousin.

I overflowed with rage. "Do you ever listen to yourself? You're talking about people, for God's sake."

If Cut went after my unknown cousin, that didn't explain the previous generations that'd had no children or were killed off before carrying on the bloodline. How did it continue for so long when having a child was never a guarantee?

I knew how. They'd amended it. Tweaked the so-called unbreakable contract to fit with the Hawks' demented ideals.

Marshall plucked the paper from my hands. "I believe we're getting off topic, Ms. Weaver." Waving the parchment, he said, "Let's focus on today's subjects. Happy now you've seen the evidence with your own eyes?"

"Happy isn't a word I know anymore." I bared my teeth. "She wouldn't have signed that without being threatened. I don't care what you say."

That fleeting afternoon when my mother returned home, adorned with the diamond collar and hugging me so tightly, came to mind. She'd been terrified but resigned. Broken but strong. I hadn't understood back then, but now I did.

She'd reached the same stage I had. The stage where nothing else mattered but getting even, claiming justice.

There's a point to this meeting.

My heart froze solid, finally understanding. "I won't sign anything. I can assure you of that. You might as well pack up and piss off because I'll tear apart anything you put in front of me."

Jasmine growled; Cut merely chuckled. "I'm sure if you did that, you'd make Daniel a very happy man."

Daniel draped an arm over me. "Oh, please, Weaver. Do it for me. You have my full permission to refuse the amendment and cut Jaz out of the updated terms."

"Like hell she will." Jasmine looped her fingers together in aggression. "You'll sign, Nila. You'll see."

I didn't reply, glaring at the table instead.

Marshall shuffled the paper. "All right, let's carry on." Pinching the top sheet from the newest looking tower, he pushed it toward me. "This is the latest amendment and requires your signature."

My blood charged through overheated veins. "I told you—"

"Shut it." Jasmine snatched the paper and stabbed the bottom where an empty box waited for my life to spill upon it. "Do it. It's your only choice."

Our eyes locked. Not only did I hate her for what she'd done and how much she'd tricked me, but I hated that she looked so much like him.

Jethro.

The shape of her nose. The curve of her cheekbones. She was the closest in appearance to him, and it hurt to hate someone who looked so much like the man I loved.

"I told you. I'm not signing anything."

Jaz's cheeks flushed. I wouldn't put it past her to slap me. In fact, I wanted her to because then I'd have an excuse to fight with a girl in a wheelchair.

Could I kill her? Could I slide my blade into her heart all while knowing Jethro had cared for her?

He was tricked...same as me.

I would honour his memory by destroying yet another person who'd betrayed him.

Hartwell shifted in his chair. "You don't know the terms yet. Listen before being hasty."

Jasmine tore her eyes away from mine, glaring at the lawyer. "The terms being that I have full right to both Weavers, Nila and Vaughn. In return, Daniel can have the estate and all monetary wealth that comes from being heir."

I flinched, shivering in the sudden arctic hatred she projected.

"That has been discussed, Ms. Jasmine. I feel you'll be satisfied with the arrangements."

Jasmine sniffed haughtily. "Discussions aren't conclusions. There is no negotiation on the matter. I want to extract the Fourth and Final Debt. That right is mine."

"Jasmine, calm down. I'm sure you'll be satisfied with the new arrangement." Cut held out his hand. "Give me the contract, Hartwell. Let me see everything has been noted before we make it official."

Marshall stole the paper from me and slid it up the table.

Cut caught it; he took his time reading, his eyes darting over fine print.

I breathed hard, suffering a crushing weight of grief and revulsion.

He's dead.
But they're not.

Why couldn't Cut and Bonnie be dead instead of Jethro and Kestrel?

Because life is never fair and it's up to me to carve out justice.

Jasmine remained rigid until Cut finally raised his eyes and shot the contract over the satin wood toward us. "I'm happy with that. The Fourth Debt will be repaid slightly differently to the rest, but that will be another discussion." His eyes met his children's. "In this case, three signatures will be required—Nila, Dan, and Jaz."

He made it sound like a school permission slip for us all to go play happily together.

I snorted, rolling my eyes.

Cut gave me a stern look.

Samuel Cole, who hadn't made a sound since I'd arrived, spoke up. "In that case, it is my duty to advise all of you that this new clause will be forever known as amendment 1-345-132."

My eyes widened. How many amendments had there been to warrant such a crazy number?

Judging by the stacks of paperwork…a lot. Far too many. Was there anything left of the original contract?

Mr. Cole continued, "Due to the unfortunate deaths of the firstborn, Jethro Hawk…"

Pain slammed into me.

Agony tore out my heart.

Misery crumbled me into dust.

Jethro.

God, I wish you hadn't left me.

I couldn't sit up straight; howling winds of grief ripped me apart. I hunched into myself, holding my ribcage to keep from sobbing.

I managed to remain silent.

But Jasmine didn't.

Her lip wobbled, tears streaking her cheeks. She cracked, but it didn't last long. Sucking in a breath, she reached into the small satchel attached to her wheelchair and pulled out another handkerchief.

Bowing her head, she dabbed at her eyes.

My lips twisted in disgust. "I don't buy your crocodile tears. Don't bother putting on a show when I know you were part of this murder from the start."

Her head shot upright. Our souls duelled, violence sparking between us.

Cole cleared his throat. "In natures of the firstborn perishing, the following may occur: The Debt Inheritance can be called null and void, leaving Ms. Weaver to propagate and provide a new heir for the payment at a later date, or, if both parties agree, a new heir instated. In the case of Jethro 'Kite' Hawk's demise, the second in line, Angus 'Kestrel' Hawk also suffered an untimely end."

God, how much longer can this nightmare continue?

I huddled further into my chair, a silent tear escaping. More swelled, wanting to river, but I refused to show my pain.

Jasmine blew her nose, her cheeks glittering with moisture.

I wanted to snatch each fake droplet and ram them down her lying throat.

Daniel smirked, showing no other emotion. "Guess that leaves me in a lucky place."

Cole ignored him. "In this case, we've been asked to draft the following arrangement to protect both interests and move forward." Placing a pair of silver-rimmed glasses on his nose, he picked up an identical copy of the contract. "On this day, the Debt Inheritance will be carried out by the remaining bloodlines of the Hawk family against the crimes committed by the Weavers. Jasmine Diamond Hawk will have sole custody and responsibility for Nila Weaver's wellbeing until such a time as the Final Debt is claimed."

Daniel squirmed in his chair. "What the fuck? But—"

"Let him finish," Bonnie ordered.

"Upon his thirtieth birthday, Daniel 'Buzzard' Hawk will gain the wealth and many estates associated with the Hawk empire and become the next undisputed heir to both the estate and future Debt Inheritance. It will be his responsibility to provide a firstborn son or the next generation will be exempt."

I sagged, finding a smidgen of silver lining.

At least there would be no more Weavers from my bloodline to claim the debts from—and Daniel would be dead. I pitied my cousin's family tree if the Hawks had another heir in mind, but I would never have children and Vaughn wouldn't be stupid enough. He'd never let another one of our family go through what we had. The Hawks were screwed. They'd burned those bridges completely.

Cole carried on in his smooth voice. "The final note to be observed is the matter of who will carry out the Fourth Debt."

The room tensed.

"Jasmine will oversee the Final Debt, but Bryan Hawk has overridden the request for the right of Fourth Debt and granted it to Mr. Daniel."

Tension ricocheted out in a burst of savagery. "No way!" Jasmine glared at Cut. "Father, we agreed. You said she was *mine*. I've proven myself time and time again. Give her to me."

Cut steepled his fingers, unruffled by her disorder. "There's a method to why you won't carry out the Fourth Debt, Jasmine." His attention fell on Marshall. "Finish, please, then we can carry on to the next point on the agenda."

The next point?

My God, what else could they discuss?

I'd just learned I was the property of Jasmine with loopholes for Daniel to hurt me.

Didn't I have a say in any of this?

Daniel snickered, capturing my hand and tugging it into his lap. "Guess we have a date, after all, little Weaver." Raising my hand to his mouth, he kissed the back of my knuckles. "Including the matter of finishing the Third Debt."

I convulsed.

Cut chuckled. "Oh, yes. Unfinished business." His eyes narrowed. "Don't think we've forgotten about that, Nila. You don't wear the tally mark yet because it wasn't completed. We'll get to that a bit later, though. Give you some time to adjust."

My fingertip wearing Jethro's initials itched. His mark still existed in this world while he didn't. Would I continue to be marked in his name for debts extracted or would I wear DBH instead?

Steeling my heart, I scoffed. "Gee, thanks. So thoughtful of you."

Daniel squeezed my hand. "Watch it."

Every molecule wanted to extract myself from his slimy, grip.

Cole shuffled in his chair, barrelling through the air of hostility with a contemptuous look. "May I continue?"

Cut nodded. "By all means."

Bonnie scoffed under her breath, the diamonds of her broaches gleaming like death rays.

Cole looked back at the contract. "The first part of the Fourth Debt will be explained at Cut's discretion."

First part?

"And the second part, hereby known as the Fifth Debt, will be carried out by Daniel Hawk due to the nature and requirements of the debt."

Was there always a Fifth Debt or was that new?

I trembled to think of more pain but I was glad in a bizarre way. *It means I have more time to kill them before they kill me.*

"An able-bodied person must extract payment and..." His eyes fell on Jasmine, pity glowing. "...requires a journey not fit for someone in Ms. Hawk's condition."

My back stiffened at the look he gave her—the look I'd seen so many people give others less fortunate than them.

What was I talking about?

Less *fortunate?* Jasmine had more wealth than she could ever spend. She came from a lineage that banded together and protected their own no matter the cost. Not having use of her legs was a downside, but it didn't handicap her, nor did it make her a nicer person for her struggles.

Jasmine fisted her hands on the table. I didn't know if it

was from the misplaced condolences or anger at being denied.

Either way, I laughed under my breath, unable to stop my derisive frustration. "Don't pity her."

Cole glanced away guiltily.

Jaz flicked me a cold look. "Don't you dare speak on my behalf."

I turned to face her, war ready to break out between us. I thought I'd find the courage to fight by sparring with Daniel or Cut. Not Jasmine. I'd hoped, woman to woman, we would rally together. I'd hoped she'd be on my side.

Stupid hope. Stupid, stupid dreams.

Marshall sent a fountain pen skittering toward me, breaking the strained standoff. "If you would be so kind to sign and initial the amendment, I'll ensure it's kept safe and on record."

They hadn't listened to a word I'd said. Once again, treating me as a clause to fix, an amendment to be filed.

For a split second, I was glad Jethro and Kes were dead.

They were free from this. Free from suffering more insanity.

My heart imploded on itself as Jethro took over my mind. His tinsel hair, golden eyes, and unbearable complexities.

He's dead.

There was nothing else for me but to play their game until there was a winner and a loser.

I'll be the winner.

I picked up the pen. With steady hands, I uncapped it and had a sudden daydream of breaking it in half and splashing ink all over the so-called contract.

My mind raced with thoughts of my mother. Had she sat in this exact chair and signed the previous amendment? Why had Cut become heir and what'd happened to his brother?

Did he kill that family member, too?

I glared at him.

Cut glared right back.

I wanted answers, but how would I get them?

The Weaver Journal?

Could the diary actually have anything worthwhile inside and not just brainwashing drivel that Cut wanted me to believe? I hadn't bothered with it because every time I touched its pages, a sense of evil had warned me away.

Lies and misfortune and fraudulent deceit.

I'd suspected Kes gave it to me to keep me in line by reading about the adversity of my ancestors—striving to be better to avoid such things—but what if he gave it to me for another reason? What if he'd been trying to help me from day one?

Why didn't I study the damn thing?

Because I'd been so wrapped up in Jethro. Falling in love, attending polo matches, and accepting horses as gifts.

God, I'm so stupid.

"Ms. Weaver." Marshall slapped the table, wrenching me from my thoughts. "If you would be so kind…"

Jaz stiffened in her chair. "We don't have all day, you know." Ripping the page away from me, she snatched the fountain pen, and signed the bottom where her name and date waited.

Pushing me out of the way, she scooted the contract and pen to Daniel. "See, Nila? Wasn't so hard."

Daniel smirked. "Watch again how easy it is." He signed with an unintelligible scrawl. "Signing your life away, literally. Kinda fun, isn't it?" He placed the two items back in front of me. "Your turn."

"I'm surprised you don't expect me to sign in blood."

Bonnie gave up being the silent matriarch and slid into a caustic temper. "For shit's sake, you stupid girl. Be reasonable!"

The table froze.

My heart sprinted with hostility. She wanted to fight? I'd give her a damn fight. "I *am* being reasonable. You expect me to die for you. It would make sense to make me sign in blood—I'm sure you'd get a kick out of that, you witch."

I smiled, glowing in resentment. In the course of one

meeting, I'd called Jasmine a bitch and her grandmother a witch. Not bad considering my past of being shy and scared of confrontation. Even vertigo gave me a reprieve, keeping me levelheaded and strong.

Bonnie shot pink with fury. "Why you little—"

Marshall jumped in, waving his hands in a ceasefire. "We don't expect it in blood. Ink will more than suffice."

"And if I don't?"

"If you don't what?" Cole frowned.

"If I don't sign it—like I've been saying since I got here. Then what?"

Marshall flicked a glance at Cut. His jaw worked as their eyes shot messages above my comprehension. Finally, he bowed his head. "Then a certain type of persuasion would be used."

I laughed loudly. "Persuasion? Torture, you mean. I thought you had integrity to uphold. Didn't you just say you had evidence that all documents were signed without—as you put it—*persuasion*?"

Marshall hunched. "Well...eh...in some cases—"

"Sign the bloody paperwork, you ingrate!" Bonnie stood up stiffly, her cane in hand.

"Nila, fucking—" Cut growled.

"Shut up! All of you." Jaz suddenly wrapped her fingers around mine, pinching the pen into position. Dragging my hand over the paperwork, she muttered, "The things I fucking do."

"Wait, what are you doing?" I struggled, but found out that she might not have use of her legs, but she had strength in her arms that I couldn't fight.

"I'm putting an end to this. I've wasted too much time dealing with this as it is." She forced the nib onto the paper.

"No, wait!"

Digging her fingernails into my hand, she directed the pen and printed a rudimentary name.

My name.

Signed and witnessed on the Debt Inheritance amendment.

"What the hell have you done?"

She released me. "I did what I had to."

My chair screeched backward as I towered over her. "What the fuck is wrong with you?"

She wheeled away from the table, wobbling a little on the ramp. "What the fuck is wrong with *you*?" She stabbed me in the belly with her finger. "You're the one dragging this out when you know there's no way out." Tears gleamed in her eyes. "He's *dead*. They're both dead. The sooner you are too, the better."

My heart plummeted to the floor. Jethro's voice and touch and smell and kisses all slammed into me.

He's dead.

He's dead.

God, it hurts.

"I wish it were you!" I screamed. "You never deserved him. You should've died instead of him. He leapt in front of you to save you and this is what you do to repay him! I hope the devil—"

"Enough!" Cut soared upright, eyes shooting golden sparks. "Jasmine, calm down. Nila, shut up immediately." He splayed his arms like a messiah seeking peace. "It's done. It's unfortunate that this had to happen, but—"

"My brothers' deaths are a *misfortune*, father?" Jaz's cheeks glowed red. "I'll tell you what's a misfortune—having to deal with this bullshit!" Her hands latched around chrome wheel rims. "I'm sick of this. I want her gone. Now! I want this finished!"

The lawyers scrambled to their feet. "I think it's time we departed." The towers of paperwork quickly disappeared back into their boxes.

The men bowed. "Pleasure being of service once again. We'll be back in touch once the, eh...once the final part of the inheritance has taken place."

The final part?

The *final part*?

That was my final part—the last straw on my willpower. I cracked. I was a girl, but now I was a monster.

I've had enough.

Enough!

Darting around the table, I planted myself in Colin Marshall's path. His eyes flared. My palm twitched. And I slapped the bastard full on the cheek.

My hand blazed with fire, but I loved it.

I embraced the pain.

I gave myself over to fury.

His mouth popped open. "What on earth? Ms. Weaver!"

Chairs screeched as Hawks leapt to their feet. I ignored them.

"Listen to me." I stalked Marshall as he backpedalled. "That final part you just so loosely mentioned is my *death*. The day they cut off my head and steal back their necklace from my decapitated throat." I looped my fingers through the diamond collar. "How can you stand there discussing my life like a simple business transaction? How can you delete the lives of two men—two men who would've put an end to this insanity—and think you're upholding something legal? How can any of you breathe the same air as me and not be struck down for the devils you are?"

My arms were suddenly wrenched back, pinned on my lower spine. Daniel's fingers squeezed hard. "That's not the way we deal with lawyers, Nila." Stomping backward, he gave me no room but to trip with him. "You'll pay for that, and I'll have a lot of fun teaching you some manners."

I was too far gone to care.

Marshall rubbed his cheek. Bowing one last time at Cut, he continued with his holier-than-thou arrogance. "Like I said, we'll be in touch." Touching his hairline, he smiled at Bonnie. "Lovely seeing you again, Madame Hawk."

Bonnie's red-painted lips thinned. "I won't say likewise."

Daniel didn't let me go as the four men gathered briefcases and boxes and left the room in a sea of black suits and purple ties.

The moment they'd disappeared, Jasmine slid down the ramp and glared at her brother. "Let her go. She isn't yours to play with." Without another word, she spun her wheels and disappeared after the lawyers.

My heart stopped beating. I prepared myself for pain. My outburst filled the room with echoing bloodshed, but...incredibly, Daniel let me go.

Cut ran a hand over his face, looking at his mother. "Well, that wasn't peaceful, was it?"

Bonnie never stopped glaring at me. "No. It wasn't."

Daniel laughed, slinging an arm over my shoulders. "You're free to go, little Weaver. But don't go too far." He kissed my cheek like any lover or sweetheart. "Don't forget what I said about our private meeting."

A shudder worked through my body.

The private meeting would turn into war.

I'd slipped into murderous; there was no going back from that.

Without another look, I turned on my heel, and positively flew out the door.

I needed space to think and fortify. I needed time to prepare and commit.

Daniel will be the first to die.

Darting from the library, I careened around a corner and slammed to a halt.

My chest rose and fell as I plastered myself against the wall, spying on the scene up ahead.

I remained hidden as Jaz ran fingers under her eyes, swiping away tears.

Only, she wasn't alone.

A man crouched before her, his hand on her knee, talking quick and low. She nodded, looping her fingers through his. Their heads bowed together; she grabbed the lapel of the man's

Black Diamond jacket.

Her pinched, ghostly face animated with hissed whispers.

They didn't notice me as Jaz pulled the man closer and spoke into his ear.

I slipped deeper into shadows as the man nodded.

He said something that made her convulse and a fresh wash of tears flow.

Then my heart stopped beating as the man gathered her into a hug.

The man...

It was Flaw.

Nila

DIARY ENTRY, EMMA Weaver.

I found out what happened to Bryan's brother today. I don't think he meant to tell me, but I've learned how to manipulate him so occasionally he slips. I wouldn't normally write that, but tomorrow…it's all over. I've seen where they'll do it. Bonnie took great pleasure in having me weave the basket that will catch me. I'm beyond thinking about how sick everything is. I tried my best. I pretended to care for Cut. I made him believe I was in love with him. I willingly shared his bed and portrayed the besotted woman around his family. But it was all a lie. You hear that, you evil son of a bitch? If you're reading this, then good riddance. At least you can't touch me anymore. You told me things I doubted you would've if you knew that every time you touched me, I wanted to slaughter you with my bare hands. You wouldn't have let me into that frosted heart of yours if you knew that every time you slipped inside me, I gave myself over to the devil, all for him to fulfil one promise.

You won. But one day, you won't. One day, your sins will catch up with you and it will all be over. My daughter is already twice the woman I am, and she's still so young. If you go after her, it will be the last thing you ever do. I swear it on every religion, every sanctified God. You will die, Bryan. Mark my words, you will die—

A noise sounded outside my room.

My head wrenched up. My breath came hard and fast. I ached with the pain my mother had transcribed in the Weaver

Journal. Somehow, she hadn't used ink—she'd used her desperation and frustration. Her emotion throbbed from the pages, fisting around my heart. It made me angry, so damn angry that I wasn't there to save her.

She'd done what I had.

She'd made Cut fall for her—just like I'd gone after Jethro—to control him.

Only, unlike Jethro, Cut hadn't been so easily broken.

He'd still carried out the Final Debt. He'd killed the woman he was in love with.

And all for what?

The noise came again.

My pulse skyrocketed. With shaking hands, I closed the journal and slid it beneath the covers.

After the lawyers' visit, I'd headed to the kitchens and stockpiled food. I didn't know how often I'd be locked in my room in this new world without Jethro.

He's dead.

He's dead.

He's...not coming back.

I balled my hands, forcing the grief to stay away.

No matter how often I thought about him, I always thought of him as alive and only a corridor away.

My brain played tricks on me. Whenever the old Hall creaked, I heard my name whispered in the walls. Whenever the wind whistled and twitched my curtains, I heard him beg for me to find him.

I was slowly going mad.

I can't. Not yet. I have a job to do first.

I focused on the door to my room, ears straining for the noise. After my raid on the kitchens, I'd hauled my stash back to my quarters. The cook had given me a canvas bag to cart canned fruit, cured meat, packaged biscuits, and cereal. I'd hidden the food in the cupboard where I stored my needles, thread, and ribbon.

If they meant to trap me, at least I wouldn't starve to

death. I could stay strong and wait to strike them down.

Once I'd prepared myself for war, I'd deliberated if I should message my father. I'd wanted to tell him how much I loved him. How fortunate we were that this might be over soon.

If Vaughn and I died...there would be no more Weavers. No more children to torment.

The debt would end for our lineage—some other poor Weaver blood would pay.

Not the way I would've chosen, but it was a conclusion I had to live with, a legacy I had to leave.

Jethro.

My heart fisted, but my eyes remained dry.

The noise came again.

It was slight but there.

A scratching, scurrying sound.

Rats, perhaps?

Or one rat in particular.

My heart clanged.

Daniel.

Had he come to honour his promise of raping me tonight? Our private meeting away from the view of Jasmine and Cut?

I looked at the windows. Pitch-black reflected my room in perfect symmetry, distorting colourful fabric, swirling them into some kaleidoscopic artwork.

After the meeting, a thunderstorm had crashed over the estate, drenching everything in damp darkness. I'd had my lights on ever since, reading and engrossed in the Weaver Journal.

Only select generations had added to the large tome. My mother hadn't been diligent, and other snippets weren't signed. It made me wonder if the Hawks gave them an outlet for truth, rather than used it against them. It wasn't a requirement to write—but a *choice*.

My eyes darted to the clock above the turquoise fish tank.

11:00 p.m.

Shit!

Scrambling out of bed, I darted across the room. My bare feet padded over thick carpet, and the leggings and cardigan I'd worn all day were rumpled. My back and quads ached from the exercise I'd endured after returning to my room.

I hadn't been for a run, but I had used every muscle in my body.

How? By protecting myself.

My door suddenly swung open, slamming against the dresser I'd painstakingly emptied and pushed in the smallest increments across the carpet. The ancient wood weighed a ton, but I'd spent hours shoving it across the room—just in case.

I jumped a mile as the door smashed against the dresser again, an aggravated sigh exploding.

He might have a key to lock me inside, but I had a better barricade. He would only touch me when I was ready. And then, it would be the last thing he ever did.

I supposed I should thank him for his prior warning. Allowing me to prepare for a midnight visitor.

Not only had I manhandled the dresser across the door, I'd also fashioned pieces of fabric with sharp needles embedded to make a simple knuckleduster. I'd counted how many scissors I had, how many tools I could use to defend myself, and what would cause the most damage.

I'd hidden my arsenal around the room. Some I stashed in my bedside table, some beneath my workstation, and even tucked in pockets sewn into my duvet. My clothing had also undergone an upgrade with knitting needles and scalpels carefully sewn into cuffs and hems.

Once I'd moved the dresser, I'd replaced the drawers and heavy fabric bolts that'd rested inside its carcass. There was no earthly way someone could move it. Not unless they had ten Black Diamonds outside my door.

Which I wouldn't discount as a possibility.

Jethro was gone. But it didn't mean I would go quietly.

I'm ready, you asshole.

Just try me.

Almost on cue, the door slammed open again, smashing against the dresser with a resounding crack. A curse fell in the silence; they jiggled the knob, followed by another smash.

I stood vibrating on the other side, pulling my dirk free from my waistband.

Daniel would need a bomb to move the dresser, but it didn't mean I was safe. Who knew if he had secret passages into this room? Ancient houses such as Hawksridge had rabbit warrens of unseen pathways and secret compartments.

The door slammed again, banging louder with frustration.

I huddled into a battle stance, preparing to stab Daniel's hand through the crack. My mouth watered with the urge to hurl profanity and curses. To threaten and thwart.

"Nila, open the damn door."

I froze.

It wasn't Daniel.

Time ticked past, stretching uncomfortably.

"Nila...it's me."

Me?

The voice was feminine. Sweet and soft but hushed and worried.

Not a man with rape on his mind but a sister with grief.

A sister I couldn't stand.

I laughed coldly. "So forcing me to sign myself over to you this afternoon wasn't enough, huh?" My hand curled tight around my blade. "Come to cause more damage just like your fucked-up family?"

Jasmine sucked in a breath.

I inched closer to the door, nervousness popping in my blood.

"Just open the door. Now."

"What? So I can welcome you inside for a sleep-over and we can paint each other's nails?" I snorted. "I don't think so, Jasmine. You're a traitor to your brothers—a snake just like your grandmother." Filling my voice with venom, I spat,

"You're just like them, and I want nothing to do with you."

"You have no choice. Let me in the damn room."

He's dead because of you. He's dead because he loved you.

My teeth clamped together. God, if she were in front of me, I'd stab her through her heartless chest.

"Piss off."

"Let me in."

"No chance. The next time we see each other, it's not going to end well. I suggest you get out of my sight."

Jasmine punched the door or rammed it with her chair—the noise signalled rapidly fraying anger. "Ah, fuck, what did he ever see in you?!" She bumped against the door again, lowering her voice. "We need to talk."

"I don't talk with betrayers."

"You want me to get someone to help? 'Cause I will. And you won't like the consequences."

My hand rose, the light from my side lamps kissing the blade with promise. "Do whatever you want, but I assure you it'll be you who doesn't like the—"

"Fine!"

Silence fell.

Animosity throbbed, slowly settling the longer we remained quiet.

Finally, a small whisper met my ears. "Just give me two minutes. Just listen. Can you do that? Or is that asking too much?"

I paused.

Two minutes was nothing in a lifetime. But two minutes to me was too high a cost. I existed on borrowed time.

"Why should I?" I drifted closer to the door despite myself.

"Because...it's important."

The genuine honesty in her voice dragged me forward. She sounded more real and true in that one microsecond than she had all afternoon.

Leaning around the dresser, I looked through the crack.

Not much was visible, but Jasmine's face glowed in the dark corridor. Red-rimmed eyes, sad-bitten lips, and sorrow-dusted cheeks—she didn't look well.

In fact, she looked ten years older than when I'd seen her at the meeting. Almost as if the past few hours had drained her of everything.

I wanted to slap myself.

Don't believe it!

It was all an act. The perfect con-artist making me trust her because she looked so undone.

"It won't work, you know." I scowled. "I'm not buying into your sad sister act. Not after what you've done."

Jasmine looked up, her face haggard. "I know you hate me. I feel it. But you have to put that aside and listen to me."

If the door didn't separate us, I'd wring her neck and throttle whatever conniving words she wanted to spout. "I don't have to do anything."

She reached through the door.

I stepped backward, raising my knife. "Don't, unless you're happy with four fingers instead of five."

"God, why don't you listen?!"

"Because I don't believe a word you say!"

"No, not with your ears, you silly cow."

I laughed. "Great way to get me to listen. Call me a cow again and we'll see—"

"Didn't Jethro teach you anything?"

I froze.

Livid rage cascaded down my back, into my legs, my arms, my mind. "Don't you ever—"

"Talk about him? He's *my* brother. He's been mine a lot longer than he's been yours."

My ears bled. "*Was*, don't you mean. He *was* yours. But he's gone. He doesn't belong to either of us, and that's all your fault!"

She sighed, rubbing her face with her hands. "Why are you so damn stubborn?"

"Why are you so damn confusing?" My eyes dropped to her attire.

I paused, forehead furrowing.

A black blanket covered her legs, along with a black hoodie and black gloves. She'd either taken mourning to a new extreme and fashioned her pyjamas in darkness too, or…

"What are you up to, Jaz?"

Her eyes wrenched up. "Finally! You finally ask a decent question." She looked over her shoulder. "Let me in. I'll tell you."

I shook my head. "Nope. Not going to happen."

"I don't have all freaking night, Nila. Let me inside before it's too late."

My heart skipped a beat. "What—what do you mean? Too late?"

"I'll tell you if you open the door."

"Tell me *before* I open the door."

I wasn't naïve anymore. I wouldn't fall for any more Hawk traps.

She had her motives and secrets—same as everyone else. Only, what she'd said about listening…what did she mean? With my instincts? With my heart? What could she possibly have to tell me that I didn't already know?

She was a heartless bitch who should've died and not her brother.

She scowled, her sleek black bob pinned back from her face. The more I looked at her, the more my heart raced. Something was off—something was wrong.

She looked like a ninja about to go on a robbery spree.

She looked as if she knew something I didn't.

She looked as if everything she'd lived through the past few hours was a lie. And this was the truth.

This was real.

I lowered my knife. "What—what's going on?"

She smiled tightly, fresh tears streaming down her cheeks. "Will you believe me? Are you finally listening?"

Goosebumps scattered over my arms.

I swallowed. I nodded.

She sagged as if she could finally share the burden she carried.

"In that case…" She sucked in a breath. "I need your help."

It took an eternity for me to find courage.

I knew the moment I spoke, my world would change all over again.

Finally, I murmured, "Why?"

Reaching through the door, she grasped my hand.

Her eyes glossed.

Her lips trembled.

Her voice split me in two.

"I need your help…because…" She squeezed my fingers, joy exploding on her face. "Nila, he's alive."

Jethro

DEATH WAS WORSE than I ever imagined.

I'd hoped when the day came that it would be gentle—a tender snip when I was old and grey—a simple transition from one world to the next. It didn't matter that I never believed I would reach old age…it was what I'd fantasiscd.

However, if I had known how excruciating it would be, if I'd guessed how prolonged and agonising actual dying was—I would've put myself out of my misery years ago.

Because this? There was nothing survivable about this.

This wasn't heaven. Shit, it wasn't even hell.

It was damnation on Earth and still I clung—no matter how fucking painful.

"You still—" I coughed, unable to continue. My lungs were heavy, my body on fire. I existed on the brink. The brink of slipping far, far away and never coming back.

I wasn't dehydrated or starved.

I wasn't cold or unprotected.

But none of those simple human requirements could save me. I'd run out of time, and it was now a simple matter of gambling on which malady would kill me.

The steady bleeding?

The spreading fever?

The bullet hole?

I'd given up trying to choose. I thought I'd faded hours ago, finally giving in to the pain.

But no.

I still clung, dangling off the proverbial cliff, too weak to let go and too weak not to.

God, please let it end!

I flinched as I sucked in a deeper breath.

Breathing...funny how I hated and loved the action.

Hated because another breath meant I'd survive another few minutes. Loved because another breath meant I still existed for Nila.

Nila...

My heart tried to hurry, conjuring the dark-haired seamstress who'd captured my heart. But all it managed was a pathetic patter.

Groaning with the weight of a thousand daggers, I looked at the cot across the dungeon from mine.

How we arrived down here, I had no fucking clue.

Why we had drips in our hands, blankets bundled around us, and crudely administered medicine was an utter mystery.

Who did this?

How long had we been here?

How much time had passed?

Was this perhaps purgatory? A place of in-between, a deplorable existence where only the worst went to pay penance?

We couldn't possibly be alive. *Could we?*

A flickering light in the corner kept the vampires of the crypt at bay, but it offered no warmth—no reprieve from the ancient ice seeping into my bones from the godforsaken catacombs.

I stared fuzzily at the shape of a man cocooned in blankets. Only, he hadn't moved, moaned, or made a sound in hours. My gift—no, my curse—no longer worked.

There was someone else down here with me. Yet, there were no thoughts, no fears, no pleas.

I didn't want to admit it, but my brother…he was no longer alive. However, I had to try to bring him back from the dead. I had to remind him I was there for him—for him not to give up, even though slipping off the cliff became more enticing every minute. "You—you still a—alive, K—Kes?"

I never heard his reply.

The moment I finished, I fell into a stupor that lasted God knew how long. My energy flat-lined and I drifted into dreams, nightmares, and fantasies.

One moment, I flew through the forest on Wings.

The next, I was back in that hated room hurting Jasmine to fix myself.

One second, I made love to Nila, sliding inside her heat.

The next, I was shivering with ice running away from Hawksridge when I was fourteen.

Each hour, I grew weaker. Each hour, I slipped a little more.

If it weren't for the terror at leaving Nila in the heinous world I'd helped create, I would just let go and disappear.

I want so fucking much to disappear.

I wanted freedom from pain.

Sanctuary from agony.

I wasn't strong enough to live with such soul-crushing torment.

But no matter how hot and flaming my pain became. No matter how delirious and wracked with trembles I was, I couldn't die.

I *refused* to fucking die.

I can't. Not while they're alive.

It was my duty to end them. To end the madness of my heritage that'd gotten away with murder for centuries.

Only once I'd balanced the scales of right and wrong could I relax and let go.

Only once I'd saved the one who'd saved me could I say goodbye and slip into the void.

My heart occasionally stuttered, out of sync, out of

power—almost as if it recognised death and wanted to give in. I forced it to do the bare essentials, keeping me from a grave. I was in the coffin ready to be buried, but I wasn't a corpse just yet.

I squinted in the lacklustre light, following the contours of my brother's body.

He still hadn't moved.

Time had an odd context down here. It could've been decades since I'd asked if he was alive, or only seconds.

I could turn to face him, expecting to see a blood-flushed body, only to come face-to-face with a dusty skeleton instead.

Anything was possible on the cusp of death.

My dying lungs did their best at working through ash and mildew to speak again. "K—Kes…"

A minute ticked past or maybe it was an hour—but, finally, my brother shifted. His grunt of agony echoed around the walls.

I wasn't alone.

Not yet.

More time passed.

I had no way to measure it.

I raised my head off the scratchy pillow, staring at the iron bars.

Our coffin was the same catacombs that housed my ancestor's bones. The same cell where Daniel beat me on Cut's command. The same dungeon where I'd started the course of drugs to numb me.

Those memories had been sharp and recent. But now they were muddy and distant.

Same as all my memories.

Nila's voice faded from my heart. Jasmine's promises disappeared from my ears. My life deleted itself as if I wasn't allowed to carry any memento from this world to the next.

I didn't want to forget.

I don't want to forget!

I willed my dried-up, malnourished brain to remember: how we arrived here. How a night of intimacy and love had transformed into my murder.

But try as I might, I couldn't.

There was nothing but splatters of mismatched images.

Blazing hot pain.

Jasmine's screams.

Bonnie's barks.

Nila's sobs.

Then more pain shoving me deeper and deeper down the drain of consciousness.

My blood was weak, diluted with agony. My soul broken but refusing to abandon a body that was hours away from succumbing to the black shroud of everlasting sleep.

Help us...

The bars were locked. There was no way out.

However, they could've been wide open and there wouldn't have been a hope in fucking hell of moving.

We were dead.

The fact we were holding on was merely a formality.

More time passed and I stopped trying to catalogue it. I was drifting, twisting, fading...

Not long now.

A sudden burst of strength let me say something I should've said many times in the past. Something I always took for granted. "I—I lo—ove y—you, Kes."

A cough wracked my body, clutching my pain, increasing it tenfold.

As the fever bathed my skin and my lungs rattled with sickness, I sighed and gave up. I'd said goodbye. I'd done everything I needed.

My senses slipped across the room to my dying brother and I held on. Hopefully, we'd find each other again. Hopefully, I'd find Nila again when I deserved her and paid for my sins.

Hopefully, all would be better in a different world.
I'm sorry, Nila. For everything.
Brother to brother. Soul to soul.
There was nothing else here for me.
I closed my eyes.
I let go.

Nila

I CHASED HER.
He's alive!

Vertigo tried to trip me as I jogged in the wake of her wheels. Disbelief and suspicion did their best to kill my intoxicating high.

He's alive.
He's alive.
It's a miracle.

I'd never had such words affect me. Never had a voice slammed into my heart, tore it out, restarted it, and dumped me into a hope so cruel, I didn't want to breathe in case I unbalanced this perilous new world and found out Jethro wasn't alive after all.

I wanted to cry. To scream. To laugh.
He's alive!

I ran faster as Jasmine shot forward.

I'd never been friends with someone with a disability. I liked to think I was open-minded and treated everyone the same way—but society still had a stigma about equality.

Jasmine shattered every misconception I had.

I thought I'd have to dawdle beside her. Wrong—I had to jog to keep up.

I thought I'd have to open doors and offer assistance

around tight corners. Nope—Jaz manoeuvred her chair, doorway, and lock faster than I ever could.

She was fierce and strong, and even though she sat below my eye level, her personality consumed mine.

I was in her shadow.

He's alive.

But how?

She hadn't given me answers. The moment she'd told me Jethro hadn't died, I'd emptied the dresser, shoved it out of the way, and followed her with no other encouragement.

Was it a trap? A cruel joke?

Entirely possible, but I couldn't ignore the chance of saving Jethro. I had to break this heartache before it broke me.

Finally listening to Jasmine gave me new comprehension. I stopped listening with my ears and trusted with my heart. I noticed things that'd been so obvious, but I'd been so blinded. She adored her brothers. She was shattered with their pain. Yet, instead of hating me...she was...*she's trying to save me.*

Could that be possible?

Could everything that'd happened—the fighting for ownership and contract amendments all be for him?

Had he asked her to do that?

To protect me.

"You weren't going to hurt me...were you?" I whispered, darting down yet another labyrinth of corridors. No lights lit our way, and the security cameras above didn't blink. No red beacon hinted that our midnight run was recorded and ready to tattle.

I didn't know how she turned them off. I didn't know how she knew Jethro was alive. I didn't know anything.

I'm blind.

"About bloody time," she muttered, wheeling forward like a tank. "Thought you were supposed to be intelligent."

Tapestries hung silent and repressive. Paintings of dead monarchs sniffed with disdain as we scurried silently like tiny mice. The awful feeling of being swept away with no control fisted around my heart. I wanted to ask so many questions, but something held me back.

He's alive.

And I wanted him to stay that way.

"How was I supposed to know? You were so—"

"Believable?" She looked over her shoulder, her arms propelling her forward. "I've learned from the best."

Awkward silence fell. We headed deeper into shadow.

Jasmine broke the brittle tension. "What made you doubt now?"

I paused. I'd asked myself that same question. The only conclusion I could come up with was: *because I'm finally listening to the truth rather than what I hear.*

I didn't reply. Instead, I answered her question with another. "Everything that happened in the meeting…that wasn't real?"

Her lips twisted into a mysterious smirk. "You already know the answer to that."

"I don't know anything anymore."

She laughed under her breath. "That's a testament to my planning skills."

We ducked under another camera. "Aren't you afraid they'll catch us?"

She gave me a hard smile. "Nope."

"But won't Cut see the recordings?"

She smiled wider. "Nope."

I didn't bother asking again. She'd done something. And I guessed I'd never know.

My fitness level wasn't useful as we ducked and weaved through the ancient Hall. Jasmine kept up a wicked pace, and every heartbeat crushed me with the same unbelievable message.

He's alive.
He's alive.
Get to him faster.

Chasing Jasmine in her all-black attire and swiftness, my

mind filled with other questions. Where did she spend her days? How did she get around? How had she kept this a secret? "How do you move from upstairs to the ground floor?"

Her eyes widened at my seemingly random question. "I have a private elevator in the centre of the house. It leads to a few floors."

"There are more?"

She snorted. "Seriously? Haven't you seen the size of this place? There's probably hundreds of rooms you still haven't seen."

Prisons and bedrooms and secret vaults full of treasures.

Could Jethro's mum be hidden in one? Could there be countless hidden mysteries just waiting to bring the Hawks down?

A chill ran down my spine. "Tell me what's happening. Where's Jethro?"

She shook her head. "You'll just have to trust me."

"I've already proven that I do." Removing the dresser and following Jasmine had shown two things: one, that I was willing to put my life in her hands, and two, that I was willing to do anything in order to save her brother.

He's alive.
He's alive.
It's not over.

"All you need to know is he's holding on, and I need your help."

"Anything. I'll do whatever you need."

Her eyes softened. "I was hoping you'd say that." The mask of collected woman slipped, showing her terror over her brother's life.

My heart tripped into a knot. "Kes. Is he alive, too?"

My spine locked, bracing for bad news. It seemed too much to have Jethro back from the dead, let alone another.

Jasmine sucked in a breath. "He is. For now."

My hands fisted. I wanted to sprint faster. "What does that mean?"

She glared ahead, stress lining her mouth. "They were moved before Cut could dispose of them. We've done what we could, but it isn't good enough." She swallowed hard. "We're running out of time."

We...

Her and Flaw?

"Where did you put them?"

"The only place not monitored."

"And where is that?"

She lowered her voice. "It doesn't matter. You're not coming with me."

My stomach flipped. I had to see him. Had to hug him and kiss him and tell him I never stopped loving him. "You came for my help. I'm coming with you."

Jasmine pursed her lips. "It has to be this way. It has to be tonight. And it has to be now. The longer you argue, the less time we have and the worse it will be for all of us. Got it?"

I wanted to argue—to slap her and let go of the helpless anger inside. Instead, I curbed my temper. "Fine."

But the minute he's safe and well, I'm claiming him. He's mine, not yours.

Flying around a corner, Jaz whispered, "Now, hush. Answers will come later."

This part of the house hinted at its age.

We were no longer in the manicured wealth of parlours, dayrooms, and libraries.

This part had an aura of forbidden.

An abandoned aura.

An aura of death and warning.

Portraits didn't hang, showing pockmarked faded walls. The threadbare carpets misted with dust as our footsteps disturbed ancient dirt, and my cardigan and leggings weren't enough to combat the icy chill emitting from the walls.

Hawksridge Hall lived and breathed as surely as its

inhabitants, but down here...here was forgotten, only fit for cretins and rodents.

I blew on my fingers, gritting my teeth against a shiver.

"Here." Jaz suddenly stopped. "This is the room."

I skidded to a halt, staring at the imposing door with a brass locking plate engraved with weasels and stoats. "What is this place?"

"It used to be the servant's quarters, but an old water pipe burst a century ago and destroyed everything. My grandfather never got around to fixing it. This wing has been ignored ever since."

Sounded about right. The Hawks only seemed to value those worth something valuable to their needs and wants. The moment they outlived their purpose, they were either dispatched or cast aside.

A tiny shadow scurried past my line of sight. I inched closer to Jasmine's chair. I wouldn't be against leaping into her lap to get off the floor if rats came to visit. "And what are we doing here?"

He's alive.
He's alive.
Surely, she didn't keep him here.

Her bronze gaze glowed in the gloom. "Using one life to save another."

A shiver that had nothing to do with the cold shot down my back. "What does that mean?"

I'm asking that question a lot lately.

She looked away, fumbling in the black blanket over her legs. "You'll see." Pulling free an old-fashioned key, she inserted it into the lock.

With a loud groan of protest, the rusty mechanism sprang open, cracking open the large moisture-logged door.

A noise sounded inside—fleeting—like a small gasp of dismay.

"Come on." Jasmine pushed her rims, coasting from corridor to room. The moment we were inside, she closed the door. "Get the light, will you? The switch is to your left."

I spread my fingers out in the dark, tracing the chilly wall and finding an ancient nub, which I assumed was illumination.

I pressed it.

Light spilled from a single cobwebbed chandelier above. The room came into view. Out of every place I'd visited in Hawksridge Hall, this was the worst room by far. Faded, chipped mint-green paint covered the walls. Beige carpet stretched across floorboards, moth-eaten and musty.

And the cold.

I hugged myself from the bitter bite of winter.

An entirely different season lived in this place. No central heating, no fire to ward off frost and snow.

Had Jethro ever been here? Was this where he learned how to embrace the coldness, so he could hide his condition?

He's alive…

"Who—who's there?"

No! Oh, my God.

My stomach clenched; vertigo stole my vision in a blip of blackness.

I didn't have to see to know.

I'd know that voice anywhere.

"It's me!" My legs unlocked, hurling me across the large room to the single cot pushed against the wall. Condensation dripped like frigid tears down the cold surface, and the only window didn't perform its job of keeping the outside elements from entering. The stunning stained glass depiction of summer flowers had turned into a dartboard of holes. Intricate violets had been smashed, leaving a whistling draft to funnel around daisies and dandelions, slipping into the space unwanted.

Falling to my knees by the bed, I reached for my beloved twin's face. "It's me, V."

"Threads?" He rolled onto his back, revealing swollen cheekbones, bruised jaw, and cut lip. His hands were tied, resting on his belly, and a black blindfold covered half his face, flapping over his nose every time he breathed.

"God, I'll rip off their balls for this." I fumbled behind his head. "Lean forward; let me get this off you."

He did as I asked, groaning as he arched his head off the rank pillow.

Scrambling at the knot, I shoved it away the moment it loosened.

His eyes opened, blinking a few times. His mottled face turned to me. My heart cracked all over again, drinking in the signs of the horrendous beating he'd endured at the hands of Cut and Daniel.

In one afternoon, Cut had almost killed my brother and shot his sons. Yet, he hadn't hurt any of them enough to end them.

Perhaps, there is hope after all.

Good had triumphed over evil.

Good would *win* over evil.

Just wait and see.

His eyes focused, face twisting in rage. "Threads. Oh, fuck, I'm so glad to see you." He tried to sit up but cried out with pain. His fingers weren't a healthy pink but blue-white from being trapped in such an arctic cell.

"Relax." I pushed his shoulder. "Let me untie you." Moving from my knees to the edge of the bed, I pulled at the twine around his wrists. Tears sprang to my eyes as dried blood and scabs reopened. Fresh crimson seeped, making the knot too slippery to undo.

"Goddammit," I hissed.

"Here, try this." A box-cutter appeared in front of my nose. I jumped. In the rush of seeing my brother, I'd forgotten about Jasmine.

"Who the hell are you?" V snapped, his eyes drinking in Jaz.

I accepted the knife. "Thank you." My own dirk rested down my waistband, cursing me for not using it.

Jasmine glanced at my black and blue twin. Her eyes remained cool and standoffish, but her voice was warm enough. "You'll find out soon." Rolling backward, she graciously gave me some privacy as I slit the rope around V's wrists and freed him.

The instant he could move, he hitched himself up and threw his arms around me. His muscular bulk wasn't warm like normal—the ice from the room leeched everything from him, making it seem like I hugged marble.

He clutched me harder. "Fuck, Threads. What the hell is going on?"

I fell into him.

Vaughn was alive.

Jethro was alive.

Even Kes was alive.

A trifecta of happiness, yet all I wanted to do was burst into tears.

"It's a long story." I breathed in his familiar aftershave.

His body shuddered, his chin pressing on the top of my head. He didn't let me go; if anything, he hugged me tighter. "God, I thought they'd killed you, too." He shook his head. "Those gunshots. That fucking maniac. What the hell?"

I untangled myself. "Like I said, long story."

Anger curled off him. "Where are the fucking cops in all of this! They came to get you. They brought you home. Yet, you touted that bullshit for that magazine and ruined everything. You cried wolf, Threads, and now we're really fucked—"

"Stop it, alright? I know I've done a few things that don't make sense. I know I made our family a laughingstock by denying everything you said and the police want nothing to do with us, but none of that matters." Giving him a watery smile, I rubbed my eyes, doing my best to stay calm. "The main thing is you're still alive. I'm still alive, and we're going to fight back."

His jaw worked. "Damn fucking right we're going to fight back. I want every single Hawk dead."

"Not every Hawk deserves to die." Jasmine's voice carried on a puff of frozen breath.

I turned to face her, sharing a kindred smile. "Only the rotten ones."

He's alive.

He's alive.

Both our brothers are still in this world.

Vaughn growled. "They're all rotten. Every last one of them."

Jasmine scowled.

We didn't have time to fight.

"We'll talk about that later. For now, tell me if you're alright. No broken bones or anything?"

V sighed, hugging me again. His strength hinted that apart from a few bruises, he wasn't too damaged. "I'm stronger than I look, little sister." He couldn't stop touching me—tucking my hair behind my ears, tracing my cheeks and arms. It was tender, but it wasn't because of love or the need to connect.

Ever since our mum became Hawk property, Vaughn had always patched me up. He'd find me sprawled at the bottom of the stairs from tripping with vertigo and plaster the scrapes on my hands. He'd somehow be there first if I fell and cut myself—always armed with bandages and painkillers for his delinquent sister.

He was so used to me hurting myself, he had a system. A process.

Words could lie about a fall—brush it off as if it were nothing. But touch couldn't hide the truth. Touch could feel the heat of a new bruise or the bump of a broken bone.

Even hurt himself, he was still trying to fix and protect me.

I pushed him away. "I'm okay, V. Honest."

"We need to get you out of here." He swung his legs off the bed. "Now. Tonight."

"You're not going anywhere."

Both our heads whipped up to face Jasmine. She'd rolled closer, sitting with her hands in her lap. I didn't trust for a second she was as meek as she seemed. She probably had hundreds of weapons hidden in her blanket.

"I've given you time to say hello. I've given you time that I didn't have to give. But now you have to come with me."

Vaughn stiffened. "I don't have to do anything." Grabbing my hand, he squeezed. "I'm taking my sister, and we're leaving."

"No, you aren't." Jasmine's face darkened. "You'll do what I say."

I froze. Once again, my loyalties split. I used to belong to Vaughn entirely. He was blood. He was the exact replica of me in every way. But my heart had replaced him with my chosen one.

The one I thought was dead.

We would never be as close because we would never need each other as much as we once had.

It was both sad and freeing at the same time.

"She's right, V. We can't leave. Not yet."

Vaughn's eyes popped wide. "What the fuck does that mean?" Raising a finger, he pointed at Jasmine. "Wait a minute…who are you?" His voice slipped into a hiss. "Are you one of them? Because if you are, so fucking help me I'll wring your neck—girl or not."

Jasmine didn't back down. She didn't even flinch. "If you're asking if I'm a Hawk, the answer is yes. If you're asking if I love my brothers as much as you love your sister, then the answer is yes. And if you're asking if I'm on your side, the answer isn't so simple."

Vaughn let me go, pushing off the bed to tower over her. He stumbled a little, but it didn't stop him from sucking in a breath and whipping the room with temper. "If what you say is true, then you know what I feel and I'll do anything to protect my twin. I won't put your needs before hers. *Ever*."

Jasmine gritted her teeth. Her eyes flashed with frustration for Jethro and Kes. The longer we argued, the less time we had.

They need us. Now. Before it's too late.

"Vaughn, listen to me—"

"No, Nila, *you* listen to *me*. I don't know how she brainwashed you, but it's over. They're all noxious; therefore, they'll all die." He took a step closer to Jaz. "And if you don't move out of my fucking way, you'll be the first to go."

Her eyes pinned him in place; her elegant throat poised with defiance. "I'll tell you something you don't know, Mr. Weaver. And then we'll see if you'll do what you're told."

V snorted but Jaz ignored him.

"Your sister has survived my family for almost six months. She's the one who stood up to us. She's the one who helped my brother all because she believed in him. She had the power to destroy him, but she didn't. And if anyone deserves to kill those who deserve to die, it's her." She swallowed hard, forcing herself to continue. "Seeing you together is hard. You both look so similar. Twins in every sense. My brothers and I might not be the same age, but we share something in common. We share a desire for freedom. And I won't let you take that away from us."

Her eyes fell on me. "Have you told him, Nila? Have you told him who Jethro is to you? Or did you continue to let him slander his name in social media when you left us?"

I flinched.

She's right.

While trapped at Hawksridge, I lived in truth far more than I ever did in London. I hadn't had the guts to look my father or twin in their eyes and tell them that I was in love with a Hawk. That I belonged to him and him to me. That I was a traitor to my family name.

"What is she talking about, Threads?" Anger glazed V's eyes along with a faint hint of fear. "Tell me."

"V, I—"

How could I tell him that I loved Jethro as much as I loved him? How could I tell him that it was no longer simple between us?

"She took him from me, Vaughn," Jaz said quietly. "She fell in love with my brother, and overnight, I became second in his life." She gave me a twisted smile—half-accepting, half-unwilling. "He doesn't belong to me anymore, just like she doesn't belong to you."

Vaughn shifted, running a hand through his dark hair. The beard he'd sported in London had been shorn, but a few day's growth shadowed his jaw. "I don't—I don't understand."

"One day, you'll end up belonging to someone you love. But for now, you belong to me. *I'm* the one who's come to rescue you. *I'm* the one who holds your life in my hands. And I'm the one who says you'll do what I ask."

My shoulders hunched. "Probably not the best way to make him help you."

She glared at me.

I shrugged.

I'd been on the receiving end of Jasmine's willpower—her perfect deception. She could spin any tale—give life to any lie. She'd completely fooled me at the meeting, and I'd never underestimate her again. I still couldn't shake the hatred I'd felt. But she didn't know my brother or how pig-headed he could be when *told* to do something.

V turned to me. "Threads...is that true? You fell in love with that bastard?" His face fell. "Is that why you slept with him?"

Jaz sucked in a breath, watching us like some soap opera.

I moved to stand in front of my brother. "What she says is true. I love him, V. And he doesn't have much time. Jasmine needs your help." Laying a hand on his chest, I murmured, "I *want* you to help her. For me. Please..."

His heart thundered under my touch; his eyes dove into mine. "This is for real? You love the bastard who's going to kill you?" His face contorted. "Could you be any more stupid?"

"He would never have been able to do it." Jasmine rolled forward. "He fell for her before she fell for him. I knew even when he didn't."

She locked her brakes, staring up at V. "If you won't help me because I'm telling you to, help me because I'm asking.

Don't let him die. Don't destroy your sister or condemn my brother when he's the only one who can stop all of this for good."

For the longest moment, we all held our breaths, waiting for V to accept defeat and agree to help. But then his shoulders stiffened, and he shook his head. "I don't believe either of you. I think you're both fucked in the head, and we need to get the hell out of this shithole."

Snatching my wrist, he jerked me toward the door.

For someone who'd been in a fight and locked in a chiller, he moved quickly.

"V! Let me go." I stumbled after him, vertigo teasing with the outskirts of my vision.

"Vaughn, listen to her." Jaz spun around, her knuckles white on her wheels. "You can't leave."

V ignored her and reached for the door. "Oh, really? Funny, this is me leaving."

I breathed hard. "Vaughn, I'm not going anywhere with you. If you won't help us, fine. But I'm not going to leave him—"

"Yes, you are. Because I'm doing something he never did." His nose almost brushed mine as he yanked me close. "Saving your arse."

"You don't understand!"

"No, Threads. *You* don't understand. They've kept you here, treating you fucking awful for months. They've twisted your thoughts and made you suffer that Stockholm shit. Well, it's over. We're going home."

His hand landed on the doorknob, wrenching it side to side.

Locked.

He whirled on Jaz, carting me back like a prisoner. Shoving his hand beneath her nose, he growled, "Key. Now."

Her chin rose. "No. Not until you agree to help me."

"Never. Give me the key." He bent down, crazed with rage. "I won't ask again."

"And I won't ask for your help again. I'll just make you."

Vaughn raised his hand.

"Wait!" I jumped forward, barricading him from slapping her. "Don't!"

V's mouth popped wide. "You're seriously defending her, Threads? After every-fucking-thing her family has done to you?"

I couldn't believe it, either. If V had been there after the meeting with the lawyers, I would've willingly given him a gun and loaded the bullet myself. But that was before I started listening—*truly* listening. Jaz was on our side.

He's alive.

But for how much longer?

Waving my arms, I whisper-shouted, "Enough! Yes, I'm defending her. Yes, I'm in love with Jethro. And no, I won't go anywhere with you until he's safe." Trembling, I looked over my shoulder at Jasmine.

She sat unruffled, her hand curled around a black gun that'd appeared from under her blanket.

I knew it! I knew she'd have an arsenal hidden in there.

Our eyes met.

I could make a big deal out of the weapon or I could focus on the task at hand.

Jethro and Kes...

Ignoring the pistol, I asked, "What's your plan? Why do you need my brother to help?"

"Mr. Weaver here is going to carry me where I need to go and do everything I tell him."

"Like fuck I am." Vaughn paced in front of us.

"V!" I scowled. "Just...listen, okay?"

A small glisten of emotion showed before Jaz added, "I can't do this on my own and, Nila, you have to go back to your room."

I shook my head. "I'll come with you. I don't want to go back—"

"It's not a matter of what you want. It's a matter of

necessity. We'll be gone a while. I need you to lie for me if it comes to that."

"Lie for you?"

"You need to take my chair and tell them that I spent the night with you." She eyed up V as he paced like a feral animal. "While he'll be my legs and strength, you'll be my safeguard. I need you to come up with any tale you need to in order to keep the truth about my brothers' lives a secret. I don't care what you say. Just keep it hidden."

My mind swam. I had no idea how I would achieve that if Daniel or Cut came knocking.

"And why do you need me, exactly?" Vaughn asked, his voice laced with animosity. "Why should I put my life on the line?"

Jaz took in his bruised face and blood-stained t-shirt. "Do you want children, Mr. Weaver?"

V's eyebrows disappeared into his hairline. "What? What the fuck does that—"

"Answer the question. Yes or no."

My heart raced, waiting for him to reply. I'd grown up with V, but we'd never talked about what we wanted in the future. Never discussed the idea of raising our own families—too caught up in designing and promoting and working tirelessly for a company that was more parent than we'd ever needed.

V breathed out heavily. "I don't know…before, I might've entertained the idea, but now never. Not after what they did to Nila." His eyes fell on me. "Or our mum."

"Exactly. My family has cast a shadow over yours for far too long. You should have the right to have children if you want, knowing they are safe to grow old." She inched closer, her voice filling with passion and truth. "I need your help to make that a reality."

I tensed, waiting for another argument, for more curses.

But V's black eyes met mine, mirroring my unspoken begging for his help. He had the power to save, not only the man I loved, but both our futures, too.

Finally, he slouched. "If I help you, you'll keep my sister safe? You'll make sure this ends?"

Jaz held a fist over her heart. "You have my ultimate word. Keep my brothers alive and I swear to you this will all be in the past."

Vaughn closed the distance between them, his eyes lingering on Jasmine's chair. With slight hesitation, he held out his hand. "In that case. We have a deal."

Jaz blinked back tears as she dropped the gun and placed her hand in his. "Thank you. A thousand times, thank you."

I didn't want to interrupt the sudden tender moment, but my heartbeat was a clock, striking the passing minutes with terror.

He's alive.
He's alive.
It's time to go.

"What next?" I whispered.

Jaz smiled softly. "Vaughn and I have a date in the crypt."

V looked at her blankly.

Jaz held up the key, rolling herself toward the door. "This is our last chance."

"What is?" I ghosted forward, drawn by the anticipation of hope and righteousness.

She slipped the key into the lock. "Our last chance to rescue Kestrel and Jethro and get them to the hospital before they die."

Jethro

"NO. NOT LIKE that, dammit."

"Hush it, woman. I think I know how to work a cutting torch."

"No, you obviously don't. You don't have the valve open for the acetylene."

A curse, a scrape, then a loud hiss.

Images of writhing snakes and striking cobras filled my cloud-riddled mind. *What the fuck?* Had I finally left Earth and plummeted to hell where reptiles and dragons waited for my demise?

Something bright and fierce sliced through the darkness. I flinched.

Yep, definitely hell.

They're waiting for me.

Heat from their fire-breathing mouths battled away the penetrating cold.

"Now you have too much. Mix it with the oxygen, you moron."

"Moron? Keep name-calling to a minimum. Otherwise, you'll have to find another donkey to help."

"Just—let me." Shuffling sounded, followed by another gust of heat and light.

The voices echoed as if they drifted through chasms of

water and rubble. Female and male—husk and lilt.

Since when do dragons talk?

"How the fuck did you get this thing down here, anyway?" The hissing grew louder, sparks lighting up the dimness behind my eyes.

"A friend put it here. The only thing we had on the estate that would open the lock."

"Never heard of a fucking key?"

More light. More hissing.

"He made a mistake. He closed the door to keep them safe, not realising there was only one key."

"And you didn't feel like using it? Too easy? Wanted to go the James Bond route?"

A curse followed by a rain of sparks brighter than any firework.

"Shut it. For your information, it wasn't possible to get it."

"Why? Dear ole dad has it?"

A squeaking, followed by another blast of heat. The girl growled, "Yes."

"I've never known anyone so under the thumb of their old man."

A pause followed by a loud curse. "That's what you get for talking about things you don't understand. Now, shut up. Get the mixture right. And get my brothers out of there before I hit you again."

"Anyone ever tell you that you're evil?"

"All the time. Now do what I say."

Their talking ceased, replaced with the lullaby of fire and burning.

I lost track of reality and life. I wasn't human anymore. I wasn't pain or death.

I was just...*time*.

No sensation or memories. No hardships or heartaches. Only time ticking past unwanted and unseen.

I was nothing, no one...gone.

"God's sake. Pick me up again. I'll freaking do it."

"I'm doing it, woman! How many fucking times do I need to tell you that?"

"You're not going fast enough."

The yellow light turned white with power, beckoning me forward, promising a better existence than the one I endured.

I wanted to reach for it, squinting in my mind as the light grew larger, brighter, inhaling me into its orb.

I'd never seen something so pure—as if I stared at the nucleus of the sun or the entrance to heaven.

Am I worthy of paradise, after all?

"Hurry. We need to leave."

"Woman, give me a damn moment, okay?"

The light supernovaed. Hissing increased in decibels until it echoed in my teeth. Electricity sparked in my muscles, slowly bringing me back to life. I tried to move, to see what beast hissed so loudly, but my body was no longer mine to command. It was weak and broken and past listening to such requests.

My foggy mind wouldn't focus; wisps of thoughts and flickers of images all faded with every failing heartbeat.

I didn't know why I continued to cling to whatever semblance of life I had.

This was no life.

This was just damnation.

"Shit, it's not cutting."

"I know it's not freaking cutting. You've got the ratio wrong!"

"If you're such a fucking know-it-all, you fix it."

My ears rang with bickering.

I didn't know the man, but the girl reminded me of my sister. A little girl who I'd loved since childhood but also drove me nuts. She'd constantly pinch my favourite toys and hide them where I could never find them.

She ran circles around Kes and me. Driving us mad, proving that love wasn't enough to protect an infuriating sister from retaliation—usually in the form of frogs in her bed or beetles on her cereal.

I attempted a smile, thinking of happier times.

The light went out, followed by a scraping noise.

"Now, turn that gauge to the left and that to the right. See those two lines...that's the ideal ratio."

"Fine. Done. Now what?"

"Now, I want to work the wand."

"What? No way."

Something clanged off the earthen walls. My ears twitched, reminding me they still worked, even when other parts of me didn't. I'd long since stopped feeling the soft splash of internment droplets on my forehead or tensing when a fresh wash of agony bathed my skin with fever.

"Pick me up and then give me the wand. Got it?"

"God, you're such an arse."

"Kind of you to notice. Now...pick me up."

"But it should be me who—"

"Why? Because you're male and playing with power tools is a man's job?"

A heavy sigh. "No...because it's—"

"Look, the original plan was for me to use the torch. If you hadn't gone all *'He-man'* on me, they'd be free and halfway to London by now."

Silence again.

For a while, minutes swept me away, granting that odd sensation of no time passing but hours slipping anyway.

"They're probably already dead. They haven't moved since we started this."

A livid curse littered the rank air. "If they don't make it, our bargain is over. I promised Nila would be safe if you helped me rescue my brothers. If they die...why should I honour that?"

Nila...

The name...

Like an angel.

Nila...

My heart suddenly woke up. Shedding death, sending lethargic blood through my veins.

Nila.

Mine.

The woman I want but failed.

"Threads is walking out of here—regardless if they don't."

"Guess the only way to know for sure is to bust my brothers out of here before it's too late."

I sucked in a useless breath—it was like breathing cremated ash.

Before, the void I existed in had no emotion, no feeling to suck me dry. But these two people? Fuck. They had so much to say and no correct words in which to say it. The woman wept with helplessness and despair, hiding it beneath bluster and rage. The man…he was just as helpless and lost; only he wrapped his in confusion and disbelief.

"Alright, alright, I get your point." Boots thudded on the dirt floor. "How should I do it again?"

A derisive laugh trilled, chasing back ghouls and monsters. "I told you how. Arms under my knees and around my shoulders. You can't break me."

"No, but I've heard about people like you—"

"People like *me*?"

"Shit, I just meant people with your—"

"My disability—is that what you were going to say? People like 'me' who can't feel anything below their waist?"

An awkward cough. "I just meant, I know you can bruise easily and it's not so simple to heal like a normal—"

"Wow, this just gets better and better. You're saying I'm not normal?!"

"Whoa, fucking chill—"

"You know what? I don't have time for this. Pick me up, give me the damn torch, and shut the hell up. When they're safe in the hospital *then* we can discuss the politically appropriate ways to discuss my condition. Got it?"

A deep sigh. "Fine."

I couldn't make sense of anything.

What the hell did this mean?

Was my brain playing tricks? Giving me an angst-loaded argument, all for what? To keep me strained enough to stay lucid? Or were there truly two people trying to save me?

"There. You okay?"

"I'll be okay once we get them out of here. Right, hand me the wand."

A pause.

"Good. Take me closer."

A few seconds later, the hissing began. I wanted to raise my head and see. But all I could do was bask in the meagre happiness the sound gave and slip again.

The brightness suddenly flared, cutting past my eyelids, imprinting on my retinas. No talking, no bickering, only the licking of flames against whatever enemy it destroyed.

Time skipped again—like a faulty record, jumping ahead, screeching backward, never playing the track in order.

"You're almost there," the man said.

Almost on cue, a snapping sounded, followed by a skeletonish groan.

"Ah, see. How little you trust me."

More shuffling. "I take it back. You're a girl, and you know how to use power tools."

"Damn right, I do."

Silence fell except for the occasional footfall and clang of metal on metal.

I sighed as the tempers eddying around me faded as companionship and victory stole their frustration. Inner peace settled, and I gave up trying to hold on.

The excitement disappeared, giving me a body that was cold, hungry, and riddled with pain.

I'm ready to go now. I'm ready to leave.

But then another sense came back to life.

The sense of touch.

"Kite…can you hear me?"

The softest warmth flittered over my cheek and forehead.

I wanted to moan with sheer pleasure. To answer their question and prove I hadn't given up, no matter how much I craved sanctuary.

"You're okay. You'll be fine." Warmth darted over my chest, my arm.

Then the sweetest voice whispered in my ear. "I've got you, Jet. You're safe now. Just hang on."

Nila

"SHE'S IN THE bath."

"She's not feeling well and can't come to the door."

"I have her chair—see? Of course, she's in here with me."

"She's in bed. We had a sleepover and can't get up."

I groaned, wiping both hands over my face.

"Nothing will work."

The empty room swallowed my words, keeping my fibs from reaching Hawk ears.

Ever since leaving Jasmine and Vaughn in the corridor leading toward the kitchens, I'd practiced a believable lie. Only thing was, there was nothing believable. After the visible hatred between Jaz and me at the meeting with the lawyers, no one would buy the excuse of a sleepover or girl chat or time willingly spent together.

It's hopeless.

The best I could hope for was no visitors and for V and Jaz to get back as soon as possible.

My mind skipped back to last night.

My spine had tingled with foreboding as V bent down in the dark and hesitantly plucked Jasmine from her chair. I'd never seen her legs in full view without baggy pyjamas or a blanket hiding the emaciated muscles but seeing them dangle over V's arms hit me hard.

Once upon a time, she could run and ride horses and chase her brothers.

Now, she had to rely on the brother of her enemy to be her transport.

A brutal price to pay for a payment I didn't know.

The look in V's eyes as he'd turned his back on me and left me in the empty corridor with an empty wheelchair squeezed my heart until I couldn't breathe. Helping a Hawk went against everything he believed in. In his mind, he betrayed his stance on blackmailing with social media, slandering the Hawk name, and standing up for our mother and me.

Yet, here he was, abandoning his sister in order to help another save her brothers.

It wasn't easy, but he showed me more loyalty and strength than I'd ever seen. Gone was the cocky joker who summoned women with one smirk. Gone was the slight player who'd worked hard but somehow managed to indulge in life with a silver spoon.

As he disappeared with a black-dressed Jaz in his arms, he grew from boy to man, and I'd wanted to run after him and thank him for saving Jethro—for once again putting my happiness above his own and doing what I bade.

It'd taken all my control not to follow. To clutch the handles of Jasmine's chair and wheel it in the opposite direction.

They're coming for you, Jethro.
They'll save you.

It killed me that I wouldn't be there. That I wouldn't be the one coaxing him to liveliness, rescuing him from pain. But, at the same time, that right belonged to Jaz. Jethro had sacrificed his life to save hers—it was only fair she did the same.

Then again, she'd dragged my brother into her plotting. There was no telling her plans—whatever they were—would be executed without a hitch. No saying they would be safe.

If Cut found out, Jaz would be punished, Jethro and Kes

killed for real, and Vaughn repeatedly beaten. I had no doubt they would destroy him until he begged for death.

And all for what? For the unfortunate curse of being my blood.

Stop thinking about it.

I glared at the wheelchair, lurking in the shadows by the door. It looked so sad, so empty without its owner. The metal machine grieved for its occupant, no longer wanting to provide a purpose without her.

Dawn lurked on the horizon.

Pink swirls and purple splashes slowly pushed aside midnight black.

For the fiftieth time, I looked at the clock.

6:37 a.m.

I'd returned to my room at ten past twelve. Over six hours ago.

Where were they?

What had they been doing?

Are you still alive, Jethro?

Are you safe?

I hadn't slept. I hadn't relaxed. How could I when they were out there, sneaking beneath sleeping cameras and saving men who in Cut's mind were dead?

The dresser was back across the door, firmly wedged and protective. But that didn't stop my growing panic as each hour traded night for day and the chance of getting caught increased.

"What do you mean Jasmine's missing? No, she isn't. She's here…in the bathroom. And no, you cannot see her."

I groaned, pacing at the end of my bed. That would fail. If she were in the bathroom, she'd need her chair to move around.

"She's taking a nap; I don't want to disturb her."

All Cut would have to do was bang on the door and 'wake her up' to realize there was no nap to disturb.

"God, this isn't going to work."

Please, hurry!

The last of moonlight turned to sunlight, glinting off the silver rims of Jasmine's chair. I had the strangest feeling of not being alone. As if the inanimate object was somehow alive, as if it had a presence in the room—the ghost of Jaz, leaving her impression with me even while she ran escapades with my brother.

What are you doing?
Has it gone to plan?
How much longer will you be?

I couldn't stop thinking about it. I hated being left behind, left to worry and fret and create insane theories on what'd happened without me.

I would've given anything to be with them.

He's not dead.
He's alive!

Joy effervesced.

I held a hand against my chest, forcing the happy bubbles to disperse. It was too soon to celebrate. Too soon to believe he was safe. In some awful way, I didn't want to jinx it by believing in the best when the worst might still happen.

Time continued onward, turning my fear into depression.

What if Jasmine underestimated her plan to save them? What if they'd waited too long? What if? What if? *What if?*

Looking at the clock, I bit my lip as the hour hand struck 7:00 a.m. No one in Hawksridge was an early riser, but Jasmine was playing with fire. She had to get back and *soon*. She had to return my brother.

I paced the thick carpet. Every creak of the ancient house warming in the early winter sunshine made me jump. Every crank and glug of old plumbing sent my heart racing.

She has to have made it.
She has to have saved him.

A tapping sounded. Faint and fleeting.

I slammed to a halt, eyes flying to the ceiling, the walls, the window, the door.

It came again.

The softest rap and the quietest voice. "Threads, open up."

After pacing tens of kilometres and biting off my nails in concern, they were back.

I flew.

With super-human strength, I shoved aside the dresser and opened the door.

"Let us in. Quickly." Vaughn's voice was raspy and tired, but alive.

Thank God.

I stepped aside. The dark corridor hid my secretive visitors until they traded the gloom and darted inside. Vaughn prowled forward with Jasmine locked in his arms, moving through puddles of sunlight, as he headed straight for her chair.

Immediately, I closed the door again, deliberating whether to put the dresser back or not.

Jaz's arm was slung over his shoulders, her body relaxed in his embrace. Something was different.

When he'd picked her up and disappeared seven hours ago, they'd been awkward and stiff. Now, they shared an experience, a mission I hadn't been privileged to participate in.

Vaughn's back bunched beneath a new t-shirt as he placed Jasmine gently into the wheeled contraption. I eyed him. *He wasn't wearing that last night.* The previous wardrobe had been a bloodied dark blue shirt. This was a dark grey tee with a sports brand tagged on the front—not at all what my brother would wear.

My heart thudded with mysteries. What had they seen and done together? What rapport had they built? And why couldn't I have been a part of it?

My jaw clenched as Jasmine smiled at V.

He tucked her useless legs onto the stirrups and took a step back. "You good?"

She nodded. "Thanks."

I moved forward, feeling left out, lost, and entirely too close to tears.

She was on our side. She'd done what she could to save the men we both loved, but at the same time, I couldn't forget how nasty she'd been. The ruse of making me hate her caused my feelings to split. I wanted to like her, but some part of me was still wary, still on edge.

She asked me to die for her brother.

But...wouldn't I do the same if it were V?

Swallowing my hurt, I crossed my arms. "How did it go?" *Please tell me it was a success.*

The rest of it: the sadness at not sharing their adventure and the grief at not being able to see Jethro would diminish the moment I knew he was in the hands of those who could heal him and Kes.

Jasmine adjusted herself in the chair as Vaughn took a step back.

Her eyes met mine. "We got them to the hospital."

"Oh, thank God." My heart tried to leap from my chest. "Did the doctors say anything?"

"Lots to tell you, Threads." Vaughn came closer. His arms banded around me, squeezing tight.

Tears pricked my eyes.

I hadn't realised how lonely I'd been, so afraid and on tenterhooks all night.

I accepted his embrace but quickly wriggled out. I couldn't handle his hug when every part of me was jealous that I hadn't been the one to help. I couldn't find comfort in his arms, otherwise I'd burst into waterworks. "Tell me. Tell me everything."

V let me go. "We stayed as long as we could. We got them there, filled in the paperwork, and waved goodbye as they took them to surgery, but we couldn't wait any longer to find out the prognosis."

His stomach growled loudly, shredding the taut atmosphere.

"But they'll make it?"

His tummy grumbled again. Finally given a task I could

perform, I headed to my secret stash in the fabric cupboard.

Vaughn looked at Jaz.

Her face was pinched. Her black hoodie and leggings painted her like a thief in the night. If anyone saw her dressed like that, she'd have a lot of explaining to do. "They were when we left them. But they're with the experts now. All we can do is hope."

Unwilling to fall into another pit of despair, I forced my mind to focus on one scenario.

They'll make it.

Wrenching open the cupboard, I pulled out a box of muesli bars. Glancing at Jaz, I asked, "How did you keep them alive for so long? And where?" Ripping the box open, I tossed a bar to V and one to Jaz. They both caught them.

Jasmine smiled in thanks, tucking hers into the satchel of her wheelchair. V, on the other hand, tore off the wrapper with his teeth and devoured it in a few mouthfuls. "Fuck, I haven't eaten in forever."

Hadn't they fed him? My heart hardened. More daggers of hatred grew toward Cut and Bonnie. I wanted to murder them slowly, *painfully*—to do to them what they'd done to innocent men and women.

Jasmine replied, "It wasn't just me. I had help."

"Damn right you did." V winked. "Me."

She smiled, a scowl plaiting with genuine amusement. "No, hotshot." Her eyes met mine again. "Flaw."

I froze. *I was right.*

My mind skipped to our conversation. Something about me not judging him, and how he was a good person. "He helped? How?"

Yesterday in the corridor.

They'd huddled together...discussing Jethro.

Jasmine sighed, "I was a freaking mess when Cut shot them. I'd wanted to walk again ever since I lost the ability, but in that second I'd wanted to *fly*. To soar across the room and tear out his motherfucking heart."

My hands curled around the box of muesli bars. "I know that feeling."

"Afterward, Bonnie took me upstairs and tried to calm me down. The rest I'm not entirely sure about, but Flaw was given the task of cleaning up." She swallowed, eyes turning dark. "He noticed they...weren't dead."

"They had drips and shit...medical paraphernalia down there." Vaughn jumped in. "Who did that?"

"Flaw again. He dropped out of medical school after he discovered diamonds were a lot more lucrative than sewing up flesh. We had the equipment, but he didn't tell anyone. He moved their bodies, set up what they needed, then came to me the minute I was alone. Everything went according to plan, apart from the mishap of shutting the cell door."

That was happening all while she came to save me from Daniel.

How had she come up with a plan so fast? And why did Cut listen to her demands as oldest child?

My mind raced. "So...Flaw kept them alive?"

She nodded. "If it hadn't been for him, they would've drained out on the carpet."

I shook my head. "But there was so much blood. They were unconscious."

Jaz rolled closer. "He performed a miracle, Nila. I'll be forever grateful for that. But there's no guarantee they'll pull through. The doctors tried to be optimistic when we arrived, but..."

Vaughn picked up where she trailed off. "The docs' faces, Threads. You could tell they didn't have much hope."

The joy of knowing Jethro and Kestrel were rescued punctured, deflating like a hot air balloon, crashing faster toward Earth. "So...they might still..." I couldn't finish.

Jaz smiled tightly, her eyes glittering with unshed tears. "Let's focus on the positive. They're away from Hawksridge with people who know what they're doing. That's all we have."

Terrible silence fell, like a curtain already stealing Jethro and Kes from us.

Vaughn finally muttered, "Why keep them down there? It was a fucking dungeon."

His train of thought gave me something to focus on.

Jasmine jumped to answer, as if unable to handle the quietness when we couldn't stop our minds from picking at *'what if'*.

What if they don't make it?
What if we were too late?

"It's the only place in Hawksridge that has no cameras. All rooms, bathrooms, cellars—they're all monitored. We couldn't run the risk of Cut seeing them."

I straightened. "What about the cameras last night?"

Her hands dived into her hair. Unpinning the clip, she let her sleek bob fall into place around her chin. "A few months ago, Kes taught me how to upload a virus that put the cameras into hibernation for a few hours. After a time, they reboot as if nothing happened. If anyone attempts to fix them while they're down, the virus hijacks the hard drive and ruins two months' worth of data." She shrugged. "Either no one noticed and will think the lack of recording was a technical fault, or someone did and will put it down to a damaged hard drive."

"Interesting." Vaughn rubbed his face. "You'll have to show me that handy trick." His stomach growled again, even louder than before.

I couldn't help Jethro or improve his prognosis, but I could help another man I loved. Turning back to the cupboard, I grabbed an armful of apples, biscuits, and another box of muesli bars. I shoved them at my brother. "Here. Have these." Dashing to my wardrobe, I pulled free a few extra-large jumpers that I liked to wear off the shoulder with a belt and gave those to him, too. "And these. To keep you warm."

Jaz wheeled forward. "That's a good idea. That room is freezing." Her shoulders rolled. "V, it hasn't exactly been easy dealing with you tonight, but you've been amazing. Helping move Jet and Kes, driving the van, filling out the paperwork at the hospital. Don't think I'm not grateful because I am. But…"

Vaughn had his mouth full with a crisp green apple. "But you have to take me back."

Jaz nodded.

"No, surely you can just let him go—" I moved between them.

Vaughn swallowed his breakfast. "No chance of a warmer room? Something without a broken window?"

She smiled sadly. "Sorry. We have to make it seem like nothing happened. Cut can't know Jet and Kes are alive. Any escapes or room changes will make him suspicious. However, I'll do what I can and move you in a few days."

I stood in front of V, cutting Jaz off. "I won't let them keep him in that place." Putting my hands on my hips, I glared. "Why can't you just let him go? You were off the estate tonight. Just take him back to London and let him hide until this is all over. Cut can just blame me if he gets suspicious."

Vaughn grabbed my shoulders. "You think I'd do that? Run away and leave you here?"

I shrugged him off. "If you're not here, they have nothing to control me with. I'll be free to do what needs to be done."

Vaughn's eyes flashed. "Don't be so stupid, Threads. I'm not going anywhere without you. End of fucking story."

Jaz stiffened. "You do realise saying 'when this is all over' is accepting your death, right?"

I groaned. *Great.* Perfect thing to say in front of an overprotective twin.

"*What?*" Vaughn demanded. "What the fuck does that mean?"

I rolled my eyes. "I'm not accepting death. I have my own plan to end this. Either way, I need you gone, V. I can't have people I love here."

Jaz suddenly shot forward and grabbed my hand. "Don't do anything reckless, Nila. I made an oath to Jethro to look after you. I can't break that promise."

My eyes widened. "When did you make that?"

Her face softened. "There are a lot of conversations and

stolen moments in this house that you don't see or hear. The day the police came for you after the Second Debt, I knew you'd changed him. He refused to speak to me. He pushed me out of his life completely, but he didn't need to tell me for me to understand."

"There is so much shit I don't know about," Vaughn grumbled. "I need some education. Someone needs to fill me in on what I missed. Second Debt?"

Jaz and I ignored him.

My heart galloped, drunk on the thought of Jethro. Imagining him alive and happy. The fact he'd talked about me...that his sister knew how he felt about me—it made our love so real. Even if it was forbidden.

My voice dropped to a whisper. "You're like him...aren't you?"

"Like who?" V asked around a mouthful of hobnob biscuits.

Jaz lowered her gaze. "He told you?"

Her tone was both awed and slightly miffed.

"Does that offend you?" The residual dislike for her tainted my voice.

She shook her head. "Offend? No. Surprise? Yes. But...I knew he'd fallen in love with you. I could feel it in him."

"Feel it?" V wiped crumbs off his t-shirt. "That's a strange thing to say."

I turned to face him. "She's a VEP." After Jethro's lesson the other day, I felt cocky to know the term. To know the technical name for a condition so common in people that it'd become a regular flaw, according to society.

V scrunched up his nose. "What the hell is that?"

Jaz chuckled. "No. And Nila has it wrong. I'm empathic to the point of emotional sensory but nowhere near as bad as Jethro. I don't call myself anything different. Just attuned to my brother—same as you're tuned to each other." She waved at V and me. "You're twins. There are differences between you, but overall, you share enough genetic make-up to sense each other on a deeper level."

Vaughn nodded. "That's twins for you."

Jaz smiled. "Twins and Empaths."

A loud noise slammed a few rooms down.

We all froze.

The inhabitants of Hawksridge were waking up.

I hated that answers had to come later, but I would hate it even more if we were caught. "As much as I want to continue talking, I think...it's time to hide."

Jaz nodded, rolling toward the door. "You're right." Without looking over her shoulder, she said, "V, I'll take you back to your room."

My heart twitched at the casual way she called my twin by his nickname. I wanted to tell her she had no right. But, then again, I *had* stolen her brother. I'd forced myself into his life and replaced her with myself.

Suddenly, I understood Jaz a whole lot more. She liked me because I was good for her sibling. But at the same time, she despised me taking him away from her.

Rushing forward, I opened the door a crack but put my foot out to prevent her from disappearing. Bending down, I whispered, "I just want to thank you. You have my word I won't hurt him—ever again. I'm in this for life, and I hope you know that I would never take him away completely." I smiled. "I'm very good at sharing."

"Sharing what?" V asked, coming to place his hands on Jaz's shoulders.

The unthinking action after a night of escapades and contact spoke more than words ever could. They were relaxed around each other. Whatever had happened had formed a trust far quicker than Jethro and I had built.

I'm...I'm jealous.

But also, strangely happy.

"Nothing." I backed up, smiling at V.

Jaz understood, though.

She shrugged, dislodging V's touch. "I think there's hope

for you and me, yet, Nila Weaver." Patting my hand, she wheeled into the corridor.

V followed, pausing to kiss me on the cheek. He'd draped the two jumpers I'd given him over his shoulder and hugged his pilfered food. "I'll see you when I see you, I guess."

Sooner, rather than later.

I squeezed him hard. "Everything will be okay. You'll see."

Jaz sucked in a breath. "I hope so. If Kes and Jet make it, there will be hope for all of us." Her eyes captured mine, dark thoughts lurking in the depths. "One thing's for sure. It's no longer Hawk versus Weaver. We're the new generation. We've inherited the sins of our forebears.

"But we'll be the ones who will change history."

Jethro

NILA LAUGHED.

I looked up from my report on the latest smuggling shipment and covered my eyes from the overwhelming sunshine behind her.

She stood haloed in golden warmth—like the goddess I worshipped daily. She was ethereal, magical...mine.

"What's so funny?"

She skipped to my side and took my hand. The instant her skin touched mine, my heart tripped over. Even after all this time together, even after entwining our lives completely, I was still hopelessly smitten. She was my queen—the custodian of my soul—just like I'd promised when I'd given in to her the night I told her everything.

With a tender smile, she placed my hand on her growing belly.

My jaw clenched with a mixture of all-consuming love, pride, and protectiveness.

She's carrying my child.

We made this unborn creature together.

Half her, half me. It would be a Weaver and Hawk. Seamstress and diamond smuggler.

Ours.

"He kicked."

"Really?" I pressed my hand harder.

The firmness of her belly didn't move.

Nila's face fell. "He's stopped."

I gathered her close, pressing a kiss on her cotton-covered bump. "You keep saying he. We haven't found out the sex yet. It could just as easily be a girl."

She shook her head, her long black hair soaking up the sun as if she somehow harnessed its power. I loved her hair. I loved how free it made her.

"It's a boy."

Tugging her onto my lap, I kissed her lips. This woman utterly beguiled me. "What if I don't want a boy? What if I want a little girl who is as perfect as you?"

"He's coming to."

"Move aside, please."

Loud beeps filled my ears. Pain swamped. Heaviness shackled. Agony battered from all directions.

Fuck, make it stop.

I didn't like it here. I wanted to go back. Return to where the sunshine glowed and my wife carried my child.

More pain crescendoed. I gave up fighting.

Fuck, make it stop…make it stop!

My heart accelerated, shoving me head-first into my wish.

With a sigh, I let go of my body, ignored the summons trying to drag me back to life, and fell.

"You want a girl?"

I nodded. "More than anything."

"And what if I want a son?"

"You'll just have to wait."

Nila giggled. "Wait?"

I pulled her close, inhaling her soft scent of wild-flowers and summer. "Until we have another one."

"Mr. Ambrose. Come on."

The warm illusion shattered again.

I tensed, preparing for pain to welcome me back. There was no pain. Only a fog. A metallic blanket blocked the fever and excruciating agony. For the first time in forever, I could think without being handicapped by suffering.

With the discomfort gone, it opened the gates for everything else to become known.

My body was *tired*. Beyond tired. Bone weary and sluggish.

I don't want to be here.

I missed my dream world where everything was sunshine and smiles, away from whatever memories snarled on the outskirts of comprehension.

I want to forget...just for a little longer.

Sleep gripped my mind, tugging me backward, slipping me under the surface and delivering me back to Nila.

"Another one?" She swatted my chest, laughing in the bright afternoon. "Getting a bit greedy, don't you think?"

I nuzzled her neck. "Greedy? I wouldn't call it greedy."

Her lips parted as I trailed kisses up her throat, skirting her chin, hovering over her mouth. Her breath cracked and shortened, waiting in anticipation of a kiss. "Oh? What would you call it?"

I paused over her lips. I wanted so badly to kiss her. To drink her taste and pour my love down her throat. I wanted so desperately to heal her. To forget about the past and remind both of us that it was over. That we were free.

"I call it building a better future."

Nila's head tipped back. I captured her nape, keeping her locked in my control. My mouth watered, still millimetres from kissing her.

"How many?" she whispered as my lips finally touched hers.

My tongue slipped into her mouth, tangoing with hers, dancing the same dance we knew by heart. I would recognise Nila even if all my senses were stolen. I would know her if I was blind, deaf, and mute. I would always know her because I could feel *her. Her love had a certain flavour—a sparkling liquor that intoxicated me whenever I let down my walls and felt what she felt, lived what she lived.*

I murmured, "As many as we can."

"Mr. Ambrose, you have to open your eyes."

That damn voice again. And that name...it was wrong. That wasn't my name.

Once again, I tried to ignore the tugging, wanting to fall backward into sleep, but this time the gates were shut. I couldn't slip.

I hovered there—in an in-between world where darkness

steadily became lighter and the world slowly solidified.

The pain was still blanketed, the tiredness not as consuming, but there was strangeness everywhere.

Strange smells.

Strange noises.

Strange people.

Where am I?

"That's it, wake up. We won't bite."

I cringed against the false, upbeat tone. I didn't tolerate insincerity and whoever encouraged me hid his true thoughts.

My condition was the first sense to return with full force, feeding off the man beside me—the man who cared, worried, and clinically assessed me. In his mind, I belonged to him. My progress, my recovery—it was all testament to his skills as my…

Doctor.

The unfamiliar place and unfamiliar smells suddenly made a lot more sense.

Bright lights were brighter and the blanket hiding me from pain lived deep in my veins.

Drugs.

I couldn't move. I couldn't speak. I could barely breathe.

But I was alive.

And mistakenly being called Mr. Ambrose.

The beeping sound flurried faster as I slipped back into all facets of my body. Fingers to fingers. Toes to toes. It was like dressing in expensive cashmere after weeks of wearing scratchy wool. It was *home*.

"He's coming to."

"That's it. We're here. No need to fear. You're safe."

The doctor's voice reached into the remaining darkness in my brain, plucking me to the surface. My eyes were heavy drapes, musty and full of moths, refusing to open.

A wash of frustration came from nowhere—tugging me faster from my haze, slamming me into a body I no longer wanted.

My eyes opened.

"Great. Awesome job, Mr. Ambrose."

I promptly closed them again. The room was too bright, too much to see.

"Give it a moment and the discomfort will pass." Someone patted me on the shoulder. The drumbeat resonated through my body, awakening everything else.

I tried again, squinting this time to limit the amount of light.

The scene before me crystallised from a sea of wishy-washy watercolours to shapes I recognised.

I knew this world. *Yet I don't know these people.*

I was back in a broken body, battered within an inch of my life. I was cold and feeling nauseous, and interminably tired. I preferred my dream world where Nila was safe, we were happy, and there was no mad evil threatening to tear us apart.

The doctor clasped my hand—the one free of an IV needle.

I tried to tug away but my brain failed to send the message, leaving me in his grasp. "You gave us quite a scare, Mr. Ambrose."

I swallowed, forcing my emaciated throat to lubricate. "Th—that isn't m—my—" I cut myself off before I could finish.

My name…what was my name…?

It only took a fraction.

I'm Jethro Hawk. Heir to Hawksridge, firstborn, and recently murdered by his own father. Everything of my past, my trials, and my love for Nila slotted into perfect place, leaving me clearheaded and aware.

As far as my father knew, I'd died when the bullet meant for Jasmine tore into my body. Whoever had delivered me to the hospital was on my side. And the name was a mask keeping me safe.

A flash of agony made its way through whatever painkillers they'd given me, kick-starting me onto another subject. "W—who are y—you?"

The doctor studied me. His brown handlebar moustache and shock of unruly hair didn't match the somber light green scrubs he wore or the softness of his hand around mine. He looked like an eccentric farmer, someone more at home hugging a chicken, than nursing a patient back to life.

"My name is Jack Louille. I was the surgeon who operated on you." His eyes cast down to my stomach, covered in starchy white sheets. "It was touch and go for a bit, but you responded well to treatment."

"W—what treat—treatment?"

He beamed, a rush of pride emitting from him, his emotions of a job well done and workplace satisfaction buffeting me. "I don't know how much you remember, but you were shot."

I nodded. "My m—memory is fully in—intact." The more I spoke, the more my throat found it easier to talk.

"Ah, that's great news. As you are aware then, a bullet sliced through your side." He leaned over me. "I don't need to tell you how close it came to being a fatal wound. An abdominal injury can rupture intestines, liver, spleen, and kidneys. There are also major vessels that can be nicked—all of which equal a lower possibility of survival—especially in your case, since you were unable to seek treatment straight away."

Why was that?

I couldn't recall.

Memories of time skipping and fire hissing tried to make sense. Kestrel had been beside me…

Kes!

I lashed out, grabbing the doctor's wrist. My body flared with agony, but I ignored it. "The other m—man. Is he here, t—too?" I didn't dare say his name. I doubted he would be under it anyway—same as me.

Doctor Louille paused, his happiness at my recovery fading as helplessness smothered his thoughts. "Your brother is still with us, but…we don't know for how long. His injuries were more extensive, less straightforward to operate." He cleared his throat. "I'll tell you about him soon. First, let me explain your condition and then you need to rest. There is time for everything else later."

No, there is no time.

If Kes wasn't doing well, I wanted to see him before it was too late.

I need my brother. My friend.

"You're what I call an extraordinary luckster." Louille smiled. "I once had a patient who slipped in the bath and shattered a window. The glass sliced his neck but missed the jugular and carotid artery. Do you know how nearly impossible that is? But he was lucky. I've had many patients that, by right, should be dead but somehow tricked death into leaving them alone." He patted my shoulder. "You're the latest luckster. The bullet sliced through the high side of your abdomen, passing through the muscles surrounding core vitals, and never entering the abdominal cavity. You would've passed out from the overload of adrenaline and pain, and it would've been horrendously messy and bloody, but here we are."

My head pounded.

Here I was.

I've been given a second chance.

I wasn't so rotten that I deserved to die; wasn't so evil to merit a one-way ticket to hell.

I'm not going to waste it.

I would use this new life to fix all my wrongs and ensure I deserved the luck I'd been given.

"H—how l—long?"

Doctor Louille ran a hand over his moustache. "You were in surgery for three hours and asleep for three days in intensive care. Your vitals were finally strong enough to wean you off the sedative and let nature take its course."

Three days?

Three fucking days!

Shit, what about Nila?

My heart clanged out of control. An exorbitant amount of adrenaline swamped me. Hurling myself upward, I lurched for the edge of the bed. Pain be damned. Motherfucking bullet wound be damned.

Three days!

"I—I have to g—go."

Louille slammed his hands on my shoulders, pushing me back against the mattress. "What the hell are you doing? I just told you you were lucky. You trying to ruin that luck?"

I struggled, seeing a clock ticking closer to Nila's death everywhere I looked.

Nila!

Three days!

What had they done to her in that time?

"Let—let me g—go!"

"No chance in hell, buddy. You're my patient. You'll follow my rules." Louille's fingers dug into my biceps, holding me in place. "Calm down or I'll restrain you. You want that?"

I froze, breath wheezing in and out. My stomach gnashed with agonising pain.

Three days...

My energy disappeared. A wash of sickness almost made me vomit. *Oh, fuck*. The room turned upside down.

Louille sympathised, letting me go. "The nausea will pass. It's the morphine. Just lie still and you'll be okay."

All I could think about was Nila and the fact I'd abandoned her.

Fuck!

"Molly, perhaps increase Mr. Ambrose's dose and arrange a sedative."

"No!" I'd already lost so much time. No way in hell would I lose anymore. I needed every minute awake to heal and run back to my woman.

My eyes fell on a girl in the background. A nurse with blonde hair in a bun and a clipboard in her hand. Her emotions were shuttered, barely registering on my condition. Either she guarded herself well or the nausea kept my sensitivity to a minimum.

Forcing myself to remain sane—at least until the doctor left so I could plan my escape—I asked, "H—how long will I h—have to s—stay here?"

"Why? You got some skiing trip to attend in Switzerland?" Doctor Louille laughed. When he noticed I was dead serious, he cleared his throat. "I estimate three weeks to be fully fixed. Two weeks for the wound to heal and another week for the internal bruising to recede. Twenty-one days, Mr. Ambrose, then I'll sign the discharge papers and send you on your merry way."

Three weeks?

Fuck, I couldn't wait that long.

Even three days drove me insane.

I shook my head. "I can't be a—away for that l—length of ti—time."

Don't give up on me, Nila.

I had to be there to keep her safe. She couldn't be subjected to more horror—especially at the hands of my bastard father and brother.

Fuck, fuck, fuck!

My heart squeezed like a fucking lemon, cauterizing my insides with citric acid at the thought of her being so vulnerable and alone.

"I'm sorry, Mr. Ambrose, but you're not fit to leave. And you're under my care until I say you are." Turning his attention to the nurse, he waved her closer. "Give me that phone number. We best let the family know he's awake."

My heart burst through my ribs. "Wh—what family?"

Don't tell my bastard father.

I'd be poisoned or slaughtered before the day was done.

Doctor Louille reached for the phone on the white bedside table. Everything in the room was either white, glass, or light blue. A flat-screen TV hung on the wall, while a small table and chairs squashed in the corner.

"The woman who dropped you here, of course." He gnawed on his bottom lip as he dialled a number and put the phone to his ear. He waited for it to connect. "Yes, hello, Ms. Ambrose? Yes, it's Doctor Jack Louille calling."

A pause.

"I have some good news. He's just woken up. I'll put him on."

Covering the mouthpiece, he passed the phone to me. My mind whirled, trying to keep up. I shook my head. What if this was a trap? What if it was Bonnie?

The doctor didn't take my hesitation as any sign to stop his persistence. "It's your sister. She's called every hour for the past few days. Get her off my back and let her know you're okay." Nudging the phone into my hands, he said, "Talk to her. Rest. I'll be back later to answer any more questions and assess your pain levels. And keep your arse in bed, or else."

My fingers curled around the phone.

No promises.

I was running as soon as I could breathe without wanting to throw up.

I trembled, battling tiredness and the thought of talking to someone still at Hawksridge, someone I loved, someone I'd failed as much as I'd failed Nila.

Waiting until the doctor and nurse had left, I held the phone to my mouth. "H—hello?"

The longest pause crackled in my ear.

"H—hello? You there?"

A sniff came down the line. "About bloody time, you bloody arse."

My heart beat stronger.

I might have failed Nila.

I might have been dead for a few days.

But Jasmine had achieved the impossible. If she'd kept me alive, I had to trust she'd done the same for Nila.

"You al—always had a gr—great way with your t—temper, Jaz."

"God, it's truly you…" Her voice broke then she burst into noisy tears.

I found out later what she'd done for us. How she'd saved us. How Flaw had kept Kes and me alive long enough to smuggle us from the estate unseen. How he'd hidden us in the crypt, providing medicine, leaving us to slowly fossilize and turn into skeletons beneath the house I'd lived in all my life—working against the clock to get us somewhere safe.

I owed Flaw a huge debt. I would pay him handsomely. But I would also never underestimate my sister or take her for granted ever again. I couldn't believe she'd willingly left Hawksridge.

After a lifetime of chaining herself to the Hall, she'd commandeered one of the many vehicles in our garage and somehow delivered Kes and me to the hospital. From the way the doctors spoke, it sounded as if she'd only just made it. Another hour or two and Kestrel would've been dead and me not long after.

How she managed to do that, I had no idea. The phone call had been brief, hushed—a quick catch-up so Bonnie wouldn't overhear. Her relief had been genuine, but she'd also kept something from me.

Something I meant to find out.

After I hung up, the nurse had slipped back in and against my wishes fed more sedative into my drip.

I couldn't try to run. I couldn't assess how weak I was. All I could do was slip into empty dreams like some drugged arsehole. Nila didn't come visit me and I awoke pissed and hurting a few hours later.

Kestrel stole my thoughts for the billionth time since I'd woken. My heart splintered for my brother.

According to Louille, he still hadn't woken up. He was in intensive care and an induced coma. The bullet I'd saved Jaz from had been a clean shot. By Louille's own admission, I was a 'luckster', a fluke of nature, a fucking miracle. No bones shattered, no organs ruptured. A single entry and exit wound leaving me bleeding and infected but otherwise intact.

But if I was a miracle, then that came with certain obligations and privileges.

Privileges I would call on in order to end the man who'd killed me.

Obligations I meant to uphold now I was free.

I'd returned from the dead.

And I'd bring the wrath of hell toward my enemies.

DIARY ENTRY, EMMA Weaver.

He told me tonight. Lying in my arms, believing he was safe, he told me what he did to his brother. Part of me can understand it—to spend a lifetime being told you're second best, only to snap when something you want more than anything torments you. But another part of me could never understand because I could never be that selfish, self-centred, or cruel. One thing is for sure—his children are damned. Even the ones not infected with his madness are ruined because of what their father did to their mother and uncle.

A shrill ringing pierced my concentration.

No!

I had to find out what Cut did. Why were Jethro and his siblings damned? What the hell happened all those years ago?

Three days had passed. Three nights where I slept in sheets fading with Jethro's scent. Three mornings where I'd paced and fretted and begged. Daniel had been offsite, leaving me to boredom rather than torture. I hadn't seen Vaughn or Cut, and I'd been kept isolated, locked inside my room like a true prisoner.

Wasting three days in limbo was sacrilege. I wanted *vengeance*. However, my mind couldn't stop swimming with worry. Jethro, Jethro, *Jethro*. Nothing else mattered. Nothing else was important.

The discordant ringing persisted; I wrenched my eyes from the remaining blank page. There was no more. My mother had left the mystery unsolved.

The Weaver Journal was the only thing with the power to steal me away from repeating thoughts of Jethro. However, reading the journal's pages gave me the strangest sensation—as if I'd lifted up the veil of time and looked at Hawksridge in a capsule of *then* and *now*. Hearing about Jethro when he was young, about Bryan loving my mother, and even Bonnie thanking Emma for making her dresses—it was surreal.

Wrong.

Ring. Ring. Ring!

Tossing away the journal, I scrambled out of bed. Dashing across the room, I peered at yards of apricot fleece, searching for the origin of the ringing. Pushing aside fabric and opening a small cubby inside the storage cupboard, I found the source.

What on earth? Why have I never seen this before?

Plucking the phone off its tarnished cradle, I held it to my ear. "Hello?"

Instantly, a female voice said, "He's awake."

My knees gave out.

Slamming against the dresser, I clutched the edge. Adrenaline drenched my system like a tropical rainstorm. No matter how much I'd prayed and hoped he'd stay alive, I hadn't truly believed it.

"Are—are you sure?" My voice was quiet as a mouse. "How can you be sure?"

Don't give me false hope. I won't be able to stand it.

"I'm sure." Jaz sniffed happily. "I spoke to him myself."

My heart leapt over mountains of joy. Bending forward, I placed my forehead on trembling hands. "Thank heavens."

Jaz didn't speak for a moment.

I stayed silent, too.

Both of us breathed loudly, living in happiness bought with hard-earned fortune.

Things would be better now.

Letting the knowledge settle, I focused on the other man in my heart. "V...did you move him?"

"Yes. He's in a different room. Warm with regular food." She paused. "I'll keep an eye on him. I promise."

I squeezed my eyes. "Thank you."

An awkward silence fell, amplifying our unspoken need to talk about Jethro.

Jethro is still heir. He'll end this. I know he will.

"Jasmine? How—how long—?"

How long will he be gone?

I was greedy. He'd been awake for only minutes, yet I wanted him now. I wanted to touch him, kiss him, hold him—cradle the truth in my hands. But that wasn't my only reason. The real reason sat like a sinister splodge on my joy. *How long will I have to endure Cut's whims?*

I'd been lucky these past three days. I had no illusion that luck would last.

Jasmine read between the lines. "How long is irrelevant. You're mine. I'll do what I promised, Nila."

Fresh tears sparked into being. "I know."

You'll do your best, but ultimately, I'm alone.

Just like I'd been alone when Jethro controlled my fate. I guess nothing had changed. It was still up to me to slice out their loathsome hearts.

"And Ke—" I cut myself off. *Stay in riddles and code.* Who knew what lines were tapped and which walls had ears. "The other one...is he awake?"

Jasmine sighed heavily. "No."

The single word throbbed with sadness, giving no room for questions.

A loud rustle, then a quick, "I've got to go." A second later, the dial tone rang loud and empty.

Pushing away from the cupboard, I placed the phone back onto its cradle. Her phone call left me jumpy with hope and desolate with sorrow. I wanted them both to make it—hearing only Jethro was awake was bittersweet.

He's awake!
I hugged myself.
He hasn't left me.
Slowly, I padded toward the bed where I'd set down the Weaver Journal. At the last second, I changed my mind. I couldn't handle reading about ancient conspiracies and pain. I needed to cleanse my thoughts with something I had utter control over.

Switching direction to the chaise lounge, I upended the basket where I'd stuffed a damask panel and Georgian lace.
He's awake.
Those two words were now my favourite in the entire English language. I smoothed out the damask and pulled a needle free from a pincushion.
He's awake.
Better than alive.
He's awake.
Fate had finally been kind—the tables had finally turned.
Everything will be different now.
Cut, Daniel, and Bonnie would take Jethro and Kestrel's place in the ground. The balance of good and evil would right itself. And Vaughn and I would continue with whatever dreams we had with no guillotine hanging over our future.

Switching on another side lamp, I bent to my task of repairing the lace with painstaking needlework. It wasn't late, but the sun had set a few hours ago and Hawksridge creaked around me, depositing its residents into the night. The growls of motorbikes shattered the wintery air, Black Diamonds disappearing to run another smuggling delivery.

I lost myself in the exquisite craftsmanship, giving myself over to scattered thoughts. Jaz and Vaughn's rescue mission had gone unnoticed. Flaw had done the impossible. Jethro had cheated death.
We won.
Could Cut tell? Could he feel that his sons weren't dead? It didn't matter.

His arrogance was his undoing.
Tick tock. Tick tock.
His time is running out.

"She wants you, Nila."

My head snapped up.

My room was no longer empty. It had invited a visitor while I napped on the chaise. The lace I'd been working on littered the carpet and the needle harpooned my denim skirt, sticking upward like a tiny lance.

Flaw headed toward me, hands in his pockets. "Did you hear me?"

I blinked.

By day, I left the dresser pushed away from the doorway in case legitimate requests meant I had to open it quickly. But by night, I shoved the heavy armoire across, allowing a false sense of safety.

How long have I been asleep?

Sunshine sparkled on the horizon, turning my side lamp mute with fresh daylight.

Oh, my God, I slept all night?

I didn't feel rested. I felt tired and foggy.

Jethro...

He'd been in my thoughts all day. All night. All my life.

He's awake!

I missed him so much—missed his golden eyes, his hesitant smile. I missed the epiphany when he finally broke and let me put him back together again.

I miss you...

"Nila...you awake or sleep walking?" Flaw clicked his fingers in front of my face.

I flinched. "I'm awake. Sorry, just a bit fuzzy."

"When was the last time you slept properly?"

I shrugged, plucking the needle from my skirt and stabbing it into the pincushion. "Can't remember." My eyes burned from tiredness; wooziness existed in my brain.

He scowled. "You do realise they're safe. You can relax a bit without grief ruining your sleep."

Standing, my body creaked in protest from sleeping on the chaise. I stumbled forward with vertigo and my cell-phone thudded to the carpet by my feet.

Huh. *I don't remember retrieving it from my bedside.*

Flaw stayed silent as I blinked away my illness and collected it from the floor. I must've grabbed it while dreaming, hoping for a text.

Did he message?

I swiped it on.

Nothing.

No messages. No calls. No emails.

I've been completely forgotten.

Some part of me hoped that now Jethro was awake, he'd text me. That for the first time in months, we'd talk like we had before this mess started. Kite to Threads. Inbox to inbox.

"Has he been in touch?" Flaw glanced at my phone.

My lungs deflated; I shook my head. "No." Brushing stray hair from my eyes, I said, "I heard that he's awake, though. You?"

A slight smile tilted his lips. "Yes. She told me."

I smiled back. I'd entered Hawksridge believing everyone was my enemy. Turned out, only a few people were worthy of that title. Most of them were kind and honourable, wrapped up in their own issues, but ultimately generous and just like any stranger—frightening and mysterious until the boundary of no acquaintance distorted into friendship.

Kes had proven that. Then Jasmine. And now Flaw.

I knew all along I could win Jethro.

In a way, I think I'd known he was mine ever since I was young.

Once this was all over, I wanted to find out how many times we'd met. How many instances we'd spoken in our childhood—being groomed for our roles.

"Anyway." Flaw swayed on his heels. "I'm not here for a social call. Been instructed to bring you to her majesty."

My eyes widened. "What?"

"Not the Queen of England." He smirked. "The Queen of Hawksridge." Jamming his hands deeper into his pockets, his eyes darkened. "She wants a word."

"A word or a beating?" I clutched my phone. "A conversation with the old bat, *alone*, isn't high on my list of priorities."

If you're alone, though, you could kill her.

The thought welded me to the carpet.

"I wouldn't recommend calling her 'old bat' in person, if I were you."

My mind ran away, forgetting Flaw existed. The only way I could kill those who needed to die was to be strategic. I couldn't do it around others. I couldn't do it in plain sight. I had to be sneaky and wily and smart.

Every night, I stared into the darkness, using the black emptiness as a chalkboard for my plotting. I wished I had a treadmill in my room. Running always helped me problem solve. But even though my body remained stationary, it didn't mean my mind did.

I'd never been so enamoured with death before or so hyped on hypothetical murder.

I knew from television to expect copious amounts of blood and a struggle if I stabbed my victims to death. I also knew that strength would mean nothing against Cut and Daniel, so I had to have the element of surprise.

A gun would've solved my problems, but the noise and lack of experience in aiming could potentially be my downfall.

All opportunities led to one conclusion…I had to be quick and quiet. I had to be *ruthless*. And it had to look like an accident or remain hidden long enough to steal three lives before I was slaughtered in retribution.

I can't kill Bonnie.

Not yet. It had to be Daniel or Cut first…then her.

She'll be my last.

"You better go. I doubt she'll make allowances for lateness even if you haven't written her on your social calendar." Flaw's voice dripped with sarcasm. "New day. New psychological plague to administer."

I narrowed my gaze. "Ha-ha. Not funny."

Taking a deep breath, I placed my cell-phone on the end of the bed. "I guess I have no choice." Spinning to face him, I gathered my long hair and secured it in a messy ponytail with an elastic band from my wrist. "Did she say why at least?"

"Do I look like I have tea and crumpets with the fucking woman?" Flaw rolled his eyes. "All I was told was to get you." He held up his hands. "And no, I don't have insider knowledge like I did with the lawyers. This time, you're on your own."

His eyes skated down my white jumper with a filigree seahorse and denim skirt. "I, eh…don't have to tell you what happened a few days ago has to remain secret…no matter what she, eh…does?"

My heart spiralled into a tailspin. "What are you saying? She'll torture me?"

I was no stranger to pain but deliberate extraction of information through agony? *How long can I endure something like that?*

He stiffened. "If she knew you had something you weren't telling…I wouldn't put it past her." Coming closer, the strain around his mouth and eyes was prevalent.

I'm not the only one not sleeping.

"I don't need to tell you how—"

"How important it is that those who shall not be named remain dead? Yes, I understand." I placed my hand on his arm. "I won't tattle. What you did to help them has firmly earned my loyalty. My lips are sealed."

The air in the room turned heavy with seriousness. "I'd understand if she did something to make you tell."

I blanched. "You think I'll crack? I'm in love with him. There's no way in hell I would jeopardise their lives."

His shoulders slumped. "Okay. Sorry for pushing. My neck's on the line, too."

I dropped my touch. "I know. You've gone above and beyond…only…"

My forehead furrowed. Details were often the crux of impending ruin. Flaw and Jaz had freed them, but now Jethro and Kes were in the hands of doctors, nurses, and people who would talk.

"Only what?" Flaw prompted.

"How did you do it?"

He pursed his lips. "Do what?"

I lowered my voice to a whisper. "Get them to the basement. How—"

"Easy." He ran a hand through his hair, wincing at memories. "Don't suppose you know how many secrets live on the estate. How many animals exist—all bred for different purposes."

"What do you mean?"

"Well, you've seen the pheasants for shooting, horses for riding, dogs for hunting. But I doubt you'll have seen the pigs."

I took a step back. *"Pigs?"*

"Pigs are an excellent way to dispose of things you never want found again."

My mouth hung open. "Excuse me?" In the months I'd lived in Hawksridge, I hadn't seen a single pig. "Where?"

"They're hidden over the chase. Having a few pigs and not a pig farm can be suspicious these days, thanks to the recent mobster movies, serving shall we say 'alternative food.'"

I wrung my hands. "You're saying Cut feeds his enemies as food to his pigs?" My gullet churned, wanting to evict all knowledge of this conversation. "Shit, he's barbaric."

Worse than that—he has sewage for a soul.

Flaw raised an eyebrow, neither confirming nor denying it. "Whatever you think, it's smart business." His voice lowered to a sepulchral whisper. "Anyway, Cut asked me to get rid of their bodies. Only, Kes and Jethro had already come to me first.

They knew something like this might happen. After all, they've been playing with their lives for months. We'd all agreed that I would remain in Cut's good graces and do what I could to give them a second chance."

I kept my voice quiet—hidden from microphones trying to record our treason. "But how did he not notice they were still alive?"

He frowned. "What do you mean?"

Pacing away, I scowled. "Didn't he ask if they were dead? Didn't he get on his knees and see for himself if he'd killed his sons?" Even asking those questions turned my saliva into a sickly paste. How could a father not even stand over his children and say a prayer or goodbye? How could he just pass off their remains to a servant without a backward glance?

A monster, that's who.

Flaw grinned, a calculating glint in his eyes. "Aren't you glad he didn't? If he had, the outcome of this would've been entirely different."

Ice ran through my blood. *He's right.*

In a way, Cut's cold-heartedness had destroyed Kes and Jethro but saved them, too.

"Once I'd removed them from the lounge, it was a simple matter to take them where I needed. Cut didn't question me. In fact, I happen to know Jasmine kept him and Bonnie plenty entertained with her screaming about wanting revenge on you." His eyes warmed. "That girl thinks fast on her feet. It was a good diversion."

Yes and kept me safe from the full Debt Inheritance.

I ought to be nicer to Jasmine. The risk she'd played would've silenced any lesser woman. She truly was Jethro's sister—strong, formidable, and slightly scary with her temper.

"After I returned from hiding them and setting up the medical equipment, I reported to Cut that it was done." He rubbed the back of his neck. "All he cared about was if the carpet was cleaned."

My heart shattered under an anvil of hostility.

Cut was more worried about an object than his sons' souls.

Utter bastard. Sick, twisted freak.

And who taught him those qualities? His dear old mother. Bonnie—the female version of the devil.

My hands balled. "I've heard enough."

Bonnie had summoned me. She'd scared and intimidated me but she was no match for my sheer hatred. I wanted to throw her in a cauldron and watch her bones bleach white. I wanted to behead her and witness her body twitch with death throes.

That'll come true before this is over.

"Take me to her. It's time we had a little chat."

"About bloody time." Bonnie sniffed as Flaw beckoned me over the threshold.

The second my sock-covered feet padded onto the pale pink carpet of Bonnie's domain, he cocked his chin in goodbye and abandoned me behind the closed door.

All alone.

An opportunity or a disadvantage?

She couldn't hurt me. Names and slurs weren't enough to subdue me anymore.

Screw surprise and secrecy.

If I have an opportunity, I'm taking it.

"What do you have to say for yourself, girl? Tardiness is a dirty sin and must be abolished." Bonnie tapped her cane like a cat flicked its tail.

No matter how much time I spent in the Hall, I doubted I would ever explore all the rooms and levels it offered. Bonnie's quarters were yet another surprise. Flaw had guided me up the stone staircase where Jasmine and Cut's study rested, only to pace down a different corridor and up another set of stairs made of winding red carpet and unicorn spindles.

Straightening my shoulders, I looked down my nose at the

shrivelled old woman. "I have nothing to say for myself. I was in the middle of something important. I couldn't let a simple summoning derail me."

She made a strange wheeze—like wind through wheat or ghosts over a graveyard. "You insolent little—"

"Guttersnipe. Yes, I've heard it before." Moving forward, I didn't ask permission as I inspected her domain. Every part of me shook. I was angry, afraid, livid, *terrified*. Lying in the dark, bolstering my courage and fermenting in hatred hadn't prepared me for face-to-face duelling. This was new—putting my thoughts into action.

Now that I knew Jethro was alive, I had something to risk. A future.

Jethro's alive.

I'm alive.

We can be alive together—far away from here.

If I became too impertinent, I could ruin my plans and destroy my future. But if I didn't stand up to them, I might not see the next debt coming—just like I didn't see the Third Debt until it was too late.

I had to be strong but aware, vengeful but intelligent—it was an exhausting place to be.

Bonnie's room wasn't what I expected. The peach coloured walls, white fireplace, and rose fleurs on the ceiling plasterwork all spoke of a law-abiding, cookie-baking grandmother.

How can a room fulfil the stereotype of elderly nana when the woman is anything but?

The wainscoting gleamed with gold wallpaper, while cross-stitch framed artwork graced every inch of wall space depicting bumblebees, dragonflies, and multihued butterflies.

I expected torture equipment and the blood of her many victims on the wall.

Not this…

I hated this room because it made me doubt. Had she been nice once upon a time? Had she become this hard-hearted dinosaur thanks to situations in her past? What had Cut done to his brother in order to turn his mother into such a beast?

Because it had to be his doing. Whatever happened with his brother reeked of sedition and backstabbing lies.

It doesn't matter.
She is what she is.

And she'd pay for what she'd done.

Bonnie didn't say a word, watching me with the signature Hawk attentiveness. The room throbbed with power; subjugation coming from her and rebellion from me. If our wills could battle, the tension would suffocate with unseen clashes.

I paused over a particular stitched oval, trying to make out if it was a praying mantis or a stick insect.

"Jasmine did them for me." Bonnie's voice was sweet venom. "Such a wonderful, obedient granddaughter. It was part of her etiquette and decorum training."

My eyes widened. "She did all of them?"

Bonnie nodded. "You're not the only one good with a needle and thread, girl." Snapping her fingers, reminding me so clearly of her grandson who rested in some hospital, she said, "Come closer. I refuse to scream. And you need to pay strict attention."

My socks ghosted over the pale pink flooring, sinking into a few sheepskin rugs before stopping beside Bonnie Hawk. My nose wrinkled at the familiar smell of rose water and overly sweet confectionary. I didn't need to know her diet to guess she loved desserts.

She was rotten—just like her teeth from consuming too much sugar.

In my head, I cursed and hexed her, but outwardly, I stood calm and silent.

Do your worst, witch. It won't be good enough.

She narrowed her eyes, inspecting me from head to toe. I let her, glancing out the window instead. Her chair rested beside a long table pressed up against the lead light glass overlooking the south gardens of Hawksridge. A water fountain splashed merrily, depicting two fawns playing a pipe. The colourful pansies and other flowers that'd run rampant when I first arrived had long since gone dormant, replaced by skeleton shrubs and the dull brown of winter.

"Do you have any skills in this arena?" Bonnie pointed at the hobby scattered over the table. The array of dried and freshly cut flowers painted the table in a rainbow of stamens and petals. Roses, tulips, lilies, orchids. The perfume from dying flora helped counteract the sickly stench of Bonnie.

"No. I've never arranged flowers, if that's what you're asking."

She pursed her lips. "Hardly a lady fit for society. What skills apart from sewing do you have then? Enlighten me." Reaching for a crystal vase, she snapped off a piece of green foam and shoved it into the bottom. "Well...go on then, girl. Don't make me ask twice."

What the hell is going on here?

The past few days had a strange consistency, as if I was stuck in quicksand. If I moved, it sucked me further into its clutches, but if I stayed still, it treated me as a friend—keeping me buoyant in its greedy granules.

What's her point?

My back stiffened, but I forced myself to stay cordial. "I run my own fashion line. I can sew any item of clothing. My attention to detail—"

"Shut up. That is all one skill. One lonely talent. A frivolous career for a trollop such as yourself."

Don't retaliate. Do not stoop to her bait.

If her aim was to make me snap so she could punish me, then she'd lose. I'd learned from them how to fight.

My hand rubbed my lower back, checking my dirk was in place and ready to be used.

Wouldn't now be the perfect time to dispatch her?

We were alone. Behind closed doors. Regardless of my past conclusion to kill Cut and Daniel first, I couldn't waste an opportunity.

My arm tensed, agreeing.

Do it.

Almost as if she sensed my thoughts, Bonnie cooed, "Oh, Marquise? Can you come in here, please?"

Immediately, a door I didn't see, camouflaged with matching wallpaper, opened. Marquise, a Black Diamond brother with shoulders like a submarine and long greasy hair pulled into a ponytail, appeared. "Yes, Madame."

Shit.

Bonnie's eyes glinted. "Could you keep us company, dear? Just sit quietly and don't interrupt. There's a good chap."

"No problem." He flicked a glance at me.

I hid my scowl as Marquise did as bade and perched his colossal bulk on a dainty carved chair. I was surprised the tiny legs didn't snap under his weight.

"Now, what were we saying?" Bonnie patted her lips with a fresh rose.

I didn't know how she'd read my body language so perfectly, but it put me on the back foot. I swallowed, letting go of my dirk. Grabbing a lily, I twirled it in my fingers. "Nothing of importance."

Bonnie glared. "Ah, that's where you're wrong. It was *very* important." Snipping the end of the rose with sharp shears, she jabbed the stem into the green foam at the bottom of the vase.

She caught me looking. "It's called an oasis. It's flower arranging basics. If you'd applied yourself at all, you would know that."

My skin prickled. Hemmed between Bonnie and Marquise, my hands were tied, my mouth effectively gagged.

Damn you, witch.

"Applied myself? I was working until 10:00 p.m. most nights before I'd even turned twelve. I sewed my way through high school and college—I had no free time to indulge in useless hobbies."

Bonnie swivelled in her chair. Her eyes shadowed, cheeks

powered white. "Watch your tongue. I won't put up with such contumelious talk."

I sucked in a breath, doing my best to be quiet even though I wanted to stab her repeatedly. My eyes skittered to Marquise.

Damn him, too.

Grabbing a sprig of leaves, she wedged the plume into the oasis. "Know why I summoned you?"

My fingers tightened around the lily. I wanted to crush the white petals and scatter them over Bonnie's coffin.

A coffin I'll put her in.

"I've long since given up trying to understand you." I narrowed my eyes, unable to hide my livid hatred. "Any sane person could never guess what madness will do or not do."

Bonnie scowled.

Her tiny stature sat proud and stiff; arthritic fingers tossed aside a newly snipped tulip and wrapped around her walking stick. Never breaking eye contact, she stood from her chair and inched forward.

I stood my ground even though every part of me vibrated with the urge to smash the crystal vase over her head.

We didn't speak as the distance closed between us. For an old woman, she wasn't bowed or creaky. She moved slowly but with purpose. Hazel eyes sharp and cruel and her signature red lipstick smeared thin lips. "That mouth of yours will be taught a lesson now that you're in my youngest grandson's care."

Not if I kill him first.

I balled my hands, keeping my chin high as Bonnie circled around me like a decrepit raptor. Stopping behind me, she tugged my long hair. "Cut this. It's far too long."

Locking my knees, I forced myself to remain tall. She'd lost the power to make me cower. "It's my hair, *my* body. I can do whatever the hell I want with it."

She yanked on the strands. "Think again, Weaver." Letting me go, she continued her perusal, coming to a stop in front of me. Her eyes came to my chin. The height difference helped me in some small margin to look down on her—both physically and metaphorically.

This woman was as twisted as the boughs of an ancient tree, but unlike a tree, her heart had blackened and withered. She'd lived long enough. It was time she left the world, letting bygones be bygones.

Her breath rattled in antique lungs, sounding rusty and ill-used.

Minutes screeched past, both of us waiting to see what the other would do. I broke first, but only because my patience where Bonnie was concerned was non-existent.

Jethro's alive.

The sooner I evicted Bonnie from my presence, the sooner I could think about him again.

"Spit it out."

She froze. "Spit what out?"

My spine curved toward her, bringing our faces closer. The waft of sugar and flowers wrapped around my gag reflex. "What do you want from me?"

Her gaze tightened. "I want a great deal from you, child. And your impatience won't make me deliver it any faster." Snatching my wrist, she grabbed a thorny rose from the table and punctured my palm with the devilish bloom.

I bit my lip as blood welled.

She chuckled. "That's for not knowing how to flower arrange."

She let me go. Instead of dropping the rose, I curled my hand around it, digging the thorn deeper into my flesh. If I couldn't withstand the discomfort of a small prick, how did I hope to withstand more?

This is my weapon.

Conditioning myself to pain so it no longer controlled me.

Blood puddled, warm and sticky, in my closed fist. Taking a breath, I reached around Bonnie and elegantly placed the rose into the oasis, opening my palm and raining droplets of blood all over virgin petals and tablecloth. "Oops."

Bonnie's face blackened as I wiped the remaining crimson on a fancy piece of ribbon. "Anyone can arrange flowers, but it takes a seamstress to turn blood into a design." My voice lowered, recalling how many nights I'd sliced myself with scissors or pricked myself with needles. I was used to getting hurt in the process of creation.

This was no different.

I would be hurt in the process of something far more noble—*fighting for my life*.

"You can't scare me anymore." I held up my palm, shoving it in her face. "Blood doesn't scare me. Threats don't scare me. I know what you are and you're just a weak, old woman who hides behind insanity like it's some mystical power."

Marquise stood from his chair by the wall. "Madame?"

I glanced at him, throwing a condescending smile. "Don't interrupt two women talking. If she can't handle a silly little Weaver, then she has no right to pretend otherwise."

"Sit down, Marquise." Bonnie breathed hard, glaring at me. "I've never met someone so unrefined and uncouth."

"You obviously never paid close attention to your granddaughter then."

She's rough as sandpaper and tough as steel.

Jasmine could lie like the best of them, but beneath that silk and satin façade, she outweighed me in strength of temper ten to one.

Why tell Bonnie that then? Shut up.

Bonnie shoved her finger in my face. "Don't talk about her. Jasmine is a woman of eloquence. She knows how to speak three languages, play the piano, stitch, sing, and run a time-worn estate. She outranks you in every conceivable way."

She has you fooled as wonderfully as she did me.

My respect for Jasmine increased a hundred-fold.

If any of us were playing the game best—it was her. *She* was the true chameleon, pulling the wool over not just her grandmother's eyes but her father's and brother's, too.

She's a powerful ally to have.

I couldn't stop pride and annoyance from blurting: "Shame you're delusional as well as decrepit."

Bonnie's papery hand struck my cheek. Her palm didn't make a sound on my flesh, merely a swat with no sting. She might have the power of speech and ferocity, but when it came to physical threats—she was brittle and weak.

"My family eclipses yours in every way. It's a shame you didn't have such an upbringing. Perhaps you would be more pleasing company if you—"

I couldn't listen to her cackling drone anymore.

"You're right. It *is* a shame I didn't have someone there to teach me how to do my makeup or bake cakes or learn an instrument. I'm sure I would've been happier and more rounded if I grew up with a mother. But she was taken from me by *you*. Don't twist my past and make it seem like I'm some underprivileged girl who's here by the grace of your family because I'm not. I'm your *prisoner*, and I hate you." I backed away from the table. "I hate you, and you *will* pay for what you've done."

Her face twisted with rage. "You ungrateful little—f'"

"I agree. I *have* been ungrateful. I've been ungrateful for falling in love with a good man only for it to be too late. I've been ungrateful for a brother I adore and a father who's been lost since his wife was taken. But I'm not ungrateful for this. I've found a fucking backbone, and I mean to use it."

Marquise stomped forward. "Madame. Just give the word."

I threw a caustic look at both of them. "You're proving Bonnie's too weak to discipline me herself."

"Enough!" Bonnie brought her walking stick down onto the table with a resounding *thwack*. "Don't you dare use my name without my permission!"

"Tell me what you want then, so I don't have to look at you. I don't want to be here another minute."

Don't go too far.

Bonnie convulsed. Her face turned puce, and for a second, I hoped she'd die—just keel over from exploding blood pressure or ruptured ego.

Don't get yourself killed over pettiness.

I had a lot more to achieve before that day.

Swallowing hard, Bonnie clasped both hands on her cane. Her thick skirts rustled as her ancient carcass bristled. "Fine. I'll take great pleasure in doing so."

God, I feel sick. I don't want to know.

"Just let me leave. I've had enough." Storming to the door, I tried the handle, only to find it locked. The air turned thick, the heating too hot. I'd drenched my system in too much adrenaline and now paid the price.

Pacing in a circle, I ran my hands through my hair. "You hear me? You make me sick, and unless you let me out, I'll just vomit all over your precious study."

Vertigo swooped in, throwing me to the side.

Jethro's alive.

He's alive.

I need to stay that way, too.

I gulped, needing fresh air. I'd never been claustrophobic, but the walls loomed closer, triggering another vertigo wave, forcing me to bend forward to keep the room steady.

Bonnie limped closer. "You're not going anywhere. You want to know why I summoned you? Time to find out."

Every cell urged me to back away, but I held my ground. I refused to be intimidated. Swallowing back nausea and dizziness, I gritted my teeth.

Bonnie pointed at the wall behind me with her walking stick. "Go on. Look over there. You want me to get on with my point? The answers are there."

Suspicion and rancour ran rampant in my blood, but I found the courage to turn my back on her and face the wall. My skin crawled to have her behind me—like some viper about to strike, but then my eyes fell on a few grainy sepia-toned photographs. The pictures' time-weathered quality hinted that they were old. Older than Bonnie, by far.

Drifting closer, I inspected the image. In browns and sienna, the fuzzy photograph depicted a man in a fur coat with a pipe furling with smoke. Snow banks hid parts of Hawksridge, making it seem like some fantastical castle.

There's something about him.

I peered harder at the man's face and froze.

Oh, my God.

Jethro?

It couldn't be. The picture was ancient. There was no way it could be him.

Bonnie sidled up beside me, dabbing her nose with a handkerchief. "Notice the resemblance?"

I hated that she'd intrigued me when I wanted nothing more than to act uninterested and aloof. My lips pinched together, refusing to ask what she was obviously dying to say.

"That's Jethro's great, great grandfather. They look similar. Don't you think?"

Similar?

They looked like the same person.

Thick tinsel hair swept back off sculptured cheekbones and highbrows. Lips sensual but masculine, body regal and powerful, even the man's hands looked like Jethro's, wrapped around his pipe tenderly as if it were a woman's breast.

My breast.

My cheeks warmed, thinking what good hands Jethro had. What a good lover he was. How cruel he could be but so utterly tender, too.

My heart raced, falling in love all over again as memories bombarded me.

Jethro, I miss you.

Having a likeness of him only made our separation that much more painful. My fingertips itched to trace the photograph, wanting to transmit a hug to him—let him know I hadn't forgotten him. That I was fighting for him, fighting for a future together.

Bonnie coughed wetly. "Answer me, child."

"Yes, they look similar. Eerily so." My eyes trailed to the following photographs, hidden between cross-stitches. One picture had the entire household staff standing in ranking order on the front steps of Hawksridge. Butlers and housekeepers, maids and footmen. All sombre and fierce, staring into the camera.

"These are the few remaining images after an unfortunate fire a few decades ago." Bonnie inched with me as I moved from picture to picture. I didn't know why I cared. This wasn't my heritage. But something told me I was about to learn something invaluable.

I was right.

Two more photographs before I discovered what Bonnie alluded to.

My eyes fell on a woman surrounded by dark fabric as if she swam in an ocean of it. Her tied-up hair cascaded from the top of her head thanks to a piece of white ribbon, and her eyes were alight with her craft. Her hands held a needle and thread, lace scattered like snow around her.

It was like staring into a mirror.

No...

My heart bucked, rejecting the image, unable to make sense of how it was possible. Unable to stop myself, one hand went to the photo, tracing the brow and lips of the mystery woman, while my other sketched my own forehead and mouth.

I was the perfect replica of this stranger. A mirror image.

She's me...I'm her...it doesn't make any sense.

"Know who that is?" Bonnie asked smugly.

I shook my head. There was no date or name. Only a woman caught in her element, sewing peacefully.

"That was your great, great grandmother, Elisa." Bonnie stroked the photo with swollen fingers. I wanted to snatch her hand away. She was my family, not hers.

Don't touch her.

Why didn't our family albums contain images of Elisa?

Why had we kept no records or comprehensive history of what happened to our ancestors? Were we so weak a lineage that we preferred to bury our heads in the sand rather than learn from past mistakes and fight?

Who are we?

Dropping my hands, I breathed deeply. "What is her image doing on your wall?"

"To remind me that history isn't in the past."

I turned to face her. "What do you mean?"

Bonnie's hazel gaze was sharp and cruel. "I mean history repeats itself. You only have to look through generations of photographs to see the same person over and over again. It skips a few bloodlines; cheekbones are different, eye colours change, bodies evolve. But then along comes an offspring who defies logic. Neither looking like their current parents, or taking on the traits of evolution. Oh, no. Out pops an exact imposter of someone who lived over a century ago."

She looked me up and down, her nose wrinkling. "I don't believe in reincarnation, but I do believe in anomalies, and you, my child are the exact image of Elisa, and I fear the exact temperament, too."

A chill darted down my spine. "You say it like it's a bad thing." My eyes returned to the image. She looked fierce but content—resigned but strong.

She chuckled. "It is if you know the history."

Wrapping her seized fingers around my elbow, she pushed me onward, following a timeline of photos of Elisa and Jethro's great, great grandfather.

Seeing Jethro's doppelganger in images side by side with Elisa sent goosebumps scattering over my skin. "What was his name?"

"Owen." She paused by a particular one of Elisa and Owen staring sternly into the camera, spring buds on rose bushes and apple blossoms in the orchard behind them. They both looked distraught, trapped, *afraid*. "Owen 'Harrier' Hawk."

Did you have the same condition Jethro has, Owen? Were you the first to hate your family? Why didn't you do anything to change your future?

Bonnie let me go. "I could rattle off tales and incidents of what befell those two, but I'll let the images speak for themselves. After all, what is the common phrase? A picture tells a thousand words?" She laughed softly as I repelled away from her, drinking in image after image.

The copper and coffee tones led me from one end of the room to the other, following a wretched timeline of truth.

Bonnie was right. A picture did say a thousand words, and seeing it captured forever, imprisoned and immortalized, sank my heart further into despair.

Elisa slowly changed in each one.

I gasped as I stumbled onto the First Debt. An ochre image where blood wasn't red but burnt bronze, trickling from lash marks on Elisa's creamy back.

It was as if time played a horrible joke, slapping me with the knowledge that my life was on repeat—my very existence following in the footsteps of another, no matter how unique I felt.

Just like when Jethro came to collect me.

That night in Milan when I'd found out my life was never mine. That Jethro was just as indebted as me. That we were both prisoners of a tangled predetermined fate.

My limbs quaked as I moved to the next.

The tarnished image showed Owen, standing with the First Debt whip in his hand, a tortured expression on his face. He was more than just Jethro's ancestor—he could've been his identical twin. Seeing another man look so conflicted brought tears to my eyes. He tried to hide it, but regret and connection blazed through the grainy picture.

We weren't the only ones to fall in love.

Owen and Elisa had defied the Weaver-Hawk boundary and fallen hard.

Photo after photo.

Trial after trial.

Their love deepened and blossomed, only to be slowly hacked away as time went on.

The Second Debt and the ducking stool. Elisa dangled on the same chair I'd been strapped to, the black lake glittering below her.

The Third Debt in the gaming den. Owen fisted crumpled playing cards, his mouth tight and unyielding, eyes begging for a reprieve.

Amongst the extracted debts were personal images. Photos of Elisa sewing, sitting in the gardens, trailing her fingers in the fountain, looking up at the cloud congested sky as if she could fly away. There were also secret images taken of Owen watching her, his fists in his pockets, his face transmitting apology, sorrow, *anguish*.

We're living their history.

An exact replica of two people's lifetimes that'd taken place decades ago.

Yet another example that I was no different from my ancestors. That I had no hope of changing my fate.

I jumped as Bonnie brushed aside my hair, her swollen knuckles hot against my throat. "See, child. You think you're different. You think you'd won by claiming the heart of my grandson, but I had forewarning." She waved at the timeline boldly placed on her walls like jewels. "I saw what happened with my ancestors before you even arrived. The day I saw the resemblance between Jethro and Owen, I studied the records. I armed myself years before you came to us. I knew you wouldn't behave. I knew this generation wouldn't be straightforward and I planned accordingly." Her smile was priggish. "There is no winning, Nila. Both of our families are cursed to bear such a trial, and only the worthy are permitted to inherit."

I couldn't reply.

Taking my wrist, she guided me toward the last seven images all framed in one intricate gilded frame. "Study this well, child. This is what happened to Elisa once Owen was dealt with for his infractions. And this is what will happen to you."

I clapped a hand over my mouth.

Owen was dealt with? He was killed, too?

My eyes burned as the sepia photos engraved themselves on my brain.

Torture after torture.

Misery after misery.

Methods I never knew existed.

Barbarous items I couldn't even name.

Elisa faded in each image from a fierce, heartbroken woman into a ghost already departing the world.

She suffered horrendously, subjected to methods of persecution no one could endure for long.

My soul wept for her. My temper broiled for her.

Poor woman. Poor girl.

Was this my fate? Would I become her?

Will I break eventually?

Bonnie stabbed the bottom picture where the only visible part of Elisa was her head. A large barrel with spikes driven through the sides encased her body. "Each of those is…what shall we call it…an extra toll you must pay. Disobedience is never tolerated—from a Weaver or a Hawk. Elisa watched Owen die and tried to return the favour by killing his father." She tapped my nose. "Just like I suspect you think you'll do, too."

I choked.

No…how could they…

"Are you planning on killing my remaining family, Nila?" Bonnie's voice dropped to a hiss. "Because let me tell you, you'll never achieve that. Not over my dead body."

My pulse exploded into supersonic beats, gushing blood, preparing to bolt.

Run!

I needed to be far away. Far, far away where they could never touch me again.

Slapping my cheek, her strike brought heat and clarity. "Look at me when I'm talking to you, child." Standing to her full height, she glared into my eyes. "I have news for you. Whatever plans you think you have, whatever backbone you think you've grown, and whatever revenge you think you'll deliver—forget all of it. You're done, you hear me? Jethro is dead. Kestrel is dead. There is no one here who will save you—including yourself. Starting tomorrow, you will pay for your sins. You will repent so your soul is pure enough to pay the Final Debt. You will lose, Ms. Weaver. Just like Elisa lost all those years ago.

"You're already a corpse, and there is nothing, absolutely *nothing,* you can do about it."

Jethro

FOUR DAYS.

A full ninety-six hours since I'd awoken from surgery.

An eternity of staring at the powder blue ceiling with a cheerful puppy poster going out of my fucking mind with worry for Nila.

What were they doing to her?

How was she coping?

Jasmine had said she'd do everything in her power to keep her safe, but as much as I trusted and loved my sister, I knew what my brother and father were capable of.

She's not safe there.

I have to get her out.

I also knew what Bonnie was capable of and that scared me to fucking death.

Sighing heavily in the stagnant room, I gritted my teeth and pushed upright. I was sick of lying horizontally. I was pissed at being told what I could and couldn't do. And I'd had enough of trading one imprisonment for another.

Louille had threatened me on a daily basis with restraining me. Especially, when he'd found me on the floor the day after my surgery, bleeding from launching myself out of bed, believing I was cured enough to fight.

I was stupid to try—but I *had* to. I had no choice.

I couldn't just lie there. That wasn't an option. Nila needed me. And I wouldn't let her down again.

It's time to do things my fucking way. Otherwise, it will be too late.

The first three days, Louille had been a damn Nazi on my attempts to walk. I got that he was responsible for my welfare. That he'd done his job and patched me up to ensure I lived another day. But what he didn't get was I didn't *want* to live another fucking day if Nila wasn't there with me.

It's my responsibility, goddammit.

I wouldn't fail her. Ever again.

Yesterday, I'd won one battle. I positively despised my demotion to a lump of decomposing meat, lying in bed with drains in my side and a catheter in my fucking cock.

I'd shown just how healthy I was with a shouting match, ensuring the removal of the catheter and the drains. Time was an enemy but also a friend. Every *tick* left Nila out of my protection, but every *tock* healed me so I could finally set right my wrongs.

I just wished I had a magical device that paused time at Hawksridge and sped up my existence so I could be strong once again.

Wait for me, Nila.

Stay alive for me, Nila.

Swinging my legs over the side of the bed, I looked at the sterilized linoleum floor. At least I felt more like a man rather than a healing vegetable. The past few days had been awful, but I was getting better—no matter how weak I was.

I hated being so fucking feeble. Too feeble to be of any use.

But no matter my frustration, I couldn't battle through the tiredness or soreness of my body knitting back together. It healed as fast as it could. I just had to learn patience.

I snorted. *Yeah, right. Patience when my deranged family has my woman.* Like that would ever fucking happen.

You have no choice.

If only I could heal faster.

Taking a deep breath, I pushed off the bed. My bare feet slapped against cool flooring. The room swam, reminding me all too much of Nila and her imbalance. *We're perfect for each other.* Both slightly broken. Both slightly flawed. But perfectly whole once we let our hearts become one.

My toes dug into the smooth linoleum, keeping me upright. The back of my hand twinged as the drip line tugged. I groaned, wiping away sweat already beading on my brow.

I'd learned the hard way when I first attempted a bathroom visit that I had to roll the contraption feeding my drip with me; otherwise, the needle in my hand jerked me back.

That'd hurt. But not nearly as much as my heart did whenever I thought of Kes still holding onto this world. He hadn't died; no matter how adamant Doctor Louille had been that he might never wake up.

Don't think about him.

I had too much to worry about. Being in a high-traffic public place meant my emotions were scrubbed raw. Luckily, I had a private room, but it didn't stop emotions from soaking through the walls.

Snippets of grief and misplaced hope trickled under my door from family members visiting loved ones. Horrible pain and the craving for death drifted like scent waves from patients healing from trauma.

I fucking *hated* hospitals.

I have to leave—if not for Nila's sake, then my own.

I would be able to heal a lot faster away from people who drained the life right out of me.

Gritting my teeth, I shuffled forward. The large bandage around my middle gave my broken rib some support but agony radiated anyway. Doctor Louille had cut down my painkillers at my request. I needed to know the truth—to monitor my healing and be able to cope with the discomfort on my own terms.

Because three weeks was far too fucking long.

I'm not waiting that long.

The minute I could get to the bathroom without it taking fifteen bloody minutes, I was checking out, and I didn't care what anyone said.

Every step fed energy to atrophied muscles.

Every shuffle forced my body to revive.

And every stumble ensured I could leave that much sooner.

Eleven minutes.

An improvement from sixteen minutes yesterday.

Not the best achievement to go from bed to bathroom, but I'd whittled off five minutes in just under twenty-four hours. I was healing faster—bolstered by my unrelenting pressure.

Wobbling back toward the despised mattress, I paused in the centre of the room. The thought of getting back into the starched sheets and staring yet again at the powder blue ceiling with no fucking purpose other than to torture myself with images of Nila didn't inspire me.

I was no good to her yet. I had to be sensible and heal before saving her, but I couldn't lie there another moment without talking to her. Without telling her how much I loved her, cared for her, missed her, *craved* her. I needed her. I needed her smile, her laugh, her touch, her body.

I need you, Nila, so fucking much.

After talking to Jasmine the first day, we'd agreed to keep communication few and far between. It was hard not to know what happened at Hawksridge, but Cut didn't know we'd made it out alive. For all my dear doting father knew, Kes's and my bones were now pig shit at the back of the estate.

And I want to keep it that way.

Jaz had done all she could to hide our reincarnation from everyone. The doctors and nurses called me Mr. James Ambrose. No one knew my true identity. She'd even taken us to a hospital we'd never been to before—boycotting our usual medical team in favour of strangers who would keep us unknown.

It didn't mean I trusted anyone, though.

I risked anonymity by contacting Nila, but I couldn't deny myself anymore. Just thinking of messaging her like we did before I claimed her made my heart beat stronger and blood pump faster.

She was my cure—not drugs or doctors. I was stupid to avoid contacting her for so long when all I wanted to do was drag her into my embrace and keep her safe forever.

Wrapping my arm around my waist, adding pressure to the throbbing wound, I inched barefoot out of my room, dragging the drip on its little wheels behind me.

I'm a fucking invalid.

The hospital was quiet.

No emergencies. No visitors.

It was a nice reprieve from daylight hours when I had to focus entirely on the itching of my stitches and ache from my rib to negate the overpowering overshare of emotions from such a busy place.

I didn't know the time, but the bright neons were dimmed, giving the illusion of peace and sleepiness. However, the morbid silence of death interrupted the false serenity, lurking in the darkness, waiting to pick off its latest victim.

Move along, death. You're not taking me, my brother, or Nila. Not this time.

My mind jumped back to the images that Bonnie had shown me a month or so ago. Her study had always been a festival of flowers and needlepoint, but when she'd invited me to tea, she had a new acquisition.

Photographs.

Images of a Weaver, who looked exactly like Nila and my great, great grandfather.

I'd always known I looked like Owen Hawk. Cut had told me a few times as I grew up. But that'd been the first time I'd heard how similar Owen and Elisa's tale was to my own life.

It was meant to scare me. To keep me in line and show me what would happen if I followed that path.

It hadn't stopped me.

I snorted under my breath.

And it came true.

Owen was murdered, just like I'd been. But that was where the similarities ended. Owen had died and left Elisa to suffer.

I'm still alive and I will *save her.*

My forehead dripped with sweat, and I gulped agonizing breaths by the time I finally shuffled down the corridor toward the front desk of the recovery wing. A nurse I'd seen once or twice looked up from her keyboard.

Plaited dark hair crowned her head while no makeup painted her face. Mid-fifties, matronly, and no-nonsense dress-code, she suited the role of caring for others rather than herself. But despite her lack of jewellery and personal adornment, her eyes were caring. In one glance, she gave me more motherly affection than I'd ever had in my youth.

For the first time in a long time, my mother made an appearance in my thoughts.

My heart thudded hard at the intrusion. I never liked thinking about her because I couldn't stomach the memories that came with it. She'd been such a good person just stuck in a bad place. She'd done her best and given birth to four children before her strength deserted her, leaving her only legacy to fend without her.

For a while, I hated her for being so weak.

But now I understood her.

I *pitied* her.

The nurse shot from her chair as I stumbled forward, grabbing the desk for balance. "Mr. Ambrose, you really shouldn't be out of bed." Darting around the partition, she wrapped an arm around my waist, flaring my injury.

Dressed in a backless gown, and already feeding off her caring impulses and frustration at having an unruly patient out of bed, I waved her away. "Just give me a moment. I'm fine."

"You're not fine."

I narrowed my eyes, blocking off her thoughts and focusing on my own. "Truly. I promise I won't keel over and die on your shift."

She huffed but moved away, staying within grabbing distance. I just hoped my arse wasn't hanging out of the godawful gown.

Wedging my back against the desk so she wouldn't get an eyeful, I smiled grimly. "I needed some fresh air and a change of scenery."

That's not all I need.

She nodded as if it made perfect sense. "I get that a lot. Well, the media room is just down there." She pointed further down the corridor. "I can get a wheelchair and settle you if you like? Lots of DVDs to keep a night owl entertained."

I cocked my head, pretending to contemplate the idea. "Sounds tempting. But you know what I'd really like to do?"

She pursed her lips. "What?"

"Is there a convenience store in the building? Somewhere I can buy a phone? Something that can connect to the internet as well as basic calling?"

She frowned. "There's a small shop on the bottom floor by the café, but I can't let you go down there, Mr. Ambrose. It's four floors and late. Besides, I doubt it will be open at this time of night."

My heart squeezed with dejection.

Nila.

I have to speak to her.

I couldn't wait any longer. Grabbing the nurse's hand, I flicked a glance at her nametag. Injecting as much charm into my voice as possible, I murmured, "Edith, I *really* need that phone. Any way you can help me out?"

She tugged in my hold, blinking. "Um, it's against hospital policy to assist with patient requests outside of medical requirement."

I chuckled, wincing as my muscles heralded another wash of agony. "I'm not asking you to grab me a burger or something bad for my health."

She laughed softly.

"Surely, popping downstairs and grabbing me a phone would be okay?" I ducked to look deeper into her gaze. "I'd be forever in your debt."

Debt...

Shit, I hated that word.

Nila would never be in debt again for as long as she lived. I would eradicate that word for motherfucking eternity the minute this was all over. No rhyme or reason existed for why my family did what they did to the Weavers. What'd started as vengeance swiftly became entertainment.

Boredom.

That was the cause. It had to be.

My ancestors were never equipped to deal with vast wealth having nothing better to do than pluck the wings from innocent butterflies and hurt those less fortunate.

There was such a thing as too much time and decadence, turning someone into a heartless monster.

Edith bit the inside of her cheek. "I don't know." Looking down the corridor toward my room, she said, "I'll tell you what, head back to bed. You can discuss it with the morning manager and see what they can do."

My stomach clenched.

It has to be tonight.

"No. I can't run that risk. You're here now. One request, then I'll leave you alone. What do you say?"

Fuck this backless gown and lack of worldly possessions.

I was so used to towering over people in rich linen and tailored cotton, pulling out a wallet bursting with money. Money always got what you wanted. Cash always enticed someone to say yes.

It truly was a double-edged sword.

"If you go now, I'll pay you triple what the phone is

worth."

Her entire body stiffened.

Shit, shouldn't have said that.

"I don't accept bribes, Mr. Ambrose."

Pain shot through my system, drenching me in sweat again. I couldn't be vertical much longer. My shoulders rolled in defeat. "Please, Edith. I wouldn't ask if it wasn't very important." Going against all instinct, I let down my walls and begged, "Please. I need to speak with someone. They think—they think I died. I can't let them continue worrying about me. It isn't fair." Hissing through my teeth as a hot wave of discomfort took me hostage, I muttered, "You wouldn't do that to a loved one, would you? Let them sit at home and fear the worst?"

Her face fell. "No, I guess you're right."

Thank God.

Suddenly, she moved back around the desk and grabbed a purple handbag. Rummaging inside, she passed me an older model cell-phone. "Here. Text them now. My shift is almost over. I'll get you the phone tomorrow when I come back into work."

It wasn't ideal, but beggars couldn't be choosers.

My hand shook as I reached for it. "I can't thank you enough."

She waved it away. "Don't mention it."

The moment I held the phone, I wanted to sprint back to my room. To hear Nila's voice. To beg for her forgiveness. To know she was okay.

I shoved away pain, holding the gift and the knowledge that I could finally reach out to her.

Hating that I couldn't steal Edith's phone and find some privacy, I shuffled away a little and swiped on the old device.

The time blinked on the home screen.

2:00 a.m.

Where are you, Nila?

Are you in bed? Sneaking out to ride Moth to find some peace like I used to do? Is your phone even charged?

Questions and worries exploded in my heart.

Cut had said her life would continue unmolested, but that was before he shot us. Who knew what new rules and madness he'd put in place now we were gone.

If he's touched her, I'll make him fucking pay.

My shakes turned savage as I opened a new message. My memory was rusty as I input her number. I hoped to God I got it right. I'd sent hundreds of messages to her but never took the time to imprint her number on my soul.

Please, please let it be right.

Using the keypad, I typed:

From one indebted to another, you're not forgotten. I love you. I miss you. I only think of you.

I pressed send before I could go overboard. Already, that gave away too much, especially if Cut had confiscated her phone.

Then again, the number was from a stranger. It would look like any other reporter digging for a story or publicity stunt. Even with our *Vanity Fair* interview, the dregs of magazines looked to revive a has-been tale by piecing together fabricated facts.

That was another issue of recuperating in a hospital with nothing to do. Daytime television was enough to rot anyone's brain—demented or otherwise.

I didn't leave my name. I didn't send another.

But she would know.

She would understand.

She would know that I was coming for her.

The next night, Edith fulfilled her promise.

Her shift started at 10:00 p.m. and by half past, she appeared in my room bearing a gift in the form of a brand new phone.

I couldn't speak as I took the box, digging my fingers into

the cellophane. Motherfucking tears actually sprang to my eyes at the thought of finally having a way of contacting Nila while we were apart.

Fuck, I need to hear her voice.

Edith's emotions washed over me. Pride for helping a broken man. Compassion for my predicament. And attraction mixed with guilt over our age difference.

Sniffing back my overwhelming relief, I smiled. In one action, Edith had given me the strength to sit up taller, knit together faster.

I'm leaving soon. I'm ending this soon.

Taking her hand, I squeezed. "You have no idea what this means to me."

She blushed. "I think I have an idea." Tugging free, she looked away. "She's a lucky young lady."

And I'm a lucky fucking bastard.

I remained silent.

Awkwardness wafted off her, mirroring my own. No matter how much I appreciated Edith's help, I wanted to be alone. Now.

A thought snapped into my brain. "Oh, did you receive a reply?"

Edith tilted her head. "Excuse me?"

"From the message I sent on your phone last night?"

"Oh…uhh." Her emotions stuttered, shadowing with grief that she didn't have better news.

Goddammit.

I didn't need her to vocalize what my condition told me. Nila hadn't replied.

Why not?
Is she okay?

Edith shook her head. "No, I'm sorry."

I sighed heavily.

What does that mean?
Nila didn't see the message?
She's hurt and imprisoned and suffering?

Fuck!

My heart bucked against my ribs, feeding anxiety to an already strained nervous system. Jaz said she'd keep her safe. *Please, Jaz, keep your word.*

My attention left Edith, unable to wait any longer. Ripping into the plastic, I unwrapped the box like a spoiled brat at Christmas and grabbed the phone. With trembling fingers, I tore open the SIM package and battery and inserted both into the device.

I pressed the power button, waiting for it to come alive.

"Oh, almost forgot." Edith passed me a receipt with a recharge pin. "That will get you on the internet and unlimited calls for a month."

Shit, I'd forgotten that part of prepay. My old phone had been on an account, deducted and sorted by our personal accountant, along with other menial bill payments.

"Thanks." I took the docket, anxiously entering the code once the phone illuminated. "I'll bring the money to you tonight."

I had no idea how I would do that seeing as I had no identification, bankcards, or way of leaving the hospital, but I would pay her a small fortune for such kindness.

She waved it away. "Just when you can. No rush." Smiling one last time, she made her way to the exit.

My mind immediately discounted her as I focused entirely on the phone. A text pinged saying the voucher code was accepted and the number was ready for use.

The wave of indecision from Edith and small creak of the door wrenched my head up. "Anything else?"

Edith blanched, her eyebrows knitting together. "I was going to ask something, but it's not my place."

It killed me to pause when I was so close to contacting Nila, but I grinned softly. "You've earned the right to ask me anything."

She bit her lip. "Do you know?" Her eyes darted to the floor. "You were shot. There's secrecy about how it happened and only one number on your next of kin."

I waited, but she didn't go on. Only the gentle pulse of curiosity from her inquisition.

"What's your question?"

She patted her plaited hair. "Like I said, not my place. But I wanted to know…if…you knew the person who did it?"

I froze. What sort of answer should I give? Pretend amnesia and hide yet another aspect of my life?

I'm sick of hiding.

All my bloody life I'd hid from my condition, my obligation, my future.

I was done pretending.

"Yes, I know who did it."

Her hand curled around the door handle. A wave of injustice for my situation washed from her.

I grinned, letting myself indulge in my condition without repercussion. "In answer to your next question, yes, I will make them pay."

Her eyes popped wide. "How did you know I was going to ask that?"

Her surprise reminded me of Nila's shock when we spent the night together, when I truly let down my guard and felt her tangled thoughts.

Someone like me had the ability to seem as if we read the future. The perfect mystic able to decipher palms and speak with the dead—all the information you ever needed to know about a person was right there ready to be felt if more attention and empathy was used. Pity the human race was so wrapped up in themselves that they forgot to think about others.

"Just a knack I have."

Edith blushed again. "You're quite the interesting patient."

I managed to keep it together while she vibrated with more embarrassment.

"Anyway, I have to start my rounds." Giving me one last look, she slinked around the door and disappeared.

I breathed a sigh of relief as the room quietened and the

door shut me away from the outside world. The instant I didn't have an audience, my heart crumpled. I gritted my jaw to stop the overwhelming pain from eating me alive.

Only this pain wasn't from the bullet but the terrifying fear that Nila had been hurt.

She didn't respond to my previous text.

She had to have known it was me.

I swallowed against more agony. I wished I could sense her from this far away—tune into her thoughts and find out if she was safe like Jasmine promised or needed my help before I was any use to her.

My muscles quivered as I fumbled with the phone's menu, inputting her number and opening a new message. I didn't want to be reckless, but I also couldn't lie there another moment fearing for her safety.

The debts she'd lived through were nothing to what was ahead. I had to kill my father before that happened. Before he took her away from me. Nila hadn't been told how many debts she had to pay and to be honest, I'd read paperwork where more were added and less were taken, depending on how bored or cruel my ancestors were.

The Fourth Debt was coming. But the Fifth Debt…

I shuddered.

That won't happen. I *would* never let it happen.

Sighing, I forced happier thoughts and typed a message.

Unknown Number: *Answer me. Tell me you're okay. I'm okay. We're both okay. I need to hear from you. I need to know you're still mine.*

I pressed send.

Nila

I STOPPED COUNTING time by hours.
One day.
Two days.
Three days.
Four.
Nothing had meaning anymore.

I thought the Hawks couldn't hurt me once I'd sunk to their level and played their games. I thought I'd be safe to plot my revenge and hold on until Jethro came for me.

I was such a stupid, *stupid* girl.

Bonnie proved that over and over again. Breaking me into pieces, scattering my courage, burning my hatred until there was nothing left but dust. Dust and cinders and hopelessness.

Five days or was it six...

I no longer knew how long I'd existed in this hell.

It no longer mattered as they slowly broke my will, ruining my conviction that I could win. However, Jethro never left me. His voice lived in my ears, my heart, my soul. Forcing me to stay strong, even when I couldn't see an end.

If it wasn't for the passing of autumn into winter, I might've thought time stood still. The ticking of clocks was only punctured by pain. The passing of night and day only pierced by Bonnie's whims and wishes.

I'm dying.

On my lowest moments, I thought I was dead. On my highest moments, I still fantasised about killing them. It was the only thing that got me through the hellish week they subjected me to.

My hate evolved into a living, breathing thing. There was nothing left but loathing.

What else was there to feel when I lived with monsters?

My mind often tortured me with thoughts of happier times…Vaughn and me laughing, of my father being so proud, of the sweet satisfaction I got from sewing.

I wanted this to be over. I wanted to go home.

Every time my thoughts turned to Jethro, I shut down. The pain was insurmountable. Every day, I stopped believing he'd survive and worried about the worst instead. In my rapidly unthreading mind, he was dead and I believed a lie.

Jasmine tried her best to keep me from the worst.

The Rack she'd denied.

The Judas Cradle she'd flat-out refused.

But there were others she couldn't reject—she couldn't disobey her grandmother, no matter that her eyes screamed apologies and our unspoken bond knitted tighter.

Jethro was no longer there. But Jasmine was.

And I learned to love and hate her for helping me.

Her help wasn't love and kisses and tender stolen moments. No. Her help was selecting the punishment I was strong enough to survive, carving my soul out dream by dream, keeping me alive as long as possible to find some way out of lunacy.

The worst part of my punishment was Vaughn saw it all.

He witnessed what the Hawks did.

He knew now what I was subjected to.

His screams were what undid me; not Bonnie's laughter or Cut's smug chuckles—not even Daniel's demented cackles.

Love was what ruined me the most.

Love was the ultimate destroyer.

But no matter how much I tried to let go…I couldn't.

"Do you repent, Nila? Do you agree to pay the Final Debt?"

I squirmed in my bindings, choking on terror as Daniel marched me toward the guillotine. All around me stood ethereal figments of my exterminated family, their detached heads hovering above their corpses.

A wail howled over the moor. Was it death? Was it hope?

I would soon find out.

"No, I do not repent!"

Cut came toward me. His face was covered by an executioner's black mask. In his hands rested a heavy gleaming axe, polished and sharpened and waiting to sever my neck.

Bending toward me, he kissed my cheek. "Too late. You're already dead."

"No!"

"Oh, yes." Daniel chuckled. Shoving me forward, the guillotine grew from simple bascule and basket into something horrendous. "Kneel."

I crashed to my knees, sobs suffocating me. "Don't. Please, don't. Don't!"

No one listened.

Bonnie pressed my shoulders, forcing me to lean over the lunette and stare at the woven basket below. The same basket into which my head would roll.

"No! No! Stop! Don't do this!"

"Goodbye, Nila Weaver."

The axe swung up. The sun kissed its blade.

It came slicing down.

A bell woke me.

A tiny tinkle in the heavy swaddling of darkness. My heartbeat clashed with cymbals, and my hands swept up my throat. "No…" The diamonds still imprisoned me. My neck was still intact.

"Oh, thank God."

I'm still alive.

Only a dream…

Or was it a premonition?

I coughed, chasing that question away.

My fever had brought many hallucinations over the past day or two: images of Jethro walking into my room. Laughter from Kestrel as he taught me how to jump on Moth. Impossible things. Desperately wanted things.

And also dread and dismay. The torturing didn't stop when Cut had had his fun...my mind continued to crucify me when I was alone.

The bell came again.

I know that sound...but from where.

I was tired and sore. I didn't want to move ever again but deep inside, I managed to find the strength to uncurl from my nest of bedding and reach under my pillow.

Could it be?

My fingers latched around my phone, my heart trading cymbals for drums. The rhythm clanged uncertainly, drenched in malady and doing its best to keep me alive. My nose was stuffy, eyes watery, body achy.

I was sick.

Along with my hope, my body had given in, catching dreaded germs and shackling me to yet another weakness.

I'd come down with the flu four days ago. A day after Bonnie told me what would happen. Twenty-four hours after I'd seen what'd happened to Elisa in those feared photographs. But none of that mattered if the bell signalled what I so fiercely needed.

For days, I'd hoped to hear from him. But every day, I was disappointed. I drained my battery so many times, trancing myself with the soft blue glow, willing a message to appear.

I squinted in the dark, malnourished and fading from what I'd endured. Luckily, the fever had crested this morning. I'd managed a warm shower, and changed the bedding. I was weak and wobbly but still clinging to Jethro's promise.

I'm waiting for you. I'm still here.

The screen lit up. My heart sprouted new life, and I smiled

for the first time in an eternity.

Unknown Number: *Answer me. Tell me you're okay. I'm okay. We're both okay. I need to hear from you. I need to know you're still mine.*

I dropped the phone.

And burst into tears.

For so long, the world outside Hawksridge had been dark. No messages from my father. No emails from my assistants. I'd been dead already—not worthy of vibrations or chimes of correspondence.

But I *wasn't* dead.

Not yet.

No matter how many times I died in my awful nightmares, I was still here.

Jethro had found a way to text me.

Sniffing and swiping at tears with the back of my hand, it took a few minutes before I could corral my fingers into replying.

Needle&Thread: *I'm okay. More than okay now I know you're okay.*

I pressed send.

My sickness and fever no longer mattered. If I ignored it, it would go away. I didn't have time to be sick now Jethro had given me an incentive to get better.

Is he coming for me?

Could it all be over?

I wanted to say so much, but suddenly, I had nothing to share. I couldn't tell him about the past few days. I would never share because I didn't want to hurt him any more than he already was.

My mind skipped backward, forcing me to relive the horror ever since Bonnie showed me Owen and Elisa's fate.

My door opened.

Jasmine sat with one hand on the doorknob and the other around her wheel rim. "Nila..."

The moment I saw her, I knew something awful was about to happen. My spine locked and the beaded fabric I'd been working on fell from my hands. "No. Whatever it is, I won't do it."

She dropped her eyes. "You have no choice."

I shot to my feet. "I do have a choice. A choice of free will. Whatever that witch thinks she can do to me, she can't!"

Jasmine huddled in her chair—an odd mix of apologetic frustration. "She can and she will." *Her bronze gaze met mine.* "I've kept you out of Daniel's hands but I can't keep you out of Bonnie's. I've given you all the time I could." *She looked away, her voice filling with foreboding.* "It's going to get worse, Nila. I've never been told the exact details of the debts—I'm not a man, and therefore, Bonnie insisted I be protected from such violence—but I do know Cut is planning something big. I need to find a way to save you before..."

I didn't want to listen but her anguish gave me strength. "You need me to stall by giving in..."

"Yes." *She sighed heavily.* "Forgive me, but I have no choice—just like you. No matter what you think."

I had no reply. But my body did. A last ditch attempt at fleeing.

My feet moved on their own accord, backing away until I stood against the wall. I wanted to scream and fight. I wanted to shove her out the door and lock it forever.

But there was nowhere to hide. No one to save me. Only time could do that. Time that neither Jasmine, Jethro, Vaughn, nor myself had.

"Have you heard from him?" *My hands fisted against my denim-clad legs. The large grey jumper I wore couldn't thaw the ice around my heart. My mind kept splicing images of Jethro and Owen. Elisa and myself.*

Their demise had been terrible—especially hers.

Bonnie told me my punishment would begin immediately. She hadn't lied.

"No." *She rolled further over the threshold.* "We agreed to minimum contact. It's for the best."

That made sense, even though it was the hardest thing in the world. If only I could talk to him. It would make me so much braver.

"Nila, come with me. Don't let her see your fear any more than you have to. It will hurt but it won't harm you. I give you my word. You've withstood worse."

"I've endured worse because I knew it hurt Jethro to hurt me. It gave me strength in a way."

She smiled sadly. "I know he's not here to share your pain, but I am. I won't leave you." Swivelling her chair to face the door, she held out her hand. "I'll take his place. We'll get through it together."

My shoulders sagged.

What other choice did I have?

I'd made a promise to remain alive, waiting for Jethro to return. His sister was on my side. I had to trust her.

Silently, I followed Jasmine away from the Weaver quarters toward the dining room.

We entered without a word.

Jasmine's wheels tracked into the thick carpet as we made our way around the large table. Unlike at meal times, the red lacquered room was empty of food and men. The portraits of Hawks stared with beady oil eyes as Jasmine guided me to the top of the large space where Cut and Bonnie stood.

They smiled coldly, knowing they'd won yet again.

Between them rested a chair.

Bonnie had said the first punishments would be easier.

Once again, I'd been stupid and naïve.

The chair before me had been used for centuries to extract information and confessions. A torturous implement for anyone—innocent or guilty. It was a common device but absolutely lethal depending on its use.

Did Bonnie suspect I was hiding something?

But what?

Was this her attempt at ripping out my secrets?

She'll never have them.

My heart thundered faster. My blood thickened in my veins.

The chair wasn't smooth or well-padded with velour or satin. It didn't welcome a comfortable reprieve. In fact, the design mocked the very idea of luxury.

Every inch was covered in tiny spikes and nails, hammered through the wood. Seat, backrest, armrest, leg rest. Each point glittered in the late afternoon sunshine. Every needle wickedly sharp, just waiting to puncture flesh.

I swallowed hard, forcing myself to hide my terror. Jasmine was right. Their satisfaction came from my reactions. I was stronger than this—than them.

I won't let you get pleasure from my pain.

"Do you know why you're paying this toll, Nila?"

My eyes flew to Cut. He stood with his hands by his sides, his leather jacket soaking up the dwindling sun.

I shook my head. The power of voice deserted me.

All my courage at killing them vanished like a traitor.

"It's because you must be stripped of your nasty plots and wishes to harm us. It's because you caused the death of two Hawk men." *Bonnie shuffled closer, rapping her cane against the horrific chair.* "Along with the repayment of the Third Debt, you must endure a few extras—to ensure you are properly aware of your place within our home."

I flinched as Bonnie closed the gap and stroked her swollen fingers along my diamond collar. "You've lived in our hospitality for six months. The least you can do is show a bit of gratitude." *Grabbing a chunk of my long hair, she shoved me toward the barbaric contraption.* "Now sit and be thankful."

Jasmine positioned herself beside me, holding out a hand to help me lower onto the spikes. I thanked my foresight for wearing jeans. The thick denim would protect me to a degree.

Trembling a little, I turned around to sit.

Unfortunately, Cut must've read my mind. "Ah, ah, Nila. Not so fast." *Gripping my elbow, he hoisted me back up.* "That would be far too easy."

My heart stopped.

Laughing, he tugged at my waistband. "Clothing off."

Jasmine said, "Father, the spikes will hurt enough—"

"Not nearly enough." *His glare was enough to incinerate her.*

Sighing, Jaz faced me. "Take them off." *Holding out her arm like a temporary hanger, she narrowed her eyes.* "Quickly."

Gritting my teeth, I fumbled with the hem of my jumper. I should be comfortable being naked around these people—it'd happened often enough—but being asked to strip brought furious, degrading tears to my eyes.

Breathing hard, I yanked my jumper off and undid my jeans. Shimmying them down my legs, I shivered at the biting air. The dining room had a fire roaring in the imposing fireplace, but the flames hadn't extinguished the wintery chill.

A resounding thud landed behind me.

Oh, no!

Cut's eyes dropped to the ruby encrusted dirk lying in full view.

I wanted to curl up and die. I'd become so used to it wedged against my back, I forgot the knife was there.

Cut gave me a sly smile, bending to pick it up.

Quick!

Squatting, I scooped up the blade before he had chance. His eyes widened as I brandished it in his face. "Don't touch me."

He chuckled. "I wouldn't do that if I were you, Nila."

My mouth watered at the thought of somehow stabbing everyone in the heart all at once.

Jabbing the air between Cut and me, I snarled, "I should've done this months ago. I should've murdered you the moment I met you."

His body stiffened. "Just try it." His eyes flickered behind me. "You have two choices. Try and attack me and pay. Or hand over the knife and pay."

"I'd rather kill you and win."

"Yes, well, that will never happen." Snapping his fingers, he ordered, "Colour, take the knife."

I whirled around but was too late. Colour, a Black Diamond brother who I'd seen once or twice, yanked the dirk from my hand like a rattle from a baby. My fingers throbbed with emptiness as Colour handed the blade to Cut.

My fight evaporated.

I'd tried.

My one rebellion was over, and what was my reward?

Pain and humiliation.

"Thank you, Colour."

Colour nodded, retreating back to his hidey-hole by the fireplace. The large rococo style fire-surround hid most of him from view, giving the illusion of privacy.

Cut waved the blade in my face. "Rather interesting piece of equipment to have down your jeans, Nila." Running the sharp edge over my collar, his face darkened. "Not only are you a troublemaker, but you're also a thief."

Placing the dirk down his own waistband, he smiled evilly. "I'll remember that for future payments."

Standing in a black bra and knickers, I squeezed my eyes. Nothing was going as I'd planned. Where was my courage—the belief that I would plunge that blade into his heart the moment I had the chance?

My chance was gone.

"Get rid of the bra," Cut said. "Unless you want me to use the knife to help you."

My hands flew between my shoulder blades, grabbing the clasp.

Bonnie coughed. "No, I think not. Keep your undergarments on."

My eyes soared open.

"What?" Cut scowled.

She wrinkled her nose. "Seeing a naked gutter rat will ruin my appetite."

Cut chuckled. "You have the strangest ideals, mother."

She sniffed. "Excuse me if I prefer to enjoy my meal without being repulsed." Swatting her cane at the chair again, she added, "Sit down. Shut up. And reflect on what you've done."

Jasmine nudged me forward, playing the perfect role of enemy.

The cold tightened my skin, flurried my heart, and pinpricked my toes as I bent my knees and sat. I bit back a cry as thousands of nails kissed my butt and thighs.

My legs shook as I lowered myself slowly, doing my best to stay aloft and hovering over the sharp, stabbing needles.

"Stop fighting the inevitable, Nila." Cut stepped behind the chair.

I tensed.

Then I screeched as he pushed on my shoulders, pressing me cruelly onto the nails. Pulling me back toward him, he wrapped an arm around my chest, hugging me from behind.

His breath wafted hot in my ear. "Hurts, doesn't it? Feeling thousands of pins slowly sinking into your skin?"

I couldn't concentrate on anything but the millions of tiny fires slowly *worming their way through my flesh.*

Bonnie stole my wrists, yanking my arms forward and pushing them against the spiked armrests. The entire chair bristled with armament and agony.

"Stop!" I fought her, but Jasmine took her grandmother's place, forcing my arm against the nails and wrapping the leather cuffs around me.

She couldn't make eye contact, fumbling with the buckle. "This isn't to kill you, so the binds won't be tight. It's merely to keep you in place."

Tears ran unbidden down my cheeks as every inch throbbed with pain and tension. I couldn't relax—I kept every muscle locked, so I didn't sink further onto the spikes.

"Don't fight it, Nila." Jasmine tested the cuffs before rolling away. "It'll get easier."

Easier?

Every inch of my skin smarted. My sense of touch went haywire, flicking from my back to forearms to calves to arse. It couldn't distinguish which part hurt the most. I couldn't tell if certain areas bled or pierced or if the nails were blunt with age and only tenderising instead of stabbing.

Either way, it was awful. As far as torture equipment went, I wanted off the chair immediately. I would take the First Debt again because at least the pain came in waves and was over quickly—this...it would strip my mind, throb by throb, until I was a quivering mess of agony.

Panting, I breathed through my nose. My scattered mind bounced like a wayward squash ball, not letting me tame my anxiety.

Cut chuckled as he dropped to his haunches before me. "The beginning is the easy part." Rising, he pecked my cheek with a gentle kiss. "Just wait and see what'll happen as the clocks tick onward."

He looked at Bonnie. "How long did we say, mother?"

Bonnie checked a dainty gold watch around her wrist. "Elisa suffered two hours during dinner."

Cut grinned. "Perfect. Make it three."

I slammed back to the present, coughing with a rattling explosion. My fingers rubbed the healing scabs dotted like constellations down the back of my thighs, back, and arms. The sores had switched from blazing to itchy as my body healed, but the remnants of the nails had marked me far more than superficially.

Even now, days later, I still felt the numerous stings.

I fell asleep with phantom nails stabbing me and woke up hyperventilating, dreaming of being trapped in a coffin lanced with millions of needles.

Three hours in that chair had been the worst three hours of my life.

I supposed I should be honoured that they went out of their way to destroy me. I'd proven to be an anomaly, a challenge they hadn't anticipated. I'd screwed up their grand plans and set in motion things that no one should have to endure.

And that was just the start.

That night, after the Iron Chair, I succumbed to a rattling flu.

I had no reserves. Barely eaten. Lacked sunlight and love.

Living with such evil and negativity stripped my immune system, shooting me straight into chills and body aches.

And there was no one to nurse me better.

Vaughn was banished from my sight. Jasmine was missing.

The rest became a blur as I'd huddled in a sweat-riddled bed and shivered.

My room never rose above a chill. I had no energy to start a fire, and even if I did, I'd been given no fresh wood to start one.

I was cold and hungry and desperately wanted to leave. I tried to remember what life was like before Hawksridge, before Jethro left, before my mother died. But I came up empty. All those happy memories were blank.

Unknown Number: *Fuck, I miss you. Knowing you're okay...I can't tell you how thankful I am. Is that the truth? Is she keeping you safe?*

My heart fell off its pedestal, splattering on the floor. I was okay. I was stronger than I looked, but I wasn't as brave as I believed.

I coughed again, wracked with sick shivers.

Jethro, I want to tell you everything.
Tell you what you mean to me.
Tell you what they've done to me.

I wanted to cry on his shoulder and share my burdens—to eradicate what I'd lived through, so I could let go and forget. Instead, I bottled it up and kept my secrets.

Needle&Thread: *Yes, I'm safe. She's been wonderful. They haven't touched me. Don't worry about me. Just get better.*

Keeping the truth from Jethro was the least I could do for him. I shuddered, unable to stop the memories of what'd happened once I'd been strapped to the Iron Chair.

The Black Diamond brothers entered an hour into my torture. They watched me with sympathy but didn't go against Cut's command to leave me be. Apart from Flaw, I hadn't spoken to any of the brothers since the shooting. They'd been ordered to keep their distance, cutting me off from any ally I might've found.

Dinner was served and I squirmed as my body weight pushed me slowly onto the spikes. The burn of each spread into one blanket of painful horror.

Blood smeared the arms of the chair and I didn't dare look at the floor to see if I dripped over the carpet. I was hot and cold, covered in sweat and goosebumps. My muscles seized; every twitch sent wildfire through my system.

And then Vaughn arrived.
His eyes met mine.

"Threads!" He almost collapsed in rage. "Fuck! Let her go!" Charging up the room, V moved so swiftly and furiously, he managed to sucker punch Cut in the jaw before anyone reacted.

"V, don't!" Part of me loved that he'd landed one on Cut. The other was horrified. "I'm okay. Don't get yourself—"

"Stop hurting her, you fucking bastard!" V swung again but missed as Cut ducked and snapped his fingers for the Black Diamonds to grab V.

"Leave him alone!"
My screaming didn't do any good.

Commotion shot to mayhem. Men shoved back chairs. Fists swung. Grunts echoed.

"Stop! Please stop!"

They didn't stop.

Not only did millions of tiny nails trap my body, but I was forced to watch my twin beaten and kicked and left gasping by my feet.

It'd only taken a few minutes.

But the punishment was severe.

I groaned, slapping my forehead.

Stop thinking about it.

After the Iron Chair, I'd been locked in my room with no bandages or medical salve. I wasn't allowed to see Vaughn, and I'd tended to my injuries in a lukewarm bath that I lacked the strength to climb out of.

I was exhausted.

They'd found a recipe that could well and truly break me forever.

Unknown Number: *I'll be back as soon as I can. Every day I'm getting stronger. Just a little longer, then this will all be over. I promise.*

I sighed, curling around the phone. My fever came back, dousing my insides with frigid unwellness. I had every intention of fighting back. I would make them hurt. *I will make them pay.*

Somehow, I would keep my oath.

But a little longer? It made time sound like it was nothing—such a flippant phrase, a small segment of moments—but to me, it was a never-ending eternity.

I don't have much longer, Jethro.

Not judging by Bonnie's antics. Every day she had something worse.

I truly was Elisa, fading hour by hour, wasting away beneath torment.

Swallowing more tears, coughing with wet lungs, I typed:

Needle&Thread: *I'll be here waiting for you. Every night I dream of you. Dream of happier times—times we haven't been lucky enough to enjoy yet. But we will.*

As if fate wanted to banish those dreams, to prove to me

that I should've given up months ago, it brought forth the memory of what'd happened the day after the Iron Chair.

I'd been summoned to the kitchen, believing Flaw had some good news for me or Vaughn had been given free rein. It'd taken my last remaining strength to shuffle to the kitchen. Perhaps, the cook would give me some warm chicken soup and some medicine for my flu.

Instead, Bonnie found me. "Seeing as you refused to confess your sins on the Iron Chair, you will pay the opposite price."

"Confess my sins?" I coughed. "There's nothing to confess. You're doing this for your own sick pleasure."

She chuckled. "It is rather pleasurable, I must admit." Coming forward, she wrapped her fingers around my arm and dragged me through the kitchen to a small alcove where herbs and small plants grew.

My fever turned everything hazy. My blocked nose and stuffed sinuses granted everything a nightmare-like quality.

Cut stepped around the corner, dangling something in his hands. "Good morning, Nila."

I stiffened, yanking my arm from Bonnie's hold. Looking at them, I tried to understand what this would entail. Whatever swung in Cut's hands glinted with wicked silver and barbarism.

My skin still oozed from the Iron Chair. I could barely stand. "I'm sick. For once, have mercy and let me go back to bed." I coughed to prove my point. "I'm no good if I die before you want me to."

Cut chuckled. "Your physical health is no longer my primary concern." He held up the shiny mask, waving it from side to side. His golden eyes gleamed with haughty smugness. "Know what this is?"

Nerves careened down my back. Their role playing and games slowly conditioned me to cower even when standing fierce before them. Jasmine wasn't here. Daniel wasn't here. It seemed that the older generation had taken control.

"Stop wasting time." I coughed again, looking for a way out of the herb alcove. "I don't care for guessing games—" An explosive sneeze interrupted me. "I just want to be left alone."

Bonnie swatted the back of my thighs. "None of that backtalk, trollop."

My heart quivered in fright even as my stomach turned to stone.

Standing up to them came with its own kind of torture—a fleeting aphrodisiac of rebellion followed swiftly by suffocating regret.

No matter that I would do everything in my power to kill them, I couldn't stop their power over me.

They took my knife.

I hated *being defenceless.*

I hated being so weak by my body's own design.

Damn this sickness!

Cut came closer. "This, Nila, seeing as you refuse to play along, is known as a Scold's Bridle." He held it up, blinding me as a ray of light caught the silver, turning everything white. "It's given to harlots and gossipers for spreading lies. They're gagged and their ability to speak is taken away until they've learned their lesson."

Every instinct bellowed to run.

Who was I kidding? I couldn't run with my lungs drowning in mucous.

Cut moved behind me, bending around to hold the silver mask in front of my face. "Let me explain how it works."

I staggered sideways trying to dislodge his embrace. How had he trapped me so effortlessly?

The flu turned everything gluggy and thick—slowing time down, using it against me.

My eyes devoured the mask, already understanding. The textbook Vaughn had shown me when we were young had a similar instrument. Unlike the medieval item in the book, this was rather sleek and refined.

It wouldn't make it any more pleasant.

Two holes for eyes, a hole for the nose, but the rest was solid silver. Where the mouth hole should've been there was a silver spike, fairly wide and sharp, waiting to wedge on my tongue to force silence or wretched gagging. The back was curved to cradle its victim's skull, trapping their entire head in its nasty hug.

Cut rocked against my back, inhaling my hair. "You already know how it works, don't you?" Bringing the mask closer, he chuckled. "Good. That dispenses unnecessary conversation."

"Lock her in, Bryan." Bonnie shuffled forward.

My heart galloped as the silver came closer. "No wait! I won't be able to breathe! My nose is blocked."

"Yes, you will. Open wide." Cut tightened his arms as I tried to run. "Do it. Otherwise, I'll just hurt you until you do."

My lungs gurgled as Cut wrangled me into position. I thrashed and moaned, but it didn't help. "Stop, please!"

The world went dark as the icy metal settled over my face.

"No!" I clamped my lips together, preventing the spike from entering my mouth.

But Bonnie ruined that by swatting my shins with her cane.

"Ahh!" The pain forced my lips wide, welcoming the silver wedge.

I gagged and yanked away, only succeeding in slamming backward into Cut's arms. The cool metal on my tongue sent spasms through my body. Water sprang to my eyes as I choked.

His elbows landed on my shoulders, keeping me pinned. "Don't struggle, Nila. No point in struggling."

I fought.

But he was right.

There was no point.

All I could do was ignore my body's begging to gag and do my best to breathe.

Bonnie brought the back piece of the mask behind my head, securing it with a tiny padlock by my ear.

The instant it was locked, the worst claustrophobia I'd ever suffered swallowed me whole. Vertigo entered the darkness, spinning my brain, throwing me to the floor. I gagged again.

It terrified. It degraded. I was trapped.

My nose blocked worse.

My head pounded.

My ears rang.

My fear consumed me.

I

Lost

Control.

I screamed.

And screamed.

And screamed.

Cut let me go.

I no longer saw, heard, or paid attention.

My cries echoed loudly in my ears. I gurgled and coughed and lamented for help. My blocked nose stopped oxygen from entering; I inhaled and exhaled around the silver tongue press, recycling my screams in a rush of poisoned air.

I suffocated.

I panicked.

I spiralled into craziness.

My world reduced to blackness. Hawksridge Hall, with its sweeping porticos and acres of land, condensed into one tiny silver mask. Condensation rapidly formed from my breath. I gagged again and again.

I lost everything that made me human.

My screams turned to whimpers.

I'm going to die.

Each breath was worse than the one before. I fell to my side as vertigo got worse.

Nausea crawled up my gullet.

Do not throw up.

If I did, I'd drown. There was no way out, no mouth piece. Only two tiny nose holes that didn't provide enough oxygen.

Images of the ducking stool came back.

This was just as bad. Just as heinous.

Claustrophobia gathered thicker, heavier, chewing holes in my soul.

I can't stand it.

"Let me out!" The words were clear in my head, but the paddle pressing on my tongue made it garbled and broken.

The faint sounds of laughter overrode the hiss and gallop of my frantic breathing.

My hands shot to the fastenings, fighting, tugging. I ripped hair and scratched the side of my neck, doing my best to get free. I broke a nail, scrambling at the padlock. Screams and moans and animal caterwauls continued to escape.

I couldn't form words, but it didn't stop me from vocalizing my terror.

Bonnie kicked me, laughing harder. "I think an hour or two in the

Scold's Bridle will do you a world of good. Now be a good girl, and endure your punishment."

The tiny bell saved me.

My heart asphyxiated all over again, remembering the dense heat, the overwhelming panic of the bridle. I never wanted to relive that again. *Ever.*

You're free. It's over.

I didn't think it was possible, but the bridle was worse than the chair. Even remembering it caused the walls to warp, squeezing me uncomfortably tight.

I had a new affliction: claustrophobia.

Unknown Number: *I sense you're not telling me something. Remember what I used to call you? My naughty nun? God, I was such an arse. I fell for you even then. I think I was in love with you even before I set eyes on you.*

All residual fear and ailments from the past week vanished. Fear was a strong emotion, but it had nothing on love.

Fresh tears cascaded over my cheeks.

You have no idea how much I wish to return to such innocence.

To only suffer worries of fashion lines and unpaid custom orders or whether Vaughn had ordered enough taupe buttons. Such frivolous problems—such easily solved concerns.

Not like what I deal with now.

My heart broke all over again. The punishment of abuse slowly turned my mind and body into rubble, fit only for sleep or death.

Needle&Thread: *I love you so much.*

Unknown Number: *I love you more. I love you with every breath I take and every heartbeat I live. I love you more every day.*

Tingles shot from my scalp to my toes.

Needle&Thread: *I wish you were here. I'd kiss you and touch you and fall asleep in your arms.*

Unknown Number: *If you fell asleep in my arms, I'd hold you all night and keep you safe. I'd trespass on your dreams and make sure you know you belong to me and give you a future you deserve.*

Needle&Thread: *What do I deserve? What sort of future do you envision?*

Unknown Number: *You deserve everything that I am and more. You deserve happiness on top of happiness. You deserve protection and adoration and the knowledge that we will never be apart. You deserve so fucking much, and I mean to give you all of it.*

I sighed, feeling the warmest, softest blanket covering me. Jethro might not be here physically, but spiritually he was. His unwhispered words were hugs, and his concern the sweetest of kisses.

Needle&Thread: *Just tell me we'll get through this. Tell me that we'll be together and grow old together and build a life that no one can take from us ever again.*

His reply took a moment, but when my phone chimed, he somehow gave me everything his family had stripped from me. He deleted the appalling events and gave me hope.

Unknown Number: *Not only do I plan on having you by my side forever, but I want you as my wife. I want you as the mother of my children. I want you as my lover and best friend. We'll get through this. It will all be over soon. And when it is, things will change for the better. I'm going to spend the rest of my life making it up to you, Nila, and proving that you took a coward and made him want to be a hero. Your hero.*

My lips wobbled with happy tears. I whispered, "I love you, Kite."

Staring at my phone, I read and reread his messages. As much as I wanted to print them off and sleep wrapped up in his words, I had to delete them.

I couldn't run the risk of Cut finding them.

I had no choice.

Die or kill.

Fight or defeat.

It killed me to drag the entire conversation to the trash and remove it.

Come save me soon.

Come end this before it's too late.

My happiness suddenly squashed as the walls squeezed in on all sides. My mind ricocheted backward, probing old memories.

I couldn't move from the floor in the alcove. I didn't know which way was up. I couldn't breathe. I couldn't speak. All I could do was hold onto the slate tiles and ride wave after wave of vertigo and claustrophobia.

My racing heart deleted years off my lifespan with undiluted panic.
I passed out.
It was a blessing.
By the time Bonnie returned to undo the padlock, I was no longer coherent.

Shaking my head, I rubbed my face.

How many tortures had Elisa suffered before she'd been 'purified'?

Unknown Number: *Goddammit, Nila. I need you so much. I need to show you how much I love you. How much I miss you.*

My heart was in pieces without him.

Needle&Thread: *I need you, too. So much. Too much. When we're together again, I'm going to—*

A noise wrenched my head up.

No!

My eyes fell on the unprotected door.

Please no!

The one awful thing about being so sick was I'd had no strength to push aside the dresser to keep me safe.

The phone came alive in my hands, claiming my attention.

Incoming call from Unknown Number. Answer?

The device vibrated urgently, begging me to accept its challenge.

Jethro...

My soul wept. I wanted so, so, *so* much to answer.

But I can't.

Locking the phone screen, I shoved it under my pillow.

You didn't delete the last message.

The door swung open.

Too late.

Daniel appeared, gloating and cocky. "It's time for another game, Nila. And we can't be late."

Jethro

I LEANED OVER my brother.

The tubes and heart monitor made him look like some Frankenstein monster—pieced together with scraps from the man I once called friend, held together by sorcery and sheer luck.

His skin held a slightly yellow hue; his lips cracked and dry, parted to allow the tube down his throat.

The doctors had done all they could—patched him up and kept his heart pumping. It was up to him now.

A week and a half had passed. Ten excruciatingly long days. If it wasn't for regular messages with Nila, I would've gone out of my mind with worry.

Her texts kept me sane.

Every hour, I grew stronger. I pushed myself until pain bellowed and my endurance improved. Every minute, I plotted my game plan, and every second, I thought of Nila.

She replied at night. Both of us under the same sky, writing by starlight, sending forbidden messages. She was in the world I used to inhabit; I was in a grave sent there by my father.

Yet nothing could keep us apart.

Soon, we'd both be free.

However, her messages weren't like before. When Nila

was still at home with her father and brother, she'd been timid and easily embarrassed. She'd been sweet and so damn tempting in her innocence. But now her texts were shaded with what she *didn't* say. She kept so much back, only telling me what I wanted to hear.

It was fucking frustrating.

Why don't you answer my calls, Nila?

Every time I'd dialled in-between our messages, she'd always ignored me and disappeared. Almost as if lying to me by innate characters was all she was capable of.

I needed to talk to her. I needed to find out the truth.

What I really need is to get out of this fucking place.

My side twinged, reminding me that I might be going out of my mind with impatience but I still wasn't fight worthy.

Goddammit.

Kes's heart rate monitor never stopped its incessant monotone beeping. I willed it to spike, to show some sign of him waking up.

Clasping his hand, I squeezed. "I'm here, man. Don't give up."

My other hand drifted to my torso, prodding the tender rib. Louille said I was lucky the bullet had passed so cleanly. He couldn't explain the trajectory to miss such vital organs, but I could. Flying through the air, twisting into position to save my sister had kept me alive.

The bullet hadn't found a perfect target.

Tracing the puckered skin through the thin cotton of a t-shirt I'd been given, I gritted my teeth. This morning, they'd removed my stitches. They'd discontinued my antibiotics and announced the good news.

I was healing quickly.

I'd agreed that was good news. I'd demanded to leave early.

But Louille just laughed as if I should be moved to the psych ward rather than recovery. His emotions shouted he was pleased with my irritation—it proved he'd excelled in his profession as healer—but his mouth said it wouldn't kill me to wait another few days.

What he didn't know was his words were too close to the truth.

Kestrel, on the other hand…

I squeezed his fingers again. He hadn't woken up. He'd been in an induced coma for almost two weeks, giving his body time to heal. The bullet had entered his chest, rupturing his left lung, shattering a few ribs. Bone fragments had punctured other delicate tissues, ensuring his body had a lot more mending to do than mine.

His left lung had taken the full impact, deflating and drowning with blood. He'd been on the ventilator since arriving. Louille said if he caught pneumonia due to his system being so weak, there wouldn't be much they could do.

I couldn't think about that 'what if.'

For now, he breathed. He lived.

You'll get through this, brother. I have complete faith.

He'd always been the stronger one.

Louille also said Kes was alive thanks to the small calibre bullet Cut used and the rib that'd taken a lot of the original impact. He said it was surprisingly hard to kill someone with a gun—despite the tales—and proceeded to tell me a bedtime story—completely unsolicited—about a gang war in south London. A sixteen-year old had five bullets fired into him— one lodged in his skull, the other damaged his heart—yet he stayed alive and healed.

Kes would, too. I had to keep that hope alive.

The gentle whooshing of air being forced into my brother's broken body soothed my nerves. Even though he wasn't awake, I offered company and acceptance.

Hovering by his side wasn't just about companionship.

I had a purpose.

My senses fanned out, waiting to see if any of his thoughts or emotions tugged on my condition. Day after day, I hoped he'd wake up. My sensory output stretched, seeking any pain or suffering—if I could sense him, then he was awake enough to emanate his feelings.

However, just like yesterday, I sensed nothing but blankness.

Sighing, I smoothed back his unruly hair. "You'll get better. You'll see. You're not going anywhere, Kes. I won't allow it."

Nila

DANIEL'S LITTLE GAME turned out to be tic-tac-toe.
Only there was no winning, under any circumstance.

At the beginning, I'd refused to play, but he'd soon taught me that that wasn't an option. Jasmine couldn't do a thing about it. She was a spectator while I was the pawn for entertainment.

Family night, Bonnie called it.

An evening spent huddled in the gaming room where the Third Debt had been attempted. With no care or comeuppance, they played Scrabble, Monopoly, and cards.

Cut smiled smugly whenever I shuddered with memories of that night, peering at the walls and chess chequered carpet.

Kestrel had been so kind and honourable. Jethro had been so conflicted and hurt.

Jasmine did her best to keep me in one unbloodied piece, but Daniel was given free control that night. His rules: play the game he wished or submit to a kiss instead.

And not just any kiss. A sloppy wet slurp with his tongue diving past my gag reflex and hands pawing my breasts.

After the second kiss, I gave up rebelling and played.

Cut merely laughed.

Bonnie nodded as if she was a lioness teaching her cub how to play with its food.

Something had fissured deep inside. My soul folded into pieces, trying to protect my final strength and endurance.

My memories, my happiness, my passion...all slowly dried up the more I drank their poison.

It was happening. They were winning. I was so close to giving up.

They wanted me to submit by playing a stupid game? Fine. They won.

Unknown Number: *Are you around? I want to speak to you.*

The seventh time he'd asked since we'd started messaging last week.

How many days had passed since then? Four? Five? *I've lost track.*

Every morning was a new challenge to break me. Two days ago, Cut had given me a bucket of icy water and told me to scrub the stoop of Hawksridge while snowflakes decorated the air. Yesterday, Bonnie summoned me to her quarters, forcing me to take her measurements and create her a new gown.

I preferred scrubbing the stoop to making that witch a dress with the same skills she'd belittled.

They've done other things.

My heart filled with fury and rage—welcomed after so much weakness and grief.

No! Don't think about it.

I refused to sully my mind with them when I finally had a moment's peace on my own. I wouldn't tarnish this precious time with Jethro with memories of his demonic family.

Clenching my jaw, I replied:

Needle&Thread: *It's not safe. Anyone can hear me. Just message...it's easier.*

I sighed as the message sent.

Easier to lie to you, to keep you from knowing how bad things have become.

Unknown Number: *That's bullshit. I'm calling you right now. If you don't pick up, I'll have Jasmine drag a phone to you so you can't hide from me anymore.*

Shit!

Sitting stiffly against my pillows, I jumped as the phone buzzed with an incoming call.

Shit. Shit. Shit.

How could I talk to him? How could I pretend I was still the same woman, when I'd faded into someone I didn't recognise? How could I keep my voice steady and lie through my teeth?

I've always been a terrible liar.

The phone jumped and danced in my grip. It's vibration repeating what I knew: *Li-ar. Li-ar.*

You have no choice.

Running a hand through my tangled hair, I pressed 'accept.' Taking a deep breath, I held the phone to my ear. "Hello?"

"Fuck." The curse whispered its way into my heart, warming me, kick-starting happiness that I'd forgotten how to feel. "Nila…thank God, you picked up."

Him.

My friend. My soul-mate.

Why was I scared of talking to him? Why had I waited so long?

Curling into a ball, I breathed, "Jethro…"

"Fuck, I miss you."

My eyes closed, fighting a wash of sorrow. "I miss you, too." *So unbelievably much.*

"Are you okay? Tell me the truth. I know you're keeping things from me."

Don't do this to me, Kite….

I attempted diversion, deflecting the conversation to him. My heart flip-flopped with tragedy. "I'm fine. How are you? Have the doctors been good to you?"

"Don't change the subject. Tell me, Nila. Don't make me

beg." He sucked in a shaky breath. "Hearing you, knowing you're there and I'm not—it's fucking killing me. The least you can do is reassure me with the truth."

Reassure him with the truth? I almost laughed. There would be no reassurance—only lies would do that. Lies and blatant dishonesty.

"Kite...honestly, I'm fine. Jasmine has done an amazing job. She made Cut amend the Debt Inheritance so she has full control."

Liar.

Half control. And not over the debts.

I'd been lucky the past couple of weeks. Yes, I'd been hurt and tormented, but there'd been no mention of a debt. No extraction of the Third or hint of the Fourth.

Long may it last.

"What have they done to you?"

Everything.

"Nothing. Honestly, I'm alive and waiting for you. I'm just so happy you're safe."

"Nila...you're lying."

I swiped at a renegade tear. "What about Kes?" I kept my voice to a murmur. "Has he improved yet?" I asked daily in my messages, but there was never any change.

Jethro sighed. "Goddammit, you infuriate me." He paused. "No, he's still unconscious."

"I'm sorry."

"You can make it up to me by telling me how you truly are."

I glared across the room at the tropical fish tank with its finned creatures swimming unmolested in their perfect environment. They were free to be happy. I wasn't. And I refused to make someone else unhappy when there was nothing they could do. "Don't badger me, Jethro."

Don't be like them.

I hung my head. "I'm alive. That's the truth. I'm not happy. That's another truth. But what good is it to tell you what they've done when you can't do anything to fix it?" My voice hardened. "Just accept that I'm okay and move on, alright?"

Silence.

My heart thundered against my ribs.

"Jethro?"

A hitch sounded in my ear. "I'm sorry. So fucking sorry."

I melted. "I know. But it's not your fault."

"I'll make them pay."

"I know. We'll do it together."

"I wish I could hold you. Kiss you. My arms are empty without you."

I felt that same emptiness—a terrible void ripping me into ribbons with its aching vastness. "I would give anything to be with you."

Both of us fell quiet. What was there to say when we couldn't talk about what we needed? What words could offer solace when only pain awaited?

"How long?" I finally whispered. "How much longer before I can kiss you again?"

"Too long." Jethro sighed. "They said three weeks, but I'm almost ready. I'm not waiting that long. It's already been too much. I refuse to leave you there another hour more than necessary."

His passion soothed me even though I didn't believe him. He thought he'd be here in time.

I wished with every fibre of my being that he was right.

But there was something monstrous inside me...slurping me deeper, telling me that my time was running out. I didn't know where the countdown beast had come from, but it was snarling louder and louder.

Jasmine was right. Cut had planned something big. Daniel knew it. Bonnie knew it. *I* knew it.

My life was quickly running out.

Hurry, Jethro.

Hurry...

Before it's too late...

Jethro

NINETEEN HOURS SINCE I'd spoken to Nila.

I'd waited until nightfall to message her again; I'd almost torn myself apart with impatience. The only thing that'd kept me inside the hospital and prevented me from hijacking a motorbike and hurtling toward Hawksridge was the lingering throb in my side.

I was better, but I wasn't one hundred percent.

Not that I needed to be completely whole to destroy my father but I wouldn't be stupid this time.

I wouldn't ruin my surprise.

Finally, after my nightly check-up and disgusting hospital dinner, it was safe to message Nila without fear of her being caught.

Unknown Number: *I need to speak to you again. I want to touch you—even if it means I can't do it physically. Call me.*

Hearing her delicious voice last night had turned me on, angered me, and set my nerves on edge. It felt as if I was the one with a guillotine blade over my head—punished by the desire to protect and love her.

My cock hadn't softened all night but I'd refused to satisfy myself.

I wanted to wait for Nila.

We can offer each other a small measure of comfort.

I'd never had phone sex before, but if it granted a smidgen of contentment in our separation, I'd give it a shot.

My heart fisted.

Nila's messages were so selfless. So concerned about Kes and me. She barely spoke of herself, no matter how many times I begged. Last night, when I'd talked to her, only confirmed my suspicions. She'd deflected a lot of her replies. And I fucking hated it.

She's hiding things from me.

After ten minutes of only receiving blankness, I tried again.

Unknown Number: *Call me. I need you.*

No reply.

No notification.

Nothing.

My heart hollowed out, bleeding with every tick of the frustrating clock.

Unknown Number: *Answer me. Are you okay?*

Still no reply.

Snow flurried on my soul, dragging me quicker toward a horrible conclusion.

Nila...what's happened?

The landline beside my bed jarred the silence.

The ringing imitated an awful alarm, ripping my eardrums.

Wrenching the receiver off the cradle, I tossed my cellphone onto the sheets. "Yes?"

"Jet...are you safe to talk?"

Instantly, my body stiffened. *Fuck.* Sitting up too fast, my rib throbbed. "Jaz...what's happened?"

She paused for too long.

Something's gone wrong.

Nila!

That was it. I couldn't heal any longer. My body had rested long enough. I was done with this fucking place.

Swinging my legs over the bed, I leapt to my feet. I didn't give in to the gushing pain. I didn't let my body rule me.

I'm done. I'm ending this.

"Spit it out, Jaz. Right fucking now."

I needed to leave. I was strong enough to kill Cut and steal Nila away.

Jasmine sniffed loudly.

"Talk to me!"

Tears immediately sprung into her voice. "I—I tried, Jet. I did my best."

My blood turned to sleet. "What did they do to her?"

Not the Third Debt. Fuck, if they touched her—!

Jaz's voice was water and grief. "They lied to me. They told me I would be present at every punishment. I found out today that wasn't true."

"What punishments, Jaz?" The room closed in. My heart rate exploded. "What have they done?"

"Bonnie had the elevator blocked for maintenance. I couldn't get downstairs, Jet. I—" A loud sob escaped her.

Fuck this.

"What did they *do*?! Is she alive? For fuck's sake, talk to me!"

"They've been tormenting her, Kite. I'm so sorry! So sorry."

I had no winter clothing. Nothing to change from the sweatpants and t-shirt I'd been given. I didn't care.

I'd run buck-fucking-naked to Hawksridge if I had to.

"Get Flaw here, now. Have him bring clothing and supplies. I want him here in an hour. Do you hear me?"

She sucked back a sob. "I'll—I'll tell him. Kite…they've been using the old equipment. They used it on Elisa in those pictures. You know?"

I froze to the linoleum. "What the fuck did they use?"

Jaz went quiet.

"What did they use, Jasmine?!"

"The Iron Chair, the Scold's Bridle, the Scavenger's Daughter." She cried again. "I'm so sorry, Jethro. I was there for most of them. I did my best to comfort and support her.

But I couldn't say no. I couldn't run the risk of them knowing you're—" More tears.

Conflicted emotions ran through me. I hated that she couldn't save Nila. But I understood at the same time. It was too much to ask from my crippled sister. Too much for anyone living in that insane asylum.

My soul sank further. "What else, Jaz?"

Her voice shook. "Tonight…they hurt her. I tried to stop it, but I couldn't. I didn't even know until it was too late."

My heart shattered. "Tonight. Fuck, Jaz. What happened tonight?"

She sniffed loudly. "They used the Heretic's Fork. She…slipped."

"Shit!"

The fork was lethal. One trip and it was death. My mind swam with images of the neck brace padlocked around the accused's throat, forcing them to hold their head high for days. The deadly sharp prongs wedged against sternum and throat, just waiting for tiredness or a fall to jerk their head down and stab them through the heart and jaw.

"That—that's not the worst of it," she stammered.

My body turned to lava and hate. "Goddammit! What else could they do?!"

"Part of the Fourth Debt. They—they—" She couldn't finish.

No.

No.

Fucking no!

I tore off the hospital wristband and traded patient for wrathful avenger.

They wouldn't get away with this.

Not anymore.

They're motherfucking dead.

"Get Flaw here. I'm coming home."

A Few Hours Earlier...

"NICE OF YOU to join us, Nila."

Cut clasped his hands in front of his black jeans. His salt and pepper hair glistened from the sconces around the room.

Daniel shoved me forward. I tripped on the blood-red rug in the centre of the space. A cough escaped as my eyes danced around yet another never before entered part of the Hall.

Amber drapes and bronze accents. War memorabilia along with a few glass cabinets displaying Luger pistols and bloodied ribbons from some battle long ago. Dust motes hovered in the air, swirling a little from the heat escaping the fireplace. The low ceiling and dark orange walls made the space den-like and cosy, full of history and artifacts.

"It's time we moved forward with the next stage...don't you think?" Cut sipped his goblet of cognac. "You've had time to repay a few of the smaller sins, but my schedule is running behind, and I can't delay my upcoming surprise any longer."

Vertigo tried to tackle me, but I did my best to stand tall. Furious tears froze in my eyes, glinting like daggers but not daring to fall.

I will not cry.
Not for them.

Not for anyone.

"You're gonna enjoy the surprise, Weaver." Daniel laughed, circling me like a vulture. "Gonna go on a little trip soon."

A trip?
Where?
Why?

Bonnie shifted in her chair beside the fire. A woollen blanket covered her knobbly knees. "Don't ruin the surprise, Buzzard. She'll find out soon enough."

Sour mistrust and hate filled my mouth. "Whatever you're planning, I hope you've arranged your own funerals."

Cut coughed on his liquor; Daniel burst out laughing. Slinging an arm over my shoulders, he whispered, "You're becoming so much fun. I like this side of you."

"What side? The side that doesn't give a shit about you anymore?"

My illness had left me weak but Jethro had made me strong. His messages and assurances that we would have a future allowed me to stand up and be heard, even if it fell on deaf ears.

Dragging his foul tongue along my chin, Daniel cocked his head. "No, the side that pretends she doesn't care but she does." His spicy aftershave polluted the air.

It was late and I'd believed I'd avoided yet another night in this nest of vipers. When he'd come to collect me, I'd been plotting how to end it. Sitting on my bed, dressed for sleep, I wasn't thinking empty thoughts anymore. Hidden in my fabric chest was a large piece of black cotton with chalk scribbles on how to kill each Hawk.

Poison.
Shooting.
Bludgeoning.

I'd explored every avenue, and Jasmine even offered me the use of her personal gun. She'd told me that if Cut died from unnatural causes, the estate and his children's futures died with him. She told me that his Last Will and Testament pretty much screwed everyone. However, she had faith I could come up with a way to revoke the fine print and somehow save them.

Our relationship had changed into a mutual liaison. She leaned on me. I leaned on her.

"Know why we've summoned you here, Nila?" Suits of armour watched me as Cut smiled. "Care to guess what you'll pay tonight?"

No...

Jethro...

"Before we begin, we're going to have a little 'show and tell.'" Daniel left me on the rug, heading toward a small table covered with black cloth. "I'm sure once you've seen what's under here, you'll thank your fucking stars that you have the power to stop us from using them."

My heart charged, pumping blood through my veins. "What power?"

"Obey and do what we say and they remain purely ornamental." Removing the cloth, Daniel grabbed something and held it behind his back. "Know what this is, Nila?"

I hated that question.

Every time I'd heard it, it delivered yet more torment.

I wanted to dismantle the sentence, burn the vowels, tear apart the consonants. I never wanted to hear that jumble of words again in my *life*.

Keeping my head high, I didn't look at him.

"You'd be best to answer me, Nila." Daniel came closer, stopping in front of me. His voice hammered nails into my coffin.

I looked into his demonic eyes, nostrils flaring with anger. My hands opened and closed for a weapon. "No, I don't know what that is and I don't care. You're like a bloody child looking for your parent's approval."

Bonnie chuckled. "Oh, tonight will teach that tongue of yours a lesson."

"Take me back to my room. I'm done playing."

Daniel laughed, catching my wrist and holding me steadfast. "Not so fast, Weaver." Stroking my nipple through my white nightgown, he murmured, "Did you forget who called it quits the other night? You were tired. I could tell. The Scavenger's Daughter would've driven you mad if I hadn't stepped in." He pinched me. "I was the one who unbuckled the iron and let you go."

He's right.

His concern for my wellbeing could've come across as kind and caring—if he hadn't also been the one who'd swatted me with willow reed while I was bowed and imprisoned by the awful Scavenger's Daughter.

He'd been tasked with teaching me manners after I'd refused to eat with them. He'd been told to make me bleed.

Surprisingly, he hadn't.

He'd been happy just drawing my tears.

However, according to Cut, I was a spoil-sport.

The Daughter had been used to crush its victims. Bowing with my head on my knees, the iron bars had been excruciating, slowly tightening with a winch, folding me into fatal origami.

"What do you want from me? Appreciation? An award for mercy? What?"

Daniel narrowed his gaze, holding out the item. "What I *want*, Nila, is for you to play along."

I snorted, unable to hide my disgust. "Play along while you torture me? Sure, why didn't I think of that?" My eyes fell on the object. For once, I had no clue what it was. I didn't recall seeing it in the torture book that V owned, and I couldn't piece it together.

Bracing my spine, I said, "I told you. I have no idea what it is. Hurry up and get it out of my face."

He ignored my command, smiling like a Cheshire cat. "Good. Gives me the chance to teach you something for a change."

You've taught me a lot, Buzzard.
How to hate.

How to crave death.
How to plot your demise.

Daniel laughed, stroking the roundish brass device with a corkscrew in the middle and petals lodged together with a small circular handle. It was pretty in an old-fashioned, barbaric way.

"This is a Pear of Anguish." He shoved it beneath my nose. "Ever seen one before?"

"I just told you I didn't know what it was."

He beamed. "Allow me to show you how it works." I recoiled as he held the pear and twisted the small lever at the bottom. Slowly the petals expanded outward, forming a morbid four-leaf flower. "This ingenious device has three uses."

I swallowed hard as he kept spreading the petals.

"Use number one was for liars and instigators. The pear was forced into their throat and slowly opened until their jaw cracked."

I shuddered.

"Use number two was for gay men or priests who broke their faith. It was shoved up their arse and cranked wide until their arsehole ripped." He laughed, flaring out the pear to full expansion. "The third was for women. Adulterers and nuns who'd lied about being virgins for their God or faithful spouses. It was shoved up their twats, and only once they'd been stretched were they deemed repentant enough to deserve the Judas Cradle or Brazen Bull."

I closed my eyes. I didn't want to imagine the rest of the torture devices. There was too much joy in creating so much pain. I couldn't stomach it. I'd seen photos of the Brazen Bull—of stuffing a poor person inside a bronze statue and lighting a fire beneath. The victim roasted alive, while the smoke of their charred remains escaped through the nostrils of the bull.

I shivered.

His fingers caressed my cheek. "Don't worry. I won't use it tonight. Only show and tell, remember?" Snickering, he placed the Pear of Anguish on a side table and picked up a wicked pincher device.

Cut said, "You'd do well to behave, Nila. One misstep and they become part of the toys used. Got it?"

I glowered, not stooping to his level with a response.

Jethro…

Keep my thoughts on him.

Whatever they planned to do tonight would be bearable as long as my mind found a way to be free.

Daniel waved the next piece in my face. "Any clue?"

I shook my head, hating him more every passing second.

"It's called a Breast Slicer." Daniel opened the pinchers which were formed into two wicked spikes. "This would be stabbed into the outer edges of a woman's tits, impaling her."

My nipples twinged as blood raced faster.

"Then they'd be ripped out as fast and as hard as possible." He demonstrated with a quick jerk. "No more tits." Fondling the awful item, he laughed. "Women had it pretty hard in medieval England. Wouldn't you agree?"

That one I did agree with.

I nodded.

I expected more tormenting, but Daniel grew bored.

Tossing the Breast Slicer to clang against the Pear of Anguish, he looked at Cut. "Can I start, or do you want me to do something else first?"

What's going to happen?

Whatever it was, he'd given me fair warning. It would be only fair to use that knowledge for my benefit. My mind charged ahead with gruesome plans. If I remained untethered, I might be able to use the Breast Slicer on him and then ram the Pear of Anguish down Bonnie's throat. Cut would have to wait—or I could skewer him with a poker from the black marble fireplace.

Cut steepled his fingers. "You can start, Buzzard."

Daniel clapped his hands. "Hear that, Nila? Permission. Fucking sister has done a good job at keeping you out of bounds, but tonight she's not invited." He grinned. "She's also not invited to the secret surprise we have for you. That will just be you, me, and Cut. Jasmine thinks she's won. But she won't be coming with us." His golden eyes darkened. "And that means there won't be anyone to stop me."

Loathsome repugnance ran through my body.

He's talking about the Third Debt.

"Get on with it, Dan," Bonnie muttered.

Daniel prowled around me. "Don't rush me, Grandmamma. I'm enjoying myself." He gathered my long hair, playing with it.

I couldn't unglue myself from the rug.

"You're very pretty, Nila. I can see why Jethro thought with his cock rather than his brain." Braiding my hair, he inhaled me. "But unlike my broken brother, I can keep a level head around you." His entire body reeked of greed and gluttony—not on food or money—but power over another's life.

My life.

His hands dropped from my hair, ensnaring my wrists. "Because of that, I don't trust you. And tonight, it's all about obedience."

I gasped as he yanked my hands behind me, binding them with a rope I hadn't seen. I squirmed in his hold, wanting to escape whatever would come next. *So much for my plan of killing them.*

"Don't do this." My voice was heavy with fury. *Don't take me away from Jethro when he's only just come back to me.* To have such love and hope granted and then stripped away was the height of cruelty. I loathed my fate. I despised my karma.

Daniel laughed loudly, his baritone bouncing off the den walls. "Don't worry. You have full control over tonight."

"You keep saying that. What does it mean?"

Spinning me in his hold, he stroked my cheek. "I mean that you'll have a choice of what happens."

"If I have a choice, then I choose for this to end. Right now."

He chuckled. "Not that simple, Weaver."

My wrists fought against the twine. I forced myself to ignore the discomfort and rapidly building fear. My unhappiness didn't matter to Daniel. He only saw what he wanted—a girl to torture and daddy's approval to do it.

It's all over.

Jethro had come back from the dead. But it was too late.

Cut placed his goblet on a side table, standing upright. "Are you ready to begin, Nila? Ready to pay the Fourth Debt?"

What answer could I give? I reverted to illiteracy. I forgot how to talk because speech never saved me. Only actions would, but I couldn't do that, either. My arms were fastened tightly.

Daniel pushed me forward. Cut caught me but I refused to look him in the eye. Instead, I looked over his shoulder—back ramrod straight, chin tilted with defiance.

Cut's golden gaze glowed. "I'll take that as a yes." Chuckling, he stroked my diamond collar. He bent closer, his breath echoing in my ear. "It's a new era, Nila. And I can't wait to share my secrets with you when we get to where we're going. Tonight you'll pay the easier part of the Fourth Debt. And later…you'll pay the rest."

I shivered. The depths of depression I'd crawled from tried to tug me back. I had to look strong, even if I didn't feel it.

"Where are we going?"

"You'll find out when we get there. But I'll give you a name…*Almasi Kipanga.*"

My nose wrinkled. It didn't give any hint. "What the hell is that?"

He smiled. "You'll see."

Bonnie stood. The rap of her cane was a third footstep as she inched toward her family and victim. Her hazel eyes met mine.

Without the black blanket covering her legs, her outfit was visible: a maroon skirt and dark brown jacket. Cynical thoughts ran riot in my head. *She's wearing colours that won't show blood.*

My heart unhinged, racing erratically.

What the hell will they do?

Bonnie smiled, showing yellowing teeth and far too much smug exhilaration. "Let's begin, shall we?"

Daniel wrapped his fist in my hair, yanking me against him. The long strands licked around his wrist, binding us together. "I'm up for that."

Horror consumed my reflexes, nulling me from intelligence.

Think.

There must be something—

There is something.

I could call for Jasmine. I could scream as loud as I could for Bonnie's protégé and hope to God she could save me.

But then I'd ruin her life, too.

How many more people had to die before this was over? Kestrel was dying. Jethro was healing. Jasmine had already paid more than I knew.

Bonnie snapped her fingers. The door behind me opened and shuffling feet announced we had visitors. I held my breath as the guests made their way to stand by the fireplace.

"No…" My heart layered in tar as Vaughn marched to a stop, courtesy of the mountain of malice, Marquise. His black eyes met mine and in twin language we held an entire conversation. Possibly our last conversation forever.

I'm so sorry, Threads.

I'm so sorry, V.

I love you.

I love you, too.

"Mr. Weaver here is going to help us extract the first part of the Fourth Debt," Bonnie said, limping closer. "You've paid the First, Second, and Third—well, not quite, but we'll get to that—you've paid debts for our ancestor, his daughter, and son. But you're yet to pay for his wife."

"Whatever this is about, just leave her alone." Vaughn

struggled in his identical bindings. Hands behind his back, wrists locked together—I felt a kinship with him that I hadn't had in the other debts.

All of those, I'd been on my own. Jethro had been beside me, but he wasn't family.

This one was personal.

My brother would see just what I'd been dealing with.

I hated that but was grateful, too.

His presence would force me to be stronger than I might have been.

Jethro...I'm sorry I lied to you.

Cut cleared his throat. "Daniel will inform you of your history lesson, and then we shall begin. You *will* consent to this debt being claimed, Nila. Just like you'll consent to the rest."

"Stop. Wait! Leave her alone." Vaughn struggled against Marquise, his eyes frantic. "Whatever you're about to do. Fucking stop it. She's suffered enough, goddammit!"

Bonnie sighed. "Marquise."

The big man quirked an eyebrow, holding on to my brother as if he were a fly on a string. "Yes, Madame?"

"Gag him."

"Of course." Marquise let V go with one hand and dug into his back pocket. With inhuman strength, he slammed my brother against his mountainous chest and forced the black bandana through his lips.

"Wait!" I launched forward, only to be jerked back by Daniel. "This is between us. Let him go."

Bonnie sneered, "Oh, he'll be let go, alright."

My heart slipped from tar to fossil. "What do you mean?"

Please don't mean death. Please!

"I mean if you play this game correctly, Vaughn can go home tonight."

My heart exploded with hope. "Truly?"

Do I dare believe them?

Disbelief shook its head, but the cruel spark of optimism begged it to be true.

Bonnie smiled. "Play correctly, and he goes home, untouched. He returns to his family because of your sacrifice out of love."

Vaughn mumbled something unintelligible behind the gag.

"However, if you play incorrectly, he'll stay here. He'll suffer right along with you and we'll end his journey the same moment we end yours."

He'll die with me.

That could never happen. I couldn't be responsible for my brother's death.

"You have my word, I'll play. Send him home now. You don't need him to make me behave." I couldn't look at Vaughn while I traded my life for his. He'd be full of guilt and rage at not being able to stop me.

Cut rubbed a hand over his mouth. "If you are a good girl, Nila, and he goes home, don't think he's untouchable. Don't think this is mercy or that we've overlooked his ability to bring havoc to our world again. This is another checkmate in a game you're too stupid to understand."

A question burned in my chest. I needed to know the answer, but at the same time, it led to such confusion. "Why?"

Cut paused. "Why? I just told you why—if you don't obey—"

"No, not that." *I can't believe I'm doing this.* "*Why* let him go? I thought you were keeping him until I paid…"

My voice trailed off.

I know why…

Cut chuckled. "Answered your own question, didn't you?"

My head turned into a bowling ball, sagging on my shoulders.

Vaughn was going home because *I* wouldn't be. Whatever Cut's surprise was…it was the Final Debt. Somehow, he believed he could keep the police at bay. That my brother wouldn't bring down their empire. That he was safe to continue with his murdering schemes.

Imbecile.

He's truly slipped from malicious to insane.

Vaughn exploded in Marquise's grip. He kicked and wriggled, yelling at the top of his voice, nonsense curses spilling from his gagged mouth.

"Shut him up," Bonnie snapped.

Marquise clamped a hand over Vaughn's nose and mouth, slowly suffocating him.

"Stop!" I wriggled in Daniel's arms.

"Don't make me hurt you before we've begun, Weaver."

I couldn't tear my gaze away from my brother as his face turned pink and eyes bugged for breath.

Cut checked his gold Rolex. "Right, let's begin. I have somewhere else to be tonight."

Daniel let me go, and Marquise dropped his hand. Vaughn sucked in wheezing breaths as Daniel planted himself in the middle of me and Vaughn. "Grandmamma, the dice?"

Bonnie inched forward, her arthritis turning her stiff. Pulling a dice free from her jacket pocket, she handed it to her grandson. With eyes ordering obedience and no room for error, she stepped back.

Daniel puffed out his chest. "As you know, Nila, you've paid the debts for the original Hawk family, but you haven't paid for the glue that held the family together. The mother was the reason we outstripped your family in wealth, power, and rank. However, before you learn what she did to make such a thing happen, you must learn the daily struggle she went through to keep her family alive."

Cut nodded proudly, giving Daniel the limelight.

In a sick way, the history lesson was a reprieve. Storytelling by a monster before he ate me for dinner.

"You're not a mother, so I doubt you'll understand completely, but this little game will prove how far she'd go to save her children."

Daniel held up the dice. "For every roll, I'll give you two scenarios. Option one, you have the ability to save yourself. Option two, you'll have the ability to save your brother. You will learn the depth of my ancestor's compassion. She wasn't a martyr—she was a fucking *saint*. Putting everyone she cared about first."

Daniel rolled the dice in his fingers. "If there was food, she'd feed her family and starve herself. If there was shelter, she'd make sure her children were warm while she would freeze. If there was pain, she'd put her loved ones first and accept the punishment. She truly was an exemplary woman."

His voice deepened. "And your fucking ancestors took advantage of her kind-hearted spirit. They tortured her by holding the lives of her children over her. They went above and beyond to make her suffer. Weaver used a dice, similar to this one, whenever he wanted her to do something. Fuck him or sleep in the pigsty. Crawl on her knees or go hungry. She was the strongest member of our lineage because, not only did she never break, but she also singlehandedly destroyed the Weaver's stature, became friends with the sovereign, and ensured the Hawk name became one of the most feared and wealthiest overnight."

He laughed. "Strong fucking woman, huh?" His eyes darkened. "Bet you wish you were half as strong as her."

He wasn't wrong. My emotional sadness and bodily weakness from the past few weeks haunted me. I'd let them get to me. I'd cracked, if not broken completely.

I'm weak.

Knowing I came from such an awful bloodline made me guilty for our wealth and success. Our prosperity was built on the destitution of others, but just like the crown and church terrorized its people, the gentry picked on lower class. It didn't make it right, but that was the world back then. Corrupted by power and free to torture.

It wasn't my responsibility to pay for their sins. It wasn't anyone's. It was evolution from barbarism to better behaviour.

Daniel smirked. "What are the most basic instincts of a mother? What is the fundamental requirement for having children?"

I pursed my lips. My eyes remained locked on Vaughn.

To defend against people who mean them harm. Just like I'll defend V from you.

Daniel continued, "We all know it's a mother's job to sacrifice herself for her children. Let's see if you can be that strong for your sibling." He shoved the dice under my nose. "This isn't an ordinary dice. No numbers. See?"

I flinched.

"Only two colours. Red and black. Want to know what those colours mean?"

God, please let this end.

"Red is for blood—a physical toll you'll have to submit to, in order for your brother to avoid the punishment for you." He chuckled. "And black is for psychological—those hard to swallow decisions where there's no right answer but only two shades of fucked-up."

"Wrap it up, Dan," Cut said. "Let's get on with it."

Daniel nodded. "Fine." He tossed the dice from palm to palm. "What should your first trial be, Weaver? Something easy or hard?"

Vaughn fought in Marquise's hold.

I ignored him. This wasn't about him. This was about me *protecting* him. The Hawks already knew I'd accept every task, no matter what it was. It wasn't a choice, but a necessity. Bearing pain myself was doable, watching my twin go through it...unthinkable.

Rubbing his chin, Daniel murmured, "I think my first roll will be..." Shaking the dice, he released it. The plastic bounced against the thick carpet, coming to a stop on black.

Black...psychological.

I stiffened as an idea lit his face. Leering at Vaughn, he said, "You have two choices, Nila. First, stay where you are and watch your brother suffer two blows to his gut, courtesy of Marquise. Or..."

I stood taller. "Or what?"

"Or...do what my ancestor had to do every night. She had

to fuck her employer."

My stomach bubbled with disgust. My tongue desiccated with horror. "I—I—no."

Daniel grabbed his cock. "Gonna fuck me for the Third Debt. Might as well get used to it, bitch."

I wanted to throw up.

Vaughn wriggled and groaned in his binds.

Visions of willingly submitting to Daniel in front of my brother caused tears to swell. I couldn't…could I?

Incredibly, Bonnie came to my rescue. "I'm not watching a rutting. Kiss him, Ms. Weaver. Save the rest for a room without my presence."

My heart scurried like a terrified rabbit.

Daniel bared his teeth. "Don't override me. I'll get her to do whatever the fuck I want."

Cut crossed his arms. "Not tonight. You'll have her. And it's going to be a far sight better than a quick fuck on the floor." Coming toward me, his eyes lit up with secrets. "We'll be somewhere no one can touch you. And you'll do whatever we say."

Vaughn struggled as Cut pressed a fleeting kiss on my mouth. "Now, go kiss my son to avoid your brother being punched, and then we can move on."

Daniel grumbled, "Fine, kiss me, whore. But not just any kiss; something that will make me *believe* you mean it."

V jerked in Marquise's hold, the groan in his chest a resounding plea for him to take the punishment. Didn't he see? I couldn't live with myself if I had a way of sparing him more pain.

A kiss is nothing. A kiss I can do.

A small price to pay for my brother's wellbeing.

Linking my hands together, I lashed myself tighter than the twine. Holding my chin high, I turned to Daniel.

His eyebrow rose, intrigued and eager. His eyes slowly filled with lust as I crossed the small space and stood on my tiptoes before him. His chin came down, lips parted, but he didn't cross the final distance.

He waited for me.

He waited to accept a kiss I swore I'd never give him—no matter how much they tried to break me.

Incredulously, I felt as if I cheated on Jethro.

I'm sorry.

Holding my breath, taming my roiling stomach, I pressed my mouth against his. He was warm and tasted slightly salty, but he didn't force me to deepen or stick his tongue down my throat.

It all hinged on me.

I have to make him believe.

Otherwise, it would've been for nothing.

Repulsion worked my gag reflex. I wanted to pull away. But I pressed my mouth harder against his, squeezing my eyes to annul the truth of who I kissed.

I'm stronger than this.

Finding my last remaining strength, I licked Daniel's bottom lip.

He groaned as I slipped my tongue into his mouth. I wasn't tentative or hesitant. I'd learned how to kiss thanks to Jethro's majesty at drawing desire from me.

If Daniel wanted me to make him believe, I'd make him bloody believe.

His chest rose and fell, brushing my nipples, reminding me of what Jethro had done to me. The anger inside him seemed to pause, lulled by whatever magic I held over him.

My throat closed; I ran out of breath.

I reached my limit.

Pulling away, I spat on the rug by his feet. "You believed me. You can't deny it."

Breath was hard to catch as I stared triumphantly at his trousers. "There's evidence that you can't hide, Buzzard." I cocked my head at the tented material. "You can't touch him. I did what you asked."

The softness of him taking what I gave vanished. Lashing

out, he grabbed my hair. He shook me, rage darkening his face. "Just wait till we make you repay the Third Debt, whore. You'll regret that."

Vaughn grunted again, but no one paid him any attention.

Bonnie remained quiet, letting her youngest grandson do what he wanted.

Letting me go, Daniel plucked the dice from the floor. Shaking it, he tossed it down again.

Red.

Pain.

I swallowed hard, doing my best not to show fear.

Vaughn didn't do such a good job. He fought and squirmed, earning a punch to his gut—even after I'd kissed Daniel to prevent it.

"Don't! I paid the damn requirement!"

Cut clucked his tongue. "Marquise. She's right. Don't hurt him unless she refuses."

Vaughn doubled over, his legs buckling in Marquise's hold.

Daniel pointed at the dice. "Pain, Nila." Tapping his chin, he pretended to think. "What can I make you do?"

Cut murmured, "Hang on, I'm calling rights on this one."

I tensed.

He tilted his head in my direction. "Nila will pay that one for me with no complaints but she'll do it when we get to where we're going. Isn't that right, Nila?"

My eyes flickered to V.

Cut's voice licked around me. "You'll know what it is when I ask, and you'll permit it. Because if you don't, I'll just kill your brother and be fucking done with it."

V growled. I stayed quiet. I'd played this game longer than he had, and I knew how to deal with Cut now.

Narrowing my eyes, I asked, "Why drag it on? Why not just kill me here?"

Cut clenched his jaw. "If you have to ask that, you haven't been paying attention." He stalked forward. "Agree to what I just asked and you'll learn before the end."

There was no other answer I could give. I glowered. "Fine."

He smirked. "Good girl."

Daniel pouted but shook off his disappointment by collecting the dice. "Oh, well, my turn again." Shaking the dice, he snickered, "Ready for another?" He rubbed his lips in lewd reminder. "Maybe I can have you blow me next."

Acid drenched my insides.

Daniel rolled the dice. The horrible thing bounced off the rug, coming to a stop on red.

Shit.

I sucked in a heavy breath.

You can do it. Do it for V.

Daniel grinned. "Red, huh? Pain..." His eyes drifted to the table where the Pear of Anguish sat.

God, no!

Marching over, he picked up an awful looking contraption peeking out from under the black cloth. "This will do."

I stiffened as he came back, dangling the torture equipment just like Cut had with the Scold's Bridle.

"This ought to be painful enough."

My eyes drank in the leather collar and long metal bar on the front. Each end was carved into two sharp prongs.

"Know what this is?"

That damn question again.

Unfortunately, I knew the answer this time. "It's a Heretic's Fork."

Was this a manor house of the fucking Tower of London? Where did they keep these barbaric devices?

"Smart girl." Daniel grinned. "And you know how it works?"

I made the mistake of looking over at Vaughn. Saliva dripped down his chin from the gag, his eyes blazing with sorrow.

I looked away. "It's strapped to the accused throat and the

fork forces the person to keep their head high to avoid the prongs from entering their chest and throat."

Bonnie smiled. "You've finally shown some aptitude, Ms. Weaver." Cocking her head, she ordered, "Strap it on her, Daniel."

"Be my pleasure." The thread of insanity that infected Cut glowed in Daniel's eyes as he moved behind me. His cold hands brushed aside my hair as he brought the horrible thing beneath my chin. "Put your head up."

Tears prickled my eyes as I raised my chin, staring at the ceiling. The square wooden panels kept me company as the fork buckled around my throat and diamond collar.

My neck arched, keeping the delicate skin safe from being stabbed. My teeth hurt from clenching, and my head pounded with a rapidly spreading headache.

You're failing again. Don't give in.

I blinked back tears, straightening my spine as if that would bolster my courage.

You're breaking. They're winning.

I wished I could tear out my brain from tormenting me. The Hawks did that enough without my mind disabling me, too.

Once the buckle was firmly fastened, Daniel inspected his handiwork. "You look rather regal like that. Guess I can't make you blow me this round; otherwise, you'd kill yourself with every suck." He cackled at his tasteless joke.

Vaughn groaned in the corner but I didn't look over.

I let my vision unfocus, granting a small reprieve from everything.

Please, let this end soon.

Slapping my arse, Daniel commanded, "Walk a few laps. Show me how well you can move with your head high and your wrists bound."

My heart chugged hard as my worst enemy swooped into being.

No, not now!

The room swirled with vertigo. Sickness fogged my head, and I lost all sense of balance.

Don't fall!

I'd kill myself.

Moaning, I did my best to equalize.

It didn't help.

The room shot black; I stumbled forward, falling, *falling*.

Someone yelled, "Catch her!"

Arms wrapped around my body as I plummeted. I jerked to a stop, hanging in some horrible embrace as the world dipped and swelled. Slowly, I traded oppressive blackness for the orange den.

Swallowing hard, I shoved away the remaining episode. "I'm—I'm fine."

Daniel planted me on my feet. "Got a fucking death wish, Weaver?"

I wanted to shake away the cobwebs left in my head, but I didn't dare. I trembled in place, itching with claustrophobia. My neck strained beyond comfort, aching already.

"You gonna faint on me again?"

I calmed my breathing. "I didn't faint. It's vertigo, you arsehole."

"She's had it since she arrived," Cut said. "Three laps, Ms. Weaver. Get through that without killing yourself and we'll remove the fork."

Three laps. Three lifetimes.

"Can you untie my hands?"

"Nope." Daniel pushed me forward. "Go on, be a good prancing pony and show us what you can do."

My knees wobbled, but I shuffled forward. I didn't know the room enough to avoid ottomans and small coffee tables. My eyes couldn't look where my feet went. I was basically blind.

Their gaze burned into me as I made my way to the perimeter of the room and followed the wall as best I could. Couches forced me to go around; I bashed my knee on a magazine rack and stubbed my toe on a desk.

I felt like a prized pony on a race-track—keeping my head high, my knees higher, prancing for my life, only to fail and be shot for my efforts.

It took a long time to navigate and vertigo kept playing with my balance. I had to stop a couple of times, swaying uncomfortably. By the time I made my way past V for the third time, silent tears spilled from my eyes and I was on the precipice of breaking.

I wanted it over with. I wanted to be free. I wanted to *run*. Run. Run. Run.

Vertigo grappled me again, hurling me headfirst into a vicious attack, scrambling me like whisked cream.

Shit!

I fell, tripping over something and colliding with air. There was nothing to catch me, nothing to stop me soaring from standing to dying.

Time slowed as I tumbled forward. My hands fought against the rope, and my mind screeched instructions.

Keep your head up! Keep your chin high!

My hands were tied. I couldn't stop my trajectory. All I could do was pray I survived.

The thick carpet cushioned my knees as I slammed to the ground. My shoulders crumpled, and I cried out in agony as the prongs bit into my jaw and chest, biting their way into my flesh.

Am I dead?

I couldn't tell.

Pain smarted from everywhere.

A shadow fell over me as Cut ducked to my level. "Whoops." His lips spread into a horrific smile. "Sorry, my foot got in the way."

And that was it.

That final tiny straw that made it almost impossible for me to keep going.

I withdrew into myself. I felt myself disappearing. My hate fizzled. My hope died. I had nothing else to give. Nothing else to feel. The throbbing of the wound no longer bothered me because my senses shut down.

There came a point when the body ceased feeling pain. The receptors were tired of transmitting an important message—only to have that message ignored.

I'd neglected my body for far too long and now it'd abandoned me.

Cut paused mid-chuckle, understanding I'd reached rock-bottom. Without a word, he unbuckled the fork and left me alone on the carpet.

Silence reigned heavily in the den. No one moved.

I didn't care if I never moved again.

You won.

I don't care what you do anymore.

They'd taken my innocence. My vengeance. My love. My life.

I had nothing to go back to. Nothing to move toward.

Stagnant. Locked in a present I could no longer survive or endure.

"Get up, Weaver." Daniel stood over me.

I stood.

"Come here." He snapped his fingers.

I went.

"Let's roll again, shall we?"

I nodded.

Monochromatic and hell-bound thoughts. That was all that remained of me.

I didn't notice as Daniel tossed the dice.

I didn't look as it rolled to a stop by my foot. I didn't care when it didn't flop to one side, staying poised on its edge—neither black nor red, both physical and psychological pain.

As far as the debts went, as far as their fun continued, I'd checked out and left.

I had no future. What did I care about my present?

Daniel ducked to collect the dice. "It's as if the ghost of our ancestor controlled it."

Bonnie nodded. "It *is* rather serendipitous."

Cut came forward, pulling free a large pair of shears from his back pocket. "Here you go, son." His eyes met mine, but he faded once again to the side-lines. Deep in his light-brown eyes was the smallest level of concern. He sensed I'd given up. His enjoyment had been taken away from him.

Daniel held up the scissors. "Know what these are for?"

I remained mute.

"Know what I'm going to use them on?"

I rejected his every taunt.

"These are to take something from you. Something they took from my ancestor." Wrapping his arm around my shoulder, he pointed the scissors in Vaughn's direction. "The Hawk woman did anything she needed in order to feed her family. She sold her every asset until she had one last remaining. Know what that was?"

V's red-rimmed eyes howled with sadness.

I tried to care, but couldn't.

V would move on.

I'd stay here.

Locked in this world with dice and Hawks.

Daniel squeezed me, trying to cultivate a response. "It was her hair. She cut off her hair in order to keep her family alive for a few more days." His voice turned to gravel. "Now it's your turn to sacrifice. Your choice is simple. Allow me to cut off your hair—suffer a psychological toll—all in order to save your brother from a painful handicap."

I continued to stare blankly.

Take what you want.

I no longer cared.

"Marquise, hold up his hand," Bonnie ordered.

Marquise spun V around to face away and splayed his fingers. I glanced at the swollen blue digits from being tied so tightly. My own fingers felt the same—numb and dying from lack of blood.

"Hair or his finger, Nila. That's the deal."

His voice sliced like a sickle through my blankness. But I didn't move.

Daniel vibrated with anger. "Hair or finger, bitch." He gnashed the shears together. "One or the other. You have ten seconds to decide."

I didn't need ten seconds.

I already knew my decision.

I wasn't vain enough or alive enough to care.

"Hair. Take my hair."

Daniel scowled. "Where's your fight gone? You're being a fucking wet fish."

I found a magic in ignoring him.

He couldn't torment me anymore.

None of them could.

I didn't think about Jethro or Jasmine or home. I didn't think at all. About anything.

Prowling behind me, he gathered my hair in his fist. "You have such beautiful hair. Last chance to change your mind, Weaver."

My voice held no fear or objection. If my tone were a colour, it would be colourless. "Do whatever you want."

I'd never cut my hair.

Ever.

It was a stupid reason but one I'd done for my mother. She'd loved to play with it. To plait it, thread it with flowers and ribbon—show me off as her little princess.

That was my last remaining memory of her, and Daniel had stolen that, too.

"Gonna slice every strand off your head," Daniel promised. His touch tugged on my hair, twining it into a rope. "Ready to say goodbye?"

My heart didn't hurry. My eyes didn't burn.

"Don't fucking answer me. See if I care." Daniel's fingers yanked harder and the rusty yawn of the scissors bled through my ears.

My eyes closed as the first snip turned me into a stranger.

Physically, I couldn't feel pain, but spiritually, I *howled* in anguish. It hurt. It hurt so *so* much to have such a poignant piece of me stolen without fighting, without screaming, without protecting what made me *me*.

The second snip broke me.

It hurts, it hurts, it hurts.

The third snip destroyed me.

Stop, stop, stop...

The fourth snip completely annihilated me.

I have nothing left.

"Can't tell you how satisfying this is." Daniel laughed, cutting with no finesse, hacking through the thick black strands.

I was alone in this.

Alone and shorn like some animal for slaughter.

All I could do was mourn silently.

Snip, snip, *snip*.

My curtain of ebony hair disappeared with every scissor-slice. Cascades of thick blackness puddled, devastated and dead, on the blood-red rug. I'd given up the last part of me—the final toll for my brother's freedom.

I'm doing it for him, for love, for family, for hope.

I said goodbye.

To my youth.

To my childhood.

Snip, snip, *snip*...

This was the end.

Snip, snip, snip...

It was over.

Jethro

I BECAME SOMEONE I never knew I was capable of.
A monster.
An avenger.
The hero I needed to be.
Nobody would touch her again.
Not me.
Not my family.
Not even pain itself.
I stepped onto Hawksridge land. *My* land. *My* legacy.
I'm here for you, Nila.
I'll fix this.
I just hoped I wasn't too late.

Nila

SLEEP.

It was the only peace I got these days.

Peace from my fracturing soul. Peace from breaking.

They'd won.

They'd finally broken me. Finally proven that no one had unlimited resources to remain strong. That we all break eventually.

I wasn't proud of myself.

I hated that I'd lost.

But at least Vaughn was safe. At least I'd done right by him.

I had no weapons to defend myself. No energy to push aside the dresser and protect myself. My belief that I could ruin them disappeared into dust.

Nothing mattered anymore.

I was theirs to do with what they wanted. And my heart was officially empty.

My reflection in the bathroom mirror showed a terrifying transformation. Hollows existed in my cheeks, shadows ringed my eyes, and the blood on my chest glowed with crimson fire.

But it was my missing hair that hurt the most.

Ragged and shorn, my glossy black strands were now in tatters. They hung over my ears, all different lengths, hacked into dysfunction by Daniel's sheers. I no longer looked like Nila Weaver, daughter of Tex, sister to Vaughn, empress to a company worth millions. I looked like a runaway, a slave, a girl who'd seen death and no longer existed with the living.

I look ready to pay the Final Debt.
I feel ready to pay the final price.
There was no power left inside me.
Staring into my black eyes, I shivered at my listlessness.
They didn't even let me say goodbye.
The moment the last strand hit the floor, Marquise had marched Vaughn from the room without a backward glance. I'd never seen V so wild or so helpless.

In two seconds, he'd disappeared.
I'd wanted to cry, to sob, to snap.
But I'd just stood there until Cut gave me permission to leave.

I was in a billion pieces.
How can I ever find my way back when I have no more glue to fix myself?

Bowing my head, I hated the unfamiliarity, the frigid breeze whistling around the back of my neck. My head was light as air and heavy with thunderclouds.

I'd lost everything. My backbone. My faith. They'd stolen more from me than just vanity—they'd stolen my right to myself.

I didn't look away as I washed and tended. I couldn't stop staring at my new face.

I didn't have kind words to bolster my courage. I didn't have hope to patch up my weeping heart. All I had was emptiness and the bone-deep desire to go to sleep and forget.

Using a torn piece of calico, I washed my wound as best as I could. Water whisked away the blood, but nothing could wash away the filth existing inside me.

I'd given up.
I'd vanished just as surely as Cut had won.
I was done.

Stumbling from the bathroom, I left behind the last remaining part of me. I said goodbye to the woman I once knew and fell face first into bed.

No thoughts.

No wishes.

Just emptiness.

I let sleep consume me.

Jethro smiled, holding me close.

His body heat, normally negligible with his cold temperature, roared with love and healing.

"I've got you now, Nila. It's okay. I'll make it all go away."

Having someone look after me after so long, undammed my tears, and I fell into his embrace. "I've missed you so much. I tried to be strong. I tried." I cried harder. "I tried to be so strong but it's not enough. Nothing will ever be enough. I'm empty. I'm lost. I don't know how to get back."

Jethro's lips kissed my forehead. "You're so strong. You'll heal. Hush. I've got you. You'll be alright. Hush." He rocked me, soothing my hair, never letting me go.

"I can't do this anymore, Jethro. I can't." I curled into his arms, wanting to fade away and stop everything. "There's nothing left. I have nothing...nothing!"

He kissed my hair—my beautiful, long hair. A low growl built in his throat. "You won't have to. I'm ending it. I'm going to save you. It will all be over soon."

The dream unwound from my thoughts as a tap against glass roused me.

The vacant despair inside me throbbed, but sleep had patched me together infinitesimally—letting me hold on just a little longer. Jethro's dream embrace stitched the vanishing pieces together just enough that I didn't burst into tears.

Whatever the Hawks did to me, no matter what affliction I suffered, no matter how desolate my mind became, I still existed—still survived.

I'm not done until I'm dead. And even then, I'm immortal.

Remember that and be strong.

The rapping came again, guiding my eyes to the dark window.

The heavy emerald drapes puddled velvet from ceiling to floor. They blocked the night sky and any hint of the mysterious noise.

Tap. Tap-tap.

Could a tree have fallen? Could Flaw be throwing stones at my window to get my attention?

Curiosity overrode my stiffness, forcing me from the warmth of slumber. Shuffling from the covers, the room swirled with vertigo. The imbalance was worse because I'd given in. I couldn't fight it anymore. I let the black wave take me, gripping the mattress until it faded. The cut on my chest burned as I breathed hard and slow.

The tapping came faster, louder.

Climbing unsteadily to my feet, I padded across the room and wrenched the curtains aside.

My eyes dropped to the sill, searching for answers.

I tripped backward.

What—

Something feathered and flighty hopped away, only to soar back and tap against the glass. I'd expected to see a wayward branch or even some flotsam that'd lodged against the frame.

I hadn't expected this.

Had some messenger from God come to slap me for being so lost? Was it some mystery of Mother Nature saying she believed in me?

I'm not alone...

My heart swelled as lost hope unfurled.

The people I lived with might not care about me...but others did. I couldn't stop fighting because I *was* loved. Out there, somewhere, I was loved by people who mattered.

My heart twisted as I bent closer to inspect.

The bird of prey rapped its beak on the window, hopping on the sill outside. Its beady black eyes tore through me, as if in one glance it knew what I'd dealt with and how close I was to the end.

You understand me, little bird. Are you my saviour?

Backing away from the window, I balled my hands.

You don't need a saviour…if you only believed in yourself again…

So what, your hair is gone? So what, your brother is gone? So what, Jethro is gone?

You're *not gone.*

So fight!

The bird charged the pane, rapping its beak with fury.

I froze.

Winter ice had chased away autumn far too fast. The spidery lace of frost decorated corners of the glass. The radiating cold cut through my cotton nightgown like knives.

Poor thing.

I hated to think of the poor creature in the cold. No animal should be without shelter.

I moved forward and opened the wrought iron catch. Cracking the window open, the bird immediately hopped inside.

No fear. No hesitation.

Where the hell had this bird come from?

I froze as the raptor spread its wings, ran across the interior window, and hopped onto my hand.

"Ah!" I snatched my hand back. Its talons were sharp and its beak deadly. I'd had enough pain at the hands of human hawks to let a feathered one hurt me, too.

The bird puffed out its chest. Its beak glinted wickedly while it cocked its head and stared at me with intelligent eyes.

It saw right through me.

It saw how broken I was. How tired. How desolate.

It made me drown in guilt for being so feeble.

Unwanted tears crept into my eyes.

"I don't have anything for you. I doubt cereal will impress a carnivore like you."

The bird chirped.

The noise whipped through the room, sending my eyes darting to the door. I didn't want to give any reason for Daniel to visit me. He'd done enough. He'd done too much.

Backing away, I shooed it. "Go on…get out of here."

Instead of flying away, it hopped closer, once again targeting my hand.

"No, wait—"

It didn't listen. With a single flap, it hopped off the sill and landed on the back of my knuckles. Its wings soared open for balance, its talons digging into my flesh for purchase.

My bicep clenched beneath its weight and I steeled myself against its uninvited presence. Its scaly legs shuffled, doing its best to remain in one place. Taking pity on it, I curled my fingers, creating a rudimentary perch. It chirped, wrapping its sharp talons around my skin. Its weight was surprisingly heavy, its plumage dense with feathers of coppers and brass. "Hi."

It tilted its head sideways, chirping again.

A draft whistled through the gap in the open window. I moved to close it, but the bird nipped at my knuckle.

"Ouch." I went to shake him off, but my eyes fell on its leg.

The hawk or kestrel flapped its wings, dispelling a rogue feather to flutter to the carpet. It somehow knew I'd seen its message.

My heart stopped beating as I looked through the window, squinting into the darkness. Who'd sent it? Were they still out there?

No shadows moved outside; no hint of midnight visitors.

"Who sent you?" I murmured as I glanced at the white parchment wrapped around its leg. Reaching for the red bow, I tugged it loose.

The bird screeched, bouncing up and down with impatience. Its sudden agitation forced me to yank harder. The roll of paper fell away, dropping to the sill.

With the heavy bird on one hand, I did my best to unroll the scroll and read.

However, the raptor didn't wait. It had done its duty—it had delivered its message. Without a backward glance, it soared off my hand and slipped like a winged demon through the window crack and into the sky. Instantly, the camouflage of its feathers vanished against twinkling stars.

My heart steadily increased its tempo; my breathing turned erratic. Pinching the note, I smoothed it out until the finest, tantalizing, most *miraculous* sentence I'd ever seen imprinted on my brain.

Come to the stables.
My knees wobbled.
My heart grew wings.
Jethro.
He's here.
He's come back for me.
I am not forgotten.

Jethro

MY LIFE WASN'T mine anymore.

It was hers.

Hers.

Hers.

I'd told her that, but I didn't think she believed me. But now I was back. I was alive and ready and motherfucking angry. She was mine to protect and adore, and up till now, I'd failed her.

I should never have brought her here. I should've had a fucking backbone and ended this when Cut killed Emma. I should've found help for my condition the night I hurt Jasmine. I should've ended their evil the day my mother couldn't cope.

So much history, so many lessons and decisions. At the time, I'd played the game—I'd waited and learned and prayed.

But I'd been stupid to think there was any other conclusion.

It'd taken Nila to slap me awake, electrocute my heart with her courage, and show me that I was a good person inside. That the thoughts I suffered—of torture and ruin—weren't mine. That the horrors I'd committed in the name of family values didn't make me the monster I'd been groomed to be.

I'm my own person.

And it was time to show Nila just what a transformation

I'd undergone.

The moment she appeared on the ridge, I struggled to breathe.

Nila...

The moonlight cast her in silver as she padded down the small hill, her white legs flashing beneath the white hem of her nightgown. A long black coat swamped her body, while a hood covered her head, fluttering around her face. She didn't run. She glided over the frost-glittering grass.

I wanted her to soar to me. To *fly*.

But something was wrong. She moved too slowly. Like a woman who'd lost her fire.

My heart shattered as she slowly closed the distance. She looked magical and mystical and far too precious to tame.

But I *had* tamed her. And she'd tamed me.

Come faster, Nila.

Hurry.

My hands curled as she didn't increase her pace. I stayed where I was, lurking in shadows, waiting.

My body vibrated, wanting so fucking much to charge toward her. To tackle her on the soft grass and kiss her senseless beneath the stars. I couldn't stand another second without her in my arms.

I took a step onto the cobblestone courtyard.

Don't.

Common-sense forced me back into the shade. I couldn't leave the safety of the stables—couldn't risk anyone seeing me from the Hall.

Wait.

Every second was fucking torture.

She moved as straight and true as the kestrel I'd sent her.

Kes.

His name and memory was a stain upon my joy.

My brother had to survive because he deserved to see the new future. He and Jasmine were owed a happier life than the one we'd been dealt.

I wanted them by my side when I introduced Nila to Hawksridge and showed her that this place had not been kind to her, but once it was mine, it would be our private haven.

Come. Faster. Run.

My heart thundered with erratic syncopation.

Nila skidded down the small incline, the flash of glittery ballet flats catching moonshine.

Every step brought her closer. I sighed heavily. The throb from my rib faded; the twinge from my newly removed stitches disappeared. For the first time since waking up in the hospital, I felt truly healed. My body had mended, but without her, my soul would've been torn forever.

Trading grass for cobblestones, Nila's shoes slapped quietly, closing the distance between us. Her breathing wheezed—as if she'd been sick but healing—and her hood hid her stunning long hair.

My skin sparked as she sprinted around the mounting block and sailed through the double doors of the stables.

Finally.

I grabbed her.

She screamed as my arms snaked around her, trapping her vibrating form, saying hello with echoing heartbeats. Spinning her in my hold, I planted both hands on her hips and walked her backward to the wall.

I never stopped moving.

Pushing, shoving, coming fucking apart at having her in my arms.

Her eyes met mine. Her fright disappeared, consuming me under an avalanche of love. "Oh, my God...it's true...you're here."

I smiled, opening myself completely. I fed off her happiness, loving how deeply she cared for me. I couldn't stand it. I didn't deserve such unconditional acceptance. But something shadowed her. She felt...different...quieter. She didn't have her usual spark or vibrant will.

My soul growled at the thought of her fading from me.

I'd bring her back.

I will.

Her back hit the brick wall, my hands soared from her hips to her cheeks, and nothing else fucking mattered. "Christ, I've missed you." Ducking my head, I captured her mouth in a brutal kiss.

Live for me. Breathe for me. Come back to life for me.

My lips bruised with how hard I kissed her. I hadn't meant to be so rough, but Nila exploded. The passion and ferocity missing inside her suddenly detonated into being.

I groaned as her hands disappeared into my hair, grabbing fistfuls, yanking me closer. She melted and fought; her tongue shooting into my mouth.

She whimpered as my kiss turned violent, driven by the need to affirm that this was real. That she was truly in my arms and still fighting, still surviving.

Our heads tilted, changing the kiss's direction. Her fingers tugged harder on my hair. I kissed her deeper.

"You're here." I poured words with kisses, not knowing if I spoke or yelled it from my soul. "Fuck…you're truly here."

Her tongue swirled with mine, her chest pressing hard as she sucked in rapid breaths. My side ached but nothing would stop me from kissing her until we passed out from pleasure.

She'd returned to me, but she was still quiet inside, still hesitant and unsure.

"I'm here." She kissed faster. "You're alive." Her fingers dug firmer. "God, Jethro…you're okay." Her voice broke, and the world ceased to exist.

It was just taste and love and heat.

The dam of her emotions drowned me, and I cried out as she reincarnated in my arms. Fuck, I'd missed her. Fuck, I'd worried about her.

But she was alive.

She was still mine.

Her hands swept up my back, touching fiercely. She winced as I sucked in a breath when she skated over my healing rib.

She gasped. "I'm sorr—"

I yanked her head back with a fistful of her hood, forcing her to look at me. Her lips were swollen, glistening in the darkness. "You can't break me, Nila."

I kissed her again, unable to stand the overwhelming emotion in her eyes. She opened for me, welcoming me to take whatever I wanted. Within seconds, I was drunk. Entirely intoxicated on her taste—all my forward thinking, my plans to put into action—they could all wait.

Because this goddess couldn't.

I couldn't.

I couldn't get enough of her. I would *never* get enough of her.

We stumbled sideways, my mind awash with need, my body and hands completely uncontrolled. My shoulder slammed into a stall as Nila lost her balance, falling against me. I spun her around, pressing her against the new obstruction, kissing her harder.

She moaned and we staggered again, clashing and fighting but always kissing.

Never stopping.

"I can't believe you're alive." Her hands tangled deeper in my hair, keeping my face locked with hers. "Every night I prayed you weren't gone."

I ducked to capture her throat, kissing my way along her jawline, glowering at the glittering diamonds lacing her neck.

No matter what happened and the freedom we earned, Nila would forever wear that collar. I hated it, but I would prefer to see her wear it every day for the next eighty years, than see it sitting back on its pedestal in the vault just waiting for its next victim.

I bit her neck, sucking her taste, inhaling every part of her.

I wanted those images out of my head. Forever.

She groaned as I captured her breast, squeezing the unrestrained flesh through her nightgown.

"Jethro—"

My cock fucking pounded with desire, my heart permanently located in the rock-hard flesh. I had to be inside her. Only then would this insane need to devour her cease.

Not yet.

Things had to be discussed.

It took all my strength, but I pushed away, dragging a hand over my face.

Nila stayed locked against the stall, her chest rising and falling; her coat opened, showing nipples pinched with lust. The damn hood kept me from seeing any further than her mouth and eyes.

Her gaze met mine in the gloom, tears sparkling on her eyelashes. "Why—why did you stop?"

I couldn't tear my gaze away from her lips. So plump and red and wet.

I'd done that. I'd practically eaten her alive.

The urge to do it again drove me fucking insane.

"We have to talk." My voice was hay and dust, cracked and dry.

"Oh." She looked down, her fingers pulling at her coat. The damn hood kept her face in shadow. She hurt as much as I did. Hurt with passion. Lacerated by lust.

Shit.

I squeezed my eyes, cutting off my vision but feeding more perception to my other senses. My skin begged to connect with hers. My heart growled to thump against hers. And my cock fucking punished me for not being inside her.

"Fuck it."

I gave in.

Falling on her again, she gasped as I shoved her hard against the stall.

"Fuck talking." I kissed her lips, her chin, her cheeks. "I need you, Nila. I need every inch of you."

"Take me." She cried out as my hand gathered her gown, bunching it over her hip. "Please—please don't stop."

"I've never wanted someone as much as I want you," I groaned as she opened her legs. "Never loved anyone as much as I love you."

She gasped as I grabbed the back of her knee, hooking it over my hip. Something ripped—her hem or coat—I didn't care. Her heel dug into my arse as she ground against my cock.

I shuddered. My hand slapped against the stall to prevent my body from crushing her.

"Don't stop." Wrapping her arms around my neck, she dragged me back to her.

My side twinged and my forehead pricked with pain, but I didn't care. My cock ruled me now and it wanted to be inside her that fucking instant.

Fumbling with one hand, I wrenched aside my belt and jerked down my jeans and boxer-briefs. The clothing had come courtesy of Flaw, along with a lift back to Hawksridge, sworn silence, and a note to deliver to Jasmine.

My cock leapt from my trousers, rippling with need and sticky with pre-cum. Fisting the base, I rocked against her, desperately trying to find her entrance.

Her fingers clawed my shoulders, tugging me closer but holding me away at the same time. "Wait—wait—"

"I can't wait."

"But you were shot...you probably shouldn't—" Her hands dropped, stroking my naked hips, digging her nails into my flesh. "Are you okay to do this?"

I kissed her again. "I'm going to show you how okay I am by making love to you." I thrust against her.

She shook her head. "Wait!" Her attention shot to my torso, seeking wounds. I had no intention of taking my t-shirt off and showing her the bandage hiding the stitched area or mentioning my broken rib.

Didn't she get it? None of that fucking mattered as she was the best painkiller around.

I'd never felt so good having her in my arms, trumping death, defeating the impossible.

"You argue with me again, and I'll make you come apart over and over until you believe me."

"But—"

"Stop it." Pressing a finger over her lips, I silenced her. "Quiet." The tip of my cock found her tight heat. "If you stop me from taking you, I'll die. I'll literally have a heart attack."

Her head fell backward as I teased, hovering so close but not taking her. Pushing up the tiniest bit, we trembled with pleasure. My head bowed, pressing against the stall behind her as I did my best to stay in control. My thighs bunched as every instinct bellowed to drive inside her. "I need you so much I can scarcely breathe."

Her emotions ran crazy, battering me from all directions.

Lust.

Fear.

Questions.

Love.

"Quit thinking so hard; you're distracting me." Looking into her eyes, I traced her cheek, soothing her rioting thoughts. "All I want to feel from you, Nila, is desire. All the other stuff…we can talk about it later." I kissed her softly. "Now, be quiet, stop thinking, and let me fuck you."

She shivered and obeyed.

Her emotions switched to one thought: wanting me to take her.

It would be my pleasure to comply.

Bending my legs, I drove upward.

Her back arched as I slid inside her liquid heat. Higher and higher, stretching her.

"God, Jethro—yes!"

I gathered her close, holding her tightly as I climbed deeper. Only once she fully encased me did I thrust.

Our lips glued together, and we rode each other.

It wasn't rhythmic or sensual.

It was purely animalistic and primal.

"I won't last—I can't last."

"I don't care." Her pussy tightened as I drove faster. "Just prove to me you're alive."

"That I can do."

It didn't take long.

My body had no endurance and time spent apart meant everything about Nila bewitched me into exploding far too fast.

With each thrust, the pleasure turned catastrophic; my balls tightened.

"Oh, fuck…" Lightning shards shot up my cock, spurting inside her. "Hell, yes." Waves of release crippled me as I splashed inside the woman I wanted forever. I bit my lip as my legs seized, my cock impaling her over and over again.

The last spurt left me lightheaded, but it'd been the shortest, sharpest, and most rewarding orgasm I'd ever had.

"Goddammit, it's good to see you."

Having her in my arms, coming inside her, knowing we were together again, helped wipe away my worries and just *be*.

"Where's Moth and Wings?"

Nila's voice wrapped around my satisfaction, dragging me back to her. The chill of the stables faded thanks to the heat lamps I'd turned on above.

I rolled over to face her; my unbuckled belt and jeans clinked.

Somehow, after I'd orgasmed, we'd stumbled down the corridor of the stables and collapsed on top of one of the hay bales in a spare stall. Nila had lost her shoes, and her black jacket was rumpled and dusty from rubbing against the wall but she'd never looked more beautiful. She still hadn't removed her hood though, and strange emotions trickled from her—hidden and quiet—scaring me more as minutes ticked past.

I was exceedingly aware of her every thought and also intimately mindful that Nila hadn't come.

I mean to rectify that.

Her mind raced, sending flickers of ideas and questions in

every direction. I let them wash over me, not wanting to focus on reality just yet.

This might be the only time we get to steal perfection like this before it's over.

I meant to indulge as long as I could.

"They're in the paddock behind the chase. If they're not needed for regular riding, they're turned out."

She relaxed. "Oh, that's good. I had a horrible thought that they might've hurt Wings—because you're de—well..." She smiled. "...you *were* dead."

Gathering her close, the sweet smell of clean hay threaded around us. "I still *am* dead according to my father. Kes, too."

My forehead furrowed thinking of my brother. *He has to wake up.* Being away from the hospital went against my desire to watch over him, but I had to trust that Doctor Louille knew what he was doing. That eventually, once Cut was dead and things had been dealt with, Kes would wake up and I could rib him for sleeping through all the hard work.

Wake up, brother. Don't leave me when we're so close.

"How is he?"

I glanced at Nila. The simplistic beauty of her onyx eyes and sexy lips twitched my cock again. "He's still alive." My voice hung in the stagnant quiet. No horses were hobbled tonight—the dogs slept across the yard, and the witching hour gave us our own seclusion from reality, hiding us from nightmares.

Nila plucked at the plaid blanket that I'd placed over the hay bale. "Will he remain that way?"

My heart clenched. *I hope so.* "He will if he knows what's good for him."

She smiled but didn't laugh, too full of melancholy to lighten the mood. There *was* no lightening the mood—not when a brother and friend was dying.

Changing the subject, I looped my fingers with hers. "Can I ask you something?"

She nodded slowly. "Of course."

"Can you take off the hood? I want to see you. You're in too much shadow."

Instantly, her emotions scrambled. Fear drenched, followed by despair. Sitting up, she shook her head. "I'd prefer to keep it on. I'm cold." To add value to her lie, she gathered her coat tightly and hugged herself.

I soared upright. "Bullshit. I know when you're lying. Just like I knew you were lying in most of the texts you sent."

Her shoulders hunched. Her hands went to either side of her hood, keeping it tight around her face.

Moving in front of her, I tugged on the black material. "Nila...take off the hood."

"No."

"Nila..." My voice dropped to a growl. "What are you hiding from me?"

Tears glassed her eyes.

My heart splintered. "Nila, please. I can't stand it when you don't tell me the truth." My hands pulled again, fighting against her hold.

A single tear slipped down her face. "Please...don't make me."

My heart stopped beating.

"What happened to you? When I first saw you, you were almost dead inside. I feel you coming back to life, but something's changed." My voice turned heavy. "Please, Nila. Let me fix this. Whatever happened; let me try to help."

More tears ran silently down her face. She looked away. "I—I was weak. I gave in. I didn't think I had anything left inside me." Her breath caught. "But then I saw you, and I remembered why I was fighting. You gave me purpose again. You reminded me that I'm still cared for and it's my duty. Not to stay alive for myself, but for *you*. You've already helped, more than you know."

"Fuck...Nila..." My chest seized as her sadness crested over me. "What can I do to make this right?"

She smiled weakly. "You've already done it. I'm piecing

myself back together. I'm better now. I've remembered who I am." Her fingers tightened. "Just...please, don't ask me to take off the hood."

I couldn't stand it. My temper thickened. "Take it off. I have to know."

She shook her head.

"Don't make me tear it off you. You have to show me. We're in this together, remember? That means sharing our pain and telling the truth."

Her shoulders hunched. She hesitated for too long. Finally, her head bowed. "Please...please don't find me ugly."

"What?" My air exploded. "Why would you ever ask such a thing?"

Sucking in a shaky breath, she let go of the hood.

My condition soaked up her thoughts—despair, pain, confliction, anger. But most of all, paralyzing hopelessness. My soul pulverised as I slowly slipped off the shadowy material and saw what she'd tried to hide.

I couldn't speak.

I couldn't think.

All I could do was stare and fill with such fury, such motherfucking *hate*, that tears sprang to my eyes.

She couldn't look at me, her shoulders hunched dejectedly. "I—I—" She gave up, hiding her face in her hands and letting go of her sadness.

Her stunning hair had been replaced with multiple different lengths and shapes. The bedraggled strands cascaded over her hands.

They would pay. *They will fucking pay for this.*

Trembling with rage, I gathered her to me, crushing her in my arms. "Those fucking bastards."

She turned in my embrace, wrapping her arms around me, crying silently into my neck. I stroked her back, her neck, the scruffy locks of hair. It felt so different, so strange.

That was what was so wrong. Why she felt so peculiar.

Her courage had been stripped, just like her beautiful hair.

I have to fix this.

I had no idea how, but I couldn't let her suffer.

Letting her go, I stalked to the end of the stable and grabbed a pair of scissors from the tack room. Stalking back, I sat behind her on the hay bale and without a word, brushed out the tatty strands with my fingers and kissed her neck.

With silence heavy between us, I snipped the mismatched ends.

I poured my love and commitment into her with every cut, sacrificing myself for every strand I snipped.

My heart raced as her hair fell to the hay, entwining gold with black. She shivered and hiccupped with teary breaths, but she didn't stop me. If anything, her shoulders relaxed and she let me fix the agony my family had caused.

I took my time.

I stroked her like I would any broken filly, reminding her that I cared and adored and would never hurt her. The soft thickness of her hair slipped through my fingers, slicing into uniformity the more I tended.

Not only did I fix her hair, but I fixed her soul, too. I sensed her reforming, gluing her scattered pieces, slipping back into the Nila I knew and worshipped.

I fell in love with her even more at the strength it took to come back from the brink of losing herself.

And she did it for me.

Under my touch, she came alive.

Under my willpower, she breathed freely and with a smidgen of happiness.

It didn't take long, working my way around her jaw, I combed the ebony strands. With a final snip, I sat back, drinking her in, reacquainting myself with this new woman who held my heart as surely as the one I'd left behind.

Cupping her face, I brushed aside the jaw-length hair and kissed her softly. "You're somehow even more beautiful, Needle."

She gasped.

The nickname I'd used in our texts slipped off my tongue effortlessly. The word symbolised everything I loved about her. Everything I'd grown to adore.

Her lips parted, welcoming me to kiss her deeper.

I groaned as I slinked my tongue into her mouth, licking her sadness and doing my best for her to see the truth.

I would never be free of her. Ever.

Silently, we lay on the hay, face-to-face, kissing gently. My fingers slipped into her hair, massaging her scalp, keeping her there in my arms instead of in her head with torment.

Time passed, and still, we kissed and existed. Silent and safe, falling in love all over again. We gave each other a sense of normalcy we'd never had before—pretending this was our world where nothing could ever touch us.

Finally, I pulled back, stroking her cheek with my knuckles. "I take it Bones delivered my message."

"Bones?"

"The kestrel."

Nila's face lit up for the first time since I'd seen her. The pain of her shorn hair faded a little. "Yes. I had no idea birds of prey could be trained to do that."

I flopped onto my back, hiding the wince of agony. Fucking Nila standing up hadn't exactly been recommended for a healing patient. "They can do all manner of things." My lips twitched, remembering what we'd done to Jasmine when we were younger. I over animated to keep Nila entertained, doing my best to forget about her hair and enjoy our peace together. "For example, Kes once trained a hawk to fly into Jasmine's room and deliver dead voles every evening just to piss her off. She'd screech and chase the bird all the way back to the mews."

"Mews?"

"Aviary." I waved my hand in the direction of the kennels. "Last count, I think we had six raptors on the estate. They live in the converted loft of the kennels. The bird I sent you will have returned home after delivering its message."

Nila played with a piece of hay, still quieter than normal.

"First, I find out there are pigs hiding here and now birds. The longer I live at Hawksridge the more I realise how little I know."

And do you want to know more?

As much as I hated my father's hierarchy, I loved this estate. The Hall had no hold on me—it could be rubble for all I cared, but I loved the land. The acres of freedom and sanctuary and wildlife.

Eventually, when evil was eradicated, I hoped Nila would adopt this place as hers and make it as pure as she was.

Those are thoughts for after this is all over.

I frowned as I concentrated on the other part of her sentence. "Pigs?"

Her face tightened. "Forget it."

I went to argue, but she arched her chin, dragging my eyes down her throat to the small stain on her nightgown. A few crimson droplets soaked through the white cotton. "What the hell is that?" I shot upright. My own pain couldn't stop myself from feeling hers. I let my condition strengthen, searching for her secrets, trying to learn how she'd become injured.

I know how.

My fists clenched.

Nila immediately placed a hand over the cut on her breastbone. "It's nothing."

"Like fuck, it's nothing." Knocking her hand away, I glowered. "Who did that to you?" Cold rage settled over my soul. Her tension and secrets waked around me. "Who did it, Nila? Answer me."

Her face contorted; she looked away. "Like I said, it doesn't matter. You saw my hair...this was nothing compared to that."

Catching her chin, I brought her eyes to mine. "It fucking matters to me. I need to know." All I wanted to do was storm into Hawksridge and repeatedly stab my father in the motherfucking heart. I wanted him to feel the pain of dying. I wanted him to suffer forever. "Cut?"

She squeezed her eyes. More emotion washed from her—fear, sickness, weakness, guilt. What the fuck did she have to be guilty about?

Glancing at the two deep cuts marring her perfection, I knew Jasmine was right. The marks could've only been caused by one apparatus.

"That fucking cocksucker. He used the Heretic's Fork."

She flinched. "How did you—"

"What else have they done to you, Nila? Your hair, your skin." I rubbed my face, unable to shed the self-loathing for leaving her in the hands of my father and brother. "You should've texted me, told me what they were doing."

She sat up. "How did you guess about the Heretic's Fork?"

I scowled. "At least one person tells me the truth rather than trying to hide it to make me feel better."

She looked away, anger lighting her eyes. "Jasmine."

"Yes, Jasmine." Grabbing her wrist, I forced her to look at me. "The sister who I tasked to keep you safe. The woman you were supposed to trust and tell if you needed help or protection." I wanted to shake her. "Yet you didn't. You endured and lied to me that everything was fine—"

She snatched her hand out of my grip. "What was I supposed to do, Kite? I thought you were dead. I became someone I didn't recognise. And then I heard you were alive and I made a promise to stay that way so we could end this together."

Her eyes lowered, cutting me off. "Besides, I've lived through worse. I just had a weak moment before coming here tonight, that's all."

"That isn't all and you know it." I swallowed hard as her emotions shouted the obvious while her mouth refused to speak. "You're on the edge, Nila. I sense it." Grabbing her shoulders, I shook her. "Goddammit, you're stronger than they are. Don't let them win. *Promise* me."

She'd lived through worse at my hands.

The ducking stool. The whipping.

But I'd hurt her the most by not being there for her.

"God, Nila." I brought my knees up, caging myself in. This position had been preferred when I was a kid. Knees up, arms braced, head down—a little fortress from the overwhelming intensity I couldn't switch off. "I'll never forgive myself for what I've done."

My eyes pricked with fury at who I'd let myself become. For being so fucking *weak*.

Nila darted to her knees, snuggling against me. "Stop. You don't need forgiveness. We've moved past that."

"I'll never move past that. Not as long as I live." Looking into her black gaze, I vowed, "I'll never stop making it up to you."

She smiled sadly. "There's nothing to make up." Cupping my cheek, she ran her thumb over my bottom lip. "After what you just did for me—cutting my hair, giving me back what I'd lost—we're even. You came back from the dead for me, Kite. You've proven yourself far more than words ever could."

Lashing out, I wrapped an arm around her, hugging her fierce. "I can never again feel your pain. It fucking crippled me before, but it would murder me now."

She shook her head. "The only pain I'll ever feel from you, Jethro, is if you die again." She snorted quietly, doing her best to lighten the mood. "So, promise you won't do that and the rest will be fine."

"The only pain I ever want to endure is pain endured protecting and deserving you."

She stiffened. "What does that mean?"

It means I have a plan to end this but war has casualties on both sides.

"Nothing." Brushing away her short hair, I nuzzled into her neck. "I don't want to talk about this anymore."

Silence fell between us. She wanted to ask more questions, the barbs of curiosity stuck into my skin like thorns, but she swallowed them back.

"You haven't asked me how I escaped to come see you." Wriggling out of my embrace, she lay on her back, patting the blanket beside her. "They keep my door locked now, so I couldn't run through the Hall."

Reclining again, I inconspicuously held my healing side, granting some pressure from the building discomfort. "How did you get out then?"

Her teeth flashed in the darkness. "I scaled the downpipe outside my bathroom and used the grass lattice on the turret to shimmy to the ground."

I groaned. "Shit, Nila." Hawksridge had evolved over the centuries—indoor plumbing being a new addition with unsightly pipes ruining the prettiness of the façade. My ancestors had done their best to hide them with lattice grass, growing the patchwork up the building. It would've been an easy climb, but not for someone with the inconvenience of vertigo. "That was stupid."

If I had known she'd had to sneak and risk breaking her neck, I wouldn't have summoned her.

Who are you kidding?

I would've gone after her if she hadn't gotten my note. Being on the estate—being so close but so far—I couldn't stand it. "You could've fallen." I traced her pretty neck beneath the wreath of diamonds. "You could've hurt yourself for nothing."

"Nothing? You're hardly nothing." She shivered under my touch. "I would've flown here with broken bones just to be with you."

The air switched from stagnant to electric.

"You make me a better person." Gathering her close, we lay nose to nose. "I mean to deserve you more every fucking day."

Her lips parted, her gaze latching onto my mouth. Her thoughts turned from conversation to sex, dragging me deeper into her spell.

I'd lived through years of horror.

I'd gone through so many stages of denial.

And I'd done my best to remember who I was beneath the influx of commands from Cut. But in one look, Nila shredded me into pieces and shone light upon the man I'd forgotten existed. A man who'd found happiness in animals rather than humans. A man who'd tried so hard to please but only became broken. And a boy who'd met a girl in his past, who'd been raised to hate her, told he would torture and kill her, only to find the courage to love her instead.

"I want you." I bent to kiss her. "I want you forever." Our lips touched; shockwaves danced down my spine. My cock thickened and Nila once again took me hostage.

Her breathing caught, rattling in her lungs.

I pulled back. She'd been sick with no one to help her. How many other fucking secrets had she kept from me? "You were ill?"

She flushed. "It's nothing. Just a cold. I'm fine."

It wasn't just a cold and it wasn't fine. I'd let her down again. But as much as I hated her lying to me, I loved her all the more for being so selfless.

I don't deserve this woman.

Nila's lips whispered over mine again. "Besides, none of that matters now. You're back. We can run."

I froze.

Run?

There was no more running.

She pulled away, her face slowly sinking into despair. "Wait...you *are* here for me, aren't you?" Her voice babbled. "We're leaving this place. We're running tonight. We'll get you better so we can end this when you're strong enough. You *have* to take me away, Jethro. I can't go back. I *can't*."

My heart fisted. I wanted to carve out my soul to make her understand. "I'm here for you, Nila. A thousand times here for you."

She shuffled backward, but I trapped her wrist.

Tears shone in her eyes. "But you're not going to save me

tonight?"

I'm going to save more than you. Don't you see?

So many lives rested on my shoulders—just like I'd carried all my life.

"We can't run. I refuse to run again."

She wiped away a tear, refusing to look at me.

I groaned, tracing the translucent skin of her wrist. "Running isn't an option anymore. If I run and lick my wounds, he wins again. We have the element of surprise now. They think I'm dead. It gives me the perfect opportunity to end this. To be free. But it has to be *now*."

"But you're not well enough."

Grabbing her hand, I placed it directly on my side. Gritting my teeth against the flare of pain, I growled, "I proved to you I'm alive by fucking you. I'm here to save you; you have my ultimate word. But there are others I need to save, too."

She deflated, knowing I spoke the truth but not ready to accept it. Her emotions turned selfish, wanting to keep me for herself. She already agreed we couldn't run—her thoughts blared it—but it didn't stop her from indulging in one make-believe moment.

"But if we ran, we'd be free." She looked up, speaking words she didn't mean. "You have money. I have money. We could disappear." Her conviction and selfishness faded the second she finished.

She sighed, her heartbeat slowing with resolution.

I tucked short strands behind her ear, my soul cursing the death of her gorgeous hair all over again. "You already know what I'm going to say and you agree with me, but I'll say it anyway. Running isn't an option. Vaughn is still here. Tex. Your family's company. You're saying you'd leave it all behind when just a few more days it could be over for good? Why should we be the ones to run when it's our lives that we're fighting for? Our future is here. Our families are here. I'm not going anywhere and neither are you."

She pursed her lips. "They let Vaughn go. He'll be back

with my father and hopefully be smart enough to hide. We could run." Her emotions overwhelmed with suffering. "I *need* to leave, Jethro. I can't go back. I can't. I'll break. I'm so close to breaking. I'm not strong enough. I *can't*—"

I grabbed her, holding her shaking form. "Calm down. I'm not asking you to go back for long." As much as it killed me, I added, "And do you truly believe they set Vaughn free? They haven't done anything decent yet; why would they start now?"

She froze.

"The only thing we can do to ensure your family's safety is to *fight*. You're the bravest person I know, Nila. You've proven I'm strong enough to do what needs to be done. And I *will* do what needs to be done. But in order to do that I need you by my side. I need you with me which means we aren't running. We're staying here and fighting."

She shook her head, even though her emotions agreed with me wholeheartedly.

I kissed her head. "You're so incredible, Needle. So beautiful and strong. I'll end this, okay? You just have to believe in me a little longer."

She cried quietly, snuggling into my embrace. She couldn't verbalize it, but she gave me permission. And I fucking loved her for it. For being strong enough to agree. For being with me even when I asked so much.

I dropped my voice to a whisper. "Nila…I love you. I'm never going to hurt you again. Unequivocally, deeply, totally—you have my heart and soul. I *will* make this right, I promise." Taking her hand, I kissed her knuckles. "You trust me still, don't you?"

A flicker of a seductive smile crossed her lips even as tears spilled from her eyes.

Memories of asking her if she trusted me when I'd shared my secrets came back. At the start she'd said yes, even as her heart screamed no. But, by the time I'd shown her intensity with my crop and made love to her, she'd trusted me completely.

Her skin was the palest cream in the dark. My lips ached to kiss her again. My cock throbbed to be inside her.

Her eyes tore past my humanness and into the part of me that was eternal. "I trust you."

I couldn't stop myself.

I pushed her onto her back and climbed on top of her. Her short hair fanned out like a black halo, tangling with hay. She didn't stop me as I pressed my weight over her. Her legs opened, her hands gathered the material of the nightgown, and she welcomed me to wedge between her delectable thighs.

I groaned as her body melted. My cock punched against my boxer-briefs wanting to fill her all over again.

As much as I needed to be inside her, I didn't want to rush it. My fingers threaded through her hair, keeping her pinned. Nila wriggled, softening beneath me.

Biting her bottom lip, her fingers moved to my waistband. "If you're strong enough to fight now, even after being shot, then prove it again." Her fingers dipped into my briefs, wrapping around my cock. "Prove that I can trust you."

My erection leapt in her hand. Her diamond collar sparkled as I kissed the swell of her breast. "You drive me insane."

"Good." Her breathing quickened. "I want you insane. Mad about me. Completely consumed by me."

I thrust into her palm. "I already am."

A shadow crossed her face, bringing with it a flicker of thought I didn't catch. Propping myself up on my elbows, I stared at her. What had she been thinking? Did she not trust me? Did she not believe me when I said I'd never let anything happen to her again?

"What is it?" I asked, my heart thumping out of control. "Tell me what you're not saying."

She sucked in a breath, looking at the ceiling. "Nothing. Everything's perfect." Her fingers tightened around my cock. "I want you, Kite."

Her voice echoed with love, but I didn't let her derail me.

Not this time.

"Tell me. Do you hate me? Do you secretly loathe me for what I've done?"

I won't be able to live if you do.

"How can I make it up to you?" My voice turned ragged. "How can I prove I mean what I say? That I'm so fucking sorry. That nothing else will ever—"

She hushed me, pressing a finger over my mouth. "There's nothing else you can do. I believe you."

Her voice said one thing, her thoughts another.

I hated when people lied. It tangled me into fucking knots trying to figure out their true meaning. That'd been the problem from childhood. Cut would order me to do one thing, but his cold-hearted cruelty guided me to do another. Kestrel learned from a very young age never to lie to me. I needed utmost honesty to survive living in a household with so many conflicting ideals and hierarchies.

"You can't lie to me, Nila." My blood thickened with impending doom. What wasn't she saying? Would it destroy me if she did? I pressed my forehead against hers. "You can't keep things from me. I know there's something you're not saying and until you clear the air that emotion will overcast everything until it drives me mad."

Her face tightened. "Your condition can be a real pain, you know that?"

I laughed wryly. "You've only just noticed?" The derisive humour didn't shred the tension between us. "Spit it out. Now."

A single tear escaped.

Fuck.

"Nila…don't." Ever so gently, I licked the salty drop, taking her sadness and vowing to turn it into endless happiness. She deserved so much happiness. *Eternal* happiness.

And I would be the one to give it to her.

My chest cracked open. "I'm so sorry, Nila." Burying my face in her hair, I clutched her hard. "So sorry for everything—

for what I am, for what I demand of you, for the things I can't fix."

Her arms wrapped around me. "You don't need fixing, Jethro. You're bombarded every day with stimuli. You're so strong to have endured a childhood living here. You put mechanisms in place to protect yourself. Only…"

"Only?" I traced her cheek with a fingertip. "Go on…"

She tensed, hesitation and reluctance seeping from her. Sucking in a deep breath, she rushed, "I know I love you. I've never known anything so clear, but I can't help wondering if you love me."

I reared back. *"What?"*

She couldn't have hurt me more if she'd tried.

"How can you even *think* something like that? What have I just been saying? You think I've been *lying* to you?" I rolled off her, trembling with rage. "What does that fucking *mean?*"

She sat up, twisting her fingers together. "I just mean…you feel what others feel. Could you be reflecting what I feel for you? How do you know what's real and what's not? It makes me wonder if I forced you to love me. That any woman who cared for you after a lifetime of living with Cut and Bonnie would've made you fall—not fall, but mirror her affection." Her eyes glossed with unfallen tears. "How can I trust that you know what you feel isn't just me putting those thoughts into your head?"

I shoved off the hay bale, unable to keep still. "I can't fucking believe this."

How could she be so clueless? So heartless to say I was so lost to not know my own wants and dreams. How could she even ask that after I cut her hair and almost fucking cried at her pain? "I'm a human being, Nila. I have the same thoughts and feelings as the rest of the population."

She hung her head, dark hair curtaining her face. "You do, but you also have so much more. Your condition, Jethro…I mean, I had one goal when you took me to Hawksridge: to make you love me so I could use you to free me." She swallowed, her eyes tight with confession. "What if I succeeded?"

Of course, you succeeded.

But I'd fallen for her of my own free will.

I should be appalled, but really—I'd known all along. I'd felt her conspiring, pushing me to let her in. Thing was…she didn't need to make me love her. I'd already fallen—long before she started her games. Even before she forced me to kiss her, I'd given her my heart without knowing it.

"You have no idea what you're saying."

"Don't I? Ever since you told me what you were, I've wondered. When you died, it killed me to think I'd never know the truth. Never know if you felt the depth that I feel for you—or the pain I felt when you were taken from me."

Dragging both hands through my hair, my side burned with pain. Her words whipped me like a thousand bullets. As an empath I was subjected to hundreds of emotional pulls and tugs every day. I was whittled down within an inch of sanity every second.

But that didn't mean I copied the strongest thoughts. It didn't mean I was weak and couldn't think for myself. If anything, my condition made me stronger. Not only did I cross-examine every opinion and sentiment but I also learned how to barricade my own conclusions from being tainted by others.

My true thoughts were in a fortress, untouched and pure and I knew *exactly* what I felt toward her—regardless that she'd lied to me.

She doesn't trust me.

I stopped pacing, turning to face her. "Is that what you've thought all along? That I'm not truly in love with you?"

Goosebumps covered her skin; she looked away. "Honestly, I didn't want to think. I wanted to believe in the fantasy, rather than pick our relationship apart. This past month has been hell; I won't deny that. Those first few days when I thought you were dead, I really wanted to be, too. But having you back …it all seems too good to be true. How can I trust that you're here for me? That you'll save me? End this?"

Her eyes narrowed on mine. "Do you want to do that for *me* or for *yourself?* Because if it's for me, then how can you pick your family over a girl who made you love her? How can you even consider killing your father—no matter how horrid he's been to you—when you can't be sure I didn't manipulate you the same way Cut did all those years."

I backed away.

She successfully sliced my soul into ribbons, making me doubt that her emotions for me were genuine. Had they all been an act to get me on her side?

You don't believe that.

She confused me—tore apart the only thing that'd been true in my life, and made me doubt.

Damn her. Damn all of this.

Deliberately, I dropped my guard and let my condition reach for her, tasting her cocktail of lust and panic.

I did my utmost to find a thread of lies. To see if her affection for me was bullshit. But unlike my father and his rare moments of comradery and respect, there was no sulking undertones or passive-aggressive control.

She was honest and true. She *loved* me. She might not have set out to love me, but it happened anyway.

Sighing, I dropped to my knees in front of her. "You have it backward, Nila."

She shook her head. "I don't see—"

"You don't see because you don't fully understand." I looked at the yellow stalks of hay, wishing we were somewhere safe and bright. This conversation had brought shadows between us that had no right to be there. "Yes, I'm more influenced by others' emotions but I'm still my own person. I still have the right of choice and reflection. I've been around women. I've been around friends and enemies. I've lived a normal life like any man and could've found happiness if I chose it."

She flinched. Her fingers fiddled with her nightgown.

Stopping her fidgeting fingers with mine, I smiled. "But, Nila, I'm still governed by my heart. Did I let you influence me? No. I let you in because I saw how strong and brave you were. I let you in because I remembered the girl I met and the way I used to feel around her. I let you in because I saw someone lost and just as controlled as I was when I first messaged you."

She gasped, trembling in my hold.

I wasn't done.

"I was envious that a girl destined to die for the sins of her ancestors was more courageous than I could ever be. I fell in love with your tenacity. Your fearlessness. Your flaws. I fell for you because you taught me to trust myself—to trust that I had the power to be better." Rising off my knees, I cupped her face, my voice throbbing with truth. "You made me a better person by *showing* me rather than forcing me. I fell in love with you because you're the one for me. Not because you were a woman in my home and in my bed."

I sat beside her. "How low must you think of me, to think I could ever stoop to such a level?"

My heart stopped beating. Would we ever find happiness, or would we always second-guess and be clouded with conditions and pasts?

She thinks I'm powerless.

That I didn't fight as hard for her as she did for me.

And she's right.

I'd locked away my true wants in favour of obeying my father. I let him control my life when I should've taken responsibility for my actions. But I knew that now. I was strong enough now.

Because of *her*.

Gently, I pushed her onto her back, climbing on top of her again, slipping between her thighs. "Do you believe me now?" I kissed her once. "Do you believe that my thoughts are my own? That my heart knows it's yours through *my* decision—

not your manipulation?" I kissed her again. "I'll make this right between us. You'll see. I'll prove to you that what I feel for you isn't a by-product of my condition or something I couldn't control. I'll show you that I willingly gave you my soul before you even knew me."

Her eyes hooded. "Thank you."

"What are you thanking me for?"

"For showing me how stupid I've been."

I chuckled, growing hard for her again, wanting her so much. "Just *trust* me."

She moaned, her mouth seeking mine. "I do trust you. I *will* trust you."

The instant our lips connected, we lost ourselves.

We fell into each other, desperate to reaffirm our spoken truth with bodily affection. There were too many misconstrued conclusions between us. I needed to show her I meant every word. And then reality would have to intrude. I'd have to tell her my plans and prepare her for what would happen next.

"Can I?" I slinked my hand up her nightgown, pushing aside cotton.

Her thighs quivered beneath my touch. She sucked in a gasp as my fingertips brushed her core. "Yes…"

Her permission sent my cock jerking with need. I gritted my teeth as I dragged my finger through her folds. "Now we've cleared the air, I want to know something very important."

She arched as my tattooed NTW fingertip drifted up to press against her clit. "Oh? And what's that?"

I nipped her bottom lip. "Did you miss me?" I slipped one finger slowly inside her.

She opened her mouth, sweeping her tongue into mine. "So much."

"How much?"

Her fingers slinked into my hair, holding me tight. She kissed me with every ferocious strength she possessed. My breathing accelerated until my side burned.

Letting me go, she grinned coyly. "That much."

I never took my eyes off her as I thrust my finger, stretching her inner muscles, claiming her. "Good answer."

She twitched as I pushed a second finger inside. "I can't wait to fill you. To prove that what I feel is real." She was so tight, her body fighting my invasion.

My thumb stroked her clit. She shivered in pleasure, her hands catching my t-shirt. "More..."

My mouth watered to taste her. To drink and worship her. We didn't have time. I should get her back to safety and wait until this was over, but I couldn't stop myself.

"I'll give you more." Sliding down her body, I shoved her nightgown up over her waist, revealing her glistening pussy.

Her eyes popped wide as I imprisoned her thighs in my hands and bowed my head over her dark curls.

"Kite..."

My heart leapt. I grinned. "Have I ever told you how much I love it when you call me that?"

Before she could reply, I sucked her clit into my mouth.

"Oh, God!" Her legs spasmed, latching around my ears.

I rimmed her entrance, driving both of us mad. She writhed on the blanket, trying to get free from my questing tongue.

I didn't let her go.

"Kite, oh...I need you."

I smiled. "That can be arranged." I sank my tongue desperately inside her.

"Oh, shit!"

I growled, "You didn't specify which part of me you needed, so I'll take liberties if you don't mind." I plunged my tongue again, licking her, drinking her—just like I wanted.

My cock throbbed, twitching inside my briefs.

"I want you—all of you!"

I chuckled, dragging my tongue upward, swirling around her clit before thrusting back inside her. "You already have all of me."

She grasped the hay, her legs locking tight as I licked her

harder.

Her taste drugged me. I had to have more. My pace increased, swirling, fucking, showing her I was alive and here and I would *never* hurt her again.

My teeth ached to bite.

My hips rocked needing to drive inside her, but I wouldn't stop pleasuring her—not yet. Not until she came undone and accepted my gift. The gift of everything that I was.

Her fingernails jerked into my hair. "Enough. I need your cock."

I shook my head, sucking harder. "Not yet." Teasing her entrance again, I breathed, "Every night apart was fucking torture. Every time I closed my eyes, I dreamt of you." My finger replaced my tongue while I flicked her clit, driving her skyward. "Do you want to know what fantasies I had while I healed?"

She moaned.

"I'll take that as a yes." Thrusting two digits into her pussy, I purred, "I didn't picture you as you might think. Yes, I grew hard for you, picturing you bound to my bed and accepting everything I gave you. Yes, I tortured myself with images of your hard nipples and flushed skin."

She moaned as I rocked faster.

"But it wasn't those images that undid me." I kissed her inner thigh. "Want to know what did?"

She looked down, locking eyes with me.

She nodded.

I smiled, once again bowing to my task of worshipping this woman. "It was a dream that gave me hope. A dream where we do ordinary things. Talk about ordinary life. Become friends as well as lovers. I want to know you inside out, Nila. I want to know everything about you."

Her legs trembled around my shoulders. Her onyx gaze matched the darkness of the stables. "I want that, too."

She whimpered as I bit her. With a wicked wet lick, I forced her leg over my shoulder, giving me greater access and depth.

Her skin scorched, blazing with lust. Part of me wanted to drive her to a climax. I wanted her to come on my tongue and lap up every drop. But the other part wanted her snuggled in my arms, her legs wrapped around mine, our two bodies giving, taking, driving, *craving*.

"I want you forever."

"Forever." Her hips arched involuntarily, seeking more.

I splayed my hand on her lower belly, holding her down as she bucked into my mouth.

"Jethro...please."

"What do you want?"

"You. I want you. All of you. Every part of you. Just you."

My mouth went dry. I couldn't deny her.

Her eyes were wild as I withdrew my fingers and prowled up her body. Without looking away, I licked her dampness from my digits and bent to kiss her mouth.

"Taste yourself on me. Know that I fully belong to you."

She moaned, seducing me with her trust. "I want you inside me. I want to feel you deep, driving me insane."

She was my ultimate fantasy come true. Dark hair, lithe body, vicious strength, and undeniable power. I'd licked her but instead of feeling like I'd given her a part of me, I felt as if she'd given me more. So, so much more.

Grabbing her wrists, I pinned them above her head. Hay crackled beneath the blanket, stabbing my knees, itching unprotected skin. But it was the best goddamn bed in the world because it was just us. No cameras. No locks. No fear.

"God, I want you." My voice was rough, obsessed with her.

Her lips were red and swollen, matching the colour of her nipples through the white cotton. I'd never seen her look so sexy. "I want you whimpering—I need those incredible sounds you make when I slide inside you."

Her lips parted. "I'll do whatever you want if you stop talking and fuck me."

I laughed. "Your wish is my command."

Settling over her, I shoved my jeans and boxer-briefs to my knees and wedged my elbows on either side of her head. I should've supported more of my weight, but I needed to feel her beneath me. For her to know that she was blanketed by my body and soul—that I'd protect her forever. That she was *mine*.

"Let me inside you," I whispered, nudging her pussy with the broad crown of my cock.

She bucked in my arms as I pushed upward, sliding through her slick arousal, taking her as surely as she'd taken me. My arms wobbled as she grabbed my arse, dragging me forward.

I couldn't stand it. It was too good. Too intense. Too fucking much.

I groaned, burying my face in her throat. Without warning, I surged upward, impaling my thick length completely inside her.

Her wetness offered no hindrance, accepting every inch.

"Christ, Nila." I grinded my hips against her as she whimpered.

"More. More!" The desperation in her voice took me hostage. I'd done that. I'd broken her by being shot and making her doubt my affection.

I was hers for eternity. I'd spend the rest of my life making her believe it.

Her hot wetness fisting around me drove me out of my fucking mind. I thrust harder.

We quickly turned from making love to fucking—straining to steal more from each other, driven by the need to hurt but also please.

Her lips landed on my chin.

Instantly, I brought my mouth to hers, slinking together, mimicking the action of our hips. Breaking apart, I groaned, "When I saw you coming to the stables…I fell even more in love with you." I thrust faster. "When you let me take what I wanted while licking you, I gave the last shred of my heart to you."

She threw her head back, sweat glittering in the hollow of her throat.

I licked it, avoiding the iciness of the diamonds around her neck. "So beautiful. So perfect." My stomach clenched. I tightened my fingers around her wrists, loving the rapid thump of her pulse. "I'm never letting you go."

Her eyes clouded with lust. "I don't know who I am anymore without you." She arched up, kissing me, moaning with my thrusts. "I believe in you."

I wanted to shower her with kisses. "I'll never get used to you wanting me."

"Wanting you?" Her eyes flared. "Jethro, I *am* you. I'm not a whole person anymore without you."

I winced as her words squeezed my heart. "Fuck, Nila." Hugging her closer, I plunged harder.

She moaned, inner muscles rippling.

"Shit, that feels so good." She closed her eyes, pressing her breasts against me; reminding me we were still clothed, still barricaded from being completely free. "You're so deep."

"I can go deeper." She groaned as I fucked her faster. My side hurt with every thrust, but an orgasm spiralled into existence. My balls sparked and the delicious gathering pressure at the base of my spine gritted my jaw. "I want to come so fucking bad."

"Then come."

"I want to come all over you, inside your pussy, your mouth. I want you every way imaginable. I want everything from you."

"I want that, too."

"I need you on your back, your knees, your stomach, against the wall, everywhere. I could fuck you for the rest of my life and still not get enough of you."

I kissed her, sucking her tongue, turning every whisper and touch supercharged with erotic passion.

"God, I'm close." She returned my kiss, wet and

passionate—her lips dancing, stealing my soul all over again. Her thighs squeezed my hips, imprisoning me as I drove into her again and again. "I'm coming...God, I'm coming."

I pumped harder, giving into bliss and stars. "Come. Fuck, I want you to come."

"Come with me."

"It would be my fucking pleasure."

Nothing else mattered. Nothing but bliss and togetherness.

We gave in.

Our motions turned rabid, seeking one goal, devouring each other in a fit of sin.

"Fuck me. Oh, Kite. Love me. Fuck me. Ride me."

I couldn't hold on anymore. Digging my knees into the hay, I gave her what she wanted. I lived in her begs and drove faster until red pain flashed through my system.

I plunged into her, our groans and moans drowning out the sounds of our fucking.

Her core tightened.

I rocked harder, rubbing myself against her clit. My balls smacked against the curve of her arse and the hay prickled like tiny needles. Our bodies battled each other—a perfect avenue of violent emotions.

I thrust again and again and again. "Fuck, I'm going to come."

Her back locked, her core clenched, giving me nowhere else to go.

Her legs locked tight around my waist. I cried out as her knee caught my injury.

"Yes!" She came hard and furious, fisting around me, dragging painful pleasure from every inch.

My orgasm unravelled without warning, exploding like a thunderstorm through every muscle. Lightning and rain drops, I spurted my very fucking soul into her.

One thing was for sure, I didn't just come. I came *undone*.

And only Nila had the power to stitch me back together.

Nila

TIME WAS MY worst enemy.

Nothing good ever came from time.

It passed too quickly—good moments and happy memories gone in a blink. Or it passed too slowly—bad experiences and unhappy circumstances dragging for an eternity.

And now, when all I wanted to do was fall asleep in the warm stable with Jethro wrapped around me and the sweet scent of hay in my nose, all I could focus on was…*time is limited.*

We'd carved out all we could, and now it was over.

I looked at Jethro. My freshly cut hair whispered along my jaw. My heart suffocated with love for him and what he'd done.

He'd single-handedly brought me back from the brink, giving me back my self-worth, fixing me enough to stay strong—for a little longer.

He pulled up his jeans and buckled them. Without a word, he slipped off the hay bale and helped me stand. We hadn't talked about what would happen now, but I already knew. He meant to send me back.

He's leaving me again.

Sadness and fear tingled my spine.

I can't go back.

But I had no choice.

I'll break.

But I had to remain strong.

I couldn't look at him as he smoothed down my nightgown, readjusted my coat, and plucked wayward strands of straw from my hair.

Say it. Tell me we're about to go our separate ways after everything that's happened.

Jethro stiffened, obviously sensing my frustration and terror.

Time would come between us again. I would hate it all the more.

"Nila...stop." Gathering me in a hug, he kissed my cheek. "You already know what I'm about to say. I feel it."

I snuggled into him, despite wanting to shove him away. All that talk of keeping me safe, yet he expected me to return to the monster's den without him.

Please, don't do it...take me with you.

"What are you going to do?" I inhaled his skin, flinching against the strange scent of antiseptic and musk. He normally smelled so delicious but now he reminded me of death and toil. "Whatever you're planning, don't. We could still leave. Tonight."

Time doesn't need us apart again. It's had its fun.

I wanted to create my own time where we became immortal and lived a safe, happy existence forever.

But you know he's right.

No matter how much I wanted to, I couldn't leave Vaughn and he couldn't leave Jasmine. And if Kestrel ever woke up, Jethro owed him a safe home to return to. As much as I wanted to scream and beg, I forced down my weakness. I was on his side—I would do what he asked of me, even if it was the hardest thing I'd ever do.

Damn obligations and common-sense. Hadn't I deserved some fantastical ideology where we could run off into the sunset and exist happily ever after?

Why couldn't life be like storybooks?

Jethro sighed, hugging me hard. His muscles vibrated; his heart thundered. He was alive, in my arms, and his orgasm was drying on my inner thigh.

He's alive.

I had to trust he'd stay that way to carry out whatever he had planned.

"I need to end this, Nila." Jethro pulled away, looking into my eyes. "You know as well as I do that we can't be free until it's dealt with."

The cuts on my breastbone flared, agreeing with him. We'd suffered enough—it was their turn.

My eyes fell to his waist. It hadn't escaped my notice that he refused to take his t-shirt off. However, he couldn't hide the small pinprick of blood coming through the light grey material.

I reached for it.

He jolted back, clamping an arm around himself—glaring at me, daring me to question his conviction that he was strong enough to do this. "One day, two at the most. I'll have everything in place and we can finally be happy."

I shook my head. "Something will happen. It always does." Tears rose. I hated that I was weak but I couldn't deny it—the thought of going back to Hawksridge alone petrified me. "I can't go back, Kite. Please, don't make me."

So much for not begging.

"They've hurt me. They almost won. I know you believe in me but I honestly don't believe in *myself* anymore. Please...*please* don't make me go back."

I couldn't stop shaking. I didn't have the power to walk back there.

Jethro kissed the top of my head. "You've been so damn strong—stronger than me by far. I sent a note to Jasmine telling her what I'm planning. I asked her to make up an excuse to keep you in her room. She'll watch over you. She'll say you're teaching her how to sew or something." His voice dropped with love. "She'll make sure you're safe and out of their hands for two days."

I didn't have the heart to tell him that Jasmine's power was minimal, slipping further on a daily basis. Bonnie had her ways to restrict Jasmine. I wouldn't put it past the old witch to poison her for going against dear ole' granny.

If Bonnie ever finds out Jasmine's working against her...

"What are you going to do? Two days is too much time."

Time again.

The enemy to us all.

The sands of hell.

"I'm going to call for help." Jethro's jaw twitched as if the thought of admitting he needed others frustrated him.

"Who?"

He frowned. "Just leave it to me. Don't worry about it."

"Tell me. I want to know."

"You need to get back before they find you're missing." His eyes narrowed. "Don't climb up the drainpipe. Go through the front door and ask Jasmine for a key. She'll wipe the camera footage in the morning."

I took a step backward, needing to distance myself so I could walk out of there without kneeling and begging to go with him. "You're changing the subject. Tell me what you're planning."

He exited the stall, forcing me to follow him down the aisle. "What do you want to know?"

Why couldn't he see that by asking me to trust him and willingly return to the Hall, he owed me everything?

It's taking everything that I am not to show you how terrified I am. How lonely. How defeated. You have to give me something to cling to. Something that will keep me strong.

"I want to know what you mean to do."

He looked over his shoulder, holding his side.

Was it just me or was his skin whiter than before? A fever kissing his brow?

I wanted to strap him to a bed and nurse him back to full health. He still had a long way to go—no matter how adamant he was.

His golden eyes flashed in the darkness. "Fine, I'm going to call Kill. The guy you met at Diamond Alley. I'm going to enlist his help."

"And he'll give it?"

"Let's just say, we have an agreement. He'll come."

"But he's in the States. It'll take him two days just to get here."

Jethro spun around, coming to plant his hands on my hips. "I also plan to contact someone else. Someone who's been doing a great deal of conspiring over the past month. Someone who has had enough like me."

My heart skipped. *Vaughn?* "Who?"

Jethro kissed my cheek, brushing aside my hair with gentle fingers. "Your father."

I froze. "Tex?"

He nodded. "Arch has been busy the past few weeks. While I've been healing, I've kept an eye on him. He's gathering an army, Nila—not just media this time, but a proper bought team. He's ready to hunt and I'll give him the perfect target."

"How—how do you know that?"

His teeth gleamed with anger and commitment. "I looked into his background. Pulled a few favours to find out if there's been inconsistent spending in his accounts."

"Wow—"

"Eh, Jet?" A figure appeared from the blackness.

I jumped. However, instead of cowering behind Jethro like I would've a few months ago, seeking protection and others to save me, I unthinkingly placed myself in front of him. My arms up, fists curled, teeth bared in defiance.

I might be almost broken, but I protected those I loved.

The hunchback came closer, skulking from the shadows. "Impressive stance, Nila. But if you mean to follow through with a punch, make sure your thumb is on the *outside* of your fingers. Otherwise, you'll break it."

I narrowed my eyes as the figure dumped two duffels from his shoulders to cobblestones. The dense fabric slapped loudly in the night silence.

"Flaw?"

A low chuckle reached my ears as he stepped from the darkness. "Hi, Nila." His eyes skated over me, widening with understanding of what Jethro and I had gotten up to.

Jethro hugged me from behind, planting a kiss on my cheek. "I didn't think I could love you any more than I do. You just proved me wrong. Thank you for protecting me."

My heart burst.

Letting me go, he skirted in front of me and held out his hand. "Once again, you've earned my thanks."

Flaw nodded, shaking Jethro's grip. "Jasmine's been told. I've got what you asked, and nobody is the wiser." His eyes fell on me. "I can take you back to the estate, Nila. Give you an alibi if anyone's up at this ungodly hour." Fishing in his pocket, he held up a key. "I have the key to your room."

Jethro rubbed his chin. "That might not be a bad idea. Just think up a decent excuse." He narrowed his gaze in my direction. "You've been sick with the flu—you can't deny it—I can still hear it in your lungs. Use that as a reason for midnight wanderings. You needed medicine." His face darkened. "Which I doubt you asked for while you suffered."

I looked away. "What I do when you're not around is my business. Just like you getting shot and making us all believe you were dead is yours."

Hear what I'm saying? That I'm not a victim anymore—I'll stand up for myself regardless if you're there to help me or not.

Jethro clenched his jaw.

Flaw laughed. "Tension in paradise, huh?"

Growling under his breath, Jethro changed the subject. "Did you manage to catch him okay?"

Flaw grinned, his strong jaw shaded in dark stubble. "Bit of a bugger to start with but nothing a handful of oats couldn't overcome." Pointing at the bags, he added, "Medical supplies in that one. Along with water and food enough for a week. Clothing, tent, and survival stuff in that one. I doubt you'll want to make a fire in case they see the plume, so I brought a gas heater to cook on and to keep you warm, along with an electric blanket that's solar-powered."

My eyes widened. "Wait, why does he need all that?"

Jethro turned to me. "Because you might be going back into the Hall alone, but I made a promise that I'd never leave you again." He took my hand, guiding me away from Flaw and outside where the moon drenched the forecourt. Before it'd been empty and silent. Now Wings stood patiently, saddled and bridled, his back hoof cocked with boredom.

Seeing the black beast caused hope to explode all over again.

I whirled in Jethro's arms. "You're staying close by?"

"Staying on the grounds. Yes." Pulling out a silver phone, his eyes darkened. "I'll send you messages. I sent you a couple yesterday that you didn't reply to. Did they take your phone away?"

No, I was just trapped in the Heretic's Fork and tormented.

I shook my head. "I haven't checked it. I keep it hidden—just in case."

"You have to stay in constant contact now," he growled. I need to know where you are, that you're okay. Otherwise, I'll lose my fucking mind."

My heart reacted like a love-struck teenager. "I must admit, I'm very impressed you remembered my number."

Jethro smirked, the first lighthearted reaction since he'd returned. "I haven't forgotten anything about you."

I rolled my eyes. "I suppose that's only fair seeing as I remember your number, too. I used to repeat it over and over again as I fell asleep." The seemingly normal part of dating, of secret messaging, and the delicious joy of finding that the person you were in love with felt the same way glowed inside.

He truly does love me.

It wasn't a projection of my love. Not a mirror or mirage. *It's true.*

I'd never been more thankful.

He stepped closer, eyes hooded. "I can recite everything about you. If someone asked me how you tasted, I'd have the perfect description. If someone ordered me to list every freckle, I'd have the exact number. And if anyone wanted to know how brilliantly perfect you are—or hear about any of your accomplishments—I'd be able to regale them for hours." He wrapped his arms around me. "I'll never forget anything because it's the little things that make you real."

Flaw chuckled. "Good God, man, you have no shame."

I wanted him to bugger off. My heart disintegrated and my core clenched to have Jethro inside me again. I was wet, wanting.

Jethro laughed. "I'm not embarrassed to be honest for the first time in my life. This woman is mine. I love her, and I don't fucking care who knows it."

I blushed. My soul ached at the thought of him leaving. He couldn't leave me. Not now. Not now we'd been honest and finally talked outside of debts and pain. "Don't go...we can work out something else. Stay...please."

Jethro's smile fell, sadness cloaking him. "I have to. Another day or so and then we'll be safe to do whatever we want, go wherever we please." Taking my hands, he squeezed tightly. "Go now, Nila. I need you to return." Looking over his shoulder, he held out his hand.

Flaw came forward and dropped the key into his palm.

Jethro gave it to me. "On second thought, it might be best if you go on your own. Tell them Jasmine gave you the key because she often has tasks for you outside the realm of Cut's requirements." His voice cracked with frustration. "I wish to God I didn't have to make you do this. But I promise it will all be over soon."

Flaw muttered, "Cut's been pretty fucking happy the past couple of weeks. Been a lot more lenient with the Black Diamond brothers. Doubt he'll cause any trouble for the next two days."

Jethro sneered, "I guess killing his troublemaking sons

makes everything hunky-fucking-dory in his world." Kissing me one last time, he urged me toward the Hall. "Go now. I'll message you when everything is in place and tell you where to go."

I opened my mouth to argue—to demand he keep me with him. Wherever he was going, I deserved to be by his side. "Jethro—"

I don't think I can do this...

He groaned, yanking me back to him. "God, I'll miss you." His mouth slammed on mine, kissing me roughly. As sudden as he claimed me, he relinquished me. "Leave. I love you."

As much as I wanted to argue, the desperation in his gaze forced me to obey.

I had no other option.

I'm strong enough to do this.

He would keep me safe.

I trust him.

To prove that I did, I turned my back on him and returned alone to Hawksridge Hall.

I didn't look back.
I should've looked back.
I did as he asked.
I shouldn't have done what he asked.
I climbed the small hill and turned to hell.

Dawn did its best to push aside the moon; the ground glittered with blades of frost. My heart was a lump of snow by the time I ascended the front entrance.

It was the hardest thing to ask of me—to willingly go back.

I didn't know if I'd ever be able to forgive him if he betrayed my trust.

If something happens...

I shook my head.

Nothing will happen.

Two days...it's nothing.

Pausing on the stoop of the Hall, I glanced fleetingly behind me.

There, on the horizon, was the faint outline of a black horse and its rider disappearing into the woods.

Jethro was gone.

I should never have let him go.

I should've run in the opposite direction.

I obeyed because I trusted him.

I should never have trusted him.

Unfortunately, I was right.

Two days was too long.

In two days, my world would end.

Jethro

MY NEW HOME.
For the next thirty or so hours.

I surveyed my camp. Wings stood tethered to a tree and my tent stood sentry in the small glen. It'd taken an hour or so to set up—it would've been less if my body wasn't low on fuel and the pain from my wound hadn't decided to make itself known.

Payback for ignoring the warning signs while proving to Nila that I was strong and capable and deserving of her trust.

Louille would have a fucking fit if he knew what I'd done only hours after checking myself out from the hospital.

I swore under my breath, prodding the fresh blood stain on my side. The stitches had done their job and knitted me together, but at the very edge the skin had torn slightly. A throb resonated from rib to lung.

Oh, well. It was a good test to judge what I'm able to do.

Not to mention, I would do it all over again even if my side burst open mid-thrust. Nila consumed my every thought, my every sense. I'd only been away from her for sixty minutes, yet I missed her as if it'd been sixty years.

Opening the front zipper on the duffel, I pulled out some extra strength painkillers. Popping a few, I swallowed them dry and returned to securing the last peg of the tent.

I didn't know why I bothered. I wouldn't sleep. I could never rest knowing Nila was in the Hall being mentally and physically tortured.

How fucking dare they use the Heretic's Fork and cut off her hair? How dare they fucking think they had that right?

Insane, the lot of them.

If I was stronger and had better odds, I would've stormed Hawksridge tonight and slaughtered my father in his bed. But he had the Black Diamonds on his side. He had an army where I did not.

I wouldn't kill myself by being stupid.

I'd been stupid for long enough already.

I was home.

This was my empire, and I'd had enough of my family's madness.

Throwing the smaller duffel inside the tent, I crawled in after it. This campsite wasn't a stranger to me. I'd spent many nights huddled in the glen away from the Hall—away from screaming tempers, guilt-infested excuses, and anger-laden requirements.

When Cut tossed me out to make it to the boundary in the dead of winter, I wouldn't have survived if I hadn't already self-taught how to build shelter, hunt, and navigate. I liked my little sanctuary. If I'd had the strength to climb, I could've forgone the flimsy tent and scaled the boughs of an ancient oak tree where I'd built a tree fort in my youth.

I used to take Kes and Jaz there before we were old enough to know our duties.

Before life ruined us.

It was barely sunrise, but by tomorrow morning, I hoped to change the future of Hawksridge. I wouldn't just have the glen for peace and safety; I'd have the entire estate.

I'd finally have what was mine.

No waiting for my thirtieth. No obeying a psychopath.

Not anymore.

Twenty-four hours to put into place the rest of my life.

Another few hours to implement it.

I'd told Nila two days. I would stick to that promise.

Taking a deep breath, I hoisted myself onto the fold-out stretcher. Flaw had truly come through for me. He'd even packed a small generator so I could charge my phone and keep a light against the slowly creeping dawn.

Goosebumps covered my body, hidden below the thick parka Flaw had given me at the hospital. Winter had well and truly taken hold, determined to remind me that once upon a time I'd *welcomed* the frost. I'd mimicked winter by absorbing its ice and doing my best to freeze out other emotions.

It was like an old friend, a new enemy, a family member I no longer needed for help.

Grabbing the small electric heater stuffed into the bottom of the duffel, I plugged it into the generator and placed it by my feet. My body didn't have the reserves it needed to keep warm—not while most of my cells focused on healing my side.

My thoughts drifted to Nila.

Had she arrived at her quarters safely? Was she warm in bed, thinking of me—reliving my fingers inside her, my tongue sweeping hers?

"Shit." Shaking my head, I did my best to force those thoughts away. My cock was far too eager to attempt a third time.

It didn't work.

Nila's moans echoed in my mind. Her voice vibrated in my ears as she admitted she loved me.

How am I supposed to concentrate?

Nila was replaced with images of Kestrel—slowly dying alone in a strange hospital. Then my father leapt into my head, laughing, tormenting.

He'd never grown out of the spoiled brat syndrome—just like Daniel.

I didn't know the full story of how my father became heir, but my mother had dropped hints. Emma, too—when she was alive. Cut was many things, but he'd told some of his darkest secrets to Emma, knowing they'd die with her with no repercussions.

Livid rage heated my veins, better than any heater.

Now, he'll pay.

And I knew exactly how I'd do it.

Pulling out my phone, I sent a message to Nila.

Unknown Number: *I love you with every breath and heartbeat. Stay true to yourself. Trust me. You're strong enough; you're brave enough. You're my inspiration to end this. Don't give up on me, Nila. Two days and it's over.*

I didn't wait for a reply. Waiting would drive me crazy and horrid conclusions would consume me. I had to trust that Jasmine would keep Nila safe and allow me to do what was needed.

Reaching into the duffel, I pulled out the little black address book I'd kept hidden in my room. I'd given Flaw directions on where to retrieve it when he collected me. An address book was archaic nowadays with phones and computers, but I'd never been more thankful for old-fashioned practices.

I had no clue where my old phone was. This was my last record.

Flicking through the dog-eared pages, I sighed with relief, grateful for contacts I could rely on. Men I'd met and were loyal to me, not my father. Men who were ruthless in their own right. Men who could help me win against Cut and his legalities.

My eyes skipped over numbers for acquaintances I'd met on smuggling routes. Outlaws and pioneers, tanker captains and bribed coastguards.

I might have a need for them in the future, but not for this.

I had one man in mind.

There it is.

Arthur 'Kill' Killian, Pure Corruption MC.

I doubted many heirs to an English estate would have the personal contact of a president of an American motorcycle club.

But, thank fuck, I did.

Inputting the number, I pressed call on the phone and held it to my ear.

The line crackled, lacking a proper signal in the woods—struggling to connect Buckinghamshire to Florida.

The ringing stopped, followed by a loud screech. "You've reached Kill."

My hand tightened around the phone. "Hawk calling."

A pause, followed by some shuffling. "Hang on. Let me get somewhere private."

"Sure."

I waited for faint voices to fade; Killian came back on the line. "What's up?"

"I need your help. Do you have trusted brothers in the UK?"

"I might. Why?"

"I need your help overthrowing someone. Give me some men, don't ask questions, and our alliance will be cemented for whatever you need in the future. Diamonds, smuggling—you name it. It's yours."

Now wasn't the time to mention that when I was in power, I planned on ceasing that side of the business. Diamonds to me were covered in blood and death. I wanted no part in it.

Silence for a moment.

Kill growled, "Give me a few hours. I'll see what I can do."

He hung up.

Phase one complete.

The next part of my strategy would be tricky, but I had no alternative. I didn't spread myself over Plan A or Plan B. This first attempt was my only attempt.

It will work.

Refreshing the screen, I dialled another number—one I'd never called before—but knew by heart because of our association.

It rang and rang.

A dawn phone call wouldn't be acceptable to anyone, but if he knew what was good for him, he'd answer it.

Finally, a sleepy, almost drunk, voice answered, "Hello?"

My heart squeezed to think my family had browbeaten this proud business owner into the spineless grieving father he'd become. We'd won over his family—more times than I could count. "Tex Weaver?"

He sucked in a breath. Rustling sounded; his voice lost its haziness. "*You*. You have the fucking nerve to call me after what you've done." He coughed, his temper howling down the line. "I'll fucking kill you with my bare hands. Where's my son? My daughter?"

"That's what I wanted to talk to you about."

Tex raged, "The time for talking is *done*. I'm sick of it. Sick of all your threats and promises. You took my Emma but I won't let you take our kids." Breathing hard, he snarled, "I've put things in place, Hawk. I'm ending this. Once and for all."

I plucked an oak leaf from the tent floor. "I know what you've been doing, Tex."

"Doesn't matter. Won't stop me. Not this time. You can't scare me away like you did with Emma. I'll die before I let you hurt my children anymore."

"I was hoping you'd say that."

He paused. "What—what do you mean?"

Leaning forward, I stared through the tent gap at the woodland around me. This was my office, my headquarters, and it was time to arrange a battalion for battle. "I'm on your side. I want to help you."

"I don't believe you."

"You don't have to believe me. It's the truth."

"What have you done with my children? If you've hurt Nila—"

"Sir, she's the one who has hurt me."

Tex sucked in a breath. "Good for her. I hope she tears

out your motherfucking heart."

I chuckled. "I'm in love with your daughter, Mr. Weaver. I have no intention of letting her tear out my heart."

Tex's temper soared into my ear. "Yet you'll happily behead her just like her mother! What sort of sick fuck are you?"

"You're not listening to what I'm telling you."

"I'm listening perfectly fine, you son of a bitch, but you can't scare me with these twisted phone calls anymore. Your father played the same game. Calling to tell me Emma was too sweet, too pure to die—that he'd find a way to end it. Only to call me on the eve of her death to tell me it was all a lie! He destroyed me, and now you're destroying the dregs that are left." Something crashed in the background. "I'll tell you right now—I'm not listening. I'm coming for you, Hawk, and I'm going to make you fucking pay."

My anger boiled over, meeting his. "Christ's sake. *Listen* to me. I'm in love with Nila. I'm putting an end to this feud. You don't have to believe me. Just listen. I'm offering you everything you want. Your son, your daughter…grandchildren who won't be taken for some ludicrous vendetta. Do you want that? Will you risk talking to me so we can work together to end this?"

Silence.

More silence.

What did I expect? Our families had been raised to hate each other. Archibald lost his wife to my father—of course, he'd hate me.

I can do it without him.

Maybe then he'd believe me when I said Nila was now mine and I would do everything in my power to keep her safe.

I sighed, "Look—"

Tex interrupted. "What do you expect from me, Hawk?"

My shoulders slumped with relief.

I had him.

"I expect you to help me save the woman we love."

Nila

TAPESTRIES WATCHED ME as if I were already dead. The very air prickled my skin with foreboding.

Hawksridge Hall embraced me, sucking me back into its morbid evil. Every step, I wanted to cry. Every breath, I wanted to sprint out the door and never return.

I can't do this again...

I can't...

The strength I'd found in Jethro's company rapidly dissolved, and the cracks and fissures from what they'd done to me ruined my determination.

My courage bled out, trailing like a bloody stain the deeper I travelled through the Hall.

There was no more happiness, only torment and despair. I didn't know how I'd survive another hour, let alone two days.

You can do it.

Can I?

I wasn't so sure.

Following the corridor, I swallowed a gasp as Daniel charged around the corner.

"*No!*"

His hair was wet and combed back. His little goatee gone, his face baby-smooth, and eyes bright with excitement rather than hazy with sleep.

It's not yet dawn.
How could he be up? What sick joke had fate played?
No. This can't be happening. Haven't I given enough?!
Daniel slammed to a stop, surprise painting his face.
I froze, wanting to miraculously turn invisible.
His chest puffed with glee; he grinned. "Well, well, well." He took a step toward me, then another.
I couldn't move.
Time spilled faster through its hated hourglass, sucking me into its sand.
"Where the fuck have you been sneaking off to?" He kept prowling toward me, tiny steps, baby steps, giving the illusion that I could run before he caught me.
Run!
The message shot to my legs and I bolted.
But I was too late.
Daniel's feet thundered on the carpet, scooping me up in his arms before I even ran a few strides.
"Let me go!"
He chuckled, holding me tight against his front. His erection dug into my lower back and his breath echoed in my ear. "No chance. Never letting you go again, little Weaver."
He wrenched open my fingers, revealing the key tight in my fist. "Where the fuck did you get that from?" Plucking it from my grip, he palmed it. "Not that it matters."
I squirmed in his hold, doing my best to ram his nose with my skull. "Let me go!"
You won't break me. Not again.
He laughed loudly. "Oh, I'm going to fucking enjoy this." Slamming me back onto my feet, he struck my cheek with the hand holding the brass key.
The thick metal crunched against my cheekbone, spurting hot tears from my eyes.
I clutched my face, sucking in heavy breaths. Short hair whipped around, stinging my cheeks.
Don't cry. Don't show weakness.

Daniel wrapped his fist around my throat, yanking me into him. "Know what, Weaver, I don't even care that you're out of your room uninvited. I don't care what shitty shenanigans you've been up to or how you got the key. None of that matters anymore."

Throwing my head back, I screeched as loud as I could. "Jasmine!"

"Oh, no you fucking don't." Slapping a hand over my mouth, he whispered, "You don't belong to Jasmine for this next part, whore." His tongue traced the heated imprint of the key on my cheek. "You belong to me. Remember what Cut said last night? About a surprise…well, surprise! Get ready to pay for all your sins in one."

I fought harder, screaming behind his palm.

Dragging me down the corridor, he laughed as cold as the depths of Hades. "No one can save you now, Nila. Know why?"

I screamed again, kicking anything I could.

"In a few minutes, you're going on a little trip, and there you'll learn everything there is to know about us. You'll finally understand how we triumphed over your family. How we won and you lost. How all of this will fucking end."

Daniel stroked my cheek. "Our first vacation together. Won't it be fun?" His voice turned gruff. "And the first thing I'll make you do when we arrive is repay the Third Debt."

Throwing me against the wall, he grabbed my hand and placed it on his thick erection. "I'm going to fuck you. My father's going to fuck you. And then…you'll pay the debt we've kept secret. The one that will tie all of this together. The Fifth Debt. You'll finally understand."

Fury fired through my blood. I struggled in his hold. "I don't want to understand! Just let me go!"

He grinned. "You'll never be free again. And you'll see why. It will all make sense. You'll be fucked, but at least you'll finally know how we won."

Kissing me hard, his putrid tongue tore past my lips.

I gagged.

In a flash of defiance, I bit him.

Rearing back, he slapped me hard.

My ears rang, and bright lights exploded behind my eyes. Pain registered but all I could think about was Jethro.

Come back!

Come claim me!

Come save me!

Shaking me, Daniel snarled, "You have six days, bitch. Six days to pay your remaining debts. And fuck, will I have fun extracting them."

I spat in his face. "Go to hell, Buzzard. You'll die before I do."

He sighed indulgently, his temper simmering with cockiness. "Nila, Nila, Nila, so delusional. You're not paying attention to what I'm telling you. No one can save you. No one will hear you scream. Six days. That's how long you have to live. We're leaving for *Almasi Kipanga* right now—this very fucking second."

His teeth glinted in the dark. "Do you get it? Do you understand what this means? We're taking you to South Africa, to our diamond mines, to where it all began. You'll see the last things you'll ever see. You'll hear the last things you'll ever hear. And you'll live your final moments on foreign soil."

My heart shrivelled.

No, no. God, no.

Daniel morphed from man to monster, shadowing my future, my soul, my hope.

I didn't have two days.

I didn't even have two hours.

Jethro!

They were taking me away.

They were stealing everything!

Daniel marched me from life to death, laughing with every step. "Oh, and another thing I should mention. This little trip…it'll be your last as you won't be coming back alive."

"No!"

After everything we'd been through. After everything we'd promised and planned.

It was all for nothing.

Time had fucked us once again…

…

Jethro
was
too
late.

Releasing late 2015

Updates, teasers, and exclusive news will be announced on
www.pepperwinters.com

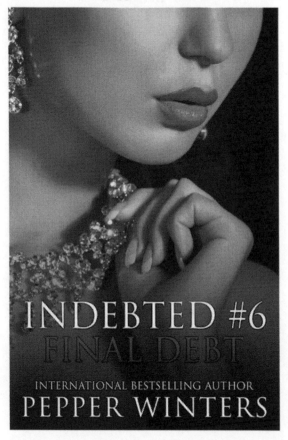

"I'm in love with her, but it might not be enough to stop her from becoming the latest victim of the Debt Inheritance. I know who I am now. I know what I must do. We will be together—I just hope it's on Earth rather than in heaven."

It all comes down to this.
Love versus life.
Debts versus death.
Who will win?

About the Author

Pepper Winters is a New York Times, Wallstreet Journal, and USA Today International Bestseller. She loves dark romance, star-crossed lovers, and the forbidden taboo. She strives to write a story that makes the reader crave what they shouldn't, and delivers tales with complex plots and unforgettable characters.

After chasing her dreams to become a full-time writer, Pepper has earned recognition with awards for best Dark Romance, best BDSM Series, and best Dark Hero. She's an #1 iBooks bestseller, along with #1 in Erotic Romance, Romantic Suspense, Contemporary, and Erotica Thriller. She's also honoured to wear the IndieReader Badge for being a Top 10 Indie Bestseller, and recently signed a two book deal with Hachette. Represented by Trident Media, her books have garnered foreign and audio interest and are currently being translated into numerous languages. They will be in available in bookstores worldwide.

Her Dark Romance books include (click for amazon link):
Tears of Tess (Monsters in the Dark #1)
Quintessentially Q (Monsters in the Dark #2)
Twisted Together (Monsters in the Dark #3)
Debt Inheritance (Indebted #1)
First Debt (Indebted Series #2)
Second Debt (Indebted Series #3)
Third Debt (Indebted Series #4)
Fourth Debt (Indebted Series #5)

Her Grey Romance books include (click for buylinks from numerous online sites):
Destroyed

Upcoming releases are (click the link to add to Goodreads)
Fourth Debt (Indebted #5)
Ruin & Rule (Motorcycle romance)
Final Debt (Indebted #6)
Je Suis a Toi (Monsters in the Dark Novella)
Forbidden Flaws (Contemporary Romance)

To be the first to know of upcoming releases, please join Pepper's Newsletter (she promises never to spam or annoy you.)

Pepper's Newsletter

Or follow her on her website
Pepper Winters

You can stalk her here:

Pinterest
Facebook Pepper Winters
Twitter
Instagram
Website
Facebook Group
Goodreads

She loves mail of any kind: **pepperwinters@gmail.com**
All other titles and updates can be found on her **Goodreads Page.**

Playlist

The Handler by Muse
Love Me Like You Do by Ellie Goulding
Crystal by Monsters And Men
Ghost Town by Madonna
Only Love can Hurt like This by Paloma Faith
With or Without You by U2
Skyfall by Adele
Do You Remember by Jarryd James
Holding You by Stan Walker
Diamonds by Rhianna
1965 by Zella Day
Stand by Me by Imagine Dragons
Best of Me by Sum 41
Give You What You Like by Avril Lavigne
Hurt by Johnny Cash
Love me Again by John Newman
Unconditional by Katy Perry
Beggin for Thread by Banks

Other Book Blurbs & Reviews

Ruin & Rule (Pure Corruption MC #1)
7th July 2015 from Forever Romance (Grand Central)
In Bookshops & Online

Learn about Arthur Killian who you just met in Third and Fourth Debt.

I love reading MC books but this has to be the best one I've read! I couldn't put it down —***Nikki Mccrae, Amazon Review***

One of the best stories I've ever read. Period. —***Tamicka Birch, Amazon Reviewer***

Ruin & Rule is another dark masterpiece from Pepper Winters. Buckle yourself in for a wild ride that is pure page-turning bliss! —**Rachel, Goodreads**

*

"We met in a nightmare. The in-between world where time had no power over reason. We fell in love. We fell hard. But then we woke up. And it was over . . ."

She is a woman divided. Her past, present, and future are as twisted as the lies she's lived for the past eight years. Desperate to get the truth, she must turn to the one man who may also be her greatest enemy . . .

He is the president of Pure Corruption MC. A heartless biker and retribution-deliverer. He accepts no rules, obeys no one, and lives only to reap revenge on those who wronged him. And now he has stolen her, body and soul.

Can a woman plagued by mystery fall in love with the man who refuses to face the truth? And can a man drenched in darkness forgo his quest for vengeance-and finally find redemption?

Buy Now on All Major Online Stores

***

Tears of Tess (Book one of Monsters in the Dark) Book two: Quintessentially Q, and Book Three: Twisted Together, are available now

6 Holy Wow This Author Took Me On A Ride I Never Saw Coming and Left Me Speechless Stars. I've never rated a book 6 stars before so this gives you an idea of just how good I believe this book to be. This story will take you by the hand and show you how both darkness and light exist within all of us. It will ultimately take you by the heart and you will be so glad that you read it—***Hook Me Up Book Blog***

DARK AND HAUNTINGLY BEAUTIFUL.....IT WILL LEAVE YOU BREATHLESS!!!!

Pepper Winters is a standout! An absolutely stunning debut!—***Lorie, Goodreads***

*

A New Adult Dark Contemporary Romance, not suitable for people sensitive to grief, slavery, and nonconsensual sex. A story about finding love in the strangest of places, a will of iron that grows from necessity, and forgiveness that may not be enough.

> *"My life was complete. Happy, content, everything neat and perfect. Then it all changed.*
> *I was sold."*

Tess Snow has everything she ever wanted: one more semester before a career in property development, a loving boyfriend, and a future dazzling bright with possibility.

For their two year anniversary, Brax surprises Tess with a romantic trip to Mexico. Sandy beaches, delicious cocktails, and soul-connecting sex set the mood for a wonderful holiday. With a full heart, and looking forward to a passion filled week, Tess is on top of the world.

But lusty paradise is shattered.

Kidnapped. Drugged. Stolen. Tess is forced into a world full of darkness and terror.

Captive and alone with no savior, no lover, no faith, no future, Tess evolves from terrified girl to fierce fighter. But no matter her strength, it can't save her from the horror of being sold.

Can Brax find Tess before she's broken and ruined, or will Tess's new owner change her life forever?

Buy Now on All Major Online Stores

***

Forbidden Flaws (Erotic Contemporary Romance) Coming 2015
She's forbidden.

Saffron Carlton is the darling of the big screen, starlet on the red carpet, and wife of mega producer Felix Carlton. Her life seems perfect with her overflowing bank balance, adoring fans, and luxury homes around the world. Everyone thinks they know her. But no one truly does.

He's flawed.
Raised in squalor, fed on violence and poverty, Cas Smith knows the underbelly of the world. He's not looking for fame or fortune. He's looking for the woman who ran from him all those years ago.

He wants her.
She ran from him.
Now she's forbidden.

What happens when forbidden and flawed collide?

Total annihilation.
Buy Now on All Major Online Stores

Printed in Great Britain
by Amazon.co.uk, Ltd.,
Marston Gate.